LOOKING FOR A GROUP

REALWORLD ONLINE BOOK 1

Geoffrey Brenna

SILVER GRIFFON ASSOCIATES
ORANGE, CA, USA

Silver Griffon Associates
P.O. Box 7383
Orange, CA 92863

Publisher's Note: This is a work of fiction. Names, characters, places, and incidents are a product of the author's imagination. Locales and public names are sometimes used for atmospheric purposes. Any resemblance to actual people, living or dead, or to businesses, companies, events, institutions, or locales is completely coincidental.

Trademarked names appear throughout this book. Rather than use a trademark symbol with every occurrence of a trademarked name, names are used in an editorial fashion, with no intention of infringement of the respective owner's trademark.

Book Layout ©2025 BookDesignTemplates.com
Cover Art ©2025 Yvonne Less, Art4artists

Looking For a Group / Geoffrey Brenna. – 1st ed.
ISBN 979-8-88908-043-5

www.GeoffreyBrenna.com

PROLOGUE
SO IT BEGINS

Atlantia, 3987 BCE

WHOOP! WHOOP! WHOOP!

"Shut that off," Xerxes yelled as he entered the command room at a run. Four underlings stood in a rough circle around him, eyes glued to the displays inside the array of crystals floating before them. "What's going on?"

His second in command, Hermes, spared him a glance before turning back to the display. "Five Kraken-class battleships and a Battle Planetoid just completely demolished our orbital defenses."

Xerxes's breath caught, the blood draining from his face. "What! How? The remote warning beacons should have detected them long before they entered the solar system."

Hermes's face was grim when he turned back toward his commanding officer. "We think a virus penetrated the gaming portal filters and rewrote the beacon software."

Xerxes scoffed. "Through the game portal? That—that should be impossible. Only one of the Ancients could override the filters. We're not significant enough to attract that kind of attention.

"This doesn't make any sense."

Xerxes started to pace, his shoulders tense. Then he flicked a glance at the technician on his right. "What are they doing now?"

"Nothing, sir. The ships took up station around the planet, while the big one dropped into low Earth orbit. Now it's just sitting there."

"It's just sitting there, in LEO? It's got to be encountering huge amounts of drag. What in Hades could they be doing?"

His mind raced as he mulled—and mulled—and came to zero conclusions, every bit as confused as the moment he'd walked into the room. But something had to be done. And fast. "Okay. Alert the Council. We need to prepare for evacuation. Tell them all to log into the game and regroup at the Keep. We'll deal with this from there." He turned to Hermes and bellowed his name to tear his attention away from his own readings.

Hermes's head snapped up. "Yes sir?"

"Deploy the scouts through the gate. Make sure there're no unpleasant surprises waiting for us there."

"Deploying scouts now." Hermes turned back to the terminal floating beside him and entered the commands.

"Now, we should—"

One of the floating crystals began rapidly blinking red. "Urgent message from the lab, sir."

Xerxes gritted his teeth and shook his head brusquely. "I don't have time for his crap right now, tell him to get back to me later." He waved the technician away and turned his attention to a status display.

"He insists it can't wait. Life or death—or something."

Xerxes blew out a breath. As if anything could get worse.... "Very well. Put him on."

An iridescent image formed in the middle of the room, displaying the life-sized, three-dimensional projection of a bald man in a black robe wearing a silver torque on his throat and a matching thin band around his balding pate.

Xerxes fought through his irritation to address the man in a barely-civil tone. "What is it, Merlin?"

Merlin spoke in that usual flat tone of his. It never changed, despite the situation, and he himself had labeled this one life-or-death. "You have to do something about that rock over the planet."

Xerxes felt his blood pressure rise as his hands curled into tight fists. "No, really? I should do something about the people who just attacked us? Well, now that you've pointed that out...." He waved his arm, giving the command to cut the transmission. "I knew that was going to be a waste of time. Turn him off."

"Wait," Merlin shouted. "It's dropping nanites."

Xerxes stiffened and raised a hand, forestalling the tech. "What do you mean, it's dropping nanites?"

Merlin's jaw visibly tightened. "Did I stutter? It's spewing nanites into the atmosphere at an alarming rate." Merlin looked aside at something only he could see, bending over as he tapped at an invisible control board. "It's also releasing some kind of retrovirus. Oh. This is bad."

"*Bad* …. Would you care to elaborate?"

Merlin let out a long sigh, shoulders slumping. Merlin, defeated? Had that ever happened?

Xerxes blinked, tension thickening between them as he waited for the answer, uttered in a weak voice. "They are erasing us."

"What do you mean erasing us? How can that even be done?" His mind whirled.

Merlin took a deep breath, spine straightening as if he were actively reminding himself to do so. "The nanites are disassembling every manmade structure on the planet—buildings, monuments, technology. As for the virus…" The man threw up his hands helplessly. "The best I can tell is that it's doing the same to our memories. From what I can calculate, in less than an hour we, as a species, will revert to stone-age savages with no memory that we were ever anything else."

Xerxes froze, stunned speechless. His body drooped in defeat. Merlin was obnoxious, thought he was better than everyone else, but he was also a genius. He'd hoped that Merlin could come up with some way to deal with this. Xerxes slumped backward, caught up into a chair that helpfully materialized underneath him just in time. "Who? Who could be doing this to us? As members of an Intragalactic—"

He was interrupted by a loud *BING* chiming through the room. Bold, glowing lines of text appeared in the air. "Sucks to be you – Haxxor666."

Xerxes, Hermes, everyone else in the room, even Merlin stared in silence.

Xerxes's mouth opened and closed several times before speaking. "Haxxor? Haxxor is behind this. Why?" Xerxes's thoughts raced, trying to grasp the enormity of the implication. "Why would one of the Elder races decide to take us out?"

The image of Merlin looked down at him, furiously manipulating his controls again. "I've done what I can. We've launched a counter-virus that should mitigate the damage somewhat."

"What?" Xerxes started in shock. "That's wonderful. Once we rebuild, we can shove this—"

Merlin shook his head, "I said 'somewhat.' I only had minutes to develop and deploy the counter-virus."

Xerxes gestured at Merlin with open palms "So…"

Merlin's features sagged sadly. "At best, we'll be left with bronze age technology and some vague memories of what once was."

Xerxes sagged once more, swallowing several times before he could speak. "Vague memories?"

"Better to have legends than nothing at all." Merlin gestured in a vague shrug. "Anywho, it's time to go. Signing off now."

The image blinked out of existence.

"Wait—!" Xerxes jerked out of his seat as if he could run after the vanished image. But it was too late. He was gone. "Asshole."

His head dropped as he let out a long, weary sigh. His men stood in a ring around him, all staring expectantly for the next order.

Slowly he stood, gave a tug on his uniform, and straightened, clearing his throat. "He's not wrong. It is time to go. Get everyone to their game portals. Log in immediately. We'll attempt to fix this later."

Hermes, who had been paying half attention to the consoles, gasped. Dread twisted in the pit of Xerxes's stomach even before he asked. "What now?"

"One of our scouts finally reported in. As far as he can tell, everything game-side is gone. The portals have been destroyed and there's a huge firestorm. Anyone who logs into the game dies instantly. He only survived because he had pushed his fire resistance to insane levels. We can't leave that way." Hermes turned back to his commander. "Sir, none of the other scouts have respawned yet. Something must be interfering with that as well. What do we do?"

Xerxes swore and scrubbed a hand over his face. But he spoke quickly in a clipped tone devoid of all the turmoil swirling inside of him. He was running on pure adrenaline now. "Update the Council. Tell them they are on their own. We need to evacuate the city and blow the power core."

"What?"

"You heard me. If we blow up the city ourselves, maybe the nanites will ignore it. It will at least leave something for our descendants to discover in the distant future. Or at least have a chance of it."

"But what about us?" Hermes fired back.

Xerxes sighed. "We'll have to learn subsistence living and dirt farming."

Another of his sub-commanders choked out. "I've never even been off Atlantia island in my life..."

Xerxes steeled himself even as his own gut sank. He, himself, had only a passing familiarity with the mainland. "There's a first time for everything. Before any of that, I'm submitting a petition to the MCP. This is an overt and flagrant violation of the game rules and the Terms of Service!"

Hermes shot him a look of shocked disbelief but said nothing.

Xerxes shrugged helplessly, his hands open and supplicating. "What can it hurt to file a petition?"

Those around him shrugged, and all looked on in uncertainty for the future.

CHAPTER ONE
ALIENS ARE REAL

Present Day

I learned two things today:

1. Aliens are real.

2. They are all assholes.

CAMPFIRE—*CHECK*. COMFY CHAIR—*CHECK*. BEER—*CHECK*. Book—*check*. No harridan ex-wife—*check* and…no kids—*check*.

That last check sucked ass though. Gareth sighed, sitting back from the glowing fire, his book lying beside him. *Stranger in a Strange Land*. Heinlein had been his go-to for comfort reads since he was a kid. And these days, he felt like a stranger in his own life, so this title seemed appropriate for his solo camping adventure in the desert.

The brightness of the fire was an anomaly against the inky night surrounding him. Only the distant pinpoints of stars broke up the darkness. Staring into the blaze stung his eyes, but inexplicably, he found himself doing it regardless. He lost himself in his thoughts, once more trying to make sense of all that had happened. Just how had his life imploded so completely—and why?

His reverie was broken by a slimy, ice-cold nose pressing against his skin in that gap between his shirt and his jeans. Shocked out of his self-indulgent replay of the past, he looked down at his only friend in the world.

"Well, Xena, I guess it's time I got the steaks on if we want to eat before the show."

He turned to a small cooler beside him and pulled out two thick, juicy, steaks still wrapped in butcher paper. Carefully extracting them, he leaned forward and placed them on an iron grill over the fire. Then he flicked a glance at the dog.

"How do you like yours?"

"*Woof.*"

He gave a decisive nod in agreement. "Rare it is. We'll be eating in minutes." He smacked his lips in anticipation and sat back, reaching into the cooler again to remove a bottle of beer. He twisted off the top and took a long pull, then sighed as he glanced up at the dark sky again. This year would be the best Leonid meteor shower yet.

"Just you and me, Xena." He gestured toward the horizon with his bottle. "If it wasn't for the Vegas glow over there, we could be the only people on the planet." Gareth looked over. Xena tilted her head and gave him a quizzical look. "What? Dogs are people, too."

Gareth took another pull, then held the bottle up toward the husky as a toast. "Well girl, here's to new beginnings. God knows we need one."

It hadn't been a good year—hell, what an understatement. It had been an absolutely horrible year. First, he'd lost his job, a job where he'd spent almost twenty years, working his way up from the helpdesk to head system administrator. Two decades. Only to get shown the door due to some dubious outsourcing scheme by his employers.

Then his marriage blew up.

He could have understood, maybe, if it had something to do with losing his job, but Tilly hadn't seemed to care about that. Her income from streaming on her game channel was more than enough. She'd even encouraged him to game more so he could join her. Couples who game together were, apparently, "lit."

"We saw how well that went, didn't we?" Gareth asked Xena, who, shockingly, had no comment. A few months into the new 'Power Gamer Gareth' plan and all talk of the dual stream had vanished. Tilly had grown increasingly short with him, endlessly going on about his shortcomings as a gamer, how he'd never make it if he didn't focus.

Finally, he'd had enough. The streaming thing wasn't for him. So, he went in search of another system admin job. Things had gone south after that. What had been tense became downright combative. Divorce papers quickly followed. He still didn't really understand why. Matilda had never explained what the problem was, even though he'd begged her to.

If he could understand the problem, he could fix it.

In the end, however, his back had been against the wall, and he'd been forced to sign divorce papers.

"I'm sure the French felt the same, when they signed the armistice with Germany," Gareth mumbled to himself. He looked over when Xena whined, picking up on his melancholy. "Don't worry girl, it'll get better. No way to go but up, after all."

His friends, of course, had taken his signing a lopsided divorce agreement as a sign that he had done something wrong. They felt justified in abandoning him, rushing to Tilly's side to "help her through this awful time." Well, *fuck* them.

Gareth closed his eyes and tilted his head back, letting the silence of the desert settle through him. He concentrated on the crackle of the fire, the sizzle of the steaks cooking, the snuffling of his dog….

"Xena," he yelled, catching her just about to grab a steak. She jerked back, giving him the patented husky *What? I haven't done anything* look. He reached out and flipped the steaks. "They'll be done in a minute. Just be patient."

He settled back again, this time leaving his eyes open, letting them slip slightly out of focus to better catch motion in the sky above. The meteor shower was due to start any minute. He'd always felt seeing a shooting star was lucky. So here, in the dark desert night, he'd let the sky bless his new beginning.

Then he'd head back home. Maybe he'd hit that new casino, *Atlantis*, on the way through town. He'd seen a billboard touting their much-advertised jackpot. Three-hundred pure gold coins. A publicity stunt, true, but someone had to win it.

That would start his new life off right. He snorted to himself—it was more likely he'd lose his gas money. Still, you had to show your luck that you believed in it if you wanted it to come. Then he'd get a new lawyer, a better lawyer. Get his life back…

"Rur-rur." Gareth glanced over at Xena. The husky perked her ears forward, watching the steaks intently. They'd started to smoke. Quickly grabbing the tongs, he flipped the steaks over again before they could burn. "Good catch, girl. I should know better than to let my mind wander while I'm cooking. They've got to be done. Gotta grab some plates."

He dug through a paper shopping bag full of utensils, and of course, more beer. "Gah—plates are on the bottom. Give me a sec—"

"Grrrrrrr." The dog stared off into the darkness, tail stiff, steaks forgotten.

Gareth froze, heartbeat automatically quickening in response to her low growl. Xena wasn't one to growl at nothing.

In seconds, he snaked his right hand around the back of his chair where he'd dropped his hatchet earlier, after chopping the kindling.

Slowly, he turned back in the direction of Xena's attention. The dog had lifted from her lounging position and now stood, hackles on the back of her neck rising. Gareth endeavored to conceal the hatchet with the paper plates in his left hand.

"Grrrrr." Xena growled again, deeper than before. Gareth squinted, his night vision non-existent due to the campfire. There was definitely something out in the darkness. Here, in the middle of literally nowhere, empty desert with only the glow of the city to the south to remind you that you weren't alone. At this hour, and at this distance from civilization, whatever it was couldn't be good.

Well, this was a load of crap. The steaks were done, so he dropped the plates on the ground next to the fire and grabbed a fork. He speared them with his left hand and moved them to a plate, being careful to keep the hatchet low and hidden in his right.

He'd be hungry enough to get to the steaks later. If there was a later.

Then, calmly as he could, he cleared his throat. "You might as well come into the light. She knows you're there."

After a moment, a figure came forward, silently. He was of average height with slicked-back, dark hair. And, bizarrely, he was buttoned up in a dark suit. Had he been standing in a used car lot, he'd have fit right in. In the middle of an empty desert night, the newcomer made the hair on the back of Gareth's neck stand up. A second figure was nearly indistinguishable behind him. With just two suits to face, he'd still get out of this. He gripped the handle of his axe a little harder but made no other move.

"Can I help you, friend?" Gareth asked as affably as he could muster.

The stranger's lips stretched back into one hell of an awkward smile. "Greetings, human." He made no move to advance further into the light. His eyes flicked toward Xena, who continued to growl at him. "The creature will not attack, will it?"

Greetings human? Creature? Gareth frowned. This got stranger by the minute. "Not unless she thinks you're going to harm me. If you do, though..." It was all bluff. Huskies were known for many things, but attacking people wasn't one of them. This guy didn't feel menacing, but the needle was pegged on the weird meter. "What can I do for you, friend?" Gareth asked again.

"I am Ygurthngjix and this,"—he gestured behind him—"is *Steve* . We were traveling to our domicile in the desert, but our conveyance has stopped. We saw your fire and approached in the hope that you are knowledgeable in the workings of these machines and can convince it to go again."

What the...? Gareth blinked hard at the stranger. Was one of those weird-ass conventions going on in Vegas? Some kind of hyper-awkward cosplayer convention? Heaven knew that normal people didn't talk like that.

Gareth shrugged. "I'm not a mechanic. Unless it's something simple, you're out of luck."

The cosplaying suit-weirdo wouldn't take the hint, though. "There was an indicator light upon the control panel. A yellow monolith."

Gareth squinted, unwilling to relinquish his wariness, especially since Xena's tail was now sticking straight out as she sniffed the air in their direction.

"I'm not familiar with that one."

"It looked like this." Ygurthngjix squatted and scratched a familiar symbol in the loose dirt beside the campfire. Gareth angled his head to catch a glimpse in the golden firelight.

"That's a gas pump. You're out of gas."

A blank stare was his only reply.

Gareth shifted his weight warily. Weirdo cosplayers demanding he play their silly game, no doubt. "Umm... your *conveyance* is out of fuel. You need to replenish the fuel tank to make it go again."

Ygurthngjix stood up and stared at him expectantly. "I require more of this fuel."

"I'm afraid I can't help you there. I don't have any."

The cosplayer blinked but made no other movement. "Then you must take us in your conveyance."

Gareth blew out a breath, out of patience. He waved toward the plate of steaks. "I'm not going anywhere, bud. My dinner is already getting cold. Besides, I don't pick up hitchhikers and I definitely don't do *weird.*" Ygurthngjix opened his mouth, but Gareth interrupted the protest. "*No.* Ygurthngjix and Steve, you'll just have to hoof it back to a gas station yourselves. Or to your *domicile.* Whatever it is, I don't care. I came out here to be by myself with my dog, and you are interrupting that. Now please, *go.*"

Ygurthngjix stood still as a statue. "We will pay."

"*No.*" Gareth waved back toward the road. "Shoo. You're wasting your time here. The city's that way. Bye bye, now."

Ygurthngjix turned toward Steve, whose mouth started to move, but all Gareth could hear was a strange whine. When the noise stopped, Ygurthngjix turned back toward him. "We will pay you. In gold."

At first Gareth thought his ears were playing tricks on him. Then, the cosplayer's words sank in.

Did he say they'd pay him—*in gold?*

Chapter Two

Hookers and Blow

GARETH BLINKED HIS INCREDULITY AT THE COSPLAYER. "Bullshit. No one carries gold around, much less uses it to pay for things."

Steve opened his mouth, and Gareth heard that strange whine again. Ygurthngjix reached into a pocket and produced a small coin, which he tossed to the ground in front of Gareth. "We will pay you twenty-five more such coins."

Gareth reached out and picked up the coin. The very heavy coin that glinted in the firelight. He brought it closer to his face to get a better look. Well, it certainly looked like a gold coin, but how would you know? He wasn't a collector. Of course, there was that thing they were always doing in the Olympics with the medals. He brought the coin up to his mouth and bit it. He was almost relieved when he didn't feel anything. He was about to throw it back and end this weirdness when he spotted the small indentation. There were teeth marks in the coin. *Holy Shit!*

It was real. Or at least it seemed so. He tossed the coin, flipping it a few times to judge its weight. It must be a good ounce or so. There had been a report on the radio about how the price of gold had gone over $2,600 per ounce, which would mean they were offering him around $67,000. *Holy crap.*

That much money would go a long way toward fixing his problems. Who the hell were these guys?

Ygurthngjix watched Gareth's examination of the coin. "Are you satisfied? The coins are real. They are yours. *If* you take us now."

Gareth rubbed his jaw and studied the guy and his companion, an unmoving shadow in the darkness behind him. This was such a bad idea, on so many levels.

But that was so much money.

"Okay. Grab Steve and get in the truck." He pointed toward his old battered F150 Crew Cab. That truck and the dog were just about all he'd gotten from the divorce settlement… and only because his ex had wanted nothing to do with either.

Ygurthngjix stood unmoving, and Gareth grew more confused. He raised his hands at the guy. "What? I thought you were in a hurry."

The cosplayer pointed at Xena. "The creature. It must stay."

Wow. The guy was really dedicated to his part, wasn't he? Gareth wondered if he ever broke his roleplaying. But if he wasn't going to do it for being broken down and stranded in the desert, he probably wasn't going to do it for anything.

Regardless, there was no way in hell he was leaving his girl behind. None. "No deal. I won't leave my dog—not for *any* money. She goes along, or it's back to plan A and you two start walking."

Ygurthngjix was stiff shouldered with clenched fists at his sides, clearly irritated. Another of those high, squeaky noises came from the direction where Steve was standing. Then they both turned toward the truck.

"Very well, human. But if the creature attacks us, you will not get paid."

"Gareth."

Ygurthngjix stopped. "Please repeat?"

"My name. It's Gareth. *Human* is a species." Gareth followed them toward the truck, then opened the front door. He paused to allow Xena to jump into her usual spot. He jerked his thumb at the two would-be passengers. "You two ride in the back."

Gareth finally got his first look at Steve. At first glance, he appeared normal—if such a term could be attributed to such hardcore cosplayers. But with a closer look, Gareth noticed an unmistakable strangeness.

Sure, he seemed like a generic, unremarkable northern European male, but his features were completely transparent, like they were 3D-printed on some kind of cellophane. Beneath that were features straight out of a bad alien invasion B-movie. Giant black eyes, gray skin, slit nose, elongated neck.

Whoa, these cosplayers were getting more and more professional with their effects. That kind of quality indicated money and since money was what they had promised him—and a good chunk of it—it made Gareth feel more like they were legit.

He was beyond the point of asking any questions about their cosplay or the convention or why they were in town. All he had to do was play along, get the money, and drop them off. Easy peasy.

"Is there a problem?" Ygurthngjix must have noticed Gareth's hesitation.

Gareth shook himself from his thoughts and swung into the truck after his dog. "Nope. No problem. Just admiring Steve's blue eyes. You don't normally see a shade like that."

The other two climbed into the back of the cab, and Gareth tried to keep his eyes ahead, rather than on the weirdness in the rearview mirror as he started the truck and popped it into gear.

"Proceed down this path to our conveyance on the side of the road. We must retrieve our bags before we go," Ygurthngjix commanded.

Gareth shrugged. "You're the one paying." He flicked his eyes up to the mirror then. "Speaking of that…"

"Your payment is in one of the bags we must retrieve."

Gareth followed Ygurthngjix's directions, trying unsuccessfully to nudge away the doubts edging his thoughts. The dog sat quietly beside him, never taking her eyes off their oddball passengers.

They traveled back down the road, quickly overtaking the parked Prius on the shoulder. Huh. Figured. Hybrid piece of crap.

"There are two bags to retrieve," Ygurthngjix said. "The smaller contains your payment."

Of course he'd have to be the one to get it but at least that gave him the chance to get a good look at what was in the bags. With a grunt, he swung open the door. "Right. Wait here."

Gareth left the truck and approached the nondescript compact car, opening the rear hatch. The stench of rotten food rose up to nearly choke him.

What the…?

He scoured the interior under the dim illumination from the car's dome light. The car was full of half-eaten and discarded burgers, along with the remains of what were obviously a great many trips to Taco Bell. Half full soda, stray French fries, and leaky shake cups were tossed carelessly in the back seat. It was like the stoner road trip from hell in here.

Gareth spotted what he was after: a backpack and large duffel bag. He scooped them up. The backpack was heavy. Encouraged by this, he unzipped it and spotted roughly twenty-five gold coins inside. Very familiar-looking gold coins. He leaned in for a closer look and pulled out the coin he'd already been given, and it was clearly the same. In the firelight it had been hard to make out any details. He'd seen these same coins just yesterday, along with two hundred and seventy-four of their friends. They'd been in the display showcasing the huge jackpot offered in celebration of the grand opening of the new *Atlantis* casino. His stomach dipped.

This made him less curious about the other bag. Nevertheless, he unzipped that one as well and nearly dropped the bag when he saw what was inside. Unmistakably, bricks of cocaine. Just like on *COPS*. Behind the coke, he could see several Blu-ray discs. *Who the fuck watches Blu-rays anymore?* They had handwritten labels in Sharpie, including a number of movies that were still in the theaters.

Not just drug dealers, but pirates, too.

Shit. Goddamn it. Fuck this. Nothing was worth the potential shitstorm about to rain down across the isolated desert night. Gareth quickly zipped the bags back up and dropped them on the ground. He closed the hatchback, only to have his eyes stabbed by the headlights of an oncoming car. He squinted. It was still some distance away, but it was headed their way. There was no way a second car was randomly heading down this forgotten road tonight.

With a resigned sigh, he hauled the two bags back to the truck, tossing them into the bed before quickly climbing in. He cranked the ignition and floored it, flipping a U-turn before turning the lights back on.

"You two expecting company?" he croaked at his passengers.

"Why would you ask such a question?"

"Because there's a car heading down the road behind us, and I don't think they're looking for *me*."

His eyes flicked to the rearview mirror, scanning the darkness for pursuing headlights but couldn't see them yet.

The weird squeaking sound Gareth was quickly associating with Steve burbled before Ygurthngjix said, "It may be the authorities. You must avoid them at all costs."

Gareth gritted his teeth, gripping the wheel until his knuckles whitened. "How about I pull over and just give you to them? This goes way beyond giving you two creeps a lift." He glanced at the mirror again. Still nothing.

"They will assume we drove out here to meet you. Thus, you will be equally culpable."

Gareth shrugged, but his pedal was still pushed firmly against the metal. "They might lock me up too—until they can check out my story. C'mon guys, time to drop the stupid cosplaying act and just be real here, or I'll slam the brakes now."

"There is no act, and these authorities will not check out your story. They will just shoot you."

"The police don't just shoot people." *Well, most of the time, at least.*

"These are not the police. I said they were the authorities. I never said the police."

Shit. Another quick glance in the rear-view mirror. Lights were hitting the Prius now. "What authorities are they, then, if not the police? The FBI?" He looked in the rearview mirror straight into Ygurthngjix's eyes, and his stomach sank. "You mean the Mob, don't you?"

"We are being pursued by representatives of the organization responsible for operating the casino. They wish to retrieve the gold coins we won. Many of the gold coins we no longer possess."

He pushed the truck faster than was probably wise, with no desire whatsoever to meet these 'authorities'.

"But why? Did you cheat or something?"

"We made an alteration to the program operating the games of chance attached to the gold jackpot. It was written to prevent anyone from winning the jackpot. We corrected this flaw."

Gareth might have forgotten how to breathe for a few seconds.

Ygurthngjix waved a hand, catching his attention. "Turn left at the four-armed succulent. *There.*"

Gareth cranked the wheel when he reached the cactus, and the truck slewed around a corner, bouncing off the track and into brush before he could recover and get it back on the road.

"Did you use the gold coins you won to buy that coke in the other bag?"

"Yes. And to pay you."

Gareth growled through his teeth. "The people running the casino are also the ones selling the drugs. You should have told a hooker your plans, so you could score the perfect dumbass trifecta. Fucking morons."

A lengthy, high-pitched squeal came out of Steve. Ygurthngjix looked at his companion. "It appears we might have miscalculated. Do you see their conveyance yet?"

Gareth's gut twisted even further. These idiots were too fucking dumb to be cosplayers.

Then who the hell were they?

He glanced into the rearview mirror and saw no evidence of pursuit.

"We are close now. Almost to our ship," said Ygurthngjix matter-of-factly.

Ship? Were they…was this…? "I thought we were going to your domicile?" Gareth squeaked out in a pitch at least an octave higher than his normal voice.

The road—more a dirt track now, really—took a turn though a field of rocks, then up a hill. Gareth had to lean forward, navigating within the scope of his headlights.

"Time to come clean about what you are and where you're from," he finally bit out.

Ygurthngjix replied without hesitation. "We are average humans, such as yourself."

"No human addresses another as *human*. Steve speaks in squeals, and his human mask is broken. I can see right through it. Are you two escapees from Area 51?"

Steve squealed at Ygurthngjix, who bowed his head in resignation. "We are, shall we say, enterprising individuals. We're visiting on a very lucrative business opportunity."

Gareth goggled at him. "Buying coke to sell to aliens?"

"Your planet is famous for its chemical creations. In certain circles, anyway." Steve let out a particularly loud squeal. "Yes, yes, I see it." He turned back to Gareth. "Pull over by the rock that looks like a *zandor*."

"I have no idea what a *zandor* is. This one? It sorta looks like a four-legged chicken."

Gareth pulled the car to a stop. Turning around to address his soon-to-be ex-passengers, he spotted headlights behind them, just down the road.

"Shit, they found us after all."

Ygurthngjix and Steve bolted from the car.

"What the hell? You're just going to leave me to face them alone?" Gareth shouted after the fleeing pair. He couldn't decide whether to follow them or dump the coke and flee in his truck. Xena jumped onto the seat from the wheel-well where she'd been sleeping, nudging him with her nose.

Gripping the steering wheel tightly, he cursed a blue streak. He needed to do something, and *now*. But what?

It was then that Gareth noticed Steve drawing imaginary patterns on the rock face. In answer to this summons, a bright flash stabbed Gareth's eyes, but he would not be deterred, blinking furiously to refocus his gaze. A silvery door had appeared *in* the rock. Was he losing it? A second later, the truck's engine sputtered and died. Gareth turned the key to crank the engine, furiously attempting to restart it to no avail.

"Human. You must hurry. Grab the bags and come." Ygurthngjix waved emphatically beside Steve. Meanwhile, his companion frantically dug his hands though the dirt at his feet, the image of someone who had dropped their car keys and was furiously searching for them.

"My truck won't start," Gareth yelled back.

"Of course not. Steve turned on the damping field to give us some time. Now hurry."

What—*huh?* They wanted him to go with them? Or just hand them their shit? Xena nipped him in the side, not hard enough to break skin but hard enough to hurt. He glanced down at the husky. She met his eyes, then poked him with her nose, looking toward the door.

Run Gareth, run, couldn't have been clearer than if the words had appeared in a text bubble over her head. "Okay, okay, Obi-wan. I'm going!"

Gareth opened the door and jumped out of the truck. He reached into the bed to grab the backpack and duffel. The dog hopped out after him and they ran toward the pair of aliens. As he got to the rock, a door slid open. Apparently, Steve had found the key.

Ygurthngjix waved him inside the doorway but stopped when he spotted the dog. "The creature stays."

"The creature goes, or I stay," Gareth replied. He held up the backpack and duffel, backing out of the alien's reach. "*With* your goods."

Xena took that moment to dart past the alien gatekeeper, into the doorway.

The alien's arm dropped. "Very well. But you must control the creature and make sure it does not eliminate before we dump you."

"*Drop* me off, you mean? *Dump* me sounds like you're pushing me out the airlock."

The alien managed to look annoyed. "Yes, yes, drop you off. Now hurry into the ship."

The ship …? Wow. This was happening. Pausing for one last look around, the thought of being chased down by the mafia overrode his hesitation at the WTF-ness of his current situation. Gareth followed Ygurthngjix into the vessel.

The inside was the size of a large SUV and resembled a spaced-up version of the Prius they'd been driving. Trash—what he could only assume where the outer space version of take-out boxes—littered the interior. Ygurthngjix joined Steve at what he presumed was the front of the ship and strapped in beside him. There was a second pair of seats behind the first, though Gareth had to shovel aside a pile of trash to sit there.

Xena rooted though the trash on the floor next to him, only stopping when he nudged her. She took a second to quickly swallow whatever she'd found, which he hoped wouldn't make her sick. Based on things he had seen her eat before, she'd probably be fine.

A loud banging noise rang off the door behind him. Gareth leaned toward the bizarre pair in the row in front of him. "Your friends have arrived. Can we go now?"

"Steve must finish priming the engine." Ygurthngjix turned back toward what was presumably a control panel.

Steve took out something that looked like a large wrench and banged it on one of the pipes overhead. Gareth's jaw dropped.

"Sometimes the fuel sticks if it isn't primed properly," Ygurthngjix supplied helpfully. A hum filled the room, and several lights on the control panel turned purple. "There, now we can launch."

"Just drop me somewhere along the I-15, south of Vegas. I should be able to make my way from there. Somewhere near Baker would be ideal."

"I do not know this Baker. Just indicate where you wish to be dropped, and we will do so." Ygurthngjix adjusted a number of switches resulting in a chorus of clangs and bangs from the back of the ship.

Gareth looked askance. "You guys might want to consider getting this thing serviced sometime soon. It sounds like something's about to break."

"Our ship is in perfect working order," the alien contradicted.

No spaceship was supposed to sound like a trashed VW bus driven by a stoner drug dealer. Everything shook, and the loud whine continued until Gareth could feel his molar fillings vibrate. He assumed that meant they were flying, though he couldn't detect any sense of motion. His mind went to the videos on YouTube showing glowing dots shooting up toward the sky, making radical changes in direction at random. Maybe they'd been real after all?

A light in the middle of the control panel flared bright orange and started flashing. At the same time, a loud squeal came from what had to be a speaker overhead. It looked like one of those old metal drive-in speakers you'd hang from your window. Both Steve and Ygurthngjix became visibly agitated, and a torrent of squeals went off between the two of them.

"What is it? Are we going to crash?" Gareth asked, tensing.

Ygurthngjix broke off his conversation with Steve and turned to face Gareth. "The ship is fine. We have been detected by the authorities and told to enter orbit and await further instructions."

"The mob has a *spaceshi* p?" Gareth asked incredulously.

Ygurthngjix shook his head. "No, not the Earth authorities. The space patrol. Our information indicated it would be absent from this area for another two hours. It must have returned early from its meal period."

"And I'm guessing that the cocaine is also illegal for you guys?"

"Visiting your planet is illegal. The interesting chemical substances your people make is merely one of the reasons your planet is proscribed. We will all be placed into detention."

Gareth waved an arm urgently. "Well, what are you waiting for? Lose him."

"That is not possible. Their ship is many times faster than ours. Attempting to run will only force them to disable our ship, and there is no certainty we would survive the attempt. We must comply. Entering orbit now."

Gareth's shoulders slumped as he fell back against his seat. "Well, that's just great. I'll go to space jail because the star police came back early from their donut run and you guys are driving a Hyundai!"

There had to be something they could do, but what he knew about space travel came from shows like *Star Trek* or *Battlestar Galactica*. But what was it they did in one of the *Star Wars* movies—that scene when Han Solo was trying to outrun the Star Destroyers with the *Millenium Falcon*? "Fly into the asteroid belt. Lose him there."

Ygurthngjix snorted. "Asteroid belts are mostly empty space. And before you ask, no we can't hide in the corona of your sun either. Anything that could protect you from proximity to a star would laugh off any known energy weapon. Your space movies are stupid. We'll have to shut down and wait to be boarded. If we're lucky, we'll only get ten of your years on a penal moon."

"*Ten years!*" Gareth practically shouted. "Fuck that. Wait, you said Earth is proscribed. Is *everyone* banned? If we dive back down, will they chase us?"

Ygurthngjix started to shake his head. Steve interrupted him, screeching in his spaceman language. Ygurthngjix replied, then Steve reached over and wacked him on the back of his head.

"Very well, human, we will try your plan. Steve feels that the authorities are too rigid in their observance of the law to violate the proscription, even to pursue us. I think both of you are wrong, but all we risk is double the term of the sentence."

"*Twenty* years? Now wait—"

Gareth was forced to grab onto something as the ship pitched over and headed back into the atmosphere. Steve watched an indicator intently and then let out a warble.

"As I feared, they are pursuing us. Perhaps if we surrender, I can convince them this was *your* idea."

"*What?* No. This ship is cloaked right?" Gareth interjected.

"No. Or they couldn't follow us."

Gareth's fist pounded down on the arm of his chair. "Not cloaked to the space fuzz. To radar."

"Of course. We hide ourselves from your primitive electromagnetic sensors." Ygurthngjix replied, his voice dripping with disdain.

"Well turn it off, then, and fly north of where you found me— about 80 miles or so. Near a small town called Rachel, Nevada." Good thing he'd kept up on his favorite alien conspiracy theories and knew exactly where Area-51 was, even without a map.

Ygurthngjix looked over at him questioningly.

Gareth gestured again in frustration. "It's a no-fly area. If you fly low and slow to get their attention, the base will scramble their jets. Then, you ditch the cops."

Steve screeched something at Ygurthngjix, who sighed. "Very well, human. It is not a good plan but at least it is a plan. On your head be it."

Ygurthngjix and Steve got busy adjusting their various controls. Gareth caught a glimpse of the familiar diorama of the desert surrounding Vegas. *Almost home.*

Lights flashed, and a screeching siren split the air. Ygurthngjix explained between tight lips. "We have been discovered by a great number of your detection devices. Several of your air-based vehicles are also headed toward us."

"And our police friend?" Gareth leaned forward expectantly.

"He is leaving."

Gareth pumped the air with his fist. "Yes! Okay, so now you can turn on the cloak and drop me off."

"No. Our only chance of escape from this planet is to leave now while the authorities' sensors are blinded by the planet. If we drop you off, it will give him time to resume his position in high orbit where he can easily apprehend us again. We will not suffer two Earth decades of imprisonment for that. Therefore, you must come with us."

Gareth shot from his chair and grabbed Ygurthngjix's shoulder. "Now wait just a damn minute. You need to drop us off. I've got a family—this is my home! I never signed up to go wandering through space."

Ygurthngjix barely acknowledged this protest and didn't even turn toward Gareth. "There is no time. We go now, human."

The alien attempted to pull away from Gareth's grip, but he was stronger and had leverage. One point for the home team. As he held Ygurthngjix down, he turned his attention to Steve, presumably the pilot. If he could somehow leverage—

A brilliant flash of light drilled into the center of each of his pupils with white-hot intensity.

He barely had time to suck in a breath before the world went black.

Chapter Three

I Don't Speak Space Walrus

GARETH AWOKE TO A COLD, WET NOSE SHOVED AGAINST his ribs. His consciousness slowly climbed to the surface through miles of fog, brain still booting up. But years of careful training snapped him out of sleep. "All right, *all right*, dog. *Jesus*, I'll let you out."

He pushed up to a sitting position, and the messages his body was sending to his brain finally started to register. He wasn't in his bed. *No*, he was lying on an icy, metallic floor. The fuzziness passed, quickly replaced by panic as he remembered the events preceding losing consciousness. Xena nudged him again, then let out a sharp bark. He put his hand down to comfort the dog. "Okay, okay. I'm up."

Xena let out a deep-throated *woof*, shifting from *wake up, human* mode to *do something, stupid human*. His alarm rising, Gareth forced himself to do what he had been avoiding—he opened his eyes.

Cold, bright light assaulted him, jabbing at his brain. He used a hand to shade his eyes. Whatever the two aliens had done to knock him out had him feeling like the day after a wild weekend bender. He was on the metal floor of what looked to be a giant metal room—huge as a hangar bay. The now-notorious backpack sat beside his leg on the floor.

Sudden movement caught his eye. To his left, he spotted a trio of aliens. These looked nothing like the glimpses he'd had of the 'real' Steve and Ygurthngjix. Two of them, who looked like giant balls of snot, were dragging a third—who looked vaguely like Greedo from *Star Wars*—along the floor away from Gareth. To his shock, the Greedo alien had his arms and legs secured and seemed to be doing his best to break the hold the snot brothers had on him.

They dragged the green dude past Steve and Ygurthngjix's ship, then they tossed the bound alien to the floor and slithered away. The bound alien's efforts to break free escalated to a frenzy as he flopped about. He emitted what Gareth could only interpret as screams in some alien tongue.

What was going on here? And where were Steve and Ygurthngjix? Gareth pushed to his feet, when he spotted the missing duo exiting a door near to the ramp into their ship.

"Steve! Ygurthngjix!" Gareth called out, voice echoing across the vast emptiness. But they didn't respond, walking quickly up the ramp and into the ship. His stomach dropped as he finished struggling to his feet. "*Wait!*"

But it was too late, or they didn't care. Gareth stared in horror as the hatch snapped closed and the ramp promptly retracted. The ship then silently levitated above the floor. The floor, ceiling and walls just behind the ship appeared to grow toward each other, until they met and created a seamless barrier between the ship and the rest of the room where Gareth stood. He could only presume it was some type of airlock that allowed the ship to leave the hangar.

And strand him here. Well... *fuck.*

A minute later, the barrier retracted, and the room returned to normal. The ship was, unsurprisingly, gone. Gareth noticed, to his horror, that the tied-up alien was also gone. Had he been sucked into space with the exiting ship? What kind of fucked up place was this?

"Well, shit. *Now* what?" He looked down at Xena as if she might have the answers. She just looked back at him with her big brown eyes and wagged her tail, upright ears fluttering back and then pointing forward again.

Gareth heaved a huge sigh, continuing the one-sided conversation. "Well, I'm glad *someone* thinks I'll figure something out, 'cause *I* don't have a clue."

He stooped to open the dusty backpack, expecting it to be empty. He was pleasantly surprised to find it still contained his promised gold, for as much good as it would do him here. Wherever *here* even was.

So, kidnapping and then abandoning him were acceptable to the dubious alien duo, but robbing him was beyond the pale.

Gareth straightened and looked around, spotting what looked like a worn metal hatch nearby. This whole place looked banged up, like the inside of the *Millenium Falcon* after Han had a particularly harrowing run-in with a squadron of TIE fighters.

Grunting with the effort, he grabbed the pack and hefted it onto his shoulder, then, after staring at the hatch for another few long minutes, he steeled himself and sucked in a breath.

"Come on, girl. Let's go see where we are."

Within a few feet of the hatch, it slid open as if waiting for him. The sound was different than he'd expected—though he soon realized that what he'd expected was the familiar whoosh of a door on the *Enterprise.* What caught his attention now—and brought him up short in mild alarm—was the presence of a large, strange being in the doorway.

The creature could only be described as a walrus-man, large and looming with rolls upon rolls of blubber, two gleaming white tusks, and a whiskery upper lip. The being spoke with a booming voice in a series of screeches, grunts and squeals.

Gareth froze, desperately trying to determine if that was a greeting or a warning. The alien walrus seemed bipedal, and approached with more ease than his earthly counterpart would have. Then it boomed at him again. Gareth threw out his hands, palm up and shrugged. "Sorry… I don't speak space walrus."

The alien boomed a third time. Then, it reached a flipper-like appendage into a pouch at its side and extracted a long needle.

Gareth lifted his hands up, palms out. "*Whoa* —no way, Jose, buddy walrus-man. I'm no pincushion for experimental alien probing." Unless the probing came from a hot chick alien who looked like Angelina Jolie with a fetish for middle-aged and supremely average earthmen. Gareth took a step back, holding his hands out in front of him like a barrier, as if that would do him any good. This thing was almost half his height taller than him and outweighed him by several hundred pounds.

Then the alien grabbed him and jabbed the needle straight into his head.

The most hideous pain streaked through his skull like a bolt of lightning. Like someone had pounded a tenpenny nail into his brain—over and over. In agony, Gareth slumped to the ground and rocked back and forth, head in hands and his eyes screwed shut. *Fuck.*

So far, aliens were assholes.

The walrus creature stood motionless, hovering over him while he whimpered and silently wished he had a way to dig into his own skull, rip out his brain, and stop the torment. He cracked his lids open just a fraction to see where the hell his dog was. From a dark corner, she cranked her head toward him, ears perked. Finally, the pain receded enough for Gareth to cock his head up at his tormenter, who studied him with no visible sign of sympathy.

Of course, what would sympathy even look like on a walrus?

"What—what the *hell* did you do to me?" Gareth choked out.

The walrus blinked. "I injected comm nanites. It's something that *should* have been done at birth. You're welcome for that."

Gareth blinked. The walrus was still doing its grunt, squeak, and squeal thing, but he understood it this time.

It spoke again. "Your full User Interface, should be available in about one hour. Once the neural pathways finish growing through your brain."

"My *brain* ..." Gareth gingerly felt around the injection site. He swore he could feel something leaking out. His ex would have had a *lot* to say about that.

"Now, as I was asking you before the discovery of your shameful lack of communication, what are you doing here? Emigres are to wait in the holding area until summoned." Mr. Walrus glared down at him.

"Emigres? What the hell? Look, I just saw someone tossed out the airlock. I need the police not the space DHS."

The Alien reared back. "You saw someone murdered? Tell me what happened. Immediately!"

Gareth paused for a second. He was no expert on aliens—though he supposed his experiences of the day made him humanity's alien expert—but something seemed off. Walrus dude's reaction didn't feel sincere. Unsure of what choice he actually had, Gareth decided to describe what he saw. "Two big blob-people dragged this tied-up green guy over to that spot." Gareth pointed down the hanger. "Then, they dropped him and left him to be sucked out into space when the ship left."

The walrus alien instantly calmed. "Why waste my time with this? That was just the cleanup crew doing their morning rounds."

"What the fuck do you mean *cleanup crew*? They tied up a man—person—*whatever* and tossed him out an airlock." Gareth felt his ire rising at the indifference exhibited by the alien.

The alien blew out his mustache and let out a sigh. "Really, do you have *no* idea how things work? The cleanup crew gathers those who have failed to pay their upkeep and ejects them from the station." Gareth opened his mouth to reply, but the alien's voice boomed right over his. "*No.* No more wasting of my time with idiotic questions. We must deal with the matter at hand. I was told you wished to emigrate."

Gareth quickly reviewed the last couple of minutes in his head before he replied, "Fuck that."

The alien gestured in a way that Gareth didn't recognize. "Return to your ship, then, human. I shall send a bill to those two idiots for wasting my time." Walrus-man turned his back and headed toward the hatch.

"I don't have a ship. The two idiots took it and left."

The space DHS agent turned back to him. "Well, if you're not emigrating, then come with me. I'll take you to the station exit."

Gareth took a step to follow him before the words sank in and he halted. "Wait—what's beyond the exit? A ship of some kind?"

"Vacuum."

Gareth froze. He should have seen that one coming. Now walrus-man wanted to space him along with no-upkeep guy?

Shit, was this some drug-addled dream inspired by binge-watching *The Expanse*?

"*Well?*" prompted the alien. "Come along."

Gareth blinked a few times. "Ah, I changed my mind. I guess I'm emigrating."

Another unrecognizable gesture from the alien. "Make up your mind. *Primitives.*" It again turned back to the hatch.

Gareth threw out a hand toward the walrus-man "Excuse me, Mr. ...?"

It stopped again, and Gareth had no idea how he knew, but it was clearly irritated. "You may address me as Chief Bureaucrat Smith."

"Smith? *Really?*"

It stood stock still, the image of forced patience, if indeed, that's what the emotion looked like on a flippered marine mammal. "The translation software's localization function assigns me a name that is appropriate to your culture. You would be unable to pronounce mine." Mr. Smith then turned and proceeded through the door.

Gareth followed his unusual escort down an increasingly complex series of corridors. Sometimes they ascended stairs, sometimes they descended long, shallow ramps. Every hundred paces or so, they turned a sharp corner. Gareth was quickly lost and struggled to keep up while glancing over his shoulder to keep an eye on his dog. She was continually distracted by the plethora of new smells to discover.

"So, where exactly are we, anyway?" Gareth finally called after the alien.

Mr. Smith replied without looking back. "Muddy River Township."

"Muddy River… *what*? That's an odd name for a space station. No, but I what I meant to ask was…*where* are we in space? Earth orbit? Out by Mars? What's our location?"

"You mean our star location. No one really cares about that sort of thing. Let me see…" It halted for a moment in the passage and cocked its head as if looking at something only it could see. "It says here the closest star is Proxima Centauri."

Gareth frowned. What the hell was it looking at? This mysterious UI-thing it had mentioned before, maybe?

Then the realization hit him. Centauri…but that meant. "That makes me the first human to leave the solar system."

"No, indeed it does not. Here we are." Smith entered a hatch that had opened at his approach. Gareth warily followed, stepping into a room that might have been labeled *Generic Office 101*. Chipped tan paint covered the metal walls. The only furnishing was a large, blocky gray desk. Smith seated himself behind it. The desk was sparsely decorated with a glass vase containing a droopy yellow flower and a framed picture of another walrus creature surrounded by what looked like a dozen walrus-lings. The alien bureaucrat pointed in front of the desk, "Sit."

Gareth looked around, blanking. There were no chairs. "Where?"

"I said *sit!*"

Gareth shrugged and sat, fully expecting to end up on the floor. To his shock, a chair sprouted from the floor, catching his butt on the way down. The metal oozed around him, forming itself to his backside like a liquid. Like the T-1000 version of a modern stool. "Cool space chair."

He tried bouncing up and down a few times, but the chair felt firmly supportive with just enough give to be comfortable. Xena curled up on the floor in front of him.

Mr. Smith waved his hands over his desk, pulling up some kind of holographic screen. "Hold still for the scan."

Scan? More needles? Possibly in his head again or even worse places? Gareth shot to his feet. "*Wait!* What scan? I don't—"

Before he could continue, Smith pressed another button which brought up a bar that slammed against Gareth's legs, knocking him back into his seat. Then, a bright light appeared over him, followed by what felt like a million ants crawling through his brain. He couldn't talk and he couldn't move. This went on for a subjective eternity.

"The scan is necessary to complete your residency application," Smith droned. "Now we must see if you can be put to use."

"I have a master's degree in computer science and information technology."

Smith made a noise that may have been a scoff. "*Useless.*"

"I worked for an internet security company?"

"Also useless." The walrus man waved his hands and scrolled quickly through reams of data. "It looks like the sludge-pits for you. It's a very important job. You will convert waste into sludge that can be fed to the bio-pits, which are then converted into foodstuffs. Very exciting." He poked at the screen hovering before him.

Gareth blinked. "A crap-processing plant? No, thank you. I'm not spending my days shoveling shit around."

Smith stopped his air-typing and stared at Gareth. "You must have a job, so you can cover your upkeep costs."

Shit! "Upkeep? You never did explain that."

"Air, food, lodging. None of these things come free."

Well, huh, obviously. Capitalism prevailed, even out here near Proxima Centauri, apparently. "And if I can't pay, I'm killed?"

"You will be ejected from the city. It is not our fault if the environment outside is not capable of supporting your form of life. It's not all bad, though. I'd make good money from bets on you."

What the hell…? He was facing a future as a space sewage worker and this guy was talking about *bets?* "I'm afraid to ask, but here goes... *Bets?*"

Smith gestured animatedly with a flipper-hand. "We haven't ejected a human before. There will be plenty wanting to see how long it takes you to pop."

Gareth stiffened, then slapped the desk with his palm, snarling through his teeth. "Now see here, Tusky. I'm not shoveling poo, and I'm most certainly not going to play *How Long Does It Take for the Human to Pop!* I have skills. Find me a job."

Smith blew air through his mustache. "You don't bring much to the table. No skills useful to us. It's not like you know anything about gaming, for example. That would make it much easier.

The scan report states you have some talent there, but no relevant experience, unfortunately."

Gaming? *Now*, they were talking. But how could that leverage him a livelihood? Gareth leaned back in his chair. "What relevant gaming experience?"

Mr. Smith sighed—it was part grunt, part growl, part snarl. "I ran a search on all of our gaming channels and forums. You don't appear on any of them."

Gareth thought back over the thousands of hours of play time he had with Dragon Epoch. If he'd been able to leverage all that into a job on Earth, he'd be a zillionaire. "I can state unequivocally that I'm qualified to play games."

Smith hesitated. "This is a specific type of game. It takes place in a virtual world and has mechanics for magic and weapons."

He blinked. Bureaucrat Smith had just described the majority of Gareth's free time—post-alimony and child-support poverty— to a tee.

"Let me surprise you by how good I am. Now, how do I make my abilities as a gamer into a job that will support me here?"

Gareth leaned forward. He couldn't wait to hear *this*.

CHAPTER
FOUR
USE THE UI, HUMAN

SMITH SIGHED AT GARETH. "I AM ONLY CONCERNED WITH your ability to pay your upkeep. Therefore, I will provisionally assign your job as gamer. Note that if you fail to earn an adequate income to cover your upkeep, you will be ejected from the station. I can now complete your application." Smith gave a final flourish of his walrus flipper-like hands. The screen before the space-bureaucrat disappeared. Simultaneously, a two-dimensional box floated in Gareth's field of vision. The box looked simple, like a Windows notification popup, but it was blank, except for the words, *Status Update*. He stretched and turned, trying to look past it, but the box stayed centered in his vision no matter what he did.

He blinked. It was still there, behind his eyes. "What the hell?"

The Chief Bureaucrat had ignored every one of Gareth's actions from the moment he'd been dismissed with the wave of a flipper. But now Smith turned from whatever had his attention. "Why are you still here? I have finished processing your application. Now, leave."

Gareth gestured wildly with open hands, fingers splayed out helplessly. "I *can't*. There's some weird box floating in front of my eyes. I can't see a damn thing!"

The large alien let out another one of his grunt-growl sighs. "Do they teach you nothing on Dirt? Click on the box. Now *leave,* before I become forceful. I must finish updating my fantasy league before tonight's matches."

Oh well, as long as he was working on something important. Sheesh.

Gareth tentatively reached out and touched the hovering words with a finger. With a snap, the box disappeared—but was replaced with a window of scrolling text.

Class Status: Changed from *None* to *Adventurer

***Bind Point: Changed from Dirt to Muddy River Township**

***Residency Status: Changed from Unwelcome Unemployed to Unwelcome Employed**

***Bank Account: Not found. New bank account created. You currently have 0 Crowns.**

***Level Up: You are now a level 1 Adventurer**

"Okay, now where do I go to play the game? And what about this bank account? I'll need funds in the game, won't I?" He remembered the backpack full of gold coins given to him by Ygurthngjix and Steve. Surely gold would be good here, too, if it was valued by his erstwhile alien abductors? Gareth spotted the pack out of the corner of his eye. "Never mind that question. But how do I deposit funds into my new bank account?"

"Go to the bank. Now—"

Idiot. Of course, he'd have to go to the bank. "How do I find places on the station?"

"Use the UI, human. There are help files, and this is all built into your link. Now *go.*" Smith boomed in a loud voice that sounded like a threat and brooked no argument.

"Okay, Okay. I'm going!" Gareth stood up and called to his dog who'd been sitting quietly at his feet. "Come on, Xena."

Chief Smith, watching him go, emitted an ear-splitting shriek, shoving himself back from his desk as if trying to put space between them.

"What is *that* doing here?" Smith waved a flipper at the dog.

Gareth squinted. Why were all these aliens terrified of his husky? "What... you mean Xena? She's my dog."

"No. *No.* NO! It cannot stay! I'm calling the watch."

Gareth held out a hand as if that could stop Smith. "Why? Calm down. She's a dog—a pet. Man's best friend?"

"No—no! It's a—a miniature Reaper."

"I don't know what that is. But Xena here is a husky. Unless you're a small furry animal, she's completely harmless."

"It must be destroyed." Smith pulled his screen up again, presumably to make the call for help.

Shit. Gareth had to act fast to save his beloved pet. He moved back to the desk and slapped his hand on it again. "*Stop*! Or I'll tell her to attack."

Smith's arms froze mid-gesture. "But you said it was harmless."

Gareth stared intently at the walrus-man, lifting a stern finger to wag at the bureaucrat. "Look—there are two options here. Either she *is* harmless, and therefore she poses no threat to you or anyone else, and therefore there's no cause to hurt her. *Or* she is one of these Reaper things and can slay you on command. In neither option is calling the watch a good choice. Can we just calm the hell down?"

Mr. Smith slowly sank into his chair. "I see. What would you have me do?"

"This is some high-tech station—at least by the standards of my planet, anyway. But even on my world, they can scan DNA. Surely you must have some way for me to prove that she is a dog and not one of these Reaper things."

"She could be scanned in the medical department. That would establish what your Xena is once and for all."

"Great, I'll do that." His shoulders fell with the relief that washed over him. Goddamn—wouldn't that just be the shit icing on the crap cake if these space assholes took his dog away? He might have to go *John Wick* on their asses. He stepped back, hands up, fingers spread to keep the fool calm. The sooner he was out of here, the sooner he'd feel safer for his girl, who had only the odd backyard rodent to atone for.

"I am ordering the scan." Smith slowly reached out, as if fearing any adverse reaction from Gareth, and then touched an icon on his transparent desk screen. "You will go directly to the medical station now. If your animal is as harmless as you say, you can keep it. But you will have to pay its upkeep as well. Now—"

"I'm going. I'm going!" He turned and left, shouldering the hefty pack. He was really hoping to hit the bank first, but this seemed more important. Who knew how many other inhabitants of the place would have similar reactions to his dog? If he had the matter cleared up ahead of time, she'd be safer. So: scan first, bank second.

Gareth and Xena had barely crossed the threshold of the bureaucrat's office when the door slid shut and locked itself with an audible click.

"So what the hell did he mean by 'Use the UI?' How the hell do I use the User Interface?" Gareth looked down at Xena. "You have any ideas?"

Xena looked up and wagged her tail weakly. *"Rur-ruh."*

Gareth sighed, the sound bouncing off the metallic hallway around them. "I didn't think so."

It had to be something easy, since that box just popped up before. Maybe it was voice activated? "Activate UI" he intoned.

Nothing.

"UI on."

Nope.

"Go UI, go?" Gareth looked back at Xena and shrugged. Well, *that* was pointless. He *really* wanted to figure this out so he could shut off the little light that'd been blinking in the corner of his eye—*and* was slowly driving him nuts.

Xena nudged his leg with her nose.

"What? Damn, I'm an idiot." Gareth focused his attention on the blinking speck and said aloud, "Click."

He staggered backward as an elaborate display unfolded before his eyes. He scanned down the menu.

- Map
- Compass
- Messages

- Quests
- Inventory

Inventory? To tell him what he already knew was in his pockets?

Gareth's eyes roamed the list, and he waved his hands around like a desperate magician. *Close, damn you. Go away.*

After a minute, things looked a lot better. He let out a long sigh of relief. "That's better. I can see, at least. Okay, so how do I find something? *Hey, Google?*" No response. "*Alexa?*"

He skimmed the menu again and clicked on *Map.* Then, *Find.* And finally, *Medical Center.* A blinking dot appeared. But it gave him no point of reference showing him where he was on the map.

Zoom out... Zoom out... Zoom out.

Damn, this place was huge. Finally, a solid dot showed up, likely denoting their current location. But navigating from this schematics-looking diagram in this maze of twisty little passages, all alike, was going to be more than a bit of a nightmare.

Gareth paced back and forth in the corridor. He was about to turn around to knock on Smith-walrus's door but thought the better of it. At this point, Gareth was pretty sure the quicker the walrus forgot about him, the better. What he needed was some kind of a path marker....

Make Path? Summon Path? Find Path? Find location...Find Medical? He heaved a sigh. Frustrating as all get-out. There had to be some way of navigating. If only it was like his favorite game, Dragon Epoch. "Hmm. What about... I wonder. *Control F?*"

***Where would you like to go?**

"There we go!" He let out a whoop of delight, startling the dog. This UI seemed to be customizing itself according to what was already in his head. He'd just have to think like he was at his PC, playing his old game. He focused his attention back on the input box in his field of vision. *Medical bay.*

As soon as he did, a series of glowing golden balls appeared in the air before him, leading down the hallway. "Looks like we're good, girl. Let's just hope it takes us where we want to go. And whoever it is on the other end is more cooperative than Bureaucrat Smith."

A twenty-minute walk through the station passages brought them to another unmarked metallic—and rusting—hatch door. He stopped and stared at it, squaring his shoulders in preparation.

"I sure hope this is it. Sure be nice if they labeled things, though. How does anyone know what anything is?" He looked down at the dog, who just looked back with a tilt of her head, a flicker of her pointed ears, and a slight wag of her curled tail.

"I bet you're telling me to use the UI, and I bet you're right." He really needed to adjust his thinking. Thus reprimanded, he focused his attention on the small UI light.

Settings > Building Labels > On

A glowing blue sign appeared over the doorway. It read, *Medical Bay One.*

So here they were. Gareth approached the door slowly, tentatively, until it slid open at his approach. Once inside, he took in his surroundings. It was a medium-sized room, empty except for a floating golden table near the center.

Near one side of the room, a mottled brown creature resembling a large potato with four tentacles, sat in a chair behind a desk. Yet another bureaucrat, he presumed. Given the fact that it didn't move and appeared that its eyes were closed, he also presumed the alien was either sleeping or dead.

This thing sure as hell didn't look like any doctor he'd ever seen or even read about in any of the wildest Asimov or Heinlein stories. Or Philip K. Dick, for that matter—whatever drugs that man had been on. Not one of them had dreamt up aliens as weird as the ones he'd encountered in the past few hours.

Well shit, what now?

CHAPTER

FIVE

SAFE MODE

T o determine whether Mr. (or was it Dr.?) Potato-head was alive, Gareth approached the desk and gave it a sound kick, making a loud ringing noise on the metal. The alien jerked awake, tentacles stiffening at its sides in alarm. Two large eyes opened near the top of its bulbous body.

The thing looked at Gareth, then at Xena, then back at Gareth, apparently trying to decide which one of them to address. Its eyes flitted between them both the entire time it spoke, as if it still hadn't decided. "Please state your emergency."

"Hello, I'm Gareth, and this is Xena." Gareth gestured to the dog. "How should I address you?"

The creature focused one eye on Gareth, twisting the other to look at the dog. "Just choose something if the nameplate is blank."

Gareth frowned. It had spoken English, but he hadn't understood a word of it. Maybe those dumb nanites had stopped working after all?

"*What?* Look, I'm new here. I don't understand what I'm supposed to do."

"New? Hmm, let me see." A data window flashed into being and hovered over the desk. The potato-alien's eyes swiveled to point at the text appearing in the air.

It read aloud the information displayed on the screen:

Gareth Fain

Race: Human

Home Planet: Dirt

Race Status: Inactive

Xena

Race: Unknown

Home Planet: Unknown

Status: Unknown

"The small being is an unknown. And your race status is inactive. How very odd. Every inactive race I've come across is inactive due to the death of the species, but you are quite clearly alive."

Potato-man turned to Gareth, correctly interpreting the expression on Gareth's face as incomprehension. He rolled his eyes in opposite directions and continued, "I'll have to explain, then. The translator takes your gibberish noises and converts them to real speech. It doesn't matter what you call things, as long as it can figure out what you mean. Therefore, you may call me anything and I will hear my proper name. Your anatomy makes it impossible to pronounce it correctly anyway. It's best to use an existing designation, if there is one, to keep mistakes to a minimum. Do. You. Understand?"

Now it was Gareth's turn to roll his eyes. "Yes, I understand everything except for this business of existing designations. How do I know what they are?"

"Just look, human. The designation should be floating over my head." The alien waved all four tentacles in that direction. "The name goes here."

Gareth squinted at the space above the alien just to be sure. "Nope. There's nothing there that I can see. Just your wavy arms flying around."

"Children can use the UI before they can speak. Your species must be particularly incompetent." It looked back at the chart again. "Hmm. It did say your species was inactive. What does it say under UI status?"

Gareth said, "UI status."

UI status: Safe Mode

"It says 'safe mode.'"

The potato emitted a sound that Gareth interpreted as a sigh. "Well, we have found the problem, then. Perhaps it's due to your inactive status. It doesn't know what setup you would prefer. You should set it to *Human Normal*."

Gareth repeated the command, like he was playing that stupid childhood game where you repeated everything your sibling said to drive them insane. "Set UI to *Human Normal*."

A line appeared over the alien's head, so he followed the alien's previous command and designated the medical officer as Dr. Head. The line vanished and the text over the creature now read *Dr. Head.*

Huh, that was pretty cool. Like wearing Google glasses. Without having to look like a complete dork but still getting all the valuable info.

"Why do you speak aloud to the UI? You can just think at it. It will read your intentions as commands."

Gareth frowned. "If that's the case, then why do you need to touch the screen and display data in front of you?"

"The display screen is visible to both of us, so that we may have a shared frame of reference for the information being discussed. You talking to your own UI is just weird."

Buddy, that wasn't the only thing weird around here. Because a giant potato with tentacles giving him lectures was straight out of some billionaire's bad acid trip.

Prudently, he kept his mouth shut.

"Now, please explain why you are here."

Gareth adjusted the heavy pack on his shoulder, unwilling to put it down just yet. He gestured to the dog, who stuck close to him here and didn't appear thrilled, much like on her visits to the vet. "Chief Bureaucrat Smith insisted on having Xena scanned to make sure she's just a dog and not a Reaper—whatever that is."

Dr. Head emitted a sound he could only imagine was a scoff. "Reapers are a myth." He waved all four tentacles over the dog. "There. No scan necessary. It's definitely not a Reaper. I have no information on what a *dog* is."

Gareth could feel his muscles steep in frustration. He just wanted to get to the bank and then to wherever his lodgings would be. He was exhausted and starving. That steak was still sitting near his campfire in the desert back on planet Earth, a little over four lightyears away, goddamn it.

"Can't you just scan her so we can get this over with and that dumbass won't come after my dog?"

"I could scan her. *But* I need a medical order. If there is no order, then no scan."

Jesus, what was it with these annoying aliens? Each one had looked so different and yet every one of them was an arrogant asshole. Well, Fain's second law was still in operation, clearly. He was four for four on the alien to asshole count.

"Listen, the Chief Bureaucrat was very insistent. I watched him send an order from his console for the scan. Then, he told me to come here."

Dr. Head waved a tentacle, and the screen vanished. "Chief Bureaucrat Smith should read his notices more often. The local network is down. He should have given you a hard copy. You'll have to go back and get one."

A hard copy? *Seriously?* They didn't even use those most of the time on Earth anymore. "He won't see me. He locked me out of his office mumbling something about a fantasy league. How long until your net access is repaired? I'll just come back."

The potato man swiveled one eye back to his screen. "The repair order was submitted twenty-four years ago. The repair crew should be here any day now."

Gareth finally unshouldered his bag, and it hit the metallic mesh flooring with a dull *thunk*. "How can you function without network access for that long?"

All four tentacles waved in different directions. Was that some kind of shrug? More importantly, how could you even shrug when you had no shoulders to do it with?

"People are too busy doing their own shit to manage repairs in a timely fashion. There are monsters to slay and loot to, well, loot. Even routine maintenance is difficult when the game pays better than menial labor. It keeps things quiet here, so there's that.

Gareth blinked at the alien. "People are playing this game instead of bothering to fix stuff? Is that why the station is so empty? I didn't see a soul the whole way from Smith's office to yours."

"The station is fully occupied—far from empty. But most people are in the game. You'll understand when you log in. Hardly anyone resists the game."

Gareth was no stranger to how addictive gaming could be. Perhaps it was part of the reason that his marriage had been trashed. Though his ex-wife had spent far more time playing than he had. He might have neglected some menial labor of his own while raiding bosses on Dragon Epoch, but Tilly never seemed to care. Until he slowed his raiding down. Just how addictive was this game?

Gareth gestured at Dr. Head. "Well, it looks like *you* can resist it easily enough."

"Not so. I was a rank seventy-four Battle Mage. But I was on the losing end of a boss fight, sustained critical damage to part of my head, and couldn't afford the repair bill. I then compounded my problems by borrowing gold from the wrong people to cover the cost. They objected to the rate of my repayments and arranged a nice little trap for me. I ended up in a Death Loop. So, no more game-net access for me."

"Oh, uh, I'm sorry. I guess?"

More tentacle wiggling. "I like it better this way. Like I said, it's quiet. Now, if you return with an order, I'll do the scan."

"Couldn't you just send the bill to Mr. Smith after the scan? This whole thing was his idea after all, because of his paranoia about Reapers."

"That involves too much work on my part and too little reward. I have a demanding nap schedule to keep." The tentacled doctor gave Gareth a look that, despite their differing species, wasn't difficult to interpret.

With a heavy sigh, Gareth scooped up his pack from the ground. The gold shifted and clinked around as he lifted it. Maybe filthy lucre would entice him? He reached in and pulled out a gold coin, waving it in front of the giant spud-man. One of the medical technician's eyes swiveled toward it. "Would this help you deal with the extra work?"

"It's a long walk, and there are lots of stairs."

Damn it. Gareth looked down at the dog who had curled up near his feet, patiently waiting. This was going to get costly, but if it ensured her safety, it was worth it. He pulled out another coin from the pack. "How 'bout now?"

Dr. Head's other eye joined the first one. A tentacle whipped out and the coins disappeared from Gareth's hand. "As a favor to the Chief Bureaucrat, I will do the scan and settle up with him after."

"Great."

"Put your creature—a *dog,* was it? Put your dog on the scanning platform."

Gareth looked around. He hadn't seen a platform anywhere when he'd come in. Or at least he hadn't noticed one, and he didn't now. The alien, without looking up from what he was doing flicked a tentacle at a floating bed in the middle of the room.

Well...that was new.

He cleared his throat. "Right. Come here, girl." He picked up his dog and placed her on the golden table. Xena ran around the metal bed, excitedly sniffing it over. After a minute, she seemed satisfied, settling into the center of the table after turning in a circle three times. Then she lay down and closed her eyes, her tail covering her nose. Her eyes drifted closed. Gareth was amazed at her ease after such a short time in this new environment.

"Good. The stasis field works on these dog creatures, too. I wasn't sure it would." Gareth jumped, startled. The potato-alien was now at his side, and Gareth hadn't heard his approach. He turned to look at the technician. It had hundreds of tiny cilia instead of legs, which it used to propel itself. That explained the stealth attack.

"Geeze. Wear a bell or something. What now?"

"It's not my fault your auditory sense organs are so inferior. You should pay more attention to your surroundings. I'm not sure exactly what scan the Chief Bureaucrat wanted. So, I will have to guess."

"Well, for what it's worth, he seemed very concerned that I prove she's not a Reaper."

The alien let out a gruff expulsion of air that seemed to denote frustration. "We've already established that a mythical creature cannot exist. But to satisfy the Chief Bureaucrat's superstitions, I could run a DNA scan." He waved his tentacles in the air and the control panel reappeared in front of him. With blazing speed only a four-armed creature could possess, he pressed virtual controls and set up the scan. Seconds later, the scan table emitted a low hum. A dim yellow light from an indeterminate source shone down on the dog.

"The noise and the light are purely for your benefit. For some reason we found that creatures became uncomfortable when they could not tell that something was happening. So, we added the effects."

"Kinda like how they added the smell to gas."

Dr. Head hesitated. "I wasn't aware that creatures of your type had to add smell to their expulsions. To each his own."

"No, I was talking about natural gas. It has no smell, but because it's dangerous, a smell was added so that it can be easily detected, and danger avoided."

"Very clever, you humans, adding smell to things." Text appeared in the middle of the screen, and Dr. Head turned his attention back to his work.

"Let's see what we have. No match for DNA type in record. Well, I expected that, given that the poor animal is from your benighted world. The analysis does suggest the creature may be related to another species that is not native to your planet. That seems unlikely, though, as that species hasn't been seen for thousands of years." He read further through the text. "Oh, I am sorry. The scan has detected damaged DNA present."

Gareth's head jerked toward the technician, all thoughts about space dogs driven out of his head. "*Damaged* DNA? What does that mean?"

"It means that your animal won't survive long." The alien swiveled one eye to face Gareth but kept the other on the screen where he continued to scroll through the readings.

"*What?* How? Was it due to something on that piece of crap those idiots called a spaceship?"

Tentacles waved again. "No, it has been present since birth, giving this creature a shortened life span. I don't understand how this creature is still alive."

"Can you fix her?"

"It's possible… but it would not be covered by the scan order."

"How much do you want?"

"Pardon?"

"Look, she's all I have left from home. I need her. How much would it cost to turn your machine on to fix her?"

"That will require ten more of those coins." Gareth opened his mouth to object, but Head waved tentacles at him. "No, do not try to haggle, human. I'm only allowed to service citizens of this town. Fixing the problems with your dog will tie up the machine for some time. If someone were to come in and I couldn't assist them because the machine is occupied with healing your pet, I could lose my job."

With some grumbling, Gareth dug into his pack to retrieve ten more coins. This place was getting *very* expensive. "Very well. Here you go."

Once again, the tentacles swooped and made the coins disappear. The alien didn't wear pants and didn't have any sort of pouch that Gareth could see. He didn't want to know where this creature was putting the coins. It was better not to know.

"Starting repair now." Dr. Head studied the screen for a moment. "Hmm, that's odd. The system is stating that it is required to install a network access node as part of the repair. That's normally reserved for sentients."

"Network access node?" Gareth frowned.

The potato creature made its weird noise like a sigh again. "It's what you have been using to interact with the station and myself."

"Oh… you mean the translator UI?"

"Translation is just one of its minor functions, though an important one."

Gareth laughed at the thought of understanding his dog's voice. "So, am I going to be hearing all day about how she's hungry or bored or wants to play?"

"I'm not sure exactly what the effect of this will be. Or why the system thinks it is required. We could abort the repair if you prefer."

Gareth held out a hand to stop him. "No, I want her to be healthy. I'll deal with the consequences."

"Very well, human. Return in forty hours."

"*Forty* hours? That's too long."

"Human, your pet's DNA is being scanned and repaired, cell by cell. You cannot begin to understand how complex this process is. Don't dis the machine."

Don't dis the machine? The translator seemed to be ad-libbing in slang now. "Well—she'd *better* be okay."

"She won't even know you were gone, as she'll be asleep. Now, you cannot wait here, and surely you have other ways to spend that time. You may leave."

Another dismissal by a second, equally bizarre, alien creature. What a day! Gareth left the alien digging through text and muttering the word *fascinatin* g over and over. Gareth wasn't sure what was going on, but if anything happened to his dog, he'd beat the crap out of Dr. Alien Potato-head. It wasn't an empty threat, either. It was a promise.

Nobody messed with his dog.

CHAPTER SIX

GAME OVERLAY: ON

GARETH USED HIS NEWFOUND KNOWLEDGE OF THE UI to quickly make his way to the bank. Thankfully, it wasn't far. Much in line with what he'd previously seen of the station, the bank was another mostly bare room decorated in grays, blacks and pitted metallic materials.

He braced himself for what was sure to be yet another weird-ass alien encounter. What kind of thing would he see next? A squid? A space turtle? Or maybe just a green tinted dude with pointy ears who preferred the way of logic?

Sure enough, an alien sat on a stool-like chair before a long counter. This new being appeared to be a large mantis-like creature with mottled white skin. It was tall, standing head and shoulders above him. Gareth craned his neck to make eye to…uh…seeing-organ contact. The alien turned toward him and spoke.

This time, as he listened carefully, he could discern the thready sound of the creature's actual voice behind the English the translator nanites provided.

"What may I do for you, gentle being?" The mantis' head tilted, giving him a gentle and almost kind demeanor, a very remarkable contradiction to its B-movie horror-show-like appearance.

"Uh, hello. I'm here to open an account."

"A new account? Really? But an account should have been created for you once you gained access to the city. Shall we see…? Yes, it's right here: Mr. Gareth, no family name on record. Current account balance is zero."

Gareth had a vague memory of seeing something like that in the status window after he'd finished his intake with the Chief Bureaucrat Smith. "Oh—yes. Sorry, I misspoke. I meant I need to make a deposit into my account."

"Very well. Please place your deposit on the counter." The mantis creature gestured at the desk. "Here."

"Okay." Gareth dumped out his pack to reveal a medium-sized pile of his remaining gold coins. There had been so much more of it before his encounter with Dr. Potato Head, rip-off artist extraordinaire.

The mantis rubbed its arms together. "Gold. We so rarely get actual gold these days. To be honest, I was dreading having to assign some sort of value to your Dirt currency. Gold, however, is universal. Much easier." He gestured and a digital scale appeared over the gold. "Your gold has the equivalent value of 254 crowns. Do you wish to deposit it all?"

"Well… will I need the gold here? Do you issue me a debit card or something? How do I pay for the things I need, like upkeep?"'

The alien tilted its head once again. "How do you *pay*? Well, you—"

Gareth held up a hand, the answer dawning on him. "Don't tell me, let me guess. I use the UI, right? I think I'm getting the picture, thank you. Yes, please deposit all the gold. I'm getting a backache from carrying it around."

The alien touched a virtual button, and the gold disappeared. Simultaneously, a status box appeared before Gareth's field of vision. It displayed his new bank balance of 254 crowns.

At the same time, a large red **254** appeared in the corner of his view.

"Why twice?"

"Excuse me?" The alien cocked its head.

"Well, I got a notice that I now have 254 crowns. A red 254 also appeared. Seems redundant."

"The red figure is the current amount of time until you can no longer pay your upkeep. As you are new, the upkeep for you and your, ah, pet is currently set to 1 crown per day."

"Ahh..." Gareth frowned. Well, that wasn't morbid at all. He had a visual representation of just how long he had until they spaced him out an airlock. He sent the command to shrink the very large notice to a more manageable size in his field of vision as there appeared to be no way to delete it. They must not want you to forget you're always on the clock.

"I have another question that I was hoping you could answer..." The alien gestured with its long arm for him to continue. "I'm going to be an adventurer."

A short nod. "Congratulations. Most of our clients are adventurers."

"Yes, well, what I want to know is how to I convert these new crowns I have into in game money, and vice versa?"

Another cock of the head. "I do not understand the question."

"Well, as I understand it, I can make a living by earning money in the game."

A whirring click from the banker. "Yes, that understanding is correct."

Gareth frowned, rubbing his jaw and the itchy growth of a day's worth of whiskers. This day just never ended, and he was beyond exhausted. "So, how do I turn the game money into crowns I can spend in the real world? Is there an alien eBay or something to sell game money?"

"There *is* a marketplace for goods, yes. But you have no need to use it to access your earnings. Just visit the bank in the game to deposit your earnings. Your balance will automatically update in the UI, and you can then use it wherever needed, whether in the game or here on the station."

Gareth rocked back on his heels. What the...? *For real?* It couldn't be *that* easy, could it? "Let me make sure I understand." The alien patiently waved an arm, encouraging him to continue.

"I earn crowns in the game."

The antennae on the alien's head twitched slightly. "Well, at your low level, it will most likely be a cup or a leaf, but yes."

Gareth opened his mouth to ask *that* question but stopped, deciding to put the coinage question off for later. "So, I take my earnings to the bank in the game and deposit them. I can then access the funds from in-game to pay for things out here in the real world?"

"Crudely stated, but essentially correct. You will find, though, that most things can be paid for in-game so you will not need to access your currency very often out here. Unless you are cut off from entering the game, of course, for whatever reason."

Gareth could hardly believe what he was hearing. Pay for everyday living by earning money in a game? It was every gamer nerd's wet dream.

The alien's antennae twitched once more. "Did you have any other questions? "

"No, but could you update my family name to be Fain?"

The alien made a notation on a screen only it could see. "There, your account has been updated. Was there anything else?"

Gareth shook his head, "No, that was everything. Thank you, you've been most helpful." A semi-polite alien, for once. Wonders never ceased.

"Good day, then."

Gareth left the bank and hesitated in the outside hallway. He had over thirty-eight hours to kill before he could pick up Xena. But what to do? He was starving and exhausted. Perhaps he should see to his own basic needs. Food, shower, and a bed to collapse into sounded just about perfect. He hardly knew how long it had been since he'd been sitting in that not-so-empty desert without a chance to ever eat that juicy barbecued steak.

He frowned, figuring he could find some kind of lodging via the UI. But how to know what was good? What he really needed was Star Yelp or Space Trip Advisor.

He pulled up the UI once again. *Let's see. Search—Lodging—By...* He paged though a list of search criteria, some of which he clearly didn't have the reference points to understand. What could an *effervescence* rating be referring to? Or *Zeitgeist* or, his favorite, *florality.*

Finally, he came across the field listed under *User Rating* s. He just hoped that meant the same thing as on Earth. He saved his search as *SpaceTrip*. Then cued the UI to *run SpaceTrip*:

•There are 432 results for search: SpaceTrip.

•1 of 432 The Golden Crown. 7.87 out of 8 stars. Rooms start at 100 crowns per night.

A hundred crowns a night? *Screw that.* He clenched his teeth, concentrating. *Edit search: SpaceTrip. Add criteria: room rate no more than 1 crown per night.* He could rough it, if necessary.

•There are 219 results for search SpaceTrip:

•1 of 219 Blacl's Inn.

•5.23 out of 8 stars.

•Rooms start at 10 leafs per night.

A leaf? Gareth quickly pulled up the help screen much as he hated to do that. Under the entry on coinage, he found.

•Coinage in the game consists of the following denominations, from most valuable to least: Oriels (Platinum), Crowns (Gold), Leafs (Silver), Cups (Copper). [System note: Equivalent coinage system familiar to the user is provided for reference.]

•Exchange rates: Each denomination is equivalent to 100 of the next lower denomination, i.e. 100 leafs equal 1 crown.

Well, at least the monetary system looked somewhat rational. He'd been afraid it would be something like 17 Cups to a Leaf, and 32 Leafs to a Crown, 3 crowns to a Stave. Like the crazy system of Ole Merry England.

So the lodging rate listed at 10 leafs a night appealed much better. Hopefully this place wasn't too divey, but the reviews were outranking places that cost a crown a night, so it couldn't be too bad. He focused his thoughts once again on the UI. *Find Blacl's Inn.* The now-familiar pathway of ethereal floating golden balls appeared before him. This one showed the inn at some great distance.

His stomach growled, and he could feel his blood sugar flagging. Great. What he could really use next was a Space Station Segway or taxi or something.

On second thought, the crown rate was probably too costly. So, he proceeded the old-fashioned way, by hoofing it.

About an hour later he arrived at his destination with a much better understanding of just how large this place really was. This time, he arrived at a blank doorway in what looked to be in the style of an open-air quad. The "roof" here was some thirty feet overhead. A smallish park occupied the center of the room, but the area was once again devoid of any sort of decoration or color. The drab gray of the walls was only broken by the floating blue sign over the door, *Blacl's Inn.*

Huh. Maybe the aliens had no taste for décor or couldn't agree on one, so they went with nothing.

Fighting back another yawn, he entered the door which, as expected, opened at his approach. Inside, he found another drab, if large, room. Here, there were several tables spread around, almost like a restaurant. Behind a counter near the door sat an alien that actually could have passed for human, if you overlooked the bright orange skin, blue spiked hair, and unusually large ears.

"Hi, there," Gareth chirped, buoyed by the thought of a meal and a bed.

"Grmph," replied the creature. He didn't even look up from his virtual display.

Huh. Was the UI translator suddenly not working? "Sorry, didn't catch that. I need—"

The clerk raised his hand, cutting Gareth off. Gareth waited while the alien stared intently at the screen. His free hand rapidly rearranged settings. After it appeared that he'd finished his task and closed the display, he finally looked up at Gareth, "Sorry," he croaked in a high-pitched, squeaky voice. "Had to get my fantasy team orders in on time. You know how it is. How may I help you?"

Gareth's brows twitched in interest. "Fantasy team, huh? That seems pretty popular around here."

"Well, you know what they say: 'Those who can, play. Those who can't, play the players.'" The alien shrugged—it looked like a very exaggerated gesture on him. "It's a way to feel a bit connected to the game."

Gareth frowned. "You don't play?"

The alien's face tightened up, and his violet eyes narrowed. "I'm guessing you're new here, so I'll give you a bit of advice. If you see someone here in meatspace, it's a good bet they can't enter the game anymore. And it's something we don't like to talk about. Got it?"

Gareth drew back and held out his palm as a sign of peace. "Sorry. You're right, I just got here, and I didn't know. No offense intended." Hopefully Gareth's hand signaled a calming gesture to the alien, and it wasn't some alien way of saying *screw you, loser*.

The alien at the counter blew out a long breath. "Very well. Just keep it in mind, okay? It's a bit of a sore point for us stuck out on this side."

Gareth swallowed, relieved that things hadn't escalated. "Thank you for your patience. I'll definitely try not to offend anyone else." The alien's face expression seemed to relax. Gareth continued, hoping to put this faux pas behind him. "I, ah, need a room, if you have one available."

"Let me see what we have." He pulled up a new virtual screen, one that looked like a floorplan of the inn and started scrolling through the rooms.

"Say, ah, I didn't catch your name. Are you Mr. Blacl?"

The clerk's face tightened again. Uh oh. Not good. "Blacl spends his time in-game. I'm here to handle the meatspace desk. Room 203 is available. That will be ten leafs a night. *In advance.*"

Well, since he'd offended the guy a second time in as many minutes, he supposed he was getting sent to the dive room. Or maybe the one with a view of the space dump. "I'm going to be here a while. Do you have a weekly rate?"

"The weekly rate is seventy leafs."

"But that's just..." Gareth noticed the clerk glaring at him now. "Yes, I'll take the room, then. At the, ah, the weekly rate. Thank you."

The clerk pressed a finger on the inn diagram, on a square that must have denoted Gareth's new room. Then, he flicked a gesture at Gareth, and a pop-up window appeared before him.

***Blacl's inn is requesting a payment of 70 leafs. Do you wish to pay? (Y/N)**

Gareth mentally pressed *Y* and was notified of the deduction from his account. A map of the inn appeared with his room highlighted on the second floor and a notification that stated he had access to the room for seven days. He turned back to the clerk. The alien was back in his previous screen, doing his level best to ignore Gareth now.

"Can I, ah, ask you a question?"

The clerk waved his hand in the air. Taking that as a yes, Gareth continued, "Is there somewhere nearby that I can get a bite to eat?"

Without looking up, the clerk replied, "Sit at a table and order from the menu. Food will be brought out."

Gareth turned around, looking over the industrial-looking bare metal tables once again. Well, it was the saddest-looking diner he'd ever laid eyes on. "You people don't go in for much decoration around here, do you?"

The clerk blew out another breath. He'd clearly had enough of Gareth's questions. "Well, *most* people turn the overlay on."

Overlay, huh? He quickly pulled up the UI, flipping through menu items until he found the setting for **Visual Overlay**. It was currently turned off. Interestingly enough, there were hundreds of choices for overlays. The first on the list was **Game Overlay**. Curious to see what would happen, he selected that one.

Instantly, the room erupted in color. The tables became hand-carved wooden trestles. The floor was covered in fresh rushes. The walls were purple plaster, with smoky sconces providing light.

Curious… Gareth knew the reality was a bare steel room with nondescript metal tables and chairs, but when he walked over and ran his hand over the surface of a table, he could feel the wood grain of the tabletop. How'd that work? He poked his finger at a small puddle where someone had apparently spilled their drink. His fingers sensed wetness, and they even smelled of stale beer when he brought his finger to his nose.

Muffled sounds came from outside the room, as if there was a living city out there—foot traffic, people calling to each other, the creaking of carts, the calls of merchants. Gareth's jaw dropped. It was like he'd been transported back in time hundreds of years.

He spun and looked at the clerk, who now wore homespun clothing and was perched on a wooden stool behind a rough-cut desk. A candle provided dim light while the clerk perused a paper ledger.

This was…this was phenomenal.

Medieval Europe, at least how he'd always been led to imagine it, and yet, he had to force himself to recall that this was located inside some bizarre and battered metallic space station light years away from his home planet.

Or maybe all of this was the long-drawn-out sustained illusion of a madman? Could he be strapped to a bed, drooling and strung out on medication in the middle of a nuthouse somewhere?

How would he even know if that were the case?

CHAPTER SEVEN

MUDDY RIVER TOWNSHIP

S O MUCH FOR THE EXISTENTIAL MUSINGS. WHETHER OR not this was some delusion of a crazed mind, it certainly seemed real to Gareth. Since all of this had occurred so quickly, and there was still so much to do, there didn't seem time to have a mental breakdown.

It felt like he was in the real world, so he was going to act accordingly.

He enjoyed the game overlay display for a moment longer. Then, with his newfound ability to mentally command the UI, he turned it off.

Immediately, everything snapped back to the sterile environment that had surrounded him moments before discovering the overlay option. With a frown of puzzlement, he sat at a table on one of the hard, utilitarian chairs. McDonalds would have been proud of this décor.

Screw this. Overlay on. The room around him snapped back into that vision of vibrant colors and medieval motif. Even his chair felt softer and cushioned beneath him. Wow. His muscles were exhausted and achy, and Gareth was reminded that he hadn't slept for a very long time. But first things first...

He looked around for a menu but couldn't find anything. The clerk said to order through the UI, but didn't say *how* to do it.

"May I help you, sir?"

Gareth's head jerked up to see someone standing beside him. He was a large, portly man wearing a food-stained apron. There was a smile plastered on his round face, and his gray muttonchops stuck out so that they resembled scrub brushes rather than facial hair. Overall, he could have come straight from a casting call for *Inn Keeper – Medieva* l. Or a Renaissance Faire. And he was decidedly human. Given the lack of other humans on the station, Gareth deduced that this was a construct of the UI too. But for the life of him, there was no way that he could see to tell that the man wasn't real.

"Uh. Excuse me?" Gareth croaked in surprise.

"Well, you're sitting at one of my tables, sir. I assume ye'd be wanting some vittles. We make the best stewed *urbog* in town."

Gareth couldn't help but smile, talk about full immersion. This was great. But what the hell was *urbog*? "Some dinner would be wonderful. But, ah, I'd kill for a burger, fries, and a cold beer."

"Coming right up." The man ambled toward what he assumed was the kitchen area. Gareth followed this closely, trying to discern any hiccups in his motion to indicate that the innkeeper was just a projection—in his mind or otherwise. Despite his best efforts, the man still looked all too real. And not even uncanny valley real, either. But *real* real.

A moment later, a scrawny boy around twelve years old emerged from the "kitchen" with a carefully balanced platter of food and a stein of beer. This was no doubt supposed to be the cook's son. Gareth was tempted to turn off the overlay to see who—or more likely *what* —was actually bringing out his food. But if the show was enjoyable, why ruin it?

The food was placed before him alongside the frosty tankard of beer. Playing along, Gareth reached into his pocket, withdrawing several virtual copper coins, and gave them to the boy. Then he blinked at the thought of it. Did he just tip a virtual boy with virtual money?

Yes. Yes, he did.

"Thank ye, sir," the boy said touching his forelock. "If yer needin' anything else, just give a shout. Someone will be right out to help ye." The boy then spun and returned to the kitchen.

Gareth watched slack-jawed with wonder.

He peered down at his plate, wondering what their idea of a burger was, outside his own solar system. However, Gareth found the burger perfectly cooked—exactly the way he liked it despite his not having specified medium rare with no pickles. Unless the UI had picked that up from his own thoughts? Just how much of his mind did it monitor? Was it some form of super Google?

The beer was also exceptional: a light lager. His favorite. The UI had to have pulled that information straight from his mind. Weird, and not a little disturbing, the invasiveness of having his mind read. But he couldn't argue with the convenience of it, either.

Having satisfied his gnawing appetite, another need slammed him hard in the face. Exhaustion pulled at every muscle, every cell of his skin, as if the gravity on the space station had doubled in magnitude.

Suddenly, the crazy events of this bizarre day threatened to catch up with him. Gareth pushed himself up from the table and made for the stairs he'd spotted earlier, toward the back. It hardly took a thought to activate the UI, and he found his doorway quickly, conveniently highlighted for him.

Without overthinking it, he reached into his pocket and found a large, heavy, old-fashioned key and fitted into the giant keyhole in the wooden door. Inside, the room was just as he'd imagined an inn room, inspired by all those years of playing fantasy role-playing games — wooden bed, large well-crafted chest, a small fireplace for heat.

He no sooner wondered where the bathroom was when a path appeared, leading to a door down the hall. The facilities also had the overlay to fit the décor of the inn, but were, mercifully, very modern. He spent a few minutes seeing to his needs and washing up, then was quickly back to his room before he could pass out.

He sank into a bed that was more comfortable than it looked and was out the minute his head hit the pillow. And he slept like the dead.

Gareth awoke the next morning, stunned to realized everything that'd happened the day before wasn't actually a crazy dream or an unintentional LSD-trip. Not that he'd ever dropped acid, but yesterday certainly fit his perception of what a bad acid trip must be like.

He'd been kidnapped by aliens, and he was on a space station light years away from Earth, in Alpha Centauri. Xena was in the middle of some kind of DNA repair being run by a giant potato.

Humans were rarely seen here, and every alien looked completely different. And people earned a living by playing an immersive VR online game where in-game money also spent in the real world.

Of all these bizarre facts that streamed through his head, the last one was the hardest to believe.

Gareth flopped back on the soft mattress, staring up at the wooden ceiling. There had been no cold wet nose jabbing him in the wee small hours, his beloved dog letting him know she wanted to be let out and have her breakfast. She seldom allowed him to sleep in. His wrist twitched to give Xena her morning scratches, before he remembered that she wasn't there.

He looked around the room once more. Apparently, the UI remembered a person's overlay preference. The four walls around him, and the contents within, all still resembled a room in a medieval fantasy inn. He frowned, curious, then commanded the overlay to turn off.

Blank metal walls, a hard, square bed on a simple platform, and a plain box for his things—not that he'd brought anything to the station beside his dog, currently in the medical bay, and the backpack full of gold that he'd deposited at the bank. So, really, how shocked could he be to wake up in an empty room?

He blinked again, astonished by how quickly he'd accepted the medieval inn as reality. But reality seemed to consist of a bland base, designed to be projected upon, like a movie screen. He wondered what other options were available. Could he turn this place into a room at a saloon from *Red Dead Redemption*? Come to think of it, would that make it look much different than the medieval inn?

He had some time to get to know his surroundings and how life worked here, since he couldn't reclaim Xena for a day yet. He'd definitely be checking out the game, but first, time to hit the bathroom and take care of his morning business. He made sure to turn the Game Overlay on again before depressing himself by roaming down stark metal hallways.

Minutes later, in the dining area downstairs, he once again found himself completely alone.

Someone had laid out some scones on a table. What looked like daylight streamed in through the windows, providing the only light in the room this morning.

"What can I get ya?"

Gareth's head snapped up. An older woman, dressed in a well-made but plain dress was his server this morning. He peered more closely at her dress, amazed at the detail, right down to the irregular stitching of the plain cloth.

The woman waved her hand impatiently. "Well, if you need more time, I'll come back later. I have other customers to serve, you know."

Gareth squinted. *Really?* Maybe her overlay showed her a full room of customers?

Who was he kidding? She was a projection of the UI. She didn't need or use an overlay. Or rather *it*. Or the program or…

Goddamn it. His head hurt. He needed some coffee or something.

He jerked his hand up to prevent her from leaving. The UI was even simulating annoyance. "Sorry, I was lost in my thoughts. I'll have two eggs over easy, bacon, hash browns, and toast – sourdough. And coffee, black, and lots of it."

He gave her a sheepish smile, and she appeared mollified for the moment. She bobbed a shallow curtsey and returned to the kitchen. "It'll be right out dearie," she called over her shoulder.

A serving lad—a different one from last night—brought him his food within minutes. Gareth chewed thoughtfully, and stared at his buttered toast, mulling. He considered turning the overlay off again so he could see what he was *actually* eating. But he gave a decisive shake of his head, happy to keep himself in blissful ignorance. Did he really want to know if it was some kind of protein paste or the space version of SPAM? Some things were better left unclear. The meal was too wonderful to spoil with overthinking, anyway.

After he'd cleaned his plate, he wandered over to the desk clerk—the same orange alien still manning his desk from the night before. Today, he was angrily flipping through pages on a virtual screen. But with one swift motion the man grabbed the screen and tossed it at the wall behind him, where it shattered into thousands of shards before disappearing.

Gareth's brows knit together. "Bad news?"

The orange man glowered at him. "The group I picked for my fantasy league wiped spectacularly on the first boss mob." He pounded a fist onto the counter. "It should have been a sure thing. I lost a bunch of crowns, and now I owe a default to the league."

Though he'd only understood half of that, Gareth offered his gentlest condolences. "I'm sorry. That sounds bad. What do you have to do in the case of a default?"

The clerk shrugged exaggeratedly. "It can be anything, really. The group I play with is pretty mellow. I'll probably just have to wear—and be seen in public with—some hideous outfit for a day." The clerk eyed Gareth. "Hey, maybe I could use yours."

The dude wanted the clothes off his back now? No way.

"Um, *no.* These are my clothes and the only ones I have. You wouldn't even fit into them."

The orange man sighed heavily. "I didn't mean your actual clothes. But I can copy them—provide you okay it."

Gareth didn't know whether to be insulted or not. Levi's were classics for any time period—and he could only presume, any place. Even outside the solar system. On the other hand, it would probably be a good idea to stay on the clerk's good side, and what would it hurt, anyway?

"Okay, fine." Gareth finally agreed. "But why do you need my permission to copy my clothes?"

The alien shook his head. "Human, you're new here, so listen to me carefully. Never—never *ever*— copy someone's stuff without getting their permission. That's one of the most egregious violations."

Gareth blinked. "Oh, okay. Good to know." Bizarre place. Could it possibly get any weirder? Oh crap, he might regret asking that. "As long as you're offering advice, could you let me know where I go to log into the game? Are there some kind of internet cafes around?" And just what would an internet cafe look like in the overlay? An aviary full of carrier pigeons? Or Ye Olde Crystal Ball Shoppe?

Clerk man shot him another derogatory look.

Gareth belted out a sigh and held his palm up. "Look, I get it. I'm new, remember? And I'm human—and apparently an idiot. Can you explain in small words how I play the game? I need to pay for my, ah, luxurious and palatial quarters."

The alien rested his pointed chin in a freakishly large hand. "Okay, *human.* It's like this. Most people base themselves out of their guildhall. The rest mostly belong to some other organization that they use as a base, like the Merchants Consortium, or the United Smiths of Muddy River, back when they existed."

He gestured as he spoke. "Or there are even some race-based organizations, Gnomes for Height Equality, for instance. "

Gareth shot him a look. "Gnomes for Height Equality? You're just messing with me now."

The clerk took a quick assessment of the room behind Gareth. Who knew what he was looking for, because it was empty as a cavern in here. Then he leaned forward conspiratorially. "Do *not* mock the GHE. They have no sense of humor and they're perfectly willing to stab you in the jimmies to get their point across—so to speak."

"Okay, safety tip of the day noted. Don't make fun of short people."

The clerk nodded his agreement. "Probably best if you don't make fun of *anyone* really, human. You have no friends here."

Gareth's mouth twisted. It wasn't news, but it was bleak, nevertheless. "On that depressing note, where do independents, such as myself, log in?"

"Just rent a room, like you already did. Use the room." Apparently, he was done with the conversation, because he turned away and started fiddling with something on the screen again. It was in stark contrast to everything around them, so Gareth assumed they must not have been able to incorporate a data screen into the overlay.

"Well, gee. Thanks for your help." Gareth left him and returned to his room, hoping to find more clues there. Perhaps he missed something. Maybe there was a console hidden in there somewhere. Or VR goggles? It couldn't be *that* hard to figure out how to access the game.

He peered around the room once more; no access port or data cable. Thank God he wouldn't have to plug something into the base of his skull like Neo and Morpheus. Was there a red pill around here somewhere?

Then he had the idea to turn off the overlay. Maybe it was just a theming issue and gaming access wasn't incorporated into the overlay. Given that the room was so plain, he couldn't see how he could possibly have missed a data port, if something like that existed.

No, it had to be something else. Something easy. Probably even obvious. Then it occurred to him that everything else so far had been done wirelessly, so maybe he didn't need an access port.

Use the UI, human. That common refrain from the day before rang through his head. Yeah. Duh. It *had* to be in the UI. Gareth focused his attention on the UI and sent the command: *Access Game.*

His body locked up solid, every muscle tensing, every joint stiffening. He couldn't move and he could hardly draw more than a shallow breath. Cold panic streaked up the back of his spine and gripped him. He started to sweat—and struggle, though since he couldn't move, it was hardly a struggle. Then he tried to scream—to call out for help, but nothing happened.

Before true terror could set in, however, a beam of light appeared above his head, lowering slowly until it touched him. Then it bathed his entire body in its glow.

And even as it did so... Gareth watched with mounting horror as his body started to erase itself—like Marty's picture at the Enchantment Under the Sea Dance when his parents hadn't kissed yet.

Fuck, Shit. Damn. What the—?

Was this what dying was like?

CHAPTER EIGHT

CHARACTER CREATION

*D*ARKNESS. HE WAS STANDING INSIDE DEEPEST BLACK. AT least he assumed he was standing. When he tried jumping around and waving his hands, he couldn't really feel anything at all. Maybe his eyes just couldn't see. At least he was alive—or so he assumed, anyway. That light that had washed over him—that disintegration beam. Jeez, what a fucked-up way to log into a game.

He was all but ready to submit his one-star Steam review. Worst. Game. *Ever.*

After what seemed like an eternity, he detected a band of glowing text materializing in front of his face. Whichever direction he looked, the text was there before his eyes.

He read what scrolled by, having nothing better to do.

•**Cleaning up old data connection.**

•**Disable access lock: Human**

•**Checking new data connection**

- **New data lock: Established**

- **Enable access lock: Human**

- **Import preferences: Human, Earth**

- **Boot**

The lights slowly rose, and he could now see that he was standing on a featureless white plane extending in every direction as far as the eye could see. White all around him. Like the worst snowstorm ever, but it wasn't cold and there was no snow.

"Hallooooo," he called into the emptiness. Not even an echo came back to him.

"Hey?" Still nothing. He commanded his legs to start walking—then running—just to see if he could. He managed it, but he had no idea if he was actually *moving* or just running in place. He stopped—no point in burning energy if he wasn't getting anywhere. Interestingly enough, he wasn't winded at all.

He was almost certainly dead. That was it. And this very, very white place was heaven—which he'd never actually believed in while he was alive.

Or maybe it was the other place?

No… not hot enough.

"Please pardon our mess." He jumped, heart pounding in reaction to a sudden disembodied voice splitting the silence. He spun, trying to spot the source. It was nowhere to be seen.

"It is taking some time to recall the human boot code from long-term storage. We will be with you shortly and appreciate your patience. Your call is very important to us."

Jeezus, a phone tree, even out here in the hinterlands of the Milky Way.

Gareth harrumphed. "You could hurry the hell up. This blank white existence is pretty damn boring—and disturbing." He'd shouted at the sky without expecting a response. Thus, he wasn't disappointed when he didn't get one.

Some amount of time later, an eon or two, or maybe just a couple minutes—who could tell? —something changed in the air around him. A being started to form in front of him—much like a person beaming in on an episode of the old-school *Star Trek*. And it was coming in on the slowest transporter ever.

Once it solidified, Gareth stared, agape with disbelief. Before him stood a six-foot-tall giant paperclip affixed with weird googly eyes and bushy dark brows.

"It looks like you need to create a new character. Would you like some help with that?"

Gareth held up his hands, appealing to he-knew-not-what. "You make me hang out in limbo for ages, and the best you can give me for a tutorial is *Clippy*?"

The apparition bounced before him as the creepy eyes roamed wildly. "I apologize. We have no reference points for a human of your era. After the scan of your mind, we perceived from your memory that this form is a helpful creature with whom you have interacted in the past."

At least now the sound had a source, even if it was the invisible mouth of a giant paperclip. *Great.*

"Wait, you *scanned my mind*? Haven't you ever heard of boundaries? If you're going to do that, you could have at least found some hot bikini babe to use." His teenaged self had viewed enough of those "for research," anyway.

The paperclip bounced again. "Such an image would be too distracting to you and therefore defeat the purpose of the avatar."

"What purpose is that?" Gareth was getting really tired of tracking the paperclip as it bounced around; it should just stand still, for god's sake. It seemed that space-Clippy was just as annoying as his earthbound cousin.

The cartoon tilted, seeming to consider. "To help you make your character, of course."

"I've created plenty of player characters. I think I can handle it." He flipped Clippy the bird. Just get on with it already.

Googly eyes blinked and black eyebrows wagged in time. "The Absolute Universe Simulator Challenge is the most complex and realistic game ever created. Even now, we are scanning your mind and making millions of adjustments to your UI to allow you to correctly interpret and interact with in-game objects. Further, there are over one thousand classes and a million playable races extant in the game. Given that you are a human of your era, you have *never* played a game like this."

The eyes spun around, then grew larger at the end as if to emphasize this was a serious point it was making. Gareth sighed and rolled his eyes. Reluctantly, he decided to at least listen to what Clippy had to say.

"Okay, fine. You made your point. I guess I need help—from a giant, talking, animated office product."

Clippy seemed to take offense. "It has been almost two thousand years since we last inducted a human into the game— aside from one aberration. You *will* pay attention, human, and not screw this up." One end of Clippy elongated and poked Gareth in the chest.

Gareth pulled back and rubbed at the sore spot in question. "*Hey!* No need to get physical. What aberration?"

Clippy's new appendage—God, he hoped it was an arm—waved through the air. "Pay no mind to the aberration."

"But if you didn't want me to ask about it, then why mention the aberration?"

If Clippy could sigh, he imagined one might come from the creepy cartoon character at this moment. "An aberration entered the game from your planet a hundred and forty or so of your years ago. But *you* are the first *official* human. Thus, moving on…" A wand appeared in the air floating beside Clippy. It waved and shot silvery sparkles everywhere.

•Status change: Human, inactive to active

"There. The human race is once again active in the game."

Gareth frowned, peering through narrowed eyes at Clippy. "*Once again? How?* I'm the first human to ever leave the solar system, much less arrive at this space station. That Bureaucrat Smith guy did make some comment when I said that to him, but he's an asshole, so I figured he was just yanking my chain. How could humans have been active before this? You said it's been two thousand years since you last inducted a human. Two thousand years ago, we thought sailing ships were the shit and liked to hit things with cleavers. There's no way we had a presence out here."

Clippy blinked, eyebrows twitching. "You are the first human *that you know of.* to have left your solar system. I can assure you that this is not the case. However, previously, most human players logged in from your starting city, Atlantia. Since its destruction—and the subsequent destruction of the satellite nodes—your people have had limited access to the game."

"*Atlantia?*" Gareth blinked, perplexed. A strange idea tickled his consciousness. "You mean Atlantis? That's a myth—a fable. There's no proof it ever existed, and even if it had—the legend says that it sank, like, six thousand years ago."

"Yes, that is correct."

Gareth stared at the animation, unable to process this. He frowned, blinked and then rubbed his jaw. "You're—ah—you're shitting me."

Clippy spun his eyes again, appeared to be thinking. "To use your idiom, *I shit you not.* The human race had its own starting city on your home planet, Earth. But they eventually drew the wrong sort of attention, and that base was then destroyed. Today, *you* are restarting the presence of your species in the game. You should be proud."

But he wasn't proud. No, he was stunned. The shock of a man who had just had the concept of his entire world rearranged and redefined—*Atlantis?* Alien attack on ancient Earth? Advanced human civilizations wiped out over a game that was played throughout the universe?

The world turned around him and he gasped for air. He even saw a few spots in front of his eyes before furiously blinking them away. This was...

He had no word for it, actually.

The animated paper clip appeared to patiently wait for him to absorb it—this new, unasked-for responsibility of representing his entire race to the universe.

Him, the washed-up, newly-divorced, middle-aged man whose prized possession now was his dog and whose own kids wouldn't even talk to him. A wave of emotions crashed over him. The revelations he'd just been given cracked open the box he'd so carefully constructed to contain his feelings about his sons. The despair and bewilderment about what had happened. Why had his sons turned on him?

He forced himself to push those thoughts back down.

This isn't helpful, Gareth. Focus, Gareth. Think about that poor guy getting spaced, Gareth.

"Look—all I want to do is earn my upkeep. You know, have a place to sleep. Oh, and being able to eat and drink would be nice, too. This whole great rebirth of the human race thing? That's not me. I'm not your guy."

Can't even keep my family together, and I'm going to restore humanity? Fuck that.

Clippy bounced only once before replying. "I understand this news must be shocking to you, and that you will need some time to process it. Perhaps we should focus for now on making your character and allowing you to earn your upkeep. We can return to the bigger picture later."

"Great." Gareth flashed him a thumbs-up before realizing how stupid it was to gesture at an animation. He did flip Clippy the bird again from his other hand behind his back. Stupid or not, it made him feel better.

Clippy took the hint and continued, "The game is a hybrid skill- and class-based system. Your class determines your basic framework. You then customize the base class with individual skills. Over time, your choices can unlock further possibilities or even lead you into a new, previously unknown, class."

Gareth rubbed his forehead, willing himself to focus on the game tutorial's words but finding it difficult in the wake of the casually delivered but reality-altering news. He cleared his throat. "Right. Okay, so you said there were over a thousand classes. Let's start there. I'll need your help narrowing them down. I mostly like to play cleric-warrior hybrids. Something like a Paladin."

Clippy used the end of his paperclip like a hand and waved it, causing a window to appear. "These are your starting class choices:"

•**Cleric**

•**Mage**

•**Rogue**

•**Warrior**

Gareth frowned, reading through the list again. "But...that's only four classes. You said there were over a thousand."

Clippy gestured again with his new appendage. "Your starting class selection is based on the classes unlocked by your race. Since your race's game-presence was destroyed, humans lost everything they had unlocked. This means you only have access to the base class list to start."

"Huh. Well, the news gets better all the time but at least that list is plenty narrow, so no narrowing-down needed. I'll choose...Is multiclass an option, as you level up?"

Clippy bounced again, seemingly happy to move on to game specifics. "When you gain sufficient experience to increase the level of your character, you can train a new level with any class trainer that will instruct you. In this way, you can have more than one class."

Gareth nodded. "I'll choose cleric for my first class, then."

A beam of light shot down from above and bathed him. When it faded away, he was wearing white cloth robes and holding a wooden mace. Huh. Robes? *Really?*

"What the fuck? What idiot game designer decided to make cleric a cloth armor class?" He hefted the mace, waving it around. "And *what?* I swat at people with a stick? Screw this shit."

Clippy's dark brows pinched together. "Cleric is traditionally a support role. You will have the most success if you find a group with whom to adventure."

"Naw. I don't do groups. I'm a soloing king." He pointed to himself. "Gareth doesn't share loot."

Clippy bounced. "You do start with four skill points you can use to customize your character."

Hmm…maybe there was light at the end of this tunnel. "Fine. Let's customize the crap outta this build, then. What are my choices?"

Clippy waved his tail-slash-hand again and a new window appeared. This one listed hundreds of skills. Gareth took a tentative step forward to get a better look, then reached out a hand to scroll through the lists.

Squinting at all the possibilities, he bit his lip, considering. "Hmm, well let's see. I'll put one point into heavy armor, because this cloth shit is for the birds—or the bird-gods, as the case may be. For my second point…hmm—oh! Sword use. Should eliminate the ridiculous stick problem I'm having. And so, for the third, I'll take shield to compliment it. Hah! An armored, sword-and-board cleric."

Clippy appeared unimpressed. "Congratulations. You have recreated a limited version of warrior."

Gareth held up a finger to point out the obvious. "Yeah. But a warrior who can cast spells—and heal himself."

"Well, yes, I suppose." Though his tone hadn't actually changed, Gareth imagined that the animation sounded annoyed.

Once again, the white light shot down from the ceiling. When it faded, he was now dressed in chain mail, with a longsword and shield on his back and a broadsword belted to his waist.

Clippy appeared to inspect him. "You have one skill point left."

Gareth scratched his head, not terribly comfortable with the chain coif that pulled at his hair. With his main objectives covered by his first three points, he peered at the list again. He scrolled quickly until he found some of the more obscure skill trees, then slowed, considering each one. "What's this—*One Random Talent?*"

Clippy appeared beside him to peer at the menu alongside him. "That option grants you a random talent."

Well, duh. Gareth shot Clippy some hard side-eye then slapped his forehead with the classic Picard face-palm gesture. "Yes, I understood that part of it. But... what kind of talents can you get from that skill slot?"

"That skill was added by the Fates. It can lead to almost anything—from the trivial, like the ability to create life-like fishing lures, to the ridiculously over-powered, for instance the ability to turn into a dragon. It is almost always something trivial, but those can be occasionally useful."

Ah what the hell. He wasn't typically a gambling man, but he had been abducted on the outskirts of Las Vegas by aliens and paid ill-gotten gambling winnings for his troubles. Seemed like a day for making exceptions.

"For my fourth point, I pick that." This time, a multicolored beam surrounded him. Thousands of different images flashed before his eyes, like a holographic TV. They scrolled by too quickly for him to identify any of them. This went on for a long time, and was starting to make him motion sick. He wobbled, thinking maybe he should sit on the floor, before he fell over, when finally, the beam vanished, leaving him with one single image. He instantly recognized the two-dimensional icon that showed a beaker with fumes bubbling out. Then it faded, to be replaced by a status window.

Okay…now what?

CHAPTER NINE
THE STATS ARE THE STATS

GARETH READ, ONCE AGAIN, THE GLOWING LINE OF TEXT in the window that described his random talent awarded by using his final skill point:

•Talent added – Natural Alchemist.

"Huh, that seems interesting, if mostly useless," Gareth mused.

Clippy scurried to move in front of him. "What talent did you receive?"

"Oh, something to do with potions, I think." Gareth shrugged. "I'll be good on healing pots, I guess. But I never was much for crafting."

"What is the name of your talent?" Clippy swooped to Gareth's other side almost frantically. "The *name*. human. The name?"

"Calm your jets, jeez. I've never seen a paperclip get so excited before. The random talent is something called Natural Alchemist. So, like I can make organic potions?"

"*Natural Alchemist.*" Clippy repeated, swooping around him in random spots before returning to his side again. "You must tell *no one.*"

Gareth frowned, puzzled. Maybe potions weren't a thing in this game? Weird. "Why? Is there some sort of potion-makers guild I need to worry about?"

"Human, alchemy is a complex skill that takes decades to learn. A natural alchemist skips all that. You will be able to create and improve potions after just one taste of an existing one. In addition, you can update formulas with ease, make exotic and powerful concoctions and accomplish it with fewer reagents. That is a *very* rare talent."

"About as rare as a human playing the game these days? Seems appropriate." He still didn't get Clippy's overexcitement, though.

"It's more than just *appropriate.* A natural alchemist's potions are only limited by his materials and his imagination. If they find out, every powerful institution in the game will seek you out and imprison you to force you to create potions for them."

Gareth frowned. That seemed…harsh. He was reminded of the childhood fairy tale of the girl imprisoned to spin straw into gold and, in her desperation, striking a devil's bargain with Rumpelstiltskin.

"Ah, ok. I'll keep that in mind." He could tell that Clippy was still annoyed with him. But really? So, he was good at making potions. No way was this an uber talent. Maybe if you were a crafting nerd like, his youngest son, Fred. But for himself... in games he just liked to hit things and collect the loot.

Clippy looked ready to start in again. Time to redirect. "So, what's left to do? I need to pick a race, don't I?"

"The only race unlocked for people of your planet is *human.*"

Boring. He would have liked to play a dwarf. Or even an elf. Welp, no special racial abilities for him. "Don't I need to pick my spells?"

"As a non-aligned cleric, you start with Bless 1, Healing 1, and Mending 1."

"I don't get to pick? Lame. And what do you mean *non-aligned?* Gareth leaned toward Clippy.

"Normally, someone creating a cleric would choose amongst the deities available to his or her race. Humanity currently has no associated deities, so you start as unaligned. That is also the option for players who wish to explore other options beside the standard, or to find their associated deity through in-game play."

"But as unaligned I can still cast spells and do cleric things right?"

Clippy nodded. "Yes. Cleric spells in the game use mana as their power source rather than divine favor, so you will be able to cast. Lack of a deity will affect your spell choice when you level up. "

"Okay. It could be worse, I guess."

"Since you already have a bank balance, we have been authorized to offer you a one-time opportunity to purchase starting-level equipment to match your current avatar for 100 crowns."

Gareth cocked a brow at Clippy. Was he being sold a bill of goods? "One time, eh? And what if I say no?"

"Then you will start with the robe and mace you were granted upon class selection."

The thought of starting the game wearing a homespun robe and wielding a stick did not appeal to him in the least. "Ah, I'll be happy to take the offer."

"Very well."

A notice appeared before Gareth's field of vision, informing him of the debit to his bank balance, which was now down to 153 crowns and 30 leafs. At the same time, the red number in the corner of his screen spun down to 153. Shit! He'd forgotten about having to pay upkeep. That was a moment to make your butt pucker, for sure. But it did light a fire under his ass to go out and start earning some crowns in the game. In fact, it made him a little giddy to know that his new job was as a professional adventurer within a game. Assuming he could avoid the whole being ejected from the station thing, that seemed like a dream gig. Hopefully, earning gold wouldn't be that hard. He had visions of fishing to turn bait costing one copper into a fish to earn a silver, as he had to do back when he played old-school EverQuest.

He shuddered, then shook his head. "Nah, they couldn't be that sadistic."

A backpack appeared in front of Gareth, so he stooped to inspect it.

30 slot adventurer's pack, containing

- **Average Steel Longsword**

- **Average Steel Broadsword**

- **Average Steel Kite Shield**

- Average Steel Chain mail
- Water skin
- Basic Rations (7)
- Feet of rope (50)

He opened it up, and pulled out the armor, weapons, and shield. The pack held a huge amount for its size, which made him think of the TARDIS—bigger on the inside.

Giant backpacks were a staple of online games, and most D&D campaigns as well, but it was surprising to encounter one here. Clippy had seemed very adamant about how realistic the game was. He supposed, like in the games he knew, the need for items surpassed the ability to carry them. That same need led to the same solution, the so-called Magic Backpack. This was definitely one case where the practical needs of playing trumped the need for in-game realism.

He quickly equipped himself, noting that the armor was a perfect fit—as if it were made just for him. Likely it *was*.

Once dressed, his eyes flicked to the status screen to inspect the change in his stats:

Armor Class: 14

Shield +1 AC, when worn

Broadsword Damage Class: 8

Longsword Damage Class: 18

The chain mail felt heavy on his body over the under-armor padding. And the coif weighed on his neck. He turned his head this way and that to adjust to the feeling. The swords and the shield also had a notable heft to them.

These facts alone promised a gaming experience like no other. His heartbeat accelerated with excitement at the thought of exploring an entire new world—and in the body of an actual adventurer rather than behind a keyboard or game controller.

"So… am I done here?"

Clippy bounced once. "Yes. Just click *Save,* and that will complete the character creation process. Congratulations."

Just as he was about to click the *Save* button, a nagging feeling told him he was skipping some important step.

"Wait. What about my stats? I haven't allocated anything yet."

Clippy's googly eyes swirled in circles and the eyebrows wagged. "Your stats are your stats. If you want to apply changes to them, you will need to accomplish that in the game."

Gareth's eyes narrowed, his arms folding across his chest. "What do you mean, the stats are the stats?"

That didn't sound good at all.

"I mean, you begin as you are. There is no adjusting them to start."

Uh oh. *No bueno.* "You mean my base stats are determined by my *real-life* abilities?"

Clippy looked at him as if he were a beloved but stupid nephew but did not otherwise respond.

Gareth blew out a breath, then checked the UI. "Fine, at least I'll get to see how I rank. Here it is, *Player Statistics.*"

A transparent window appeared in front of him.

Strength: Average

Intellect: Average

Physicality: Average

Constitution: Average

Wisdom: Average

"What's with all this *average* crap?" sneered Gareth. And why were there only five stats? He expected the standard six.

Clippy waved his tail/arm toward Gareth. "What is *this*, if not the epitome of average?"

Gareth pulled a face. "Well, thanks for that. What I *meant* is…why are there no numbers? Stats normally have numbers."

"The designers of the game were trying to emulate the real world. In your reality, there are no numerical measures of your abilities. The best you ever know about how well you perform in certain areas is based roughly on how you rank compared to your peers."

Gareth's mouth twisted for a moment in thought. "Well, isn't that special? I guess I'm done, then."

Turning to the UI, he gave the command:

Save

The UI did nothing for a minute, then a screen appeared with his newly made character sheet upon it. His new life laid out in all its glory.

Name	Gareth Fain
Level	1
Class	Cleric 1

Deity   Unaligned

AC 14

HP 20

Strength   Average

Intellect   Average

Physicality Average

Constitution Average

Wisdom   Average

Spells

Bless 1
Healing 1
Mending 1

Talents

Natural Alchemist (Apprentice 0)

Skills

None

Combat Skills

Broadsword (Apprentice 0)
Longsword (Apprentice 0)
Kite Shield (Apprentice 0)

Abilities

Armor Use, Light
Armor Use, Heavy
Shield Use, General
Weapon Use, Sword
Weapon Use, Simple Melee

Clippy bade him farewell and good luck before constructing himself a paper airplane to fly away inside, then vanishing into nothingness.

Gareth blinked, then gave the command to exit character creation mode. He instantly reappeared in his room. Nothing had changed except that now, he was wearing the equipment he'd been granted in the character creator. He still had no understanding of how to actually get into the game to play it. With a sigh, he reluctantly decided his best bet for unanswered questions was the grumpy hotel clerk. Maybe if he complimented the alien's "cool blue hair," he'd be more forthcoming with the info.

This time, as he headed down the stairs, he caught the sound of voices from the room below. *Lots* of voices. Once in the dining area, Gareth was stunned to see that it was packed with people; every table taken, empty plates and cups everywhere. Even the bar was full of people sipping drinks. Gareth snaked this way through the clusters of arranged tables—and half pulled out chairs—toward the lobby desk. Once he got a glimpse of the clerk, however, he ground to a halt. The surly orange grump with the blue hair was no longer there. Instead, there was the smiling, green face of what could only be an orc.

"Why hello!" the orc called, waving him over. "You must be our new guest." He reached out to take Gareth's hand once he was within range. "It's good to meet you at last."

"Thank you. I'm happy to meet you, Mr....?"

"Blacl, just Blacl—no Mister. Though innkeep, sluggard, oinker—most anything yelled my way will get my attention, usually. Though I would prefer if you didn't use oinker. Can't say I like that one much."

"I'll stick with Blacl, then. It seems quite busy today."

"Well it *is* taco Tuesday. But it's busy most days to be honest, thanks to our fantastic cook."

"Huh, I must be missing the busy times then. I got used to having the place to myself."

Blacl gestured with a meaty hand. "That's because you've been stuck in meatspace until now. Nobody hangs out on that side anymore. For me, I only go there for the mandatory annual checkup."

Gareth frowned, replayed Blacl's words, chewed on them for a moment until sudden realization hit. His jaw dropped. "Wait... what? You mean, I'm inside the game? Right now?" Gareth reached out and touched the desk. "But everything feels totally *real*."

Blacl shrugged his burly shoulders. "What is reality but a set of electrical impulses fed to our brain? Does it matter if they come from our organs or are fed directly via the interface? If you ask me, it's all real."

Good god. He was having flashbacks to the red pill and blue pill speech from *The Matrix*. Had he just entered a version of it here?

What the hell even was all this? He fumbled for the barstool nearby and sank onto it, his knees weak.

He'd been so excited to get into the game, he hadn't considered what that actually meant or that it might cause some kind of existential crisis about the nature of reality.

Maybe he should have listened to more of those projected reality simulation conspiracy theories on late night talk radio.

He swallowed and stared at Blacl, not feeling so great.

The innkeeper tilted his head, watching him with sympathy in his large orcish eyes. "It's okay, good sir. You'll be right as rain very soon. It takes us all like that our first time."

Gareth had a sinking feeling that he was in for a whole dizzying succession of first times.

CHAPTER
TEN
FRESH MEAT

GARETH TOOK A MINUTE TO FEEL OUT HIS surroundings, marveling at the sense of weight on his shoulders and back from the armor. He waved his hand and gasped at the sensation of air moving around him. Blacl looked on patiently with an amused smile.

The inn door banged open. Four broad warrior-types entered, their armor dented, steaming and covered with mud and a sickly green ichor.

One slapped the bar loudly. "Blacl, beer us!"

Blacl jerked his chin toward the man. "I heard you lot were on your way in. Your table's open. I'll be right there."

The innkeeper then turned back to Gareth. "Excuse me a moment. I need to see to them personally. They just got back into town, and adventurers tend to be free with their coin on the first day back."

"No problem." Gareth shrugged.

Not particularly hungry himself, Gareth decided to set out and explore the township. He left the inn with a glance at Blacl, who was sharing a laugh with the newcomers. Outside, the streets were just as bustling as the space station had been quiet. What looked like hundreds of people of every shape and size—and number of ambulatory appendages—were strolling down the street.

Anxious to jump into things, Gareth pulled up his map in the UI. Much to his relief, this map was a normal two-dimensional city map, not the confusing three-dimensional map of the station. He did notice that the map stopped at the edge of the city, and try as he might, he couldn't scroll or zoom out to see the surrounding area. And while the streets and buildings were shown, little of the map was labeled. He must have to travel to the places before the UI would fill in the missing info. He did spot an area marked *training,* and for lack of anything better to do, he headed there.

A brisk ten-minute walk brought him to the thinning outskirts of town. There, he found a roped-off area containing hay bales, barrels, and scarecrows. A group of people wearing makeshift armor and wielding weapons of dubious lethality were doing their best to kill the straw effigies. Others tried to shoot arrows into the straw bales with little success. This was *definitely* the newbie training area.

"Well, look at the fancy new meat, will ya?"

Gareth turned. A group of four people stood off to the side, watching the new players practice. Their equipment and weapons were of much higher quality than the newbies used. Two of them wore plate mail, one wore flowing black robes of rich material, and the last had on armor made of a green, scaly leather. Each of them wore tabards bearing a different crest—a mailed fist, a lightning bolt, a fierce cat creature and a bloody dagger.

The man in the leathers with the bloody dagger crest nudged the warrior with the mailed fist. "It's your turn to go first."

The other man nodded. "Right."

He approached Gareth, stopping right in front of him with a quick look up and down. "New warrior, I see. Non-standard starting equipment…hmm. Who is your patron?"

Gareth frowned. "Excuse me?"

"I need to know who your patron is. Which guild are you pledged to?"

Gareth mulled that one over for a moment before answering. "I'm independent."

"*Good.*" The man nodded. "You're with me, then. Welcome to The Elite."

***You have been invited to join the guild The Elite. Do you wish to join? (Y/N)**

Gareth ignored the text flashing before his eyes. This person's presumption that Gareth would automatically accept his offer—as if it were some kind of honor—rankled him. "I'm a cleric, not a warrior."

The guy did a classic double take. "*Cleric?* What's with the equipment, then? Clerics don't fight. They cower in the back and heal when called upon."

Hmmph. "I'm not that kind of Cleric. Thank you for your kind offer, but I'm not ready to join up with anyone right now." He made an appeasing gesture with his open palm and then selected *No* on the invitation prompt.

"*What?* But… *no* one turns us down." He turned back at the other three, "Hey boys, this one's too good for us. He says he doesn't want to join *The Elite*."

Three more glowing prompts appeared:

***You have been invited to join the guild Mage's Fury (Y/N)**

***You have been invited to join the guild Conquest Cats (Y/N)**

***You have been invited to join the guild Sudden Death (Y/N)**

Gareth sighed and selected *No* for all of them. The mildly amused expressions on the men's faces subsequently hardened in turn. All three joined their comrade to face off with Gareth.

The guy with the cat logo on his tabard folded his arms across his chest. "You might want to rethink your decision, newb. The four of us each represent the biggest guilds in Muddy River. We decide who we want, and newbs don't turn us down, not if they know what's good for them." He pushed forward, invading Gareth's personal space.

Gareth held out his hands, palms facing outward. "Look, I appreciate the offers, I really do. But I'm new here. And I want to get the lay of the land before I commit to anything."

Conquest Cat drilled his index finger onto Gareth's breastplate. "We already told you everything you need to know, newb. We are the biggest, *most powerful.* guilds. *We* get our pick of the newbies. And we want you. Not picking one of us would end badly for you."

It occurred to Gareth that he'd never asked Clippy whether this was a Player versus Player game. An oversight he was rapidly coming to regret. As if in answer to his silent question, Gareth felt a sharp pain stab his left side, where the mage was standing. A red bar popped up in the UI, dropping to about half its length.

A health bar?

"Tick-tock, newb. Tick-tock. Time's a-wasting." Well, that answered that.

Before Gareth could respond, a rough bass voice cut through the confrontation. "*What's* going on here?"

The four guild recruiters jumped back. Conquest Cat turned and yelled at his accomplice from The Elite. "What the hell, dude? Why didn't you warn us *he* was coming?"

Through the haze of health-loss, Gareth craned to look past the quivering recruiters toward an eight-foot-tall minotaur stomping toward them. He carried a massive axe in his right hand. Though Gareth wasn't an expert on bull facial expressions, it was clear that the creature was pissed, just short of steam escaping his large nostrils.

"No—nothing's going on, Clud. We were just *evaluating* the newbie. We *are* allowed to do that." Cat shrugged so exaggeratedly it was almost comedic.

The minotaur—Clud—snorted loudly. "Bullshit, Axion. I saw the damage notice. Meldurath here shot the newbie."

"A mistake, I assure you." Meldurath, the mage in the black robes, held out a nervous hand. "I was just demonstrating the spell for him but never meant to hit him." Nevertheless, the mage carefully maneuvered himself so that the two melee characters were between him and the minotaur. A literal meat-shield.

Clud straightened to his full eight feet, fists resting on his hips. "You tell Klytis that the four of you are banned. For a *month*. Now, leave!" Gareth squinted. Either he was hallucinating, or there were only three of them now. One was definitely missing— the roguish-looking one.

Cat began whining. "You *can't* do that. We have a right—"

The minotaur shifted his axe from one hand to the other, as if readying to swing it. "Tell me again what I can and cannot do, puny. Now bugger off—unless you wish to shoot that same spell at *me* and see what happens."

The two warriors looked at each other, then lowered their defiance, slowly nodding. "Our shift's over for the day anyway. But you're going to hear about this from our guild leaders." With his combined meat-shield leaving, the mage had no choice but to follow, muttering about how we were lucky he didn't show them all his true power.

Clud stared after the retreating trio until they finally turned a corner and were out of sight. Then, he set aside his axe and turned toward Gareth, this time speaking in a softer tone. "Sorry about that. Those guilds are really getting too big for their britches, starting to think that they run the town. I'm Clud, by the way."

"Gareth, pleased to meet you." He stuck out his hand and Clud grasped hand to wrist, clasping like they did at the renaissance faire. Gareth sized him up again, making a note never to be on the receiving end of Clud's anger.

The hulking minotaur regarded him, tilting his massive, horned head. "Well now, let me see about healing you up. I think

I have a potion here somewhere." He began digging through a belt pouch that was bigger than Gareth's backpack. On Clud, it looked like an average-sized money purse.

Gareth held out a hand to stop him. "No, wait. I can heal myself, I think. I'm a cleric, and that's what clerics do, right?" Otherwise, this build was really going to suck.

Gareth accessed the UI to flip through the menus until he found the one for *known spells*. Sadly, the list wasn't very long.

Known spells:
- **Bless 1**

- **Heal 1**

- **Mending 1**

Mending? Wasn't that a mage spell? Gareth frowned at that thought. Obviously, he didn't know this game as well as he knew the myriads he'd actually played before. Each one had its quirks. No matter how familiar the overall environment seemed, they all had differences. Forgetting that would only lead him into trouble.

Without knowing exactly what he was doing, Gareth studied the scorch mark that denoted the wound in his side. As he did, he directed his thoughts toward the command to *heal*. Immediately, the red bar in the upper right of his vision field replenished itself to full health and promptly vanished from his sight. He concluded that it must only be visible when he sustained some damage. A blue bar appeared just under where the red one had been. It showed about two-thirds full. Given the fact he'd just cast a spell and from his knowledge of other games, that must be the mana bar. From the looks of it, he had about three spell casts before he was out of mana.

Clud watched with interest, even going so far as to pull up Gareth's chain mail to study the healed wound. "You weren't lying. It's been an age since I've seen a battle cleric build. Very interesting."

Gareth shrugged. "I really wanted to make a Paladin."

Clud blew a forceful breath out of his large nostrils. "I bet you did." Clud looked Gareth over carefully, "From the look of things, I'm guessing you're human, and from the old stories, I know they loved to make Paladins. It was a powerful class. Too bad it was lost."

Gareth frowned. "So, how is it possible to *lose* a class?"

Clud held out a large hand, palm up, waving it instructionally. "Well. Every class—other than the base four—has a patron deity somewhere in the game environment. The Paladin patron was probably destroyed."

Gareth shook his head. "This game is so weird. Why does a class need a patron to exist? Anyway, thanks for helping with the four horsemen there." He jerked his thumb in the direction where the recruiting bullies had vanished. "What's up with them, anyway?"

Clud placed a hand on his chest. "I'm in charge of new character intake and training, as you can see. The guilds like to come by and check out the newbies, see if there's anyone they should recruit. It used to be low key, until those four guilds banded together and chased the rest off." He shook his massive head. "Now they act like this is their private recruiting ground. Unfortunately, unless they step over the line and harm a newbie, I can't do anything about it."

Gareth grimaced. "Those guys seemed like major assholes. Why were they so hot on picking me up?"

Clud gestured to the ragtag bunch of newbies in the practice area with their tattered armor and shabby weapons. "Compare yourself to *them*. Look at their starting equipment compared to yours. You obviously have some sort of patron giving you a boost to start. They were probably hoping to gain leverage with whoever your patron is. Plus, you're a human, which hasn't been seen for a very long time. With the stories floating around about your people, they probably figure you'll be leveling mountains by level 10." Clud let out a loud snort.

"Great, just what I need, unreasonable expectations. I'm afraid I'm just an average Joe, completely lacking in superpowers." Gareth scratched his jaw and looked over the training area. "So, ah, how does this work?"

"You just wade in and attack a dummy. Every so often, you'll get a skill-up. At 100 skill-ups, your weapon ability level will increase. This is just the free newbie training, so your maximum weapon level is one."

Huh. Well, that didn't sound too hard. Gareth nodded, fairly sure he understood. He waved to Clud on his way to start his practice. "Thanks again."

Clud reached out and grabbed Gareth's arm, stopping him. "Be careful of those four, Gareth. They don't take refusal well."

Gareth glanced in the direction where they'd departed. and then nodded. "I will."

Jeez, just half hour into the game and he'd already managed to make some enemies. Hopefully they'd move on to other fresh meat soon. Or Gareth was going to have to be very diligent about leveling up—and fast.

CHAPTER
ELEVEN
THINGS GET DIRE

GARETH SPENT THE NEXT TWO HOURS ASSAULTING straw men and barrels. He didn't stop until he'd leveled up in both broadsword and longsword skills. He sure as heck wasn't ready to take on Inigo Montoya, but he felt more competent than when he'd walked in. Surprisingly, he was winded, and his arms were sore. Just like they'd be if he'd done these things in the real world…

Which got him thinking once again about reality and the nature of this game environment. And his bodily needs. Because right now, he was experiencing a gnawing hunger.

Almost as if on cue, a lunch cart pulled up—quite literally. A wagon towed by some sort of giant beetle arrived. It had a small kitchen setup inside the cart. Gareth and his fellow newbies headed over. His stomach twisted and growled. He'd probably consider eating a bug or whatever other weirdness might be available. The cook—not a giant beetle, thankfully—was busily spooning out a sort of thin, brown, lumpy soup into bowls. They could just be vegetables, right? Without a word, each of the trainees ahead of him accepted the bowl and moved toward the wooden tables nearby. Gareth grabbed an empty bowl from the stack and moved in to get his share. *Please don't let it be something utterly revolting.* He wasn't quite *that* hungry… yet.

When he reached the front of the line, the cook snatched his bowl away. "Ye don't want that slop. That's for them who's can't pay. I've got just the thing for ye here." The cook pointed at some skewers of vegetables and meat roasting over coals on a tray behind him. "Just one leaf each. Exactly the thing for a hungry warrior such as yerself."

Gareth's mouth twisted. If people were going to try to shake him down for his obvious money, then he was going to have to get thrifty and make it last as long as possible.

"I'll take one of each. And *you'll* take one leaf for both."

The cook sputtered. "Snatch the dinner right out of me children's mouths, why don't ye? Fine." He handed over the two skewers on a wooden plank. Gareth frowned. That lack of return haggle told him that he'd still overpaid. Obviously, he had a lot to learn—about all aspects of the game.

When he sat down at the very end of a table, he couldn't help but notice the glares of other fellow newbs over their slop bowls. As if he hadn't already made enough enemies. It'd probably be a good idea to move along before he made any more.

And money. He'd been going through that quicker than he'd thought. He needed a way to start making more before he ran out. He glanced at the red number in the corner of his view: *153*. One hundred fifty-three days before he got tossed out an airlock.

It seemed like forever, but he couldn't help but think he'd be spending a lot more before he really started rocking this adventurer thing. And every crown he spent took a day off his life. He shook his head, willing himself to put that thought out of his mind, or he'd be too frozen in fear to do anything. Then he'd really be screwed. Better to focus on what he could do: make some more coin. Enough crowns, and he wouldn't need to worry about his upkeep.

But first, lunch.

His meal was tasty, all things considered. He pushed up from his table to hand his empty plank back to the cook.

"That was delicious, thank you. So, ah, you wouldn't happen to know of any work to be found around here, would you?"

Cook scratched at his beard. "Well, I could always use more rat meat."

"Um. *Rat?*" Ugh. Suddenly his meal didn't seem as tasty anymore.

"Yeah! You newbies love killing rats, and I love cooking them. I'll give you five cups each. And I'm here every day at lunch, so you know when and where to find me. But if you don't see me, just ask for Olofir." The cook turned away as he proceeded to pack up his kitchen.

Rats eh? Such a cliché. The ultimate fodder for newbies in games the world—or in this case, the galaxy—over. He could kill a rat—or twenty. "So where do I find rats around here?"

He had no idea he'd spoken his question aloud until he heard a reply. "Just follow this road out of town. Turn left at the burned-out farm, then right at the split tree. When you hit the swampy area, you'll see them all over the place."

Gareth turned to the source of this helpful information. Another trainee now stood right beside him. Definitely one of the ones who'd glared at him over lunch. Perhaps the joke of Gareth inadvertently eating rat had mellowed him. Or he was still being a punk and just wanted to get rid of the well-equipped and seemingly rich newcomer.

Nevertheless, Gareth nodded to him with gratitude. "Thank you. I'll remember it." Did Gareth imagine the nervousness on the other person's features when he said that?

Ah, what the hell. How bad could it get? Gareth followed the directions he'd been given. Beyond the edge of town, the path thinned significantly—odd for a typical newbie area. In his significant gaming experience, Gareth had always found the newbie hunting grounds crowded and the pickings slim. And the path to them was usually well marked. Maybe this game was different, but that didn't prevent Gareth from keeping a wary eye out for trouble.

He had no trouble finding the split tree—literally a tree that had been split in half by lightning. Soon after that, the ground softened beneath his boots, as if drenched with moisture. So, he'd arrived... but he didn't see any sign of rats—or newbies, for that matter.

However, it did look like the perfect area for nests, so he drew his broadsword, hefted his shield and began the hunt. He searched... and searched... moving deeper into the field where the grass was longer and the wind slapped the stiff blades against his armored shins. He shaded his eyes from the sunlight—every bit as bright and hot as at home, even if the color was a bit off— and kept looking. He peered at each and every bush or fallen log, even kicking at some of them. A few times, he was startled by movement and swung first, resolving to ask questions later. Those "battles" ended up being clumps of rotting vegetation savaged by his sword.

After what seemed like forever, he heard snuffling and grunting behind a clump of very tall weeds. Crouching, and attempting to be as quiet as possible, he slowly pushed through the tall grass until he could peer beyond.

A rat! Gareth drew back, startled. This was no normal rat. It was the size of a large pony and paid him no mind as it ate at the remains of a dead deer. A rodent of unusual size, perhaps? Now all he needed was to discover that he'd inadvertently wandered into the Fire Swamp. What was next? Flame spurts? Lightning sand? Dread Pirate Roberts running by with a blonde in a red dress?

Gareth inspected the improbable creature. As he carefully looked the creature over, a window with information popped up just over the rat. Wasn't that convenient? A quick notice popped up, informing him that he'd gained 1 point in the Identification skill.

Dire Rat

•**Level:** 7

•**Health:** 37

A *dire* rat? Gareth had been set up, goddamn it. There was no way in hell he could take a creature that had six levels on him.

Making the most of the rat's preoccupation with its rotting meal, Gareth backed away with as much stealth as he could muster in his clanky armor.

Unfortunately, it wasn't much. He hadn't taken five steps before the rat's head shot up, and a second later, it charged straight for him.

Gareth halted, braced his feet, then readied his shield to meet the charge. The massive rodent slammed into him at full speed, knocking him off his feet. He did manage a good jab with his sword as he fell, but that only reduced its health bar by ten percent or so.

Whoa. This was going to be a long fight. Or a short one, depending on how lucky the rat got. Gareth turned his attention to his own health bar—dropped by a quarter. Yikes. Twenty-five percent of his life, and it hadn't even bit him. Pain radiated from his side—once again shocking him that he could experience the pain of the damage he sustained. But it felt different—toned down—more like a notification of pain than true pain.

The rat reared, and Gareth struggled to position his shield between them, desperately seeking to avoid the inevitable bite. He shoved the shield upward to bludgeon the rat as it came back down. As it was momentarily stunned, he got in a few more stabs—albeit from an awkward angle, so he didn't hit with the full force of his strength.

Then it landed on him, and the weight of its body pushed the shield back onto his chest. Now pinned, he could only watch helplessly as he struggled in vain, wondering what the game's death penalty would be. The rat was too big, and his efforts had not done near enough damage.

The massive rodent scrabbled up Gareth's shield, giving him an up-close and all too personal view of huge yellow teeth. Gareth's eyes squeezed shut as he tried to remember whether he knew the Lord's Prayer—or any prayer, for that matter. He didn't really believe that any higher power would hear him, especially not in a game.

This was it. The end. Finito. El done-zo.

Thowk. Thowk. Thowk. Thowk.

Gareth let out a sharp breath. Was he dead? He pried his eyes open as the rat's head dropped onto him. But it was limp and drooling. Gareth gasped, aware of the smell of blood—his own?

Was he dead now? It took him a minute to notice the rat had stopped moving. He pushed against the shield as hard as he could and managed to shove the bulky creature off. Slowly, he tested each of his limbs before pushing out of the muck of the swamp beneath him. God, what a mess. Blood, a rat corpse, and mud everywhere. He stood, blinking. Wouldn't even help to dust himself off. The filth was way beyond that.

Four crossbow bolts stuck out of the side of the dead rodent like porcupine quills. Where the hell had those come from? He narrowed his eyes, peering around. That crossbow belonged to an owner—likely a high-level owner. Crap.

Had he managed to attract even more of the wrong attention?

Gareth's eyes locked on the figure nearby, a short and stocky person in full plate armor. The figure watched him from about forty feet away, standing on a dry hillock. If Tolkien hadn't lied, this was almost certainly a dwarf.

Hopefully he was a nice, happy dwarf. He'd already proven himself incredibly helpful by saving Gareth's life, so there was that.

Gareth sheathed his sword and approached the stranger while also giving his armor a casual brush to get the worst of the mud off his backside. On Gareth's approach, the dwarf was re-cocking an odd-looking contraption of a crossbow—a quad bow that could shoot four bolts at once. The helmeted figure never took its gaze from the landscape.

Gareth squinted, attempting to use his identify skill again. All he got back was a string of question marks. Must be some sort of level limitation—or maybe it only worked on monsters.

Gareth halted about five feet away and held his empty hands where the dwarf could see them. His equipment was of much higher quality than Gareth's. His eyes ran over the intricately detailed and gorgeously made armor that fit the dwarf perfectly. On top of that, the mysterious figure was festooned with weapons. There was zero chance that this adventurer would see Gareth as a threat. But holding his hands out and not making any sudden moves was never a bad idea.

"Greetings," Gareth called, hoping he didn't sound as nervous as he felt.

The dwarf lifted the visor of his helm, revealing a wizened, but not old, face, dark black hair, a long beard and striking green eyes. When he spoke, it was in a deep, gravelly voice. "What are you doing out here, boy? This is no place for newbs."

Despite his ease, the dwarf never took his eyes off the horizon, scanning the area even while addressing Gareth.

Gareth coughed into his fist, feeling sheepish. "I was, ah, told this was the place to hunt rats."

The bushy brow beetled. "And you *believed* them? You're dumber than a barrel of toads." Apparently satisfied that there were no more dire rats in the area, the dwarf dropped his pack and pulled out a portable stool. Setting it on the ground, the dwarf stared up at Gareth, inspecting him from head to toe in a long look. "Do you need a potion, boy? Or are you just going to stand there bleeding?"

Gareth huffed out a self-conscious breath. Duh. "Crap. I forgot." He focused on his health rating and the wounds he'd sustained. "Heal." The red health bar replenished itself and disappeared.

The newcomer nodded. "*Cleric.* Well, that explains some things." He held out a thick finger. "Never forget to heal, boy. You never know when you'll need all the hit points you can get." He sank to the stool and scooped up his fancy crossbow. "Now, come sit over here so I don't accidentally put a bolt into you while clearing out any more rats." He pointed at the ground next to him.

Well, this was certainly an odd development. What was he doing here?

And more importantly, why was he being so nice to a clueless newbie such as Gareth?

Not seeing many other choices, Gareth did as the dwarf asked, staring expectantly at his new and unusual acquaintance.

Chapter Twelve
Power Leveling

THE WIZENED DWARF STARED DOWN AT GARETH FROM this temporary perch. Gareth sat cross-legged on the ground in front of him, poised to learn more. Then, the adventurer scratched his beard and broke the awkward silence. "Kruger's the name, by the way."

"Gareth," he responded with a nod.

Kruger's gaze slid over Gareth's equipment and armor, as if inspecting them. Who knew, maybe he was using the UI to find out more information, though Gareth had attempted to do the same for Kruger and had come up with nothing.

The dwarf coughed. "So what are you, level two or three? Is this your first rat hunt?"

"I'm actually level one. And this is my first hunt for anything. First day, actually." Gareth tilted his head and shrugged. The newcomer's critical tone was grating on him. What did it take to find a friendly face in this game? Did they even exist?

Kruger choked out a harsh-sounding laugh. "Oh, wee. Aren't you an ambitious one? First day in the game, and you're already going after dire rats."

Gareth bristled. "I was actually going after normal rats. As I said, someone told me this is where they were. I wouldn't be here if I'd known they were monster rats."

Kruger's mouth twisted thoughtfully. "Someone doesn't like you, looks like. But still, you didn't wonder why the newbie zone was so far outside the city?" The dwarf shoved a hand into his pack and extracted a flask. He took a long pull, then offered it to Gareth.

In spite of himself, Gareth sighed. "Yes, that had occurred to me. But I didn't want to just assume I knew how things worked in the game." Gareth took the proffered flask, sipped at it and almost gagged. It burned like raw moonshine—a hundred proof, if he was any judge.

Kruger took back his flask and took another swig, nodding. "Assuming you don't know everything is a good start. But not finding out the things you don't know is bad." He slapped his armored belly. "Always trust your gut. If it says something is hinky, *believe it.*"

A bit tired of hearing about his shortcomings, Gareth attempted a change in subject. "So, what are *you* doing out here? Not leveling up on dire rats, obviously."

Kruger scoffed. "I don't get any XP from these little things. I'm out here looking for something I lost. One of these things might have it."

"What... the rats? How does that work? Do they carry things in some kind of pouch?" It occurred to him that the one that had nearly done him in hadn't yet been looted. He made a note to check.

The dwarf guffawed, slapping a knee. "A rat with a pouch? Nah. But maybe one of them ate it." He darted a look at Gareth. "I have a proposition for you." He dug into his pack, withdrawing a long, slender, serrated knife. "As I said, I don't get any experience from these rats. But I can buff you up, so you'll survive fighting them. In exchange, all you have to do is carve them up and give me anything you find in the stomachs. I'll even teach you how to properly skin and separate the rats so you can make more coin when you get back to town."

Gareth's stomach turned at the thought of butchering giant vermin. "Why would I want to skin and chop up rats? Olofir said he'd give me 5 cups each for a normal sized rat. I figure I could get a leaf each for one of these."

Kruger rolled his eyes and heaved a big sigh into his beard as if collecting his patience. "First off, *always* ask around at different vendors. Don't just take the first offer—*especially* for resource gathering."

Gareth frowned and scratched his jaw thoughtfully. He thought it had been a pretty good offer, to be honest. But again, what did he know on his very first day?

Kruger set his shoulders, taking on an instructional tone. "Let's take your cook there, O-whatever-his-name-is. He'll cook up the meat, for sure. But there's still a bunch of rat leftover. Once he gets the carcass from you, he'll sell the eyes and the spleen to a potion maker, the whiskers to a brush maker; the bones go to a chemist, the hide to a toy- or furniture-maker. The tails go to a baker. Essentially, every part of the rat gets used. You kill the rat, take it to him, he pays you five cups or whatever. Then he turns around and makes three leafs off it."

Gareth's brow twisted. "Wait, what does a baker want with rat tails?"

"Umm, rat tail pie?" the dwarf chuckled as if giving the most obvious answer in the world. Then he rubbed his stomach. "*Damn.* now I'm hungry. Anyway, if you part up the rat yourself, you can sell straight to each artisan. Then *you* pocket all the profit. Never take the easy way. They're ripping you off."

"Interesting." Gareth nodded. "Okay, I accept your offer. Now, what do I do?"

Kruger stood from his stool and gestured to the freshly-slain dire rat nearby. "I'll show you how to part up the rat on this first one. Then we'll buff you up and turn you into a killing machine." The dwarf grabbed his crossbow and knife and walked over to the rat with Gareth trailing close behind.

"Now pay attention, son. I don't want to do this twice." He set down the crossbow, grabbed the rat and started cutting at it.

A now-familiar status box appeared before his field of vision:

***Kruger wishes to teach you skinning, do you accept (Y/N)**

Gareth quickly accepted, eager to acquire a skill that sounded a lot more useful than his secret talent.

Quicker than Gareth thought possible, Kruger had separated the rat into individual piles of ingredients, just as he'd described.

Then he offered Gareth the knife. "I'll leave cutting open the stomach to you."

He took a step back and waved for Gareth to proceed.

Gareth quickly identified the stomach—that bag-looking, pink, fleshy lump sitting all by itself, glistening with slime. Gareth grabbed it up, and the sharp knife slid easily through. A rank smell rose up and unidentified, partially digested matter splattered his face, arms and chest.

Disgusting. Ugh. But he fought to hide his revulsion, driven by the desire to impress Kruger. Gareth used the knife to pick through the contents of the stomach. "And just what am I looking for, here?"

"Another bit of advice for you..." Kruger said from a safe distance behind him. Sure, let the newb do the messy grunt work. Seemed about right. "*Always* look in the stomach—especially in large creatures. You never know what they've eaten. I've found some damn fine loot in stomachs. Of course, picking through bile does have its downsides, which is why you're doing it and I'm standing over here. Anyway, in answer to your question, just pick out anything man-made. Or gold, of course—or jewels or—well, just pick out anything that isn't food."

Gareth swallowed his revulsion, ignored the roiling in his own stomach and continued picking through the contents. Once he was sure there wasn't anything of value, he turned to Kruger and handed him back his knife.

Kruger held out a hand and shook his head. "Just keep it, I'll get another. You'll need it to keep going. Remember, I get anything of interest in the stomachs, but everything else is yours."

As he said this, a new status box popped up.

•You have learned a new skill: Skinning, level 1

•You have learned a new skill: Search, level 1

After scrolling through and dismissing the message, Gareth turned back to his unlikely mentor. "Now what?"

"Well, first you gotta put the bits away to be sold later and make your big whopping profit. If you leave it all here, it will have been dragged away before you get back to it."

"*Put it away?* Where? In my pack?" He gestured to his own backpack. There was no way it was fitting all that crap inside, to say nothing of how gross it would be to just shlump it all in there.

"Yep. Try it."

Despite Gareth's misgivings, he did as the dwarf asked, and true to the other games he'd played, he was able to fit everything inside. Though it took a little shoving and shaking to get some of it to fit through the opening.

"So how is this going to work?" Gareth finally cinched up his bag. "Obviously I can't kill dire rats, as you just witnessed. And I don't really like the idea of becoming bait."

Kruger shook his head, deep in thought. "No worries. Give me a second and you'll be able to kill these rats just fine and all by yourself." He took a deep breath, then chanted in a strange, harsh tongue.

Icons appeared at the corner of Gareth's display from the UI:

•Bulwark

•Strength

•Smite

•Steel Skin

Kruger finished chanting, lowered his arms, and appeared well satisfied with himself, smiling faintly. "There. Now, you'll be able to kill one of these just fine."

Gareth quickly verified it. His armor rating had gone from 14 to 54. Under strength, he now had a +5 damage bonus. *Smite* appeared to be some sort of enchantment that added to the damage he dealt with his weapons—once he hit something. *Bulwark* increased his health—though by how much, he couldn't tell. The game stubbornly refused to give him any numeric value for that or for the blue mana bar.

Gareth puffed out his chest and mimed flexing his biceps. "I'm fiercer now! Let's go kill something."

Kruger held out a hand. "Don't get carried away. You're still a newbie, even with all the buffs. You won't have any trouble with a rat, but if you get more than one, run to me and I'll handle any adds."

"Gotcha. So, how do we find more rats?"

"Just stomp around and make noise. Trust me, they'll find you. You're too low-level to be viewed as a threat by them."

An hour later Gareth had killed three dire rats without incident.

And by the end of the day, the dead rat count was up to twenty-three.

Gareth parted up the rats quickly, saving the stomachs for last. The two adventurers, mentor and newbie, settled near a stream where Gareth insisted on washing off the rat guts and blood. Battling the rodents had been bloody and tiring work but piecing them out afterward had been a whole other type of mess.

And now Gareth was the proud owner of twenty-three dire rats' worth of skin, bone, meat, and piles of other sellable rat parts. His backpack was stuffed to the brim. He'd even had to bum a ratty-looking bag off Kruger to store the rat whiskers and eyes.

He'd saved the worst for last...a huge pile of slimy pink stomachs. Kruger's share of the loot, as they'd agreed. He glanced at the dwarf, curious to see what his missing item was. Maybe they'd gotten lucky.

The dwarf just frowned at him grumpily. "I don't know why you bothered washing up when you still have work to do." The dwarf said pointing at the piled organs. "Why wait 'til the very end to cut them up, instead of doing them as we went along?"

Gareth positioned himself beside the pile of stomachs and just over the bank of the brook. "Well...if I'm going to have partially digested rat food sprayed on me, I'd rather it was all at once. This way, I can wash up at the end instead of walking around all day covered in guck."

And maybe he just wasn't so much of a newbie after all, because he'd been strategic enough to use this as an excuse to keep Kruger—and his amazing buffs—around all day while he'd fought. *And* while he'd gained more experience, leveled up his skills and acquired more items to sell.

CHAPTER

THIRTEEN

HISTORY'S MYSTERIES

I T APPEARED KRUGER HADN'T CAUGHT ON TO GARETH'S plan to keep him around.

What was abundantly clear, however, was Kruger's growing impatience. "Just hurry up with it, will you? I ran out of beer hours ago, and I need to get back to civilization." Once again, the dwarf produced his portable stool and sat waiting for Gareth to get on with it.

Gareth snatched up yet another slippery stomach and slit it open, taking care to point the slit away from himself. Despite being cautious, however, he was soon filthy again from digging and sifting through the contents. At least he'd learned how to avoid the initial spray.

This stomach was no less vile than the first, but among the bile and lumps of partially digested food, Gareth detected something hard, metallic. He gingerly plucked it out and inspected it—some kind of badge. He washed it off in the stream and then flicked the item over to the dwarf. "Is this what you were looking for?"

Kruger squinted at the badge, turning it over in his hands a few times, taking long enough to inspect it that Gareth's hopes rose. Maybe they'd gotten lucky on the second try?

Then the dwarf let out a breath and shook his head. "Nope. But I think *you'll* find it of interest."

He tossed it back to Gareth, who angled it in the dying sunlight to get a better look. The front of the badge depicted an eagle with outstretched wings. A wreath encircled the body of the bird and underneath were inscribed the letters *IX.* the Roman numeral for nine. His brow furrowed in thought. "This looks like an ancient Roman badge from Earth. What the hell is it doing here in the game? And the number nine...? Huh. Like the ninth legion? Why does that sound familiar?"

Kruger shrugged. "Don't look at me. I stopped keeping track of human history a very long time ago. But I do know that a while back, some guilds paid to have groups of humans scooped up from your world and brought here. They needed more fighting power—and probably cannon fodder, too. They had primitive tactics that involved lots of people swarming the bigger creatures. It doesn't translate exactly but having skills in the real world does allow your character to start off better skilled. The game doesn't make you forget things you already knew before."

All of those abduction victims... so many stories throughout history of people—or large groups—who had simply vanished over the centuries. He glanced down at the badge again—this disappearance had occurred millennia ago. All those victims had been snatched away from their lives, just like him.

He shuddered. "That's screwed up. They kidnapped people just to get them to Zerg some mob?"

Kruger's dark gaze intensified. "I don't think you understand how serious this game is. Galactic empires have risen and fallen over what has happened in this game."

Gareth blinked, thinking about Clippy's lesson in ancient history, which felt like weeks or even months ago.

"Every time I think this game and world can't get any stranger, some new facts come to light that raises the bar again." Gareth tapped the badge again. "Ninth legion, ninth legion, I swear I've heard about them before."

Some ancient mystery or *what-if* tale? A documentary? Or—wait! It was an episode of *Doctor Who*. Bill was going on about the Ninth Legion—Legio IX Hispana. "They disappeared in Scotland sometime in the early second century. One of history's great mysteries. There are theories, but no one knows for sure."

Kruger's mouth twisted, and he nodded toward the badge. "Well, now *you* know what happened to them. Likely picked up and forced to fight here for the good of a power guild in the game."

Gareth studied the badge again. The disappearance of the Ninth. The vanishing of Atlantis. What other strange and incredible puzzles and anomalies would come to light for him in the coming days and weeks? Until...

Until what? Until he made his way back home?

Finding this badge, an actual object from his actual home world, should have made him feel more connected, more hopeful that other humans had come here and even, perhaps, survived.

But as he rolled that badge back and forth in his hands, all he felt was even lonelier than before.

"This is beyond screwed up."

Gareth's musing was interrupted by a sharp pebble hitting him on the head. Gareth looked up to meet Kruger's exasperated gaze. "I'm sure it's all very disturbing to find out what happened to your fellow Dirtlings. But it's also ancient history at this point—*literally*. Get back to cutting. Trust me, you don't want to be out here after dark, especially at your level."

Gareth inspected the sky. It wouldn't be long before dark settled on the landscape. "Fair point. Back to work, then."

He continued with the stomach dissection, settling into a pattern to get through his task as quickly as possible.

Before long, a small pile of loot grew. Gareth separated the items out by category—coins of various denominations, two crude daggers, a slimy boot, a rusty belt buckle, four twisted pieces of metal he couldn't identify, and lastly, a ring with a partially digested finger still in it. *Gross.*

"There it is!" Kruger jumped up and snatched the ring from Gareth's fingers, plucked out the dismembered finger, and flicked it over his shoulder into the grass. "Some little prick stole this from me, and I chased him into this here swamp. Little jerk was rude enough to get eaten by the rats before I could run him down. My father gave me this ring." He bent to wash it in the stream, then slipped it onto his stout finger. As if a newly engaged woman inspecting the diamond given to her by her fiancé, Kruger held his hand out to admire it in the fading sun.

"Well, looks like you're all good. And it's high time for me to get back to town." Gareth began collecting the coins.

"Nope, those are mine." Kruger bent and scooped them up in one easy motion. "Deals a deal. You can keep those though." He pointed at the rest of the junk. With a quiet harrumph, Gareth piled the nearly worthless crap into his bag. He also grabbed a

Dire Rat head and shoved it into his bag along with the corpse of an ordinary rat he'd accidentally stepped on while fighting its much larger cousins. Kruger cocked an eyebrow.

"I need to educate someone on the difference between the two." Gareth shrugged.

He wasn't thrilled with the loot he'd gotten for his day's work, but hey, the power-leveling had been great.

Kruger continued. "You should have leveled up three or four times during all that. That's the real reward."

His task now finished, Gareth hefted his full pack on his shoulders and squinted at the dwarf. "Leveled up?" Gareth fumbled, too embarrassed to admit he hadn't leveled up. "Uh, well anyway, great experience today. Nice meeting you."

Kruger shook his head with a rueful grin. "You're going to be the death of me, lad—or rather the death of *you*. For me, today was an investment in the future, though. I'd rather you lived, so I can get the return on my investment. You need to learn the UI."

Gareth hesitated. "Oh, yeah, the UI…shoulda thought of that."

Kruger gave him a stare, clearly understanding that Gareth was still lost. "There should be an indicator, somewhere, that says you gained enough experience to level."

Gareth thought about the blinking light that had popped up after defeating the second rat. "There was *something*. but it was annoying me while I was in the thick of things. I gave the command to hide it."

Kruger waved a thick hand triumphantly. "Well, then. *Un* hide it. And activate it."

Gareth pulled up the UI and mentally flipped through the menus before finding the indicator he'd hidden from view. Upon activating it, a new status card popped up.

•Character increased from level 1 to level 5 (4 unallocated)

•Broadsword increased from Apprentice 0 to Apprentice 4

•Kite Shield increased from Apprentice 0 to Apprentice 4

•Skinning skill increased from Horrible to Horrible

•Search skill increased from Horrible to Horrible

Increased from horrible to horrible? Those skills must have progressed some, but how much progress did it take to make it out of horrible? *Unallocated levels?* Now that was interesting.

Gareth quickly found the control to allocate his newfound leveling wealth. "Hey, how come I can only put levels into cleric? I was told multi-classing was allowed."

Kruger sighed again. "Learn the game, son. You need to train in a new class before you can allocate levels to it. And before you ask, you need at least one unallocated level—more for some of the rarer classes—and a trainer to train you. Oh, you also need a bunch of gold."

"Exactly *how* much gold?"

Kruger shrugged. "For a base class like Warrior? A thousand or so."

"A *thousand* gold?" Gareth goggled. "Couldn't *you* train me? You seem like a high-level Warrior."

The dwarf shook his head regretfully. "I'm a Paladin, not a Warrior. I can only train others in my same class."

Gareth drew back, annoyed at the misinformation he'd been given. "A *Paladin?* But I was told that was a lost class. Please, train me."

"Technically, I'm a Hamarfiend, colloquially known as a *dwarf* Paladin. And I'm afraid our patron, old Silver Beard, only accepts dwarves. You, quite obviously, need a human Paladin to train you. So, I can't help—unless you somehow become a dwarf. Come see me if that happens."

Gareth stared in disbelief. "You're shitting me! Different races have different versions of each class? Is Dwarf Warrior different from Human Warrior?"

Kruger sighed. "Sometimes, yes. It's a complicated game. However, warrior is a base class, so it is the same for all races. Advanced classes—not so much. Human Paladins fought evil in every form. Dwarf Paladins mostly fight demons. Each racial class has a unique set of skills. It's a fine distinction, I know."

Gareth harrumphed. "It's dumbass, is what it is."

The dwarf shrugged. "Be that as it may, it is what it is. Not much we can do about it. *Now* ... I've got places to be, and so do you. Best we both get going." He made a shooing motion with his gloved hand while he gathered his stuff into his pack.

Gareth didn't move, arms locked over his chest in defiance. "This sucks."

"A great many things in this game are unfair. It is a simulation of the real world, after all. One form of it, anyway." He studied the newbie for a moment as he fiddled with his beard. "I'll tell you what. When you get back to town, look up Grifor. Be sure to tell him I sent you. He should be able to work something out with you for the warrior training."

Gareth brightened. "Grifor? Great. I'll do that." He snatched up his pack and turned back to the dwarf. "I'm grateful for all your help today. Especially since I would've literally died without it. I don't mean to come across as ungrateful, it's just that this game is harsher than what I'm used to."

Kruger waved his hand. He appeared distant, as if already thinking about where he was going next. "Don't worry about it. Your first day is in the books, and you've done quite well for yourself." He took a few steps toward the swamp and then turned to add cryptically. "I'll be seeing you around."

The dwarf vanished into the swamp and Gareth took no time to puzzle after him, instead heading back toward town. He had leveling up to do—along with a newbie to beat the shit out of for trying to get him killed on his first day. With satisfaction, Gareth imagined the look on the creep's face when he realized Gareth had gained four levels in a single day.

He stepped back onto city streets at about the time that the sun was setting. He spared no time to dawdle as he made the rounds at the various rat-interested vendors, as Kruger had instructed. In the end, he was ten gold crowns and change richer.

Next it was off to find the original rat meat quest-giver, Olofir. The cook tried to give Gareth grief, stating that his offer was for the entire rat, rather than just the meat. With a shrug, Gareth turned to gather up his ten pounds of dire rat meat, muttering about taking it somewhere else. Olofir quickly relented.

Gareth was still undecided on how to allocate his new levels. This game was turning out to be very combat-oriented. Maybe three levels of warrior versus one more of cleric, to focus on combat abilities more, might be the way to go? Then again, that might leave him with sub-optimal healing powers. In any case, the point was moot until he found this Grifor person and was able to train his warrior class. Odds were good he might end up just becoming a level five cleric.

In the UI, Gareth pulled up the *find* function and spelled out Grifor's name. Unlike on the station on the real-world side, this time, it came back with a message stating that Kruger hadn't discovered a person named Grifor yet.

Gareth frowned. So, you weren't allowed to use the UI to find a person you'd never met before? Apparently, this *find* function was just a way of taking virtual notes then? Gareth then noticed that he could opt out of the find function, should he so wish. Likely a way to hide from enemies. After all, it could be a cheap way to track someone down. Given the day he'd had, and the many hostile players out there, including the newbie with a mark on his back, Gareth selected to be anonymous in the *find* feature.

No need to make it easier to try to do away with him. He was four levels stronger, yes, but that didn't make him invincible.

With a sigh and a squaring of the shoulders, Gareth pondered whether he should continue his search for Grifor or get a pint to quench his thirst.

Hmm... *why not both?*

CHAPTER

FOURTEEN

GRIFART AND THE ORC PISS TAVERN

ETERMINED TO FIND GRIFOR BEFORE IT GREW TOO late, Gareth decided to go the old school route. Out on the streets again, he saw the usual—horses, traders, wagons, people crossing the way. Kids playing in the alleys…

He spotted a raggedy urchin hanging out beside a fruit vendor in the market. That just might be his ticket.

"Hello, son." Gareth stopped beside him, looking down at the filthy kid.

"I wasn't doing anything!"

The grimy… *boy? Girl?* Were those terms even meaningful for a creature with four legs and one big central eye? The creature looked ready to bolt under Gareth's notice, so he held out his hands, palm up, to look as unthreatening as possible. "I didn't say you were. I'm just looking for some directions."

The cloptaur—so Gareth designated it—gave him a once-over. Apparently deciding Gareth wasn't a threat, its stance visibly relaxed. "Well, I've been all over Muddy River. If you want to know where something is, I'm your girl. It takes a lot of effort to learn the town like I have."

Girl. Well, that was good to know. Hopefully the little girl wasn't bullshitting about knowing the town. "Knowledge has value, for sure. And the sharing of it is even more valuable. I'm looking for a man named… Grifor."

The child made a big show of thinking, putting its—*her*—hand up and rubbing her chin. "*Grifor* you say? Can't say that I know any Grifor."

Gareth reached into his pouch and pulled out a silver leaf. "Would *this* help your memory at all?"

The child's eyes darted to the coin before she shook her head. "I'd like to help you. I really would. I just don't remember any Grifor."

Well crap. "He's a warrior. A dwarf, I think."

She shook her head again. "Sorry. There aren't that many dwarves in town, either. I'd definitely know one named Grifor."

"I was told he was in town, here. Are you *sure* you don't know a Grifor?"

This earned him a look of withering scorn worthy of his own teenage son. "I *said* I know all the dwarves. There're only eight— Kun, Vongus, Hulnar, Dwingle, Ignan, Brulnor, Thordrak, and…*wait*. I bet you mean Grifart."

Gareth frowned, shaking his head. "Grifart? No, his name was Grifor."

An exaggerated shrug. "Well, I don't know Grifor. That could be his actual name, I guess. I've never spoken to him myself. Everyone calls him Grifart though. But if you want to try and see if it's him, you'll find him at the back of the Orc Piss tavern."

Then she snorted out a laugh. "Good luck getting him to talk to you, though. He's passed-out drunk most of the time. The beer there makes him gassy, see? That's probably were he got his name—or his nickname."

Gareth held out the coin but pulled it back when child reached for it. "Two more things." The girl's eyes shifted sideways, as if nervous again. Gareth responded by pulling out some copper cups and placed them in his hand beside the silver coin. "I just want to know where I can find this tavern, and what your name is, in case I need your help again."

She jerked a thumb—at least Gareth thought it was a thumb, anyway—over her shoulder. "The Orc Piss is in Old Town, near the midden. Just head toward the awful smell. My name is..." She hesitated a moment, considering. "Just ask for Galxis." Then she snaked the coins out of his hand and darted down the street.

Gareth peered after her, then turned toward the direction she'd indicated. Old town, eh? Well, he could at least use the UI to find *that* on his map. And so, it was as easy as that—because, apparently, he didn't have to discover landmarks in his starting city before asking how to navigate to them.

On foot, it took about twenty minutes to reach Old Town, a decidedly seedier part of the township that was Muddy River. Guessing that the midden would be located by the river, he headed there, where it cut through this part of the town. The overpowering stench was unmissable, and by the time he saw the water, his eyes were watering from it. Apparently, his guess had been right.

When he reached the midden, he was silently gagging in the back of his throat between sucking in gulps of air through his mouth. Goddamn that was vile! And here was a clue as to why the town was called Muddy River. As he looked at the oozing, milky flow, he swore to never, *ever* drink the water here.

Pulling his eyes away from the filthy river, he only needed a quick glance around to locate the tavern in question. He was aided by a sign over the establishment which depicted an impossibly well-endowed orc urinating on some flowers. Huh. A line from the treasured movie of his childhood rose up unbidden in his mind. *You will never find a more wretched hive of scum and villainy.* Gareth mentally assured Old Ben he would be cautious as he headed in, hoping there wouldn't be criminals inside who instantly decided they didn't like him.

Inside, the tavern was no more appealing than its exterior. The lighting was dim and smoky, and the smell definitely had stale urine at its base. *Charming.* The only thing you could say about the smell was that it was better than the midden outside—but not terribly.

There were a dozen grimy tables scattered around the room. And their occupants seemed only interested in taking the shortest route from sober to drunk. Gareth waded into the main parlor, dodging flailing limbs and questionable puddles on the ground. Finally, in one dingy corner toward the back, Gareth spotted his goal—or what he thought it to be, anyway. It'd be nice to claim keen observation skills, but in actuality, the seated figure was the only dwarf here.

Gareth approached the table and stood quietly for a minute, hoping to be noticed. The dwarf just stared into his mug, taking a sip every once in a while.

Gareth cleared his throat loudly. "Mr. Grifor?"

"Fuck off." The dwarf didn't even look up from his mug.

"Mr. Grifor, I just wanted—"

"I said *fuck off!*"

Gareth dodged the mug flung in his direction. The crockery shattered against the wall, luckily missing the other patrons. None of them even looked up from their own drinks. Maybe this display of sudden violence wasn't an uncommon occurrence.

Well, apparently it was time for Plan B. Gareth left the table to go to the bar and get the barkeep's attention. To Gareth's surprise, the bartender appeared to be another one of the potato-people, like his friend from the medical bay. But, where the med tech was a healthy-looking brown color, this creature was a sickly-looking green. The barkeep put his four tentacles to good use, filling glasses and serving several customers all at once.

Once again, Gareth stood ignored, despite waving at the bartender. It was like this place was some sort of members-only dive, and he, clearly, wasn't a member—nor would he want to be. Instead of yelling at the bartender to grab his attention—and likely the unwanted attention of others in the bar—he resorted to an old trick. He slapped a silver leaf on the splintery counter in front of him. The sight of silver, rather than the copper the rest of the patrons seemed to be offering, finally drew the creature's attention, and he glided over to float before Gareth.

"Can I help you, mister?" Green potato-man breathed out, his eyes swiveling seemingly at random. Maybe he was a potato creature who was high on some kind of substance.

"I'll, uh, have two of what he's having." Gareth pointed at Grifor.

The potato man made some strange noise that was almost like a huff. "A gentleman like yourself doesn't want to drink *that*. Orc Piss will rot your insides. They only drink it because it's cheap. But you'll be wanting something suitable to your station."

Somewhere during his speech, the silver coin on the counter had disappeared. Another advantage of four arms, Gareth guessed.

He shifted on his feet, considering. If he were being honest, he had no desire whatsoever to consume a beverage named after orc urine. Therefore, he slapped his hand down on the bar.

"Two of your best beers then. In *clean* glasses. And cold." The barkeep returned a minute later with two mugs full of something that at least smelled like beer.

"That will be two silvers each."

"I'll give you one for the both. *And* I won't bitch about the silver you pocketed." Patrons at the other end of the bar began rattling their cups against the rough wood, calling and shouting, apparently seeking attention for themselves. The barkeep finally grunted his acceptance and skittered away. Gareth certainly wouldn't be ordering anything else after that, though. He had no idea what potato-man spit tasted like, and he had zero desire to find out.

When he returned to Grifor's table, he plopped the mug in front of the dwarf. "Here. For your trouble. I just want a minute of your time."

Finally, Grifor's eyes lifted from the tabletop, and his bloodshot gaze was bleary. Gareth was taken aback when he noticed the scars on the dwarf's face. Apparently, he'd gotten close to losing an eye in a fight—more than once. Also, he'd lost the end of his nose at some point.

The dwarf scooped up the glass of beer. "You have until I finish this." Then he started draining it in big, noisy, gulps.

"I'll be quick. I need a Warrior trainer."

He paused long enough to let out a loud belch and respond. "Trainers are in the guildhall by the newbie area."

Gareth sank into the chair opposite him and cleared his throat. "Yes, well, I don't have the thousand gold crowns they want."

Grifor sucked down another big swallow. "Sucks to be you, then. What's this have to do with me?"

"I met another dwarf, name of Kruger. He gave me your name, said you and I might be able to work out a deal for warrior training."

"Huh. Kruger's dead." He tilted his head back, draining the last from his glass. "And now, you're out of time."

Gareth slid his own mug across to the inebriated dwarf. "This should buy me another couple minutes."

With a sour look, he grunted at Gareth. Then took up the second mug.

I leaned in to press my point. "Like I said, a dwarf who told me his name is Kruger said that you could train me in levels as a Warrior."

"And like *I* said," Grifor began with a loud belch. "Kruger is dead. And if he were alive, he wouldn't be caught dead in this town." He raised the mug and drained half of it, the foam sticking to his beard. Clearly, what little patience he had was wearing thin.

"I didn't meet him in town, actually. We came across each other in the swamp outside the east gate."

He chuckled. "I know you're lying, now. It's even less likely that he'd be in a swamp. He always hated mud."

Gareth shrugged. "I can't speak to that. But he was there looking for a ring. A ring his father gave him. So maybe that was important enough to brave the mud."

"What ring?" Up went the mug for another gulp.

Gareth shrugged. "He never said if it had a name. It was an odd, gray-colored metal, not like white gold. It was flat, not shiny. And it had a big black gem on top. Oh and it was inscribed with griffons all the way around."

Grifor finished his drink and turned the mug upside down to show it was empty. "Well, this has been pleasant, but you'd best go now. I can't afford to get used to real beer again. Good luck with your training." He waved Gareth away as if he were some pesky bug.

Fuck this shit. Gareth stiffened, fed up with the shitty attitude he was encountering here, one creature after another. He shot out of his chair. "Fine. Enjoy your piss swill then."

But Gareth was only two steps away from the table when he was brought up short by Grifor's shout. "Get back here and sit down!"

CHAPTER
FIFTEEN
THE LOST TOTEM

GRIFOR'S VOICE CARRIED ACROSS THE TAVERN HALL, loud enough to draw stares. Gareth gingerly turned back to the drunken dwarf.

He sank into the chair opposite him with a frown. "I'm confused—"

"Shut up. Describe that ring again."

Gareth scowled, no longer amused by the drunk dwarf's gruff attitude. "It was a ring of gray-colored metal with a large black stone, inscribed with griffons all around."

Grifor's brow beetled, and he twirled the coarse hair of his beard thoughtfully. "And this dwarf—how was he dressed?"

Gareth's eyes went to the ceiling, trying to remember. It had been a very long day, and he was exhausted—and because Grifor had swilled down *his* beer, he was also thirsty. "Had a big ol' hammer. He wore some kind of plate-mail, but it was painted black with silver trim. He carried a stool with him and drank a lot of beer while I did all the dirty work."

Gareth clearly had the dwarf's attention now. He leaned forward, staring at Gareth intently. "And scars? What scars did he have on his face?"

Gareth squinted, trying to remember. He hadn't really paid that much attention to Kruger's face. Most of it had been covered by either a helmet or his long, black beard. "None that I could see."

Grifor sat back in his chair and slumped. "Well, I'll be dipped in pig shit."

Gareth cocked his head at the drunk. "Does this mean you believe me now?"

Grifor stared at him for a moment. "You'd better understand this, young one, if you want to get any older. Kruger's *dead*. And if you go around spouting lies about him being alive, some of his old enemies might pay you a visit to shut you up. Understand?"

Gareth nodded, wondering if Grifor was one of those enemies. It was hard to tell, really. But if talking about Kruger attracted attention, then Gareth wasn't about to do it. He didn't need that kind of attention.

Grifor appeared more sober than he had before, less slurring and swaying. "Now, why did this—mystery dwarf—send you to me?"

Gareth shrugged, holding out a hand placatingly. "He said that you and I could work out a deal, so you could train me as a Warrior, so I can dual class."

Grifor scowled and shook his head. "I can't do that."

"But—"

He held out a hand. "I didn't say I *wouldn't*. I said I *can't*. I'm nothing but a drunk now."

Gareth slapped his hand down on the table in frustration and fatigue. "Well, stop drinking, then."

Grifor backhanded him—quicker than he could have perceived the blow coming. Even drunk, the dwarf was still a formidable fighter. Gareth's ears rang from the blow. He shook his head, trying to clear away the fuzziness. Then he stared at the dwarf in shock.

"What did you do *that* for?"

"Trying to slap some sense into you—you seemed to need it," Grifor growled. "Learn the game. The reason I can't train anyone isn't due to the drink. It's the other way around. I drink because I lost my ability to train. Everyone who gains enough power, sooner or later, gains a totem that becomes the focus for their power. If you lose your totem, it guts your character."

Gareth frowned thoughtfully. "And you lost your totem?"

"No, I would never lose my totem. Anyone who *loses* their totem is not worthy of the class that it represents. The totem was taken from me."

Gareth scratched his jaw. "But—how could someone take a totem from a powerful character such as you?"

A heavy shrug. "Not really sure how it happened. Normally, no one besides the owner could even know what the totem is. It's a very personal thing and we don't share the knowledge of it. But...let's say that I was in a dark place and wasn't paying enough attention. One day, I awoke, and it was gone."

Well, if anything smelled like a quest, this sure did. Maybe Grifor was an NPC, for all he knew. Or maybe PCs could give quests, too? Did it matter? How would he even know the difference between a PC and an NPC? He made a note to ask someone about that later. Maybe he could access Clippy again. That little shit seemed to know a lot.

He looked up at the haggard dwarf across from him. "So, what if I get your totem back? Would you train me, then?"

Grifor huffed out a sad laugh. "If you got my totem back, I'd owe you a debt that exceeds training you as a warrior. That's a big *if*, though. But yeah, I could start with training."

Gareth made a "give me" motion with his hand. "Well then, describe it to me. I'm not sure where to start, but I *will* find it for you."

The bushy eyebrows rose. "Oh, you will, will you? I like your gumption. Well…" He leaned closer, casting a caustic eye around the room then motioning for Gareth to lean in. No one was paying any attention to them now, so the possibility of being overheard was slim. Nevertheless, Grifor spoke in a quiet voice. "It's a battle axe in the shape of a giant bat—one wing holding at the haft, the other wing forming the edge of the blade. And I know exactly where it is—not that the knowledge will do you any good. But it's hanging on the wall in the main dining room in the guildhall of The Elite. So you see, it's a useless matter. Just getting *into* that hall will be beyond you—especially at your level."

The UI flashed before his eyes once more and Gareth read the script:

•Quest offered: Recover Grifor's Mojo

•Reward: Training as warrior. Faction with Grifor increased to ally.

•Penalties for Failure: Loss of faction with Grifor.

***Do you accept? (Y/N)**

Gareth quickly accepted the quest. He'd always loved playing a good guy at heart, and this quest—to redeem the has-been old goat—seemed right up his alley. Also, having a potential powerful ally could bear fruit as the game went on.

He whispered across the table. "Don't worry, old man. I'll get your axe back for you." Now he just had to figure out *how*.

Gareth rose from his chair and hefted his pack onto his back.

Grifor watched, no hope alighting in his eyes at those words. "Just do me one favor. If you see—ah—that *other* dwarf again, please don't tell him I lost it. I couldn't bear the shame."

Gareth nodded. "Sure thing. But don't worry, I'm getting it back for you."

Grifor's mouth curled regretfully. "You're going to die, over and over. But I appreciate the effort."

Well, thanks for that cheerful parting, old fart. Gareth huffed, rolled his eyes, and weaved his way out of the tavern, ignoring the unwanted stares in his wake.

Now all he had to do was figure out how to break into the Elite's guildhall and steal back Grifor's ax. Easy peasy.

The Elite…he remembered the guild name from one of the four recruiters who were fighting over him in the newbie area earlier that day.

The armored man with the tabard of the mailed fist—yeah that was the one. He'd had an *attitude* on him, too. Had acted so affronted when Gareth had turned down his presumptuous invite.

No one turns us down, he'd sniffed.

None of them had been great, but the recruiter from The Elite had been the worst, or at least the most arrogant.

He'd have to find a way to break into their guildhall and grab that ax. That was going to take some thinking through. Especially surviving afterward. His wife's power guild, the "Harbingers of Hera" used to get real pissy when things didn't go their way or they felt they'd been disrespected. Dealing with them was a big reason he started playing solo so much. Fuck it, he was doing this. If the Harb…err…The Elite didn't like it, they'd just have to deal with him being pissy for once.

Where was the guildhall, anyway? Gareth pulled up the map in his UI. A quick search showed him all of the guildhalls in the city. There were forty-three, listed by guild in order of distance to his current location. He resorted the list alphabetically, and a quick scan revealed the entry for The Elite. Their guildhall—a fancy gothic manor built in stone—was about halfway up Twin Pines Hill, on the far side of the township from the river, where he was currently.

Well, time to get moving…

Chapter Sixteen

Kara

From the front of the stinking Orc Piss Tavern amidst the midden, Gareth could peer across the city toward a great hill. Its structure of covered slopes dominated the view to the north of Muddy River Township. If this place was anything like Earth, that hill would be the high-rent district.

Gareth was surprised that the guildhall of The Elite would be located there. In his experience, guilds tended to be thrifty with their guild halls, preferring to spend their gold on more practical things, such as spell reagents and single-use potions. Still, the recruiter had been very arrogant, and the guild was called *The Elite* after all. The location seemed on brand.

He walked along filthy streets while studying the map overlay in his UI, only half paying attention to the world around him; enough to dodge a cart here or avoid a group of children playing in the street there.

He was brought up short by the harsh grate of a gravelly shout in his direction. His feet faltered with dread.

"Hey, where do you think *you're* going?" The question was punctuated by the unmistakable sound of a meaty slap.

For once, Gareth wasn't on the receiving end of the threat—or the slap upside the head. He immediately flipped the map closed and took a discrete look around. There was no one nearby, but he couldn't ignore the presence of a very disreputable-looking alleyway not far from where he stood.

"*Please.* I don't have anything! I just want to go home." A jolt of adrenalin shot through Gareth at the sound of that voice. It eerily resembled that of Maisy, a close friend of his younger son, Fred. Gareth steeled himself, determined to get a closer look at exactly what was going on and determine if someone needed his help. What little foot traffic there had been in the street had now, strangely, disappeared. With a mental girding of his loins, Gareth crept to the edge of the alleyway and stuck his head around the corner.

The alley reeked and was absolutely filthy, having been used as a dumping ground by people too lazy to walk another block to the midden. About halfway down, Gareth spotted a trio of grungy toughs. They had a small, blue-skinned girl backed up against the wall.

Gareth toggled his *identify* skill, which tagged the three thugs as level four Ugarths. The girl was labeled a pixie, but that was all the skill would tell him.

Gareth pulled back to avoid signaling his presence while taking a moment to change their identifier from *Ugarth* to *Goblin*, since that was what they looked like to him.

A quick glance showed him at 100% health and mana. Three-to-one odds weren't good, though. Deciding to even things up a bit, he opened his character sheet and clicked over to the section for leveling up. He quickly dumped two of his unallocated levels into cleric, then closed the level-up window for later.

Shit, he forgot that leveling up granted spells. A window hovered in the UI, demanding he pick them now. He scanned the list, eyes catching on one he recognized from his time in the rat field: *Smite* . With a satisfied grin, he added it to his spell book. But the shitty window wouldn't close until he selected his level 3 spell. Given the time crunch, he had no time to read the spell descriptions. The last time he let the system pick for him, things had turned out okay. He decided to gamble on the system again and clicked to gain a random spell. With the essentials complete, Gareth closed the spell selection window along with notifications of increases to his health and mana pools from leveling up.

Then he readied his broadsword and shield—the alley was too narrow for him to swing his longsword. The broadsword glowed briefly as he cast Smite. His Smite only added 1-4 points of damage each hit, unlike Kruger's; that had done 10-40. He wouldn't sneer at it, though, willing to take what he could.

Then he rounded the corner and entered the alley as quietly as possible, hoping to get in a surprise bonus hit or two. But much like with the rat, this hope was in vain. In his full chain mail armor and big shield amidst the narrow alley, made narrower by the piles of garbage, he just wasn't that stealthy. A pile of garbage he'd barely nicked with his shoulder slid with a rumble and clatter onto the muddy ground. The tough-guy closest to him spun at the noise and faced him full on.

"Who the hell are *you?*"

Gareth braced himself. "Look boys, just leave the girl alone, and there won't be any trouble."

Goblin number one nudged goblin number two in its side. "Look, Ethot, we've got a *hero* here. A well-equipped, level *three* hero."

Ethot turned his head to look. "Finally! Someone with some loot worth more than a few cups."

The last goblin took his eyes off the girl, who promptly seized the opportunity to knee him in the groin. Then, she darted around him and fled down the alley.

Which left Gareth the sole focus of their attention. He briefly considered following the girl out, since his objective had been to help her. And now she was safe. But visions of these three taking free shots at his back as he lumbered down the street kept him in his spot. Better to face them head-on and get his own shots in, too.

The goblin in the back appeared to recover from his junk-shot, and the three started toward Gareth. He promptly put his back to a wall, keeping the pile of debris to his right. Hopefully, it would provide him with some cover—or at least inflict bad footing on anyone attacking from that direction.

The three closed in until they were just out of sword reach, then spread out in front of him. Ethot extracted a wicked-looking short sword and swung it around.

"Now look here. My friends and I, we like inflicting pain. And if you make us, we'll inflict plenty on *you* before you die. *Or* you could drop your equipment in a neat little pile right here and we'll let you go unharmed...*mostly*." He gave Gareth a wicked-looking grin, his yellowed teeth jagged and broken. "My boys here were robbed of their fun with the squirt, so they'll have some with you. But you'll be able to walk—or *craw* l—out of here. It's a better deal than you'll get otherwise."

Gareth stood his ground, waiting for their move. There was no way they were letting him out of this alley—no matter what they said. The other two unsheathed their weapons—some sort of spiked club and a long, curved knife.

He anticipated some sort of feint from them to draw his shield out of line. So, when the goblin on the right swung at him, he simply ducked and pivoted to the left. It was a long reach for the goblin, anyway, with all the crap scattered on the ground between the assailants and their would-be victim.

Gareth caught the goblin on the left with his shield and slammed him back into the wall. But before Gareth could follow up, Ethot attacked. Gareth was barely able to parry the thrust from that sword. This allowed the goblin on the left to regain his footing. The guy on the right had used this time to scrabble up the pile of junk, placing Gareth too close to his knife for comfort.

He reset his stance and awaited their next strike. This time, Ethot faked an attack, followed up by the two on the sides jumping in to fight. Knife boy slipped on some trash, and Gareth met him with his sword, deciding to just eat the attack from the other goblin. His sword slipped past the goblin's degraded defense and into his green chest. The Smite spell fired off as the blade entered flesh, blowing a chunk out of the creature's shoulder. Apparently, it was enough to cause the goblin to slump to the ground.

Gareth wasn't having it all his way, though. While he'd made his attack, the goblin on the right got a solid hit on him, reducing his health bar by one-third. Then Ethot launched another attack. Gareth barely blocked the blow, catching it on his shield. With that momentum, Gareth shoved the creature back before facing another attack by the one holding a mace. They quickly traded blows, Gareth taking a chunk out of him while receiving another blow reducing his health bar to less than half.

He couldn't afford to take any more chances. He cast healing on himself, bringing his health back up to 80%. This didn't go unnoticed by his goblin friends. Ethot shouted a command and dropped back. The other goblin launched forward. Gareth met him with a crash, and they exchanged hits. The extra damage from the Smite spell was adding up, and finally the goblin dropped. But he'd landed a blow on Gareth before doing so, which caused his health bar to start blinking—only twenty percent left. *Uh oh.*

Gareth scanned for Ethot while casting another healing spell. He barely had enough time to spot the object flying toward him before he was blown back against the wall. The combined damage of the explosion and impact stunned him, and he blacked out.

Moments later, he regained his senses to see the health bar was flashing once more—and worse, the goblin's leering face was only inches above his.

Ethot held up his sword, the tip hovering near Gareth's eye. "You know…bad wounds stay with you, even after respawn. I wonder how you'll like being a one-eyed adventurer."

The stench of his breath and the drool landing on Gareth's face almost made him welcome his impending doom. The goblin readied his thrust.

Gareth tried to throw the goblin off him, but Ethot couldn't be budged. Hopefully the goblin had lied about permanent wounds. He wouldn't look all that great sporting an eye patch. And there was no way Gareth could pull off Nick Fury's swagger. Besides, the lack of depth perception would suck.

The goblin started to push his sword down. "Bye, human."

Gareth squeezed his eyes closed and waited. And *waited*.

Nothing happened.

Chancing a peek, he was stunned to see Ethot slumped over him, clearly dead, with a gaping hole in his chest. Beside him stood a three-foot tall blue chick with a wicked grin.

She pumped a fist in the air, celebrating her victory. "Crit sneak attack, booyah! Thanks for the help. This guy really didn't know how to take *no* for an answer."

She looked Gareth over, violet eyes sliding over his form. "*Man.* you're messed up. I'd make with the healing if I were you."

Gareth checked his health bar—barely a flashing sliver now. All the blood currently leaking onto the ground likely had something to do with that. Without even getting up, he dropped three quick heals, bringing himself up to full health. With relief, he noted that his mana bar had only dropped to half. Those extra two levels had really made a difference in his mana pool.

"Thanks for the save. I was a goner."

When she made no reply, he looked up. She was running the other goblins through, ensuring their death. Then, she sifted through their gear and pouches.

"Bah, six cups and two leafs. And their weapons are crap—not even worth nabbing to sell. Ethot had a nice short sword, but it must have respawned with him, the creep. His corpse only has some pocket fob with a butt-ugly goblin chick on it. Her dress disappears when you turn it upside down. Complete trash."

"You mean he wasn't an NPC?" Gareth sat up, scratching his head. He had to figure out this whole PC and NPC thing.

Kara's purple eyes flicked to him. "Nope, most of the people you meet are PCs. There's a lot of players, and the computer only creates NPCs if there's no PC willing to fill the position. Like his henchmen, here. I guess Ethot must be repulsive even to his own kind. Go figure." She shrugged.

Once finished looting, she straightened. "Hey, so, thanks for helping me out. It was looking kinda dicey 'til you showed up." She reached her hand out for a fist bump.

Gareth obliged, bumping his knuckles to hers. Then he groaned loudly, getting to his feet. "Don't worry about it. Just doing the right thing."

She barked out a laugh in response. "You must be new here. Come on. After a fight like that, you oughtta buy me a beer. Besides, we need to get outta here before more of his Sudden Death buds show up. You're not supposed to be able to chat with others while in purgatory, but somehow they always seem to get the message across anyway."

Sudden Death—a familiar-sounding name. Another one of the arrogant recruiters.

"Great, *those* assholes again."

Gareth followed Kara out of the alley. She shot him a speculative look. "So, you've met others from that guild who were assholes? Can't say I'm surprised. There's only one guild in Muddy River worse than them."

"The Elite."

She looked impressed. "Yep. Hate *them.* too."

He looked her over, reassessing his stance on flying solo. "My name's Gareth by the way."

She looked up at him with those vivid purple eyes and smiled, then placed a hand on her chest. "I'm Kara. Pleased to meet you."

CHAPTER SEVENTEEN
The Big Four

THEY ENDED UP BACK WHERE GARETH HAD STARTED HIS day—at Blacl's Inn. Kara had explained that they'd be safe there. The troublesome guilds had long since been banned from the premises. Apparently, Blacl was a complete badass, and the guilds weren't willing to cross him. Lucky for Gareth, he'd set the inn as his bind point.

They shared a meal and bonded over their common hatred of the four guilds. Already, this game was feeling very real to him, and reality—or meatspace, as they called it here—seemed like a drab echo of another life.

"So, what's your beef with Sudden Death, if you don't mind my asking?" Gareth eyed her over his tankard of beer—his second of the night. Fortunately, he'd never gotten a taste of the stuff at the Orc's Piss, but Blacl's beer was pretty darn good.

Kara gave the room a quick glance with her odd, violet eyes before replying. "They've made themselves the main guild for players with a certain skillset. Mostly they do it by pressuring anyone they want into joining the guild. Then they apply a 50%

tax on all your earnings, payable to the guild leadership. Highway robbery. I don't need their help, and I won't pay their damn tax."

Gareth chuckled in agreement. "That's pretty screwed up. Maybe they'll drop their push to get you to join now that you've rejected their offer so forcefully?"

She shook her head. "Not a chance. They want me too much."

Gareth frowned, looking her over again. "Are you an exceptional thief or something?"

Her eyes darted around again. She hunched over the table toward him, motioning him to do the same. Then, she slid her hand between them. The skin on her hand and lower arm changed coloring to match the table—right down to the grain in the wood. Gareth could still see the outline of her hand if he stared closely at it. But it would be invisible to a quick glance. It looked like her arm ended at the bottom of her sleeve.

Gareth stiffened in surprise, and her hand snapped back to its normal blue color.

Her features shuttered, obviously not knowing how to take Gareth's reaction. After another beat, she pushed her chair back from the table.

Gareth was so stunned, he hardly noticed. "Damn, that's cool. Do it again!"

This stopped her. "What?"

"That hand thing—do it again. Can you do the rest of you? Or just your hands?"

She scooted back to the table and waved her hands at him. "Will you shut up? I don't want anyone to know. People don't react well to my gift. Like you didn't." She glared and there was definitely an accusation in her voice.

Gareth blinked. "I'm sorry. I was just surprised. Sometimes it takes a minute for my brain to catch up. But that is definitely the coolest thing I've ever seen. It's obvious why they want you so badly."

"Yeah." She sighed. "I'm sorry they ever found out. I trusted someone I shouldn't have, and he betrayed me to save his own skin. Now I'm on their most-wanted list."

Gareth frowned. He'd hoped, mostly based on his years of watching *Star Trek,* that being out in the universe would mean that people behaved better. The last couple of days, however, showed just how naive he'd been. "Well, that sucks. Frankly, I'm surprised you trusted *me* with it."

She shrugged. "At this point, I don't have a lot to lose. You need friends to survive here."

It gave him a jolt just thinking about that original plan of his—to fly solo, keep all the loot, find the good quests and keep the secrets to himself. The two of them regarded each other in silence for a few beats, then sat back, each lost in their own thoughts. His own turned in circles—spurred on by his own lack of information. Something he needed to address as soon as possible.

His eyes flicked up to his now quiet companion. "So, don't any of the other guilds push back at these jerks? The smaller guilds could band together and force those four to play nice, couldn't they?"

Then he remembered how hungry he was and leaned forward to take a bite of his burger. After his first visit, his favorite burger—two patties with melted pepper jack cheese, lettuce, tomato, and onion on sourdough bread—had been added to the menu. Or maybe it was just his own personal menu? This whole integrated UI thing was still messing with his head.

"Oh, they tried—at first, anyway. After some of the guild leaders had 'accidents'—and a few disappeared, the resistance ended. Now, the Big Four pretty much treat this town like their own private preserve." She picked at her salad, filled with bright-colored slices of some kind of fruit.

"How can they intimidate anyone? I know I'm new, but I've taken hits. It doesn't hurt that much. Why does anyone care if they threaten violence?" He took a swig of beer, which had also adapted itself to his taste. Enough of this and he wondered if he'd ever want to go home.

Well, that was stupid, of course he'd want that...eventually.

She gave him some side-eye. "You haven't died yet, have you?" She pushed her unfinished salad aside. "The death penalty is cumulative. You start off at a 1% pain setting, and like you say, nothing really hurts. Every time you die, that setting goes up between 1 and 5%, depending on how much of a dumbass the game decides you were. Once you die enough times, the pain gets real—and *quick*."

Gareth polished off the last of his burger and beer, then pushed those dishes aside as well. One of the kitchen boys promptly swooped in to collect them. "Okay, I see how that could be a problem, but there's got to be a way to reset it somehow or lower the pain setting."

Her brows bobbed up. "There's plenty of rumors and stories about abilities like that. But if someone has access to one, they're not saying. An ability like that could make you beyond rich. Some players level up pretty high and then have to quit the game due to the pain setting they're on. They'd pay anything to make it tolerable."

Gareth nodded idly. "Well, you've certainly given me a lot to think about. I suppose now Ethot's high-level buddy will be after me to even the score. Maybe kill me a bunch of times, then lock me in a room and beat me over and over." His burger turned to lead in his stomach.

Kara stared at him. "I bet you're regretting coming to my aid now, huh?"

Gareth shook his head emphatically. "Not at all. Those guys were asshats. But it does raise the stakes more than I had anticipated."

Kara quirked her head at him, as if looking at him in a new light. "Well, if it makes you feel any better, it can't happen—or at least he can't get some high-level friend to just butcher you. At least not in town. When the ancients made the game, they made a rule that limits players to an effective maximum level of ten while in a newbie zone, which Muddy River is." She sat back in her seat and continued. "That's still not great, as higher-level players will still have advantages over you, but at least they can't one-thump you. You'll stand a chance. Even if it's only a small one."

Gareth sat back as well, some tension draining away. "I can work with that, I think. It's better than I thought it would be, anyway." Fatigue washed over him. It had been a *long* day and so much had happened. And with a belly full, he had other needs to see to. "I'm about to pass out, but I still want to talk with you about helping me with a job. Can I meet you here for breakfast?"

Kara nodded. "Sure thing. Blacl's an old friend. He can squeeze me in somewhere. Best I don't keep to my normal haunts tonight."

Gareth pushed away from the table and stood. "Well, goodnight then."

She stood and crossed her arms over her chest, staring expectantly. "*Well?*"

"You want a kiss goodnight?" Gareth laughed.

Kara rolled her eyes to the ceiling. "A, you're an idiot. And B, you're too tall—and pale. But I do need your contact info so I can add you to my friends list. *Normal* people do that when they're going to work together."

Gareth blinked, unsure of what to do before remembering the old refrain, *Use the UI, human.* Then he mentally asked the UI to share his info.

She made a face. "Oh, for crying out loud...I just want your contact info—not *everything*. I don't want to know all *this* crap."

He had no idea what he'd just shared with her—that he woke up in the morning with dead horse breath or was only mediocre at his day job? "Sorry, sorry." He revised his request to just share his contact information. A second later, a popup appeared asking if he wanted to add her info to his friends list. He quickly clicked *yes.* "I'm still learning the UI."

Kara's mouth twisted as she made a face. "Obviously. What backwards place did you grow up in anyway? You should've learned how to use the UI in kinderschool." She sighed but there was no mistaking the glint of curiosity in her gaze.

In spite of himself, Gareth almost laughed—self-deprecatingly, of course. "It was ah, a wild, primitive and unsightly land. I'll try to do better in the future."

Her mouth thinned, but she nodded. "You do that. I'm not going to be associated with some backwoods hick."

Gareth took his leave and headed to the stairs that led toward his room. Kara accompanied him as far as Blacl's desk. She stopped there, no doubt to negotiate a place for the evening.

He rounded the corner and started up the stairs, frankly relieved with the knowledge that as long as he was here, he was safe from the hawks that were the Big Four guilds. Great news when you felt more and more like a freshly hatched chick, relatively.

It was even more of a relief to spy his room—the warm and friendly fire already crackling, the perfect inn room to stay in. He didn't have the heart to log off. He looked around and relished the sensations of this new world before sinking into bed and closing his eyes, succumbing to exhaustion.

CHAPTER EIGHTEEN
A NEW QUEST

GARETH AWOKE WITH A START TO THE SOUND OF insistent beeping. Flailing about, he slapped the nightstand in search of an alarm, but soon realized he was still in the game—and his room didn't have an alarm. That would be drastically off-theme, anyway. But this beeping was clearly coming from inside his head—and there was a persistent light flashing in the corner of his eye.

It was a simple matter of pulling up the status window to shut off the alarm, thank the gods.

***bing* message from medical bay one received.**

Your pet will be released from stasis in eleven minutes.

You are required to be present for decampment.

While reading the message, it ticked down to ten minutes. *Fuck.* He had to get going. Logging out of the game was, fortunately, quick. But it felt like an entire world had been sucked out of his head.

Abruptly, he blacked out.

He came back to consciousness standing in his room, in the same position he had been in when he'd logged into the game. It begged the question: just how did it work? What exactly was that whole beam doing when he logged in? Was it transferring his body into the game environment or just storing it somewhere? And *why*? Was he only allowed to exist in one place at a time, like Mickey Mouse at Disneyland?

A loud beep and a notification popped up that said he now had five minutes before he had to be at medical. Leaving the existential questions for later, he raced down the hallway and washed his face for a quick wake-up.

He pulled up the path to the medical bay and hustled to meet the deadline that was ticking down by seconds now. He arrived just as Dr. Head walked over and began accessing the panel floating over his dog, Xena. He looked her over carefully and was relieved to see that she looked exactly the same as when he'd left her.

Dr. Head swiveled one eye over to look at Gareth. "You're late. I almost woke her up without you."

Gareth held up his hands, palms out, in a placating gesture. "I apologize. I got caught up in the game and lost track of time." He reached out to Xena, but his hand bounced off some invisible screen surrounding her.

Dr. Head's eye swiveled back to the floating screen. "Wait a moment. I'm running some final checks before awakening your pet. This was an unusual case. It normally doesn't take two days to fix someone."

Gareth's eyes narrowed and he frowned. "Maybe it had slow access to Earth data. It must have been quite some time since anyone from Earth has been in here." He reached out again but remembered in time to pull back before his hand hit the screen.

"Maybe. Who knows? Don't care really." With one final flourish, Dr. Head stabbed a button with a tentacle. "There, now. All finished."

Xena blinked open her large, dark eyes. Then she uncurled herself and stood. She looked at Gareth and promptly began her soft canine protest, clearly expressing her displeasure at being left on the table. "*Raouroo.*"

"Okay, Okay." Gareth gently lifted her off the table and set her on the ground. Taking a minute to give her some proper loves, Gareth bent to scratch her head and back. She luxuriated in the attention for a minute, her ears fluttering back against her head. Then she pushed his hand away with her nose.

Hungry

He frowned, shaking his head. It was like he'd heard something, but Dr. Head hadn't spoken. In fact, he'd stepped away, headed for his desk. Gareth remembered an unfinished item of business. "Ah—I need something to give the Chief Bureaucrat in order to certify that the station is safe from Xena."

"Approach." Dr. Head's tentacle-arms flashed over his desk screen.

Gareth did as he was asked. A minute later, the unmistakable sensation of an ice-cold dog nose touched the back of his leg.

Hungry

Gareth shook his head again. Maybe this was some side-effect from playing the game? He looked down at the dog standing just beside him. "I'm sure you must be hungry, girl, I just need to get your license so we can go."

Dr. Head looked at him—almost impatiently. "*What?* I already sent the certificate to you. Check your inbox."

Gareth dutifully pulled up the UI to check, and sure enough, there was a blinking light on the mail app. He opened it and saw an official-looking report from this medical bay stating that Xena was 'a harmless creature.' The report went on to state the medical staff would appreciate it if the administration would stop wasting its time chasing after fairytales. All of that apparent in-fighting was none of his business, so he dismissed it with a shrug. Some things were the same everywhere, it seemed.

When he'd finished reading, he turned back to Dr. Head, who sighed at him. Then, without pausing what he was doing, the medical officer said, "Just flick the report at him when you're in close proximity. His UI will receive it. You really should spend some time with the user manual."

Manuals were for losers. Without comment, Gareth turned to leave but stopped and looked over his shoulder. "So, ah, what pain setting did you end up with before you had to stop playing?"

Dr. Head's tentacle-arms froze mid-gesture. He stared at Gareth for a long minute before speaking. "I was up to a 5.2 before I could no longer stand the pain. I even had the quest for a restoration spell that would lower the rating, but even my guild said it was a myth and wouldn't help me. That last failure against the boss mob was the final straw for them and they banned me from pursuing the quest any further. So, I rage quit the guild and, well, you know the rest."

Gareth considered this for a moment. "You ever think about going back?"

"*Think?* Yes—a lot. *Do?* No. Too many people would come after me—just to see me squirm. And I'd have to figure a way out of the death loop first." Head looked back at his screen, clearly done with the conversation.

Gareth stared at him a moment before speaking. "Maybe I could help, if you point me to the quest."

"*You?*" One eye scanned Gareth from top to bottom. "What could you do? You just got here." Head tapped away on his screen.

Gareth shrugged. "Don't know what I could do, but it would be more than your guild is doing now, which is nothing. If I could complete that quest, you could play again."

"It'll never happen," was the terse reply.

"But…what do you have to lose, really? Worse case, I get to share your pain." Gareth felt that cold, wet nose on his calf once again. "Yes, Xena, we're going. See you around, Head. Thanks for, ah, *fixing* my dog. I'll let you know if I ever hear anything about that quest or the restoration spell. From what I've seen, Muddy River could use more decent people playing the game. It seems like the assholes are winning over there."

As he stepped toward the exit, a notification popped up on his UI.

•Quest shared: Rediscover the secret of restoration.

•Talk to Old Man River in the Temple of the Lost.

***Do you wish to accept this shared quest (Y/N)?**

Gareth quickly hit yes, then gave Dr. Head a quick salute of farewell—unseen because the good doctor was focused on his screen—and left.

Gareth and Xena headed back to Blacl's inn on the meatspace side after stopping at the park out front for a game of chase, Xena's favorite. After ten minutes of chasing her around, she gave him a look and trotted over to examine some of the strange plants growing in the park. They weren't what he was used to, but the blue tint and the long stems with small purple flowers on the end were starting to grow on him. Xena found the plants endlessly fascinating. Gareth walked over to a bench and sat down to watch her. After a couple of days in the med bed, the dog was owed some time to stretch her legs.

The bench he sat on was fascinating. He'd avoided it at first, because it didn't appear very comfortable for someone of his stature, but as he gingerly sank onto it, the bench rearranged itself to fit him. So weird. These people had so much interesting stuff on their station, but they spent all their time playing VR D&D. There had to be a reason for it. Maybe the Robot Overlords were short of power. He snorted.

Once Xena was finally done with her sniffing and exploring, they headed into the inn. Gareth greeted the clerk as they walked past and then chose one of the bland metal tables in the dining area. Not really fond of the appearance, he quickly turned the overlay back on, though he was getting some mental backlash from changing from bare metal to rustic wood. Xena wandered, sniffing for a moment, then sat beside him, staring up at him expectantly.

"Well, girl, let's see what you can eat." He pulled up the menu and flipped through it.

"Here you go, sir."

Gareth looked up, startled from his attention to the menu. A serving boy was already setting down a plate with his favorite breakfast and coffee. Gareth opened his mouth to ask if they had anything dog-appropriate when he heard the sounds of eating from under the table. Xena already had her face buried in a big bowl of some kind of chopped steak in a brown sauce. A smaller bowl next to it held what looked like chopped up bananas.

Gareth felt uneasy, like when ads for stuff he talked about with someone suddenly started appearing on his phone. Only in this case, he hadn't even said anything. Were they stalking his thoughts? It was certainly convenient, but he'd really prefer to order first. "Who ordered this?"

"I don't know sir; I just bring the food out." He returned to the kitchen.

Gareth hesitated before turning back to his own plate. He'd really like to know where that food for Xena had come from. With a sigh, he chalked it up to some sort of need-based predictive algorithm. After all, if Google, back on Earth, could predict what he wanted online, it was likely this advanced alien computer could one- or even two-up it. He really hoped it was just a good algorithm. The other options seemed…disturbingly intrusive.

He turned to his own plate as his stomach growled. *Speaking of predictive systems…*

It was every bit as amazing as the first breakfast he'd had here.

As he polished off his last bites, he became aware of a presence at his side. A walrus-like presence. He turned toward the tusked face of Chief Bureaucrat Smith.

The hulking creature wasted no time with pleasantries getting to his point. "I see your animal is out of the medical bay."

"Yes. We were, ah… just coming to see you. She was just so hungry after being in there for so long." As he spoke, he accessed his UI inventory to flick the medical report to the Chief. "You'll see that everything is in order."

The walrus-like eyes scanned back and forth, reading what only he could see. It was a strange thing to witness. Maybe that was why they normally made the backs of their screens visible to everyone.

"It seems you are correct. I have—reluctantly—admitted your pet to Muddy River Township. But why did you choose to have an interface installed?"

Gareth shrugged, vaguely remembering something about a network access node being required. "It wasn't *my* idea. Your magic floaty bed-thing insisted on it while it was scanning her. Not my place to argue with your tech."

"Very odd." The chief shifted stance, appearing as if he wanted to pursue the subject. He was, however, interrupted by a beeping noise which he waved a hand to silence. Then, he continued, "I'm late for another meeting, so we'll continue this later. My purpose in contacting you right now was to ask you to seek out my brother. He keeps messaging me to find him someone to do a job for him. I've elected you. Find out what he wants, and do it, so he'll leave me alone."

Gareth blinked at the walrus-creature. "Okay…I guess. But how do I find him?" May as well play along. He wasn't exactly in a position to refuse.

The Chief Bureaucrat waved an arm, and a game notification appeared in Gareth's UI.

•Quest: Help out Lord Smith. The Chief Bureaucrat is being bothered by his brother. Seek Lord Smith out at Muddy River Palace, and do whatever it takes to keep him from bothering the Chief Bureaucrat again.

•Reward: faction with the Chief Bureaucrat. Possible unlocking of further quests.

•Penalties for Failure: Loss of faction with the Chief Bureaucrat.

"Wait, your brother is in the game?" Gareth asked.

"Yes. He runs the city there, much as I run the station here. Now, hurry up before he messages me again, the pest." The Chief Bureaucrat turned and stomped away.

Gareth stared after him for a moment. Well, it looked like he had a dilemma. First, he had to get back into the game so he could meet Kara and beg for her help to steal that axe from The Elite. *Then.* he needed to find this Lord Smith and see what needed to be done. However, he couldn't just leave Xena here to fend for herself all day. What to do?

As if on cue, the dog nudged his knee, then very purposefully yawned wide. Then, she rubbed his hand with her head several times, yawning again.

"Really, you're tired already? Well, that bed must not have been as restful as it looked while fixing you. But problem solved. Let's head up to the room. There must be some way to get a soft cushion or something for you."

They climbed the stairs and found their room. Someone had already been in and straightened up, leaving behind what looked like a child's bed against the left wall. Huh. He wasn't sure whether this level of service was creepy or convenient. *Why not...both?*

Xena hopped up onto her new bed, turned in a circle several times, then lay down, falling fast asleep.

Gareth made sure to use the UI to lock the door—just in case she woke up before him. He also used the UI to set an alarm to ping him in-game if she awoke and another to ping him in eight hours if she didn't. Hopefully he'd done it right, but who knew. His UI skills were still pretty feeble. The locked door would have to act as a precaution in case he'd screwed up the alert.

Gareth settled back into his own bed, quickly closing his eyes before giving the command to enter the game. That way, he wouldn't have to face any weird lights or see his body disappear.

He wondered, as the process began, if he'd ever get used to that. He could only imagine he wouldn't.

CHAPTER NINETEEN
THE RUINS

AFTER A MOMENT OF BLACKNESS, HE WAS BACK IN THE game, lying on his bed in Blacl's inn, game side. As on meatspace-side, his room had been updated to include a bed for Xena. Which was weird when he thought about it. He'd never asked for a bed, in either room. He looked around quickly, hoping for some fuzzy cuddles, or at least a musical husky discourse. Then he remembered that she couldn't enter the game. That disappointed him for some reason. It was ridiculous to feel that way. How could a dog, however smart, play a VR game? Besides, he wouldn't want to risk her getting hurt. It was for the best. Still, he missed his furry best friend—his only friend, really. If she could enter the game, he'd have someone so unreservedly on his side as to make this all a bit easier.

Gareth descended the stairs and entered the common dining area. Kara was already at a table, so he approached, sinking down opposite her. He opted against ordering more food, since his belly was already full from breakfast on the meatspace side. That was weird though, wasn't it? Why was he full in-game because he'd eaten outside of the game? Would it work the same the other way around? Would he exit the game feeling full if he ate while in the game?

This was all starting to mess with his head.

He decided to focus on the now and ordered a coffee to be social. Never hurt to have something to do with your hands, to drink, and give yourself a moment to think while you spoke. "Morning."

Her plate was nearly empty, and she pushed her fork aside. It clattered on the plate. It appeared, yet again, to be something plant-based. Blue-skinned space vegan. Who knew?

She cleared her throat as she wiped her mouth with a cloth napkin. "So, what kind of trouble do you have in mind for today? You said something about a job."

Gareth looked around the room, noting that she'd picked a table in the far corner with no one nearby. He leaned forward and spoke in a low voice, anyway. "I need to steal an axe out of The Elite's guildhall."

Her eyes widened immediately as she whistled. "You don't play around, do you?" Her brow furrowed, and she rested her chin in her hand. The fingers on her other hand tapped at the table for a few moments. "*I* might be able to break in, but *you?* Never. And I very much doubt I could get out of there all by myself."

"Getting in shouldn't be a problem."

She looked askance. "How do you figure?"

Gareth gave her a brief rundown on his encounter with their representative yesterday—and his overenthusiastic attempts at guild recruitment.

"I should be able to swing a tour of their guildhall. The public areas anyway. Supposedly, the axe is on display, in full view, in the dining hall. So, I'm thinking…we get in, you grab the axe, we leave. Easy peasy."

Kara held up a hand, palm out. "Hold your horses, there, *humie*. You might get yourself in by sucking up to them, but that doesn't get *me* in. And before you say anything, I can't use my *special* talent to get in with you. It works better at range. Besides they have two security golems out front that would detect me."

Well there goes plan A. On to plan B.

Gareth leaned forward again. "I noticed yesterday that my pack can hold a lot of stuff. As you are so petite, I figure you could hide inside. When I get in there, I put it down somewhere out of the way inside the hall. While I keep them busy with my questions, you grab the axe and jump back in the pack, then I carry you both out."

She gave Gareth a resigned smile. "Great plan. Except it won't work."

Gareth's own smile crumpled. "Why not?"

"Packs are enchanted to hold a lot of non-living things. But if you try to put a living thing in a pack, you are limited to the actual size of the pack. Just one of the quirks of the game."

Gareth fell back against his chair, shoulders slumping. "Well shit. But… you're not that big. Maybe you'd fit."

She shook her head, lips pressed together. "Not happening, stud. I'm *not* cramming myself into your pack. Besides it's not even that big a pack. Even if I scrunched inside, they'd still notice."

Plan C, I guess.

Gareth worried his lip. "You're probably right. What we need is some way to make you smaller. But then we'd need to make the axe smaller, too, or you'd never be able to lift it."

"*That* part I can handle," she said with a distinctly smug look on her face.

"How?"

She smirked. "Not telling. But given my size, it'd be hard to steal anything interesting if I couldn't deal with items larger than I was, right?"

Gareth rubbed his jaw thoughtfully. "So, we're back to making you smaller."

"Too bad we couldn't just buy a shrink potion," she said with a laugh.

Gareth shot her a quizzical look.

"The alchemists don't just sell to *anyone*. You need to gain some favor with them first. *I* currently have negative favor, and you're new. The potions are pricey—over a hundred crowns, anyway. Much as I'd love to stick it to those fuckers, we'll need another plan to do it."

"I can cover the cost." Kara's eyes widened, and Gareth shrugged. "I started the game with some extra gold—long story. But that would just about wipe me out. I mean, I'll pay if I have to. Maybe we can do a quick quest to gain some favor with the alchemists?"

"Maybe..." Her clouded features didn't look hopeful.

"Well, let's go ask anyway. Unless you have a better idea?" She shook her head. "Do any of the potion-makers dislike you less than the others?"

"Hmm. Well, there's Mabel. I never did anything to make her mad. Mostly because I was afraid to. Everyone is afraid of her, and she hates everyone."

"Who buys her potions then?"

"The desperate." Gareth gave her a pointed stare, brows raised. "Shit. I guess that's us then, isn't it?"

"Yep." Gareth stood and gestured to her. "Lead the way."

Their trip to Mabel's led them to yet another part of the town Gareth hadn't seen before—the imaginatively named Ruins. Some disaster or another had destroyed most of the buildings in the area, reducing them to rubble. The ones that were left were all damaged in some way. None of the damage looked recent, which led to some obvious questions.

Gareth shot a glance at Kara, who was walking down the middle of the road, keeping her eyes focused on nothing, as if carefully avoiding looking at anything in particular.

"So, what's the deal? How come no one has fixed any of this?" he asked.

When she met his gaze, he was struck by the sadness in her eyes. "This part of town used to have a thriving community—a mostly human community. When the humans were destroyed, it was left this way, to stand as an example to others."

Gareth frowned. There was so much to unpack there. "I can get leaving an example. That's been done more times on Earth than I can count. But from what I've been told, it's been like six thousand years. Doesn't it seem a bit extreme to leave all this in rubble after all that time? There can't be that much excess space in the township."

Kara licked her lips and darted a look at him before speaking in a low voice. "The first purge was around six thousand years ago, with a couple of lesser ones thereafter. The last one was only a couple of thousand years ago. It's been a long time, sure. No one wants the land here, for fear that whatever happened to your people will rub off on them. Also, there's the ghosts."

"*Ghosts?* There's no such thing as ghosts." Except, how could he say that, given all the bizarre things he'd seen in this game? Maybe ghosts were a thing here.

Kara's face was grim. "Stick around here after dark and you'll find out how wrong you are."

"Uh, I'll just take your word for it."

After a little while, she stopped in front of one of the more intact buildings. "We're here."

Gareth stood beside her, looking over what must have once been an impressive building. The top three floors were collapsed, the remains lying all around the building like a debris skirt, with just a small sliver of building still sticking up to reveal its former grandeur. The ground floor was mostly intact—what he could see of it, anyway. A path had been cleared through the rubble to the door.

"I thought you said no one lived out here anymore."

"Anyone *who has a choice* lives somewhere else. But not everyone has a choice. Mabel's in there."

Gareth looked up at the ruined building again and heaved a sigh. "Well, let's go see Mabel then."

He followed her inside, stepping into a surprisingly neat and clean shop. The front area was occupied by long cases with shelves loaded with potions, vials, and creams. Everything was painstakingly labeled and described. The back area of the shop held a sort of medieval laboratory, with cauldrons and beakers all happily bubbling away over small, smokeless fires. A curtained doorway divided this area from another further inside the structure.

Kara strolled through the front of the shop and approached the counter that divided the room, preventing a person from entering the lab. She looked around for a minute, then called out, "Mabel! Mabel, it's Kara."

"I'll be right there." A deep but feminine voice answered from the other side of the curtain. Minutes later, a large minotaur entered the room, wiping her face with a cloth. Her head and snout bore the brown and white coloring of a jersey cow, quite different from the flat, brownish fur covering Clud's face.

"You're a minotaur!"

The words were out of his mouth before he could even think about them. His gut tightened... because he had no idea how she'd react to him pointing out the obvious, no matter how benignly.

CHAPTER TWENTY

MABEL THE ALCHEMIST

MABEL STOOD AT HER COUNTER AND LOOKED AT THE both of them, then snorted. "You're quite observant for a..." Mabel's eyes flicked to the side briefly, "...*human?*" Mabel turned to give Gareth a much more thorough examination. "I always imagined humans would be taller." Gareth started to defend himself, but Mabel snorted and continued, "I was taking a lunch break while this latest batch of potions cooks. How can I help you?"

Gareth's face heated when he realized that he was staring like a preschooler at the zoo for the first time. "I'm sorry. You're only the second minotaur I've ever met. And the first one was yesterday. I guess I just assumed you were all more inclined to, um, physical professions rather than the cerebral."

"I see you've met my son." Mabel waved away his look of surprise. "There're only two minotaurs in Muddy River now. Anyway," Mabel blew out a long breath through large nostrils.

"Cluddious is plenty smart. He was always good with his studies as a child. He has a degree in city planning and another in advanced mathematics. He just prefers to work with his hands. You small folk make him angry all the time, so he enjoys a job that allows him to get paid to knock you around."

Gareth blinked. "Well, I'm not sure what to say to that. I don't know what's more shocking—that Clud is your son, or that he's more educated than I am. However, I was pretty sure that Clud and I were getting along."

Mabel nodded her large head. "Oh, he likes you. You didn't cave into those cow patty guild recruiters like everyone else does. He's just frustrated he's prevented from stopping them. He hates bullies."

"I'll definitely try not to bully anyone, then."

"That would probably be wise." She patted Gareth's cheek with a large hand. "Now, what can I help you two with?"

Kara had pulled up a tall stool so she could sit more less level with the others at the counter. Now, she leaned forward to insert herself into the conversation. "We need some help with a... *project.*"

Mabel looked down at Kara and smiled fondly. "Of course you do, dear. What kind of help are you looking for?"

"We need a shrink potion," Kara replied.

"Well, don't we all." The expression on the minotaur's face turned sour.

Kara's jaw dropped, then her eyes narrowed, and she looked like she was about to launch into the minotaur.

"I have gold," Gareth interjected. His attention had drifted toward a book he found lying on the counter, but he wanted to show he was still paying attention. *Hmm, Mabel's Guide to Basic Flora. That sounds interesting.*

"Gold isn't the problem." Mabel turned back to a shelf behind the counter and rummaged around until she found a large jar, which she placed on the counter before her two would-be customers. "Shrink potions require wormwood. Look in the jar."

Willing to play along, Gareth looked up from the book and into the jar. "All I see are some little fungus-covered bits of sticks."

Mabel sighed wearily. "That's my entire supply of wormwood. That fungus has infected it and destroyed any magical essence it had. The fungus has spread through the entire region. The worms are all limp now, no wood. No wormwood means no shrink potions." She waved at the bubbling cauldrons behind her. "I've been trying to replace it in the recipe, but it's almost impossible to do that. I need to find a new recipe."

"Wait, I thought wormwood was a plant?"

Mabel's huge brows furrowed together at Gareth. "A *plant?* Why would it be called wormwood, then?"

Gareth shrugged. "I don't know. It's a leaf from a plant where I come from. What's the source of wormwood here?"

Mabel shifted her stance and raised her hand, effecting an instructional tone. "Wormwood comes from Gil worms. They eat away at tree bark until they've consumed enough wood. Once they do, the worm becomes stiff and sticks out from the tree. You break the worm off from the tree and slit it open to extract the hard, woody core. Breaking it off the tree releases the worm eggs, which starts the cycle over again."

Gareth shook his head. "I'm sure this won't be the last time I say this, but this game is *so* weird."

Mabel paused and gave Gareth a scathing look, then continued. She clearly didn't appreciate the interruption. "Frogwood shares most of the properties of wormwood. I'm in the process of trying to substitute that to make a new potion. However, I need to achieve extraordinary success on the potion for it to spontaneously create a new recipe. The odds of *that* are not good. Until then, no more shrink potions." Mabel's shoulders slumped. "I'd like to help you, but I can't."

Gareth was not going to ask where frogwood came from. His attention drifted back to the book. "Mabel, did you write this?" Gareth reached down and picked up the book.

"Gareth, put that down." Kara sniped at him.

As soon as he touched the book a prompt appeared.

***Do you wish to read this book (Y/N)?**

What harm could it do? Gareth quickly thought *yes.*

A torrent of information flooded his brain. Gareth found himself with a new appreciation for what Neo went through in *The Matrix.*

He slumped back, almost stunned, hardly even noticing when the book disappeared shortly after the flood of information stopped. "Damn, I know basic botany now."

He looked over at Kara, who was just standing there with her face in her hands. Feeling his gaze on her, she looked up. "Weren't you ever taught to keep your hands to yourself?"

Gareth felt a twinge of unease as his brain caught up to the fact the book had vanished after he was done 'reading' it. He glanced back toward Mabel, who was now towering over him, glaring.

"I'm sorry, I didn't know that would happen."

"Newbs." Mabel said shaking her head. "Well, you owe me two bags of reagents now."

"Hmm?" Gareth said clearly confused.

"That book is part of a resource gathering quest I give out. Now you have to go out into the surrounding countryside and gather two bags' worth of alchemy ingredients. The book is so you know enough to bring back something useful. If you knew how many times I had someone try to sell me elfweed or ratmoss…. Two bags pay for the cost of the book. After that, I'll pay you based on what you find."

Gareth clicked over to his quest log, seeking the exact details of the quest. Gather quests were kind of boring, but they'd paid the bills in more than one MMORG he'd played. Anyway, it was always good to have a ready source of funds. "I can't seem to find the quest in the log," Gareth mumbled.

Mabel snorted. "This is just a minor gather quest. It's not going to be in the log."

Kara glared at him. "The quest log is only for significant quests. It's right there in the help files."

"Oh, yeah. Right. I'm going to get right on those." *Not.* Gareth looked up at Mabel. "So if it's not in the log, how do I remember what to do?"

"Make a note or something. It's *'more realistic.'*" Gareth could hear the air quotes as Mabel explained. "Anyway, if you forget, I'll *remind you.*"

Given the way Mabel said that last bit, Gareth doubted he'd enjoy the reminder. "I'll be sure not to forget."

Mabel looked down at him, then snorted and turned back to her lab. "See that you don't." She walked back toward the bubbling beakers, "This has been an interesting diversion, but I have another thousand or so trials to go to get this recipe to work. Come back in a year or so, and I should be able to help you out with that shrink potion."

Gareth shook his head, thinking. Something was tickling at his brain. Something about recipes and alchemy and...*special abilities.*

His secret skill! As if Clippy were there in his head again, he remembered the specifics: *a natural alchemist is a genius at alchemy, able to create and improve potions after just one taste of an existing one. In addition, you can update formulas with ease.*

It seemed his talent could help with this conundrum of Mabel's. But he hadn't forgotten Clippy's cautionary words, either, to keep it secret. That warning had been delivered almost with the same urgency as Gandalf's entreaty to Frodo about the One Ring—*Keep it secret, keep it safe.*

But how could he accomplish the change while still keeping the skill on the downlow?

While he was quietly digging around in his thoughts, Mabel and Kara struck up a conversation. Mabel was puttering about, mixing up her next trial of the potion recipe. Kara was going on about some of the other outcasts living in the area, acquaintances they had in common. While they were thus occupied, Gareth sneaked a glance at Mabel's notes on her work developing the new potion. It looked like she had a copy of the old recipe lying on top of her new work.

Gareth cleared his throat, interrupting their chatter. "Hey Mabel, can I look at the recipe? I've never seen one before."

Mabel glanced at him. "Normally, I'd charge for access to one of my recipes. But since it's useless now, go ahead." She returned to her conversation with Kara. Apparently, some neighbor named Slick liked to run around with no pants on during laundry day. Even this world had its crazies.

Gareth reached over the counter and plucked up the recipe. Turning it right-side up, he looked it over. It looked pretty much like every kitchen recipe he'd ever seen. A list of ingredients at the top together with instructions on how to combine and heat them.

As he read the recipe, a prompt appeared in his UI.

***Add recipe Shrink to recipe library (Y/N)?**

With a furtive glance at the engrossed Mabel and Kara, Gareth selected Y and was informed that he now had one recipe in his library, listed under potions. He also received a notice that a *Knowledge of Potions* skill had been created for him, at level 0.

He pulled up his library menu and selected *Potions*. There, he noticed a button at the top for *Create New Recipe*. But it was grayed out. When he tried to select it anyway, he was informed that his knowledge of potions was too limited to create new recipes. He needed to increase his skill level.

Undeterred, Gareth selected the shrink potion recipe that he'd just learned. This time, a diagram appeared, showing all the ingredients used, connected by lines. It resembled a compound structure diagram from chemistry class. He looked over all the components until he found wormwood, then selected and deleted it. This left a blank spot in the diagram. Mentally focusing on the new blank entry in the diagram brought up a short list of ingredients. He wondered if increasing his knowledge of ingredients would also increase his options. He'd have to be on the lookout for more books like Mabel's. Luckily, frogwood was listed. Selecting that, he inserted it into the spot of the diagram formerly used by wormwood.

At the bottom of the menu was another button. This one read *Compile Recipe*. He selected that, and shortly thereafter, received a new notification.

- **Recipe successfully created.**
- **Recipe Shrink (improved)**
- **Shrink duration + 1 hour**
- **Shrink amount +10%**

Right after a second window appeared:

- **You have successfully used your hidden talent Natural Alchemist**
  - **+100 experience**
  - **+500 experience for first use**
  - **Level up. Natural Alchemist is now level 1 (apprentice)**

A skill level-up and an improved recipe—not a bad deal! It made him want to find more recipes to modify. But Clippy's admonition to keep the ability secret was never far from his thoughts. He had no desire to be locked in a room and force-fed recipes to modify. With that in mind, he suppressed the urge to modify everything he could see, making note to explore this more later.

Mabel and Kara were still talking. Though it felt like toying with the recipe had taken a long time, it must have only been a minute or two. Gareth dug into his pack for some parchment paper and a pencil, then wrote out his new recipe. His companions took no notice, too engrossed with the adventures of Slick the Pantless. Gareth crumpled the paper and smeared the pencil a little to give it an aged, semi-weather-beaten look.

Then he flagged them down for their attention.

"Here's your recipe back. Thank you for letting me look at it. Once I did, I realized I found something like it yesterday when I was out hunting Dire Rats. Maybe you'll find it useful?" Gareth handed Mabel the original recipe along with his own crumpled-up handiwork.

Mabel glanced at him, setting the old recipe aside, then smoothed out the new facsimile that Gareth had created. Her eyes widened progressively as she read it. "*Where* did you say you found this?"

"Ah, well I was outside of town hunting in the swamp with a...friend. I found this in a ratty old pack sitting by a tree. My hunting partner wasn't interested, so I tucked it away and didn't think about it until now."

Well crap, where had he dug all that from? He was getting to be an even better liar than his youngest.

Mabel frowned, eyes skimming the parchment again. "Coincidentally, this is a recipe for a shrink potion, using frogwood. Just like we were discussing." Her eyes flitted back to Gareth, gaze lingering on him, full of suspicion.

"Weird coincidence. Does that sort of stuff happen in the game often?" He smiled feebly, hoping to she'd read the strong *I didn't do nuthin'* vibes he was giving.

"About as often as an adventurer passing on a recipe for their share of the loot. Do you have any idea what something like this is worth?"

Gareth shrugged, not really caring about its value. He just wanted her to make it into a potion so they could get on with their plan. He had shit to do and the list was piling up. "Actually, no. I'm still new here."

"Normally, even getting a look at a useless recipe like I showed you would cost you a hundred gold. A new recipe like this could easily go for ten times that amount. Even more, since this one is an improved version."

Gareth choked, then covered, coughing as if trying to clear his throat. "Over a *thousand* gold? For a recipe?"

Mabel snorted, though he could not tell if it was from frustration or excitement. "Recipes are the base of all crafting. They are jealously guarded."

Then she turned back to the new recipe Gareth had given her.

Gareth's gaze drifted to Kara, who was watching him with a calculating look on her face. He quirked an eyebrow at her, but she just waved for him to continue his conversation with Mabel.

He faced the minotaur alchemist again. "So, can you make the potion for us, now?"

"I *could*. But now we have another problem. Like I said, recipes are very valuable. I understand how you got this, but I can't just take it from you. Nor do I have the gold to pay you a fair price."

Gareth considered, letting his gaze roam around the shop while trying to figure out just how much he wanted to push. This game seemed to be very group-oriented. And he didn't have many friends. Gathering allies any way he could seemed like a plus.

Mabel waited patiently while he mulled things over.

"Well, you already let me look at the old shrink potion recipe. That was worth a hundred gold. And I did read your book, and you were pretty cool about that." Gareth put on a big show of thinking, putting his hand on his chin and everything. "I got this one for free. We could call it even if you make us a batch of these new potions as a rush order for us and maybe… give me a 15% discount going forward?"

Mabel eyes widened in shock, letting go a long breath through her wide nostrils. Then she tilted her head and shifted her stance. "I'll give you ten percent. *And* I get an exclusive on this recipe for a year."

He cringed. There went his plan to visit all the other alchemists in town to make piles of gold from them. Well, this deal was about forging a valuable relationship, too, and that didn't have monetary value. And since he really needed that potion ASAP, he reached over the counter to shake her hand. "It's a deal."

Mabel returned the handshake and then focused her attention back on the recipe, studying intently as if memorizing it. Then, she unlocked a drawer behind the counter and filed her new recipe away, along with the old one. Gareth's inner Scrooge McDuck wet its lips, spotting the stash of recipes she had in her files. Just how much gold could he make if he improved every one of those?

"Say, Mabel, what would it cost me to look at some of your other recipes?"

Mabel turned back to him but her eyelids lowered, her expression guarded. "Whatever for?" Then she blew out a huge force of breath from her nostrils, so fierce he could feel it yards away. Her deep brows furrowed and if ever she resembled a bovine about to charge, it was then. "You're planning to sell the recipes to my competition."

Gareth stepped back, holding a hand up in defense. Uh oh. Looked like he'd pushed it to the limit—and now the limit was pushing back.

Chapter
Twenty-One
Ghosts

GARETH FACED OFF WITH A HIGHLY-IRRITATED minotaur alchemist—not something he'd ever imagined in his wildest dreams as a situation he'd find himself in. Clippy's strict warning about keeping his talent a secret warred with his need to gain the suspicious Mabel's trust. A quandary, to be sure.

It was too early for the full truth, so he went with a lesser one. He held his hands, palms out, unthreateningly. "I'm new here, and I'm fascinated by crafting and how recipes work. I was curious about commonalities and figured I might be able to see them if I studied more recipes."

This seemed to mollify Mabel a little. She still gave him a suspicious look, as she shut and locked her recipe drawer. "*Some* alchemists might be willing to sell you a look at their library. But *I* work on the barter system. Bring me something else, and I might let you have a look. Now, get out of here. You may come back in an hour. Unless you didn't want those potions. *And* you still owe me two bags worth of ingredients. That debt predates our deal for the recipe."

Son of a bitch, Gareth muttered under his breath. "See you in an hour, then." He turned to his diminutive companion. "Let's, ah, leave her to her work." He and Kara quickly exited the shop and returned to the ruins outside.

"Well, *that* went better than I expected." Kara stood straight, hands on hips. "Mabel can be kinda prickly sometimes. She took a positive shine to you."

Gareth stared at her in disbelief. "If *that* was happy Mabel, I'd hate to see grumpy Mabel. Is that why her shop is way out here?"

Kara looked around the giant piles of rubble that were once buildings. Across a courtyard, there was a small group of people looking their way. "Let's talk while we walk, shall we? Standing around makes us a target around here."

Gareth waved for her to lead the way, and she set off down a side path. Once they were off the main road, she began to talk once more. "Mabel doesn't care whether or not she pisses people off. Given the downtown clientele, she'd probably enjoy it. Her shop is out here because minotaurs aren't generally known for their intellect. She got tired of all the insinuations that she was just fronting for one of the 'smarter' races. The jokes about her milking herself for the potions weren't helping, either. And then there's Clud, her son. He tends to take slurs about his mother personally, and it was hurting his career because he kept getting picked up for fighting. All around, it was just easier to be out of the spotlight. Here, she can do her thing, and no one cares if she tosses a rude customer out of her shop—*literally.*"

They'd stopped at the entrance to a cul-de-sac with the remains of a neatly appointed house at the end. Kara stared at it with something that looked like longing—or sadness.

Then her eyes flicked to Gareth, and she straightened, as if pulling herself out of her daze. "I, uh, grew up there."

Gareth's eyes went back to the house. What remained of the architecture was exquisite and there were, from what he could tell, once beautiful flowerbeds and carefully arranged topiaries—now merely overgrown bushes. It looked like it had once been a very nice house. A sense of dread settled in Gareth's stomach. "So…what happened?"

Kara stared at the place once more, lips thinning with what was obviously a bad memory. "I came back late one night, after running around with my friends, and everyone was just gone. All our stuff was still here. But no family."

Gareth let out a sharp breath. "Holy crap. That must have been horrible."

Kara licked her lips, shoulders slumping. "It still is. I looked for them for a long while. But I never found any clues. In my nightmares I see them locked up somewhere, waiting for me to rescue them. Sometimes I look around and think I spot one of them in a crowd…"

Gareth tensed. Even before he'd been snatched away from his home world, he'd lost everything in that wretched divorce. It ached whenever he thought of his boys. "You'll—*we'll*—find out what happened to them. I'm not sure how, or when, but we don't give up on our friends."

Kara reached up and patted him on the back. "You're a good man, Gareth. But I've looked for years. Now, I content myself with just checking back from time to time to make sure no one is abusing the old place."

Gareth stared after her, eyes stinging mildly with his own longing brought up fresh by her words. "I can relate to how you're feeling. In some small way, at least. I've lost my family, too, but in a different way."

"Because you were brought here?"

He shook his head gruffly, sniffed hard, and turned his face away from her examination. "Before that. My wife left me--well, threw me out, really. Our marriage wasn't perfect, but it felt like that came out of nowhere."

Kara looked up at him, interest in her eyes. "And you have children?"

Gareth squared his shoulders, eyes skimming the horizon around them, the rubble of the Ruins made it possible to see further than you normally could from a city street. "Yeah, two boys. I don't see them much."

She frowned. "Because you don't want to?"

He shook his head gruffly.

"Is a child not allowed to see their parents after a marriage ends? That's strange."

"Normally, that's not the case, but this was anything but normal. I had a good lawyer, or so I thought, but something weird went down. I wasn't allowed into a meeting with the lawyers and the judge. After it was over, my lawyer could hardly look me in the face. Just told me to take the deal and not fight it. He was adamant."

Kara was riveted to this tale of his misery now, probably relieved that she didn't have to dwell in her own anymore. "What was the deal?"

He turned narrowed eyes on her, reliving all the stress, anger and frustration from that time. A time he'd rather forget. "Supervised visits. *Once a month.* It was a shit deal, and that fucking lawyer screwed me."

Kara blinked. "Didn't you talk to your wife about it?"

"*Ex* -wife and I sure as hell *did*." He sucked in a tight breath. "I confronted her right away. Asked her how she could support taking kids away from their own father." He shook his head in memory of that cold look she'd given him in return. That icy frost was seared into his soul. "All she could say was something like I should know what I did and repeated I should just sign the papers, or I'd have to meet with the DA. Like I'd done something fucking illegal or something. Shit like that comes up sometimes in custody fights. Mudslinging. But I've never done anything that could remotely merit such an accusation. I could only assume that her slimeball lawyer had manufactured something on me. I figured once a month was more than I could see them from a jail cell. To say nothing of who the hell would take care of my dog." His shoulders slumped in defeat.

It had broken him, that entire day. Just a blur of pain that had set him on the course of loser-hood that had ended with him sitting alone in the desert with his beloved dog trying to pick up the pieces of a shattered life.

"That sucks, Gareth. And if there was something I could do to remove your pain, I would. But you can't believe the negative shit about yourself. You can't let that hold you down."

He sucked in a sharp breath and shrugged. "You're right, I'm sure. But it's tough." Gareth looked at Kara's old home again, fiddling with the growth of whiskers on his jaw.

Kara heaved a sigh. "Our hour's almost up. We should head back."

They turned around and started back toward Mabel's shop. But only a couple of blocks later, Kara stopped and pushed Gareth into a rubble-strewn alleyway.

"Crap. We got trouble."

"What?" He craned his head to look around. Nothing seemed out of the ordinary to him.

She whispered. "Peek around the corner. But don't make any sudden moves, or you'll draw attention."

Gareth nodded and slowly eased himself up to the corner of the alleyway, then edged his head around for a look. About a block and half further down the street, two people milled about, poking through the rubble. Gareth withdrew into the alley again and shrugged at Kara.

"It's two guys sifting through rubble. What am I missing?"

"Those same two guys were outside Blacl's when we left. I also spotted them down the street when we left Mabel's."

Gareth frowned. "That is a little suspicious." He went to lean forward for another look, but Kara grabbed a fistful of his chain mail and yanked him back.

"Don't be a doofus. You're not that stealthy. I recognize them, anyway. They're two of Thepeiros's goons." She moved the opposite way down the alley, tugging Gareth along with her.

"Thepeiros? Who's that?"

"Thepeiros is the Elite guild recruiter. What level is your *Inspect* skill at, anyway?"

"Oh, *that* fucker." Gareth glanced through his skill ranks in the UI and found *Inspect.* "It says 'Horrible.'"

Kara's mouth twisted in disgust. "You need to work on those skills, human. A child has a higher skill level than that." She grunted and gave him another yank.

"So, what do we do? Surely, the guards won't allow them to attack us."

Kara stopped tugging him and planted her feet. "What we *do* is stop waiting for them to notice we've gone down this alley. There aren't any guards in the Ruins or the whole town for that matter."

"No guards at all? How—?"

"Later." Kara gave him a push, narrowly missing a sensitive area.

Gareth needed no more convincing. He turned and followed his small companion. Given all the fallen stonework and rubble, her nimble maneuvering found the going much easier than he did. And the alley itself was unexpectedly long. After about fifteen minutes, they emerged into another main thoroughfare. This one was even more damaged than the area they'd just left. And while that area had had a few people here and there, this place was completely deserted—not a soul to be seen but the two of them.

Gareth couldn't explain why, but the sight creeped him out.

"Come on, big guy. Let's get a move on." She started down the street at a trot.

Gareth only spared a moment to glance into the alley behind them. There was no sign of their two "friends." They'd probably head back to Mabel's to pick up the trail again. Gareth took off after Kara, catching her quickly due to his longer stride.

"So, what's the hurry?" He huffed alongside her. "Why not just take our time and let those two get bored and wander off?" There was no falter in her pace. Her eyes swept continually from side to side.

"Listen. Every part of this town has its good parts and its bad parts. The Ruins is the bad part of town, and *this* is the bad part of the Ruins." She visibly shivered. "It gives me the big-time creeps. I told you that the Ruins are haunted."

Gareth nodded.

"Well, *this* is like ghost central. People who enter here after dark don't come out."

Gareth's brows rose. That explained his own creeped-out feelings. "Well, then. Let's get back to Mabel's ASAP. How far do you think we need to go before we can cut back?" Gareth was now the one to outpace Kara as she fought to keep up.

She sucked in a breath. "We keep going this way until we reach the ruined fountain. Then we can turn back toward Mabel's—"

"*Stop!*" Gareth halted in his tracks, looking along the left side of the road back the way they'd come. Something had glimmered and—there it was again. A flash from a doorway they'd passed. He stepped toward it.

"Where are you going? Ghosts—remember the ghosts? They eat people!" Kara was tugging at him, but he ignored her. Gareth was inexplicably drawn to that doorway.

It was yet another ruined building with dust and rubble everywhere, but the ground floor was remarkably intact. He walked up the pathway that led to the front door—huge, cut from thick, mottled granite. Gareth gave the barrier the once-over, unable to figure out the mechanism for opening it.

But there had to be a source for that light—that quick flash he'd seen as he'd walked by. He tried every angle and finally figured out that he'd originally spotted it from his peripheral vision, he peered at the doorway out of the corner of his eyes. From that angle, the door was highlighted with a yellow glow.

Kara continued to tug at his arm. "Gareth—we need to go. This isn't the time to be a tourist."

Gareth lifted his arm and pointed at the top seam of the door. "Look, there's some kind of figure etched into the door." He slipped his pack off his shoulders and dug through it, extracting an extra homespun shirt he'd bought at a newbie vender earlier. Using it, he was able to clean away enough of the dust to better make out the figure.

"I really need to invest in some dungeoneering gear. A whisk broom would be handy right about now."

Standing back, he could better see the image now. "Look. It's an eagle."

"I don't care if it's the magic, gold-crapping thunderbird. We. Need. To. *Go*."

"*Arrooohhhoooo*." A bone chilling howl rose up.

"What the hell was *that*?" Gareth tore his eyes away from the stone door to look around but couldn't see anything.

Kara grabbed Gareth's hand—tightly—to get his attention, then pointed to a ruin behind them on the road. At first, he didn't see anything, but then the creature passed through a shadow, and he spotted it—a spectral white figure floating through the air toward them.

"That's a *ghost!*"

"No crap." Kara searched frantically as if trying to find a way out, but another creature appeared from the left, blocking both sides of the road. They'd been cut off.

"But ghosts don't exist. They're just a fairytale to scare kids and dumb adults."

Kara let go of his hand and started digging through her pouches, mumbling to herself about dumbass humans. When another long, haunting wail sounded, she looked back at the approaching ghosts and pried herself between Gareth and the door. She continued patting her pockets. "I've got nothing that will damage the unsubstantial. We're going to die here, stupid human. I hope your dumb door was worth it."

Gareth froze, watching the ghosts approach. They were slow as hell, but they'd effectively cut off their prey. As they drew nearer, Gareth was able to pick out more details. They wore leather armor, plumed helmets and sandals. Strangely enough, they looked a lot like Roman Legionnaires.

"This must have been the base camp for the Ninth Legion. I found one of their badges earlier."

"Who cares about some old dead humans. Unless you found a key for that door, we're screwed." She shoved him in front of her. "At least you'll die first, humie."

The ghosts were now close enough he could feel the chill radiating from them—a damp, clammy sort of frigid air that wasn't unlike passing through a dank fog. Their eyes—they burned with red and amber madness and fury, as if they were about to rip the living beings apart in the most painful way possible with their fleshless fingers.

This was going to hurt—a lot. Or would it? He hadn't died yet, so his pain setting was pretty low. "Wait, what are we worried about? Won't we just respawn?"

Kara turned and gave him look of incredibility. "First off, ghosts have a special attack—it'll hurt even on a low pain setting. Second, ghosts suck up your exp, I'd rather not lose a level or two. Third, you're a dumbass."

The ghosts crept closer, the cold from their aura really starting to sink into his body. Then Gareth had a thought. They used badges, or things that looked like badges, all the time to open things in Star Trek—Kirk Trek, the only real Trek. Maybe his badge would work that way. He dropped his pack and pulled out the badge he'd looted the day before. It was shiny in the low light, bearing the symbol of the Ninth Legion of Rome.

"What are you doing?" Kara screeched. "You know if you die, you'll just drop whatever you're holding. Leave it in your pack, so it will respawn with you." Kara was trying to push her way through the door now, as if she had some mysterious skill that involved passing through solid objects.

"I have an idea." Gareth muttered. With no clue of the proper place to put the badge, he began randomly slapping it all over the door. On the sixth or seventh try, the stone slab slid to the side, giving way. Without the support, the two adventurers fell into the dark opening.

A burning pain shot through Gareth's back, and his health bar dropped by a third. He also got a notification that he'd lost 4,000 experience. He hadn't lost a level, but it had been close.

He quickly stumbled to his feet and turned toward the doorway, ready to make his escape. To his relief, both ghosts hovered outside, refusing to cross the threshold.

One of them appeared more solid-looking now, probably the one that had just hit and damaged him.

Kara bounced up off the ground and retreated further into the dark room. "Shut the door, Gareth!"

"*Shut* the door? I'm not even sure how I *opened* the door." Still, he frantically searched for some way to reverse the timely accident. That's when he noticed a smooth stone just to the right of the doorway. Reaching out—while still attempting to put as much distance between himself and the ghosts as he could—he pounded on it.

Lucky and timely accident number two in as many minutes! The door slammed shut. Gareth sagged against the wall in relief. The air warmed again immediately. He couldn't help but wonder, however, why the stone would keep ghosts out. Since they were immaterial, they could pass through solid matter, couldn't they? But they hadn't even tried to cross the threshold when it had been open so maybe there was something about this place that they avoided. Maybe, just maybe, that meant they were safe.

Thank all the gods—both in and out of the game.

"Door's shut," Gareth panted, the adrenaline in his bloodstream starting to fade.

He spun to seek out his companion in the darkness. She stood facing him off, her stance one of aggression and anger, all tension with fists clenched at her sides.

"Idiot. I *told* you we had to leave. You wouldn't listen. Now you've shut us inside with no way out."

Gareth clenched his teeth, eyes flitting from one wall to the next.

Well, shit.

Chapter Twenty-Two

Great Caesar's Ghost!

I N THE DARKNESS OF THE RUINED BUILDING, GARETH fought to heal his injuries while simultaneously calling for Kara to come to her senses. "We're safe, for the moment. Be happy."

Gareth studied the wounds he'd received with confusion. It was like the damage from the ghost was resistant to his healing. It took almost all his mana to fully heal himself. He made a mental note—*Ghosts: bad juju.* He also had a UI notification that he could recover his lost experience by killing the ghost. Yeah, like that was going to happen.

Kara took a few minutes to calm her own panic—which was exactly the same amount of time it took her to stop hitting him. After that, she sank to the ground, her back to the door, tucking her knees under her chin. She didn't say a word. Since Gareth had a pretty piss-poor record with human women, he held back from saying anything that might make it worse. Instead, he ignored the outburst and moved on.

"Well, we're safe from the ghosts in here," he reiterated. His eyes traced the outline of the door. "We just need to find another way out of here, so we can head back to Mabel's." Then, he turned, peering into the darkness. "And look at this place! It's great." He gestured around the room. This was no mere one-room shop but a much larger building. The structure was intact, though it looked like it had been stripped in a hurry. Down the hallway, he could make out doorways to other rooms. There were signs of a hurried evacuation everywhere—chairs knocked over, books splayed open face down on the ground, remains of papers littering the floor and half of a banner hanging from the wall as if someone had tried to rip it down and failed.

"You don't understand, Gareth." When Kara finally chose to speak, it was with such a tiny voice that he had to lean in closer to hear her. "I can't deal with ghosts. I...I think ghosts took my family. The day before they disappeared, I was out late, ignoring my curfew. I never had problems with the ghosts, because I was too quick, too sneaky. Then, I got caught—I panicked and ran for home. I lost them, or so I thought. The next day, my family was gone."

Gareth frowned, watching her tiny form curled in on itself. "I'm sorry, Kara. I'm sure it wasn't your fault." He patted her on her head, because he couldn't reach her shoulder, but she didn't acknowledge the gesture.

"You are correct. The ghosts, as you call them, do not kidnap people," a booming voice echoed in the darkness.

Gareth jumped, spinning around toward the voice. And though he'd never seen her move, Kara was once again behind him, probably the most proper place for a rogue. A man had entered the great room from the darkness and stood before them. Gareth squinted, trying to get a closer look at the fuzzy details. Maybe it was just the image of a man. A hologram? He did appear kind of see-through and wavey. The stranger was dressed in toga-like white robes with a laurel wreath on his head, the image of a Roman citizen of old.

"Great Caesar's ghost!" Gareth mentally groaned at the pun. He'd read a lot of Superman comics as a kid, after all.

"Nay, I am neither Caesar, nor a ghost. I could never deign to be worthy of being called after that great man. Though he did help end the Republic and usher in the Empire, and not everyone viewed that positively. Nevertheless, the empire is mighty and rules the world."

Gareth straightened to his full height. "What are you then, neither ghost nor Caesar?"

The image gestured back at him. "I guess you could say I am the embodiment of this building. Its caretaker and protector."

Gareth licked his lips, thinking.

Kara poked her head out from behind her Gareth-shield to speak. "I hope you'll forgive our intrusion then, good caretaker. We meant no harm to your building."

The image shook its head. "Not at all. You, sir, are the first human to enter here since the legion left. It has been a long and lonely absence. Which reminds me...I have a message for you."

Gareth drew back in surprise. "A message for me? How is that possible?"

"A message for the next human to enter the guildhall, which is you. Therefore, it is a message for you."

Gareth turned to Kara, who shrugged back at him. Then he returned his attention to the holographic Roman. "Give me the message then, I guess."

A second figure appeared beside the first. He was also a projection of some kind, though he was dressed as a Roman Legionnaire, complete with laced-up sandals, breastplate, plumed helmet and shield.

"I am Legatus Gaius Maximus Aurelius. As you are seeing this, my fears have been realized, and we have been sent to our doom. We were taken from our home, Caledonia, some twenty years ago, and forced to fight in this infernal existence ever since. I fear we have proved too successful, and our erstwhile masters have started to fear us. With good cause, I will admit. Our guild has fought valiantly, and we have leveled greatly. We strain against our leashes. If only we had been given a little more time. But we must have been betrayed. Trust no one, sir, especially the rulers of this town. Seek out the dwarves. They have proven themselves dependable allies. As a representative of our race, I charge you to avenge our fate. I give you this, our guildhall, and what resources remain within to help you. *Long live the Emperor!*"

With that, the legatus drew his sword, saluted Gareth, and then vanished. Immediately, a quest prompt appeared in Gareth's field of vision:

•**Quest: Discover who betrayed the human guild, "The Vagrants," and destroy them.**

•**Assistance provided: Ownership of the guild, "The Vagrants," and all its remaining assets.**

•Reward: Unknown

•Penalties for Failure: Unknown, but probably bad.

•Accept quest (Y/N)?

"How hard is it to make your own guild?" he asked Kara.

"It used to be easy, but now, not so much." Kara glanced between him and the projection with a clearly calculating stare. "The four horsemen don't like competition. They've locked down the creation of new guilds to force people to join one of their four."

"So, ah, this is a valuable reward?"

"An existing guild, with guildhall? Right now, I'd say it's priceless. Not to mention the guild bank." Kara wet her lips at the mention of the guild bank.

"Okay then, I accept." The quest prompt disappeared, and a new entry was created in his quest log. He expected a glowing light or a chime or ding or something as he was made into a guild leader. But all he got was a message:

****Error — Guild ownership cannot be transferred while guild is suspended.****

He looked over at the ghost "What the hell, Caesar?" The game automatically updated the overhead tag to read *Caesar* the moment Gareth addressed him. "I thought I was supposed to get the guild?"

The projected being squirmed for a minute, starting to speak and then stopping several times.

"Oh, for the love of all that's holy, just spit it out."

The image paused and then restarted. "The guild is suspended for lack of payment of guild taxes."

"*Taxes?* Can't escape them, even here, I guess. And the guild bank is empty, I suppose?"

"No, indeed. There are sufficient funds to bring the account up to date."

"Okay, then, pay the taxes already."

Another pause from the image before continuing. "Currently only the guild leader can access the guild bank."

"But... *I* am the guild leader."

Caesar shook his head. "Not until we pay the taxes, I'm afraid."

Gareth channeled a perfect Picard facepalm gesture to express the unique frustration of the moment. "So, let me get this straight. To become guild leader, I need to pay the taxes. But to access the funds to pay the taxes, I have to be the guild leader."

"Correct," the image said as if this were perfectly logical.

"And what is the amount due?"

"The guild taxes are quite reasonable, indeed. Only 100 crowns per year."

"And they haven't been paid for..." Gareth made a gesture for Caesar to fill in the blank.

"For 1,833 years."

"*Great.* So, I only need 183,000 crowns?" He heaved a sigh.

"Actually, it's 237,000. There are fines attached for late payment."

"Of course there are." Gareth threw up his hands. "Welp, that's that. I'll try to drop by once in a while to say hi, then." He turned back to Kara, disregarding the projection. "It's been a bit. You think those ghosts have left?"

He turned to head back toward the door. Caesar reappeared right in front of him, as if blocking his path.

"There *is* a possible solution. It has the added benefit of resolving the problems with the ghosts as well."

Gareth's hackles rose, suspicious that Caesar hadn't led with this bit of useful info. "And what would that be?"

"We had a…lapse of security. An object was stolen from the guildhall. If you return it, then it would be within my powers to reward you with enough gold to pay the back taxes. Its return would also placate the ghosts, so they will stop roaming the streets."

"Let me guess, the ghosts were supposed to guard this object, and its loss is driving them to lash out because of their eternal torment until its safe return?"

The apparition blinked at him. "Why, yes."

Gareth almost rolled his eyes. "How very stereotypical."

Caesar pursed his lips. "I don't understand."

Gareth waved him off instead of explaining that this was one of the most overused tropes in game quest storytelling.

Kara chose this moment to interject. "You lost your guildstone, didn't you?"

Gareth turned to her, confused. "*Guildstone?*"

Kara's gaze flew to his. "It's a magical power source. Normally, it powers things like the guild defenses, the portal room—if you have one—and allows for magical crafting stations. Basically, the more powerful your stone is, the more powerful your guild can become." She turned back to Caesar, hands on her hips. "Just what are we talking about here in terms of power?"

Caesar's gaze sunk to the ground before him. "It's a Class Ten stone."

"By Gaea's green teats!" Kara's jaw dropped, eyes wide as saucers.

Gareth arched a brow at her. "I take it that means it's a big one?"

"Well, I've heard of bigger, but that's certainly the biggest one that's ever been around here." Kara turned to Caesar once more, eyes narrowing. "How did you ever lose that? It couldn't have been stolen…The protections on it would have incinerated anyone who tried to take it."

The hologram began moving, floating around in tight circles as if pacing or agitated. "Another human entered. He was offered the quest and guildhall, just like you were. He said he couldn't in good conscience take on another quest until he finished his current one."

Kara blew out a breath of disbelief. "And I bet he told you that if he borrowed the stone, he could complete his quest and be free to take this one." Kara shook her head. "You're an idiot."

Caesar hung his head. "It had been so long. Centuries. Almost two millennia. And he was so convincing. The spirit guards tried to prevent it, but I stunned them. When the stun wore off, and he didn't return with the stone as promised, they went berserk. Then they started trying to kill anyone who got anywhere near the guildhall to prevent another theft."

Gareth focused on the part that really tickled his senses. "*Wait*…you said I was the first human to enter since the legion left. Then you say another human entered, making me the second. What gives?"

Caesar shrugged, clearly uncomfortable. "There were anomalies in his scan. I overlooked them at the time, attributing them to my long sleep. After review, I determined that may have been a mistake, and he was only part human. Therefore, you are indeed the first human to have entered since the legion left.

Gareth rolled his eyes. "You're splitting a mighty fine hair. When did this happen?"

"One hundred eighty-seven years ago. I'm unaware if he is still alive."

"That long ago, eh?" Hadn't Clippy mentioned an anomaly about that long ago, too? "Well, he's dead, then. Humans only live a hundred years—*if* they're lucky. Though I don't know about part-humans."

Kara shook her head vehemently. "Even if he's a hundred percent human, there's lots of magic to extend your life around here. For instance, with that stone alone, he could power a spell to keep him alive indefinitely." Kara started pacing around thinking. She turned back to Caesar. "What protections does the stone have?"

"Well, only a human can access or move the stone," Caesar responded.

"Or partial humans, apparently," Kara interjected.

Gareth held up a hand. "Wait... go back a second. Even if this guy had a spell in-game to extend his life, he'd still die when his body aged in the real world, wouldn't he?"

Kara looked at him like he was an idiot. "Weren't you listening when you were introduced to the game? Didn't you notice the big white beam erasing you when you logged in? The computer that runs the game keeps the game world and meatspace world in sync. *And* it has almost unlimited power to do so. It stores your body somewhere while you're logged in. When you log out, it recreates your body using your in-game persona as a guide. Well… kinda, anyway. There are some things that will always only stay in the game and vice versa. In any case, extending your life in-game will extend your life in meatspace, too."

Gareth blinked, staggering as his knees weakened. "So, I'm immortal? I'll respawn when I die in here...that must mean—"

"*No.* idiot." Kara jumped up and smacked the top of the his head with the back of her hand. "If you don't have something to extend your life, you'll still grow old and die. You age inside the game, just like normal. Or, if you get chased out of the game, you'll grow old and die in meatspace. Or if—" Then she cut herself off, shaking her head. "Well, there's a ton of ways to die. The easiest way to die is to believe you're immortal and then do stupid crap."

Gareth shook his head, dazed. "Right. No stupid crap, then." He stood up and dusted himself off, only feeling a little better. Caesar still hovered nearby, looking shockingly uncomfortable for an artificial person. Gareth asked him, "So, what do you know about this guy who took the stone? Just in case I run into him sometime."

Caesar hesitated. "I have no way to verify any of this, of course. All I know is based on what he told me. He was born in the highlands of Scotland sometime around the year 1810 AD. He was vague about the exact year or place. At the time, I surmised he didn't know for sure, but now I wonder if he wasn't hiding the information on purpose. From other things he mentioned, I now suspect he was running from something when he was transported into the game. I'm uncertain if the anomalies in his scan were introduced on Earth or after he entered the game."

"Yes, about those anomalies. You're being a bit vague. What exactly was so anomalous?" Gareth pressed the apparition.

Ceasar hesitated, "Normally I am unable to share the information gained via a medical scan, but I guess since you are to be the new guild leader I can make an exception. When I scanned him, the results of the brain scan were muddled, as if there were two entities residing there."

"And that didn't clue you in that something was wrong?" Gareth rubbed his forehead, feeling a headache coming on.

"As I said, at the time I attributed the results to my long sleep. It was only after, when I had time to do a full diagnostic of myself, that I realized the error had to come from him." Ceasar's voice grew decidedly snippy. "And he had entered the game via Earth, so I had no reason to suspect anything."

Gareth puzzled at that. "Yeah, how is that possible? Was he grabbed, like me?"

Caesar shook his head emphatically. "No, he made his way here on his own. He was quite proud of that fact. He must have stumbled across a bind access point from the old Atlantean days."

"I'm still not sure I buy that Atlantis was real. And that we all played some sort of space MMORPG. That's even more unlikely than space drug dealers grabbing me in the desert." The other two just stared back at him, apparently not finding it as shocking as he did. Gareth decided to focus on his current problems, "So his body is stored on Earth somewhere while he's in the game? I know we're primitive by your standards, but we'd notice that kind of power draw eventually, I'd think."

Kara answered for the projection, "No one knows what happens to your meatspace body, just that it's 'stored'. When you log out, it's unpacked at the access point you have bound yourself to."

Gareth blinked, absorbing this. Did this mean a way back home for him? If this person made his way in from Earth, he could make his way out again the same way. Which meant Gareth could do the same thing—and wind up back on Earth. With shock running through every sense at this revelation, he could hardly form the next question. "Your actual body's location gets moved when you change your bind point in game and log out? How is that possible?"

"As your small companion said, the MCP strives to keep both of its realities as much in sync as possible. How, I do not know, but your body is recreated in the location that correlates to the location of your bind point where you logged out."

Gareth started pacing in tight circles around the room. "So, if I could find the game access point he used, and reset my bind point to there, my body would appear back on Earth when I log out? I could go home?"

The apparition nodded. "In theory, yes. But that particular path would contain many obstacles."

Gareth sighed and made a dismissive gesture. "Yeah, yeah, I know. Nothing is going to be easy. Whatever I'd have to overcome, it's likely easier than jumping out an airlock and swimming through vacuum to get back to Earth, which is the only option I have now. I'm counting this as a win." He flicked his gaze back to Caesar, desperate for more vital info. "What's this dude's name anyway? I'd like to keep an eye out. He sounds like trouble."

"He introduced himself as Crush. I'm no longer aware of naming conventions on Earth, but I suspect that is a *nom de guerre* that he adopted for the game."

Kara gasped loudly.

"What is it?"

She took a deep breath and flicked a very nervous gaze at Gareth. "I only know of *one* Crush in the game. Crush the Destroyer, guild leader of The Elite. He betrayed and murdered his way to the guild leadership. Every person he ever labeled a threat disappeared soon after. You mess with him, and you're never going home, unless it's in pieces."

At that moment, a soul sucking howl rose up from the other side of the door. Seconds later, the door bucked and shuddered, as if something very heavy had slammed against it.

Chapter
Twenty-Three
Exit, Pursued by a
Bear

WHAM! WHAM! WHAM!

The incessant pounding threatened to break the stone door out of its frame, dropping it down on anyone who stood behind it.

Gareth's eyes goggled as he jumped back from the door. "If they're spirits, how are they hitting the door so hard?" He had to shout out his question to Caesar the ghost in order to be heard over the crashing against the front entrance.

Caesar stared intently at the door. "It appears that they've convinced the troll from down the street to assist them."

"A *troll?*" Gareth wasn't ashamed to admit—if only to himself—that his voice hiked up an octave on that last word, visions of the hideous hulking beast from *The Lord of The Rings* movies stomping around in his mind's eye.

Caesar's incorporeal eyes turned back to Gareth. "Oh, he's harmless." *Wham!* "Mostly, anyway. He's a bit addled and spends his days collecting moss and lichen."

"Moss and lichen?!" *Wham.* "He wants to get in here pretty bad for moss and lichen!"

Caesar's face dropped. "I'm afraid they must have convinced him that we're holding his son captive in here. When he's more lucid, he remembers his son left of his own accord years ago. But mostly he's just feeling a sense of loss regarding him." The ghost sighed a breathless breath and shook its head. "To think they preyed on an old, addled troll. The dishonor *alone* should send them to the afterlife." Caesar turned back to the door. "*Fie. fie on you.* I say! The gods above grant Gaius never discover this dishonor."

Kara, who had been darting about the destroyed room looking for a nook to hide in, popped up. "This is going to suck hardcore when they get inside."

Gareth looked over at Ceasar. "They refused to enter when they first chased us into the guildhall. Can they get in or not?"

Ceasar shook his head. "I'm afraid they are quite capable of entering the guildhall if they manage to destroy the door. There are wards on the building that prevent unauthorized entries. Breaking the door will create a hole in those wards." Ceasar looked towards the door. "It is possible that my playing the Legatus message for you, and your being offered the guildhall has pushed them to this desperate action. They probably see this as a prelude to another theft, though how the guildstone could be stolen a second time is beyond me."

Gareth held up his gauntleted hand as his mind raced. "*Wait,* I have an idea! Give me the quest to recover the guildstone." Ceasar started to object but Gareth talked over him, "Just do it!"

Ceasar looked away for a second. A prompt appeared before Gareth.

•Quest: Locate the missing Vagrant guildstone and return it to the guildhall.

•Assistance provided: none

•Reward: 237,000 crowns

•Penalties for failure: none

•Accept quest (Y/N)?

The text blinked at him, asking for his response, and he quickly hit *yes.* "There, I've accepted the quest to recover the stone. Now that I'm helping you, they should leave me—" Kara jabbed her elbow into him. "Hey! Watch the boys! They should leave *us* alone now, right? If we're helping you recover the stone, we can't be a threat?"

Wham! Apparently not, then. The ghost echoed his thoughts. "I'm afraid not. After the whole Crush fiasco, they stopped listening to me. If they get in here, they will most definitely kill you."

Wham! Gareth could now spy cracks starting to spiderweb across the stone of the door. "Well, we're running out of time, then. This was an adventurer's guild, right? No adventurers I've ever heard of would have only one way in or out of any enclosed area. That would make it a death trap." He moved to confront the ghost he'd dubbed Caesar. "There must be another way out of here, even if it's an entrance into the sewers. Isn't there?" He poked toward Caesar's chest to drive home his point, momentarily forgetting the guardian's lack of corporeal form. Gareth's finger slid right through him. Nevertheless, Caesar still jumped back with a distinctly guilty look on his face.

"There is a sewer entrance, located in the storage cellar below the kitchen," came the dry reply.

Gareth shot a look of triumph at Kara. "There, ya see? Now let's bugger off before they make their way in here."

"Now just wait a minute, Long Legs." The pixie joined him in front of Caesar and addressed the ghost directly. "Why didn't you mention this to us until we directly asked?"

"Well, most of the sewer system collapsed when this part of the city was destroyed."

Wham! Gareth pointed at the door. "That actually doesn't sound so bad. Time to go."

Kara clamped onto Gareth's leg to prevent him from leaving. "Wait for it."

Caesar continued, "The remaining parts of the sewers are infested with giant rats and alligators."

Gareth blanched. "Alligators?"

"*Giant* alligators."

"*Giant alligators?*" Once again, his voice squeaked up an octave. He'd had a thing about alligators since that family Disney trip to Florida one year. He'd had to beat one—not so giant—off with a golf club. "And um…what do they eat?"

Caesar mulled this over for a minute, "Well the giant rats, I assume."

"*People.* They eat people. Don't be a dumbass." Kara poked him hard. "We need an *alternative* exit."

Gareth looked around him frantically. The cracks in the door had grown and dust was beginning to spill off it in waves. Yes, there had to be *another* way out.

Something sparked—likely from those years of being forced to watch *Downton Abbey* with the ex. "Wait a minute. What about a servant's entrance? A delivery bay? You can't tell me *everyone* came in through the front door."

"There is," Caesar acquiesced.

"*Great.* So where is it?"

Caesar lifted his hand and pointed. "Through the kitchen and down the hall to the left."

Kara unclamped from his leg, spun and sprinted off. Gareth spared the briefest of moments to nod his gratitude toward Caesar. Then he turned to follow the pixie down the hall. "I'll be back, Caesar. Hopefully with the guildstone."

Then, he halted as another thought occurred to him. The ghost hadn't been too generous with his details, in any case, and getting them out of him was like pulling teeth.

Wham! Shudder. "What's past the alternate exit?" Gareth yelled.

"It's an alleyway."

"*Great!*" He brightened. "We love alleys." *Wham!* Gareth's eyes flew to the crumbling door. "Maybe let them in once we're gone? It'd be good to save the door for later." With one last wave, he turned and sprinted after Kara.

Kitchen, kitchen. Where was the kitchen? Every hallway looked the same to him. Just how fucking big was this place, anyway? He may have despaired of finding Kara again until he heard her voice coming from a short passage on his right.

"Yo, Big Jobs. Over here!"

Following her voice down the long side hallway, he soon entered what had once been the kitchen. It was big enough to conceivably feed hundreds. Honestly, he could only imagine what an impressive sight it must have been in its day. Now, the sheer emptiness and dilapidated condition of it was a depressing reminder of all that had been lost.

"Where's the supposed passage?" Gareth, in all his marveling of past glory, had not paused in his search for the escape route. The banging against the front door persisted—and he could hear it just as well in here as he had in the front room.

"Right *here.*" Kara stomped her foot, drawing Gareth's attention toward another passageway. Gareth blinked, having expected a human-sized passage. This one was large enough to haul a horse-drawn wagon through.

Without hesitation, they sped down the hall and quickly came to the exit. It was one of those setups where the smaller, human-sized door was inset into a larger gate-sized one—for the presumed supply wagon, he guessed.

Gareth pulled out his eagle insignia and pressed it against the smaller door, unlocking it with a satisfying click. *Thank the gods.* It opened, revealing a debris-filled alleyway. He was getting used to the mounds of rubble in this area of the city, so it came as no surprise to him. Peering about carefully for spirits or troll-sized foes, they passed into the alley silently, taking care to shut the door behind them.

Gareth attempted some of his best sneaking, following Kara around and over stone blocks, shale and bits of ceramic roof tiles toward the end of the alley. This led them back to the main road—the same one that had originally taken the pair to the guildhall.

Gareth could make out a few spirits on their right, flitting about where the path branched off from the road toward the main entrance of the guildhall. Presumably, more spirits and the troll were further down the path, where he couldn't see them.

He took a step toward the main road, aiming to turn hard left away from the cluster of their pursuers when Kara waved him back into the alley.

She held up a finger. "*Ssh.* Listen." She cocked her pointed ear and leaned toward the end of the alley.

He squinted, trying his best to hear what she might be reacting to, but his ears were not natural sound funnels, like hers.

There was complete silence. Nothing at all to be heard. The battering on the door had stopped.

Then, a great voice boomed out. Almost certainly Caesar's.

"What is the meaning of this? Have you so forgotten your oaths that you seek to destroy the very place that you swore to protect?"

Gareth leaned in, straining to hear the reply. Its low hiss went well with the creepy ghost it belonged to. "*Give them to usssss. We know they are in there.*"

"I am the only one in here, you deluded creature. It's been too long. Your ghostly brains have turned to ectoplasm. "

"Give them to ussss, or the troll will shatter the door."

"How could you use this poor creature in such a way? Leave him be. *None* of this does any credit to you."

"Give them—"

"There is no one here!" Caesar yelled. The ensuing conversation devolved into mumbles that Gareth couldn't make out, followed by another outburst from Caesar. "Fine, if you don't believe me, come in and look around for yourself. Then you must leave, having dishonored yourself again."

When Gareth finally turned his attention back to his companion, Kara had vanished. Hopefully she'd gone to scout the area ahead and wasn't abandoning him.

Luckily, she soon reappeared beside him. "They're all heading into the guildhall, so now's our chance to scram." She exited the alley and trotted down the road in the opposite direction of the guildhall.

Gareth was just starting after her when he caught a glimmer out of the corner of his eye. He quickly jerked his head around but didn't see anybody or anything. He switched directions to investigate. The glimmer ended up being some plants growing amongst the rubble outside the guildhall. They'd been highlighted by his UI for some reason.

He leaned forward to examine them more closely, when a message popped up:

•Legionnaires' Flower: the stalks of this plant can be used to increase the duration of potions that are of medium difficulty or lower.

Holy crap! He pulled out his skinning knife and used it to gather up the glowing plant stalks and put them into the bag Mabel had given him. As soon as he finished, he took off after Kara. She stood, impatiently waiting for him further down the road.

"What the *hell?*" she hissed. "Do you want to get caught?"

"No, of course not. I saw something glowing and stopped to investigate." Gareth said, while looking back over his shoulder for any pursuing ghosts.

"*Well?*" Kara asked, starting down the roadway again.

Gareth matched her pace. "Just some plants. Something I could use for Mabel's quest."

"Didn't know you had a gathering skill?" Kara threw him some serious side-eye.

Gareth remembered once again Clippy's warning about keeping his talent secret. That probably meant from Kara, too. "Ahh...I must have gotten a skill when I read that book. I didn't notice anything. Not until I spotted the glowy plants, anyway."

Kara appeared dubious but didn't pursue the question any further.

Once they felt they were far enough away from the ghosts to feel comfortable, they let loose and picked up the pace, heading directly back to Mabel's shop.

With relief, he blew out a long breath once he clapped eyes on the shop's sign. It felt like days, instead of a few hours, since he'd been there. He looked around, but didn't see any sign of their two friends from earlier. They must have gotten tired of waiting and wandered off. Hopefully, they weren't just lying in wait to jump them somewhere else.

That one had been close. He still hadn't gotten a good look at the troll but judging from the amount of force it had been able to exert on the solid stone door, he honestly didn't want to.

He'd had his fill of the Ruins for now—including picking up a whole new involved quest chain. Time to move things along.

Chapter
Twenty-Four
SPLAT!

WITH NO SMALL AMOUNT OF RELIEF, GARETH AND Kara entered Mabel's shop to find her dealing with a gnome who needed help with "a private issue requiring the utmost discretion." Kara and Gareth puttered around trying to at least look like they weren't listening in. Finally, his business concluded, the gnome left, whistling a jaunty tune.

With the gnome gone, Gareth and Kara approached the counter. Mabel was fussing about with her array of items, apparently reorganizing and cleaning whatever she'd used for the gnome's complaints.

"Seems like yet another satisfied customer there," Gareth said and winced the moment Mabel gave him the side-eye.

"I don't discuss my customers' issues with others. I'm sure you'll agree that is the wisest course." Her rag stilled on the counter as she looked from one of them to the other quite pointedly. Then it began moving again with Gareth sufficiently quieted. "Still, I don't think I'm violating any confidences by pointing out that a 3-foot tall gnome has an—ah—*unique* set of issues when his girlfriend is a 7-foot tall half-giant berserker. Or that *I'm* the only one in the city with the skill to help him."

Kara hopped onto a stool, allowing her to see at counter height. Her eyes were lit with salacious curiosity. "*Really?* Did you…?" She put her hands up and spread them apart. "Or instead…?" She moved her hands closer together.

Gareth snorted his disdain at Kara. "She said she couldn't discuss it."

Kara turned a glare at him in response. "Look, I'm not just asking for gossip's sake. I don't know if you noticed, but this town is mostly filled with 'larger sized' people. If Mabel has figured out how to make relationships more, um, *compatible* …. Well, it could make *my* dating pool larger."

Mabel stared at Kara for a minute, then barked out a quick, "See me about that later." Then she reached under the counter and pulled out a clear glass vial containing a glowing purple potion. "As promised."

"That's the shrink potion?" Gareth reached out to grab it, but Kara smacked his hand away.

"*I'm* the one who's using it, so I'll take that, *thank you very much.*" Kara quickly made the potion disappear, stashing it somewhere in her armor. "Now all we have to do is get ourselves into that guildhall."

Mabel snorted abruptly. "I shouldn't be hearing any of this. *Go.* Come back later if you need more help with potions—or things that *won't* get me in trouble with other paying customers."

"Sorry, Mabel." Kara hopped off the stool.

Gareth spied something interesting further down the counter. "Kara, wait a second." Pointing at a package of wrapped up potions, "Hey Mabel, what's this?"

Mabel looked over, "Oh *that*. I just finished making some *Dungeoneers specials*. A package deal containing two *healing* potions, a *grease* potion, and a potion of *night vision* . Only ten crowns."

"Nine crowns for us, right?" Gareth waggled his brows.

Mabel grumbled under her breath, "Yes, only nine crowns for you."

"Great. I'll take one." Gareth grabbed the wrapped package and put 9 crowns on the counter. He noticed the upkeep counter in the corner of his UI spin down a little as he did so. That wasn't getting old *at all*. "Oh, and I found some plants for you." Gareth put Mabel's bag on the counter.

"Already? That was fast." Mabel walked over and picked up the bag, dumping the contents onto the counter.

"Legionnaires' Flower! That's a rare plant. Wherever did you find that?" Mabel looked at Gareth, eyes alight with interest.

"In the ruins, outside the old human guildhall." Gareth shrugged, trying to downplay what he'd done. He should have found something common to bring her, probably. He'd tried to look up Legionnaires' Flower on the walk over, but the book he'd read only listed common ingredients, and the stalks he'd harvested weren't among them. That should have been a clue.

"Well, you butchered them while harvesting them. What did you use, a *sword*? Still, this will cover your debt and then some." Mabel quickly pulled out a sharp looking knife and carefully cut the ends off the stalks, putting them away in a jar she pulled out from under the counter. "Come back later, and I'll settle up. I don't have enough gold on me right now. The quest I give out is only really supposed to bring in common stuff. It wasn't intended to net anything like *this*. Not that I'm complaining."

"How about some better harvesting tools and a book that lists advanced ingredients in exchange? I can use that more than gold anyway." At Mabel's quirked eyebrow, he continued, "I got lucky finding this stuff. I'd like to be ready, just in case I get lucky again."

"Sure, why not?" Mabel shrugged, then moved deeper into the store and returned with a small satchel and another book. "The satchel has everything you need to harvest ingredients without butchering them. The book lists many of the more uncommon ingredients."

"Thanks" Gareth scooped up the satchel and book. As soon as he touched the book, a familiar prompt appeared:

***Do you wish to read this book (Y/N)?**

He quickly pressed *yes* and marveled as information flowed into his mind again. Soon, he had acquired a greater knowledge of alchemy ingredients, which should help him with his Alchemy skill going forward. He still thought Clippy was exaggerating about how powerful his Natural Alchemist talent was, but at least it was starting to look useful.

Kara gave him an inquisitive look. Gareth just shrugged as they walked out. "Mabel's good people. I'm going to keep an eye out for more stuff I can gather for her."

"You know, that stuff isn't easy to find *or* to harvest." Kara remarked pointedly.

Gareth shrugged. "I don't understand how this game works— as you're well aware."

Appearing to get the message that this was all the answer she'd get, Kara let the subject drop. For now, at least.

Once outside, they ensured that they were the only souls on the ruined street before continuing the conversation about the impending robbery. Kara peered up at her newbie companion. "Like I was saying, now we need to get you an invitation to that guildhall."

"Do you have any idea where they hang out? They won't be near the training area, since they're banned right now. I'd rather not go bang on the door of their guildhall asking to be let in."

Kara nodded emphatically. "You definitely need an invitation. Not to mention—we only have this one potion. We can't afford to expend it only for them to tell you to come back tomorrow."

Gareth scratched his jaw thoughtfully. "Right. I hadn't thought of that."

They walked along in a silence only punctuated by Kara's frustrated sighs. She ground to a halt just before leaving the Ruins for a more populated part of the city. With her hands on her hips, she regarded Gareth soberly. "Well, I've got nothing. I spend too much of my time avoiding those a-holes, not actually trying to meet them."

"Hmm. Okay, so where would you *not* go if you were avoiding them?"

Her arched brow shot up. "They like douchey high-rent places. You know, where you spend tons of crowns on frothy blue drinks called *Mermaid's Piss* or *Dryad Nectar*. But there are tons of them, and we don't have the kind of crowns to go on a pub crawl looking for Thepeiros. *If* they'd even let us in. We're a bit scruffier than their normal clientele."

Gareth looked around for a moment while he thought—partially to make sure no ghosts were sneaking up on them. It was unlikely they'd wander far from the old guildhall, but why take chances?

"Back home there was a new *It place* every month. It can't be that different here. What's the newest pub? *That'll* be the place to start."

"That would be The Harpy's Nest. It opened about a week ago. Word on the street is that they only serve avian-derived drinks."

"*Avian* -derived? I don't even want to know. That should be the place to start, though."

"We can't. The place is invitation-only, so we'll never get in."

Gareth cocked his head toward Kara. "We don't *have* to get in. What we do is just hang around outside like we're waiting for someone until our guy comes by."

Kara scowled. "That plan sucks."

He shrugged. "Do you have a better one?" She grudgingly shook her head. "Well, then, let's go. Where is it?"

"Follow me." She entered the main road, and he followed closely up a steep hill that wound its way up to a lookout point. From here, the way that the hill curved, you could look over most of the town, even the distant grayed-out areas of the Ruins. Kara pointed off to the eastern side of the city. "Over there."

"*What?* Where?" Gareth squinted. "How am I supposed to pick out a club from the rest of the town from up here?" Kara said nothing but continued to hold her arm out, pointing. Gareth looked again. "The only thing over there that sticks out is the tower with the huge birds flying around it—*ohhhh.*" Gareth frowned and chewed at his lip. "Those aren't birds, are they?"

"They're harpies."

"They can't be *real* harpies. They'd attack all the nearby people."

"Well, I don't know if they're real or not. But their *shit* definitely is."

"Their shit?"

"They fly around the tower and dump on anyone they find unworthy."

Gareth wrinkled his nose in disgust. "That's just wrong. And the city allows that?"

"The town's *betters* aren't the targets. Hell, they think it's the funniest thing ever—great spectacle. There's a balcony where people can sit and watch. They even take bets on who's going to get hit next."

Gareth set his jaw and nodded back toward the tower. "That's definitely our place. I guess we'll need a harpy-proof spot so we can watch the entrance in peace."

"Ya *think?*" Blowing out a breath, Kara started down the winding avenue toward the tower. Huffing a deep sigh, Gareth followed.

***

Splat!

"Well, *this* sucks." A short time later, they'd found a table at a simple cafe across the road from The Harpy's Nest. The cafe owners had—wisely—strung up a series of tarps that *mostly* kept the harpy scat off the patrons. They'd then added small covers on the tables as a second line of defense against debris getting into the food or drinks.

But after several hours, the constant rain of splattering crap slapping the coverings above really started to wear on their nerves.

"He's not going to show." Kara was on her fourth drink, and it wasn't helping her mood.

Gareth fiddled with his own glass and jutted out his jaw. "He'll show. He's been banned from the training grounds, so he's got nothing better to do."

Whoom!

He looked up just in time to glimpse a ball of fire expanding from the spot where a harpy had been hovering moments before.

"*Filthy cur!* You'll pay for this." Nearby, a group of well-dressed toughs confronted a cowering creature. "Some of your dung got on my shoes."

Gareth craned his neck for a better look. "I know that voice. It's my 'friend' from Mage's Fury—Meldurath. But why's he yelling at that little guy? He's only, like, two-feet tall."

Without looking up from her drink, Kara shrugged. "He must've walked too close to that group, and when he got bombed, some of it splattered onto your mage."

"But that's hardly the little guy's fault. Meldurath should blame the damned harpy."

Kara rolled her eyes and looked away. "Have you met the wealthy here, yet? If you're poor, or even just less well-off, everything's automatically your fault. Being poor is proof of that. Besides, the little guy is a gremlin."

Gareth's brows knit. "So?"

"They're only a small step above goblins. They literally do all the shit jobs in the city. This guy is probably supposed to run around and pick up the harpy crap on the ground. He's probably used to abuse."

Meldurath pulled back his hand and slapped the cowering figure, knocking him into the dirt.

Gareth bristled. "Screw *this!* I'm not gonna sit here while some douchebag beats up Dobby." He pushed out his chair and stood.

Kara glanced up at him, trying to wave him back into his seat. "Gareth, remember why we're here. Let's not pick any fights we'll regret later."

"You can stay here, if you want. But I can't just sit by and watch this."

Gareth left the table and approached the site of the fracas, just out of the path of the literal shit-storm at the edge of the street.

He pushed aside his disappointment in Kara's attitude, but she didn't owe him anything. To each their own. And to that end, Gareth wasn't going to let these assholes get away with random abuse of someone much smaller than they were.

Nope. Setting his shoulders, he placed his hands on his hips and murmured a silent prayer to the Powers That Be—or possibly just the great Clippy in the sky—that this wasn't the hill he was going to die on.

Chapter
Twenty-Five
Death Penalty?

MELDURATH STOOD INDIGNANTLY BEFORE THE cowering figure, looking much the same as he had yesterday, when he'd shot Gareth with a spell in response to Gareth's rejection of his guild invitation. The skinny punk still wore rumpled black robes and knee-high black boots. Now that his hood was pushed back, Gareth could get a closer look at him.

Gareth had seen a few other fellow players of similar race characteristics—a sickly greenish-yellow cast to the skin, and colorless hair and eyes almost the exact same shade of gray. The eyes had no whites, and they bulged out. He looked a little bit like a Sleestak from the old *Land of the Lost* TV show, minus the lizard skin, three-pronged hands and bony spine.

And right now, this idiot was getting ready to put a hardened boot to the small figure on the ground in front of him. Gareth caught the boot in his hands just as it was swinging to sink into the gremlin. Gareth yanked the boot upward, dropping Meldurath flat on his back onto the street, *and* right into a pile of sticky harpy dung.

Meldurath lay stunned, appearing breathless for a few long moments until he turned his focus on Gareth. Then his gaze narrowed on the newest target of his animosity. "Well, well, *well.* If it isn't the human."

Gareth raised his eyebrows, not sure whether to be impressed by the magician's memory or his own ability to make a lasting impression. Gareth ignored Meldurath's sputtering rage to turn and offer a hand to the gremlin who, until then, had remained in a cowering ball in the street.

Gareth helped the gremlin up, then gave him a light push. "Run along, little guy." The gremlin gave Gareth a speculative look, then looked at the irate mage behind him. The small creature then made tracks for the shadows.

Gareth turned back to the mage, who'd been helped to his feet by two of his companions. A third tried his best to brush the dung off Meldurath's back.

Gareth squared his shoulders and waited for the inevitable explosion of rage, possibly a rant or threats. Perhaps he should take stock of his abilities and items beforehand? It occurred to him, then, that he had no idea what level this guy even was. Maybe he'd be joining one of the piles of refuse on the street soon. Oh well...in for a nickel, in for a dollar, as his grandpa always used to say.

Once he was back on his feet, Meldurath shoved his friends aside, pushing forward to get right in Gareth's face. He pointed a long bony finger at him. "I'm going to enjoy this, human."

Gareth quickly tried to inspect the mage, berating himself for not having done it in the time he'd bought for the gremlin to run away. The problem was that most of the information in his inspection was grayed out due to his low skill level.

All he got was:

Name: Meldurath Boltflinger

Level: 47 (reduced to 10 within city limits)

Guild: Mage's Fury.

Class: Loghtning Mage

Loghtning mage? WTF was a Loghtning mage? Was that a typo for *lightning*?

Well, regardless of what that meant, it didn't take a genius to see that he was seriously outclassed. Another one of grandpa's sayings came to mind—*he who fights and runs away lives to fight another day.*

And since this cretin was making some gestures with his spindly hands that looked a lot like he was cracking his knuckles, it was definitely time to go.

But as he turned, he caught in his peripheral vision, a jerky movement. Meldurath was throwing up his arms while spitting out a harsh-sounding word in a language that Gareth didn't recognize. Considering everything was auto-translated into a common language, Gareth should have understood. So it couldn't have been a language—not the normal kind, anyway.

Instantly, a wall of energy shot up out of the ground, encircling all five of them—Gareth, Meldurath and his three best buds. Well, shit. There's no way anything in this game could be as easy as running away, could it?

"Now, *now,* human. We just got together again. You can't leave yet. And there's no Minotaur babysitter to protect you this time."

Gareth looked around with the vain hope that there might be someone from the city guard nearby. Instead, he mostly just saw the backs of everyone quickly vacating the premises. They were the smart ones. And they'd definitely be living to fight another day.

Gareth frowned. He had yet to see anything resembling city guardsmen and he remembered Kara saying something about there not being any. The city had to have a city guard, right? Every game he'd ever played had guardsmen patrolling the city.

In yet another way this game was different than his previous experiences, clearly.

With no clear hope of receiving aid, he turned back to face the mage. Meldurath's three groupies appeared to be in the process of making wagers amongst themselves. Gareth squared his shoulders, certain they weren't betting on him. More likely, the wager was on how long he'd last against their idol.

To top off the pile of shit he now was in, Gareth had left his shield leaning against the cafe table. Maybe he could get Kara to toss it to him? But she'd vanished. Unsurprising, really. Blending in when the going got tough seemed to be her specialty.

Gareth raced through the possibilities of fighting without his shield. He'd probably need to go max DPS against the guy anyway, so he unsheathed his longsword and approached the slightly-built mage who stood smirking, waiting patiently while Gareth readied himself.

Casters normally didn't have a great deal of health. Meldurath was level 47, and, under normal circumstances, such a fight would be way out of Gareth's league. But within the city limits, the mage's level was reduced to 10. So, Gareth at least had a fighting chance—literally. A couple of good hits should take the mage down, provided he could land them. Meldurath had magic to his advantage, but Gareth had a big-ass sword. *And,* thanks to the force wall, a small distance between them. Meldurath was well within melee range.

He swung his weapon and hit the caster as hard as he could.

Wang!

The blow jolted up Gareth's arm. It was like he'd slammed his sword against a concrete wall. The feedback was too much, and he couldn't keep his grip. The sword dropped to the ground. Gareth looked up in shock, and the smug bastard grinned back at him.

And to Gareth's astonishment, Meldurath then gestured to the sword, as if indicating to Gareth that the mage would wait while he retrieved it.

With no better plan in place, Gareth bent and did exactly that. This time, however, he was more cautious in his approach. The follow-up swing was just as fruitless, though at least Gareth managed to retain his longsword this time.

Wang! Wang, wang...wang!

Still nothing. Panting from his exertion, Gareth checked his stamina bar, which had dropped by about a third. Wielding the two-handed weapon took a lot more stamina than attacking with his broadsword.

Gareth stepped back, taking a deep breath. It might help to rest a moment while he figured out what to do.

Meldurath hesitated, then, seeing that Gareth wasn't going to waste any more energy, he twirled a finger with a flourish and pointed it at himself. "Protection from normal weapons." He shook his head pitiably. "If only you had an *enchanted* weapon..." The mage rolled his eyes and shrugged. "Still, it wouldn't make a difference really. You wouldn't happen to be wearing enchanted armor, would you? *Pity.* I'm afraid this will hurt."

Meldurath gestured toward Gareth and uttered another command word. An eye-searing bolt of lightning sizzled from his hand, hitting Gareth square in the chest with a force that threw him upward and back. He slammed into the force wall, then slid to the ground like a sack of flour.

Gareth searched the UI to check the stat overlay and saw that his health bar had dropped by half. A number of other notifications had popped up:

•**Significant Lightning damage.**

•**Blunt force damage.**

•**Minor Fall damage.**

With a sweeping thought, he dismissed the notifications and stood. He was going to have to figure out how to suppress them so they didn't pop up and block his vision during the heat of a fight.

The next thing he did was use some healing spells on himself, returning his health bar to max level.

Meldurath patiently waited for him once again, smug expression still intact. Gareth's healing did prompt a response, though not the one he'd have hoped for.

The mage *laughed.*

"Oh, this is perfect. I forgot you were a *cleric.* I thought I'd have to use potions to keep this going, but I only had a couple on me. This is so much better." He actually clapped his hands at the thought of being able to shoot Gareth over and over—even beyond the limits of his normal hit point count.

Gareth's gaze flicked to a prone figure lying on the ground behind his attacker. One of Meldurath's henchmen now sprawled on the ground, leaking blood from a large gash in his leg. Given that the blood flow had slowed to a trickle, Gareth guessed he was in the middle of respawning right now. Gareth's sneaky, diminutive friend had followed him into the fight.

Gareth turned his attention back to Meldurath—mostly because he didn't want the mage to clue in that Gareth wasn't in this alone. Maybe Gareth was just a noisy distraction from the actual fight—the one that involved Kara and her very nasty black sword. If that was the case, he'd have to see what he could do to give Kara a shot at Henchman #2. She'd started at the back of the group, but if Gareth couldn't keep their attention focused on him, they were bound to notice the loss of their numbers by one, which would ruin her next surprise attack. Still, it would be nice if he could figure out a way to do some damage of his own.

Meldurath stomped his foot. "Come, come. If you're going to be boring, I'll just end this now. Come swipe at me again. I'll use something different this time for my *reply.*"

The sadistic fuck was channeling his inner Trelane now. There had to be some way to wipe—or *beat*—that smirk off the obnoxious bastard's face. So, he was protected from normal weapons, but what about magic-imbued weapons? Gareth stepped up toward the mage and fired off a Smite spell while in mid-swing. A brilliant white light illuminated his sword from hilt to point, imbuing the weapon with temporary magic.

Gareth's sword struck. This time, when it bounced off, there was a bright flash. Meldurath was thrown back, and a big scorch mark zagged across his jacket, marking where he'd been hit.

•Critical Hit

•Damage increased vs. Evil

Take that, ya bug-eyed fucker. Henchman #3 ran over to help the mage to his feet. With a quick glance, Gareth noted that Henchman #2 had joined #1 on the ground, quietly bleeding out. Perhaps due to his antics as a distraction, the other two hadn't noticed yet, but it was only a matter of time. Kara must have some kind of awesome sneak attack.

Meldurath returned to his feet throwing a glare at Gareth. "Cheater! Martial weapons and magic don't mix. You'll be paying for that." This time, Meldurath's hands flew through the air as he gestured at Gareth, a veritable flood of words gushing out. A giant ball of lightning crackled in the air just in front of the mage, then flew forward. Gareth threw himself aside, trying to avoid it, but it was too fast. It struck the ground in front of him, exploding and tossing him through the air.

Gareth blacked out and had no idea how much time had passed when he came to. He blinked, trying to regain his bearings. He was once again slumped up against the force wall. In the corner of his UI, the health bar was blinking frantically.

He laid his palm on his chest, trying to heal himself, but got a message that read:

•Unable to cast while under a stun affect.

•Stun will wear off in 10 seconds.

Ten seconds was about eight seconds too long, given the way Meldurath was stomping across the enclosure toward him. Gareth struggled to get to his feet, but the stun effect prevented movement as well.

Well fuck, here it was, then…

But *no.* As Gareth watched, helpless and motionless, a flicker of movement behind the mage caught his eye. This time, he was able to see Kara's form glimmer into visibility right behind Henchman #3.

But this one was more skilled—or maybe luckier. The henchman started to turn, throwing Kara's aim off. Still, all it gained him was the ability to scream right before a glowing black short sword entered his side, dropping him to the ground instantly. Gareth squinted—how could something *glow* while also being *black?* Because that weapon sure as hell had. Goosebumps prickled the back of his neck.

Meldurath halted, hearing the scream, and turned to look behind him. Then he paused, likely realizing for the first time that all his men were down.

"*What?*" He searched the enclosure frantically for the assailant, but Kara had already gone back into hiding. Then he muttered another quick spell. A wave of energy shot out, blanketing the area but, as far as Gareth could tell, didn't do anything. Meldurath clearly thought something should have happened, because he repeated the spell once again—and then again.

After the third time, he spun toward Gareth and yelled, "*How?* No one here should be high enough level to stay hidden through my invisibility purge spell. The zone cap would prevent it. How are they avoiding the cap?"

The duration of Meldurath's distraction had run down the stun timer for Gareth and he was finally able to stagger to his feet. The tiny sliver of health in his blinking bar was small enough that at this point, he might die if he so much as tripped. In response to the furious mage's question, Gareth just shrugged, while dropping a quick heal on himself. "I just got here, dude. Newbie, remember? I don't even know what a zone cap is."

Gareth then waved at the dead bodies behind the angry mage. "I sure as hell didn't do *that*. How sure are you that someone isn't making the most of your distraction so they can take you out?"

Internally, Gareth patted himself on the back for the insertion of that doubt as he watched the mage process what he'd said. Bluff and misdirection, for the win.

Meldurath stopped about ten feet away, keeping himself well out of sword range. His jaw tensed and then relaxed, eyes narrowing. "I hadn't considered that. Perhaps you're right." He quickly glanced around behind him. "I'm afraid I'm going to have to cut our playtime short, so I can deal with whoever this is."

Uh oh ... the mage was starting a new spell. Gareth frantically tried to cast another heal spell before whatever-it-was hit him to finish him off. Simultaneously, he wondered what had happened to Kara. She wasn't going to be able to help him with this new development. Meldurath's equipment was probably too good for her to execute her sneak attack, anyway. Hopefully she'd be able to get away once Meldurath had wiped the floor with Gareth.

He braced himself as Meldurath's hands glowed with a new spell. Gareth felt his own heal spell surge through him but doubted it would make any difference. The upshot was that Gareth was about to gain some firsthand knowledge of the death penalty.

CHAPTER
TWENTY-SIX
A HEIST

BEFORE MELDURATH COULD FINISH CASTING HIS SPELL TO attack Gareth, a silver light rained over the evil mage, bathing him in its light and freezing him in place. Then, a voice boomed out a single word and the force wall penning them in was reduced to nothing. Gareth glanced quickly around him, spotting Thepeiros, the recruiter for The Elite guild. He'd also been part of that posse of four that had confronted Gareth in the training area. Thepeiros was accompanied by two others, and they were all approaching the street where Gareth and Meldurath were battling.

Gareth used the last of his mana to heal himself, bringing his health up to around 30% and ending the furious blinking of his health bar. Maybe he'd avoid the death cycle yet.

When the trio reached them, Thepeiros faced Meldurath with hands on his hips. "Take these next couple of minutes while the spell wears off to think over just how you are going to explain yourself and your attack on a player *we* are currently recruiting. And it had better be a good excuse." Then he eyed the battlefield as he turned to Gareth. He nodded, seemingly approving.

"Meldurath was just about to kill you. Yet you managed to take out those three first. Very impressive. You *definitely* belong with us."

Gareth, exhausted from the fight, was bent over gasping, his hands on his knees. The two-handed sword did a lot of damage, but it was murder on his stamina. He'd have to learn to pace himself or better yet, do something to increase his stamina. This was why clerics generally stuck with light weapons, he supposed. Hopefully getting some levels in the warrior class would fix his stamina problem.

Once Gareth caught his breath, he straightened and sheathed his sword. Looking up, he nodded. "Thanks for the help. Much appreciated. A few seconds more and he would have had me."

Thepeiros practically preened. "The Elite look after their own. That's something you should consider before making a decision you might regret."

Thepeiros moved up to Gareth and affably put a hand on his shoulder. Slowly, he aimed them both toward the entrance for The Harpy's Nest. "*We* respect strength. And judging by what you did to Meldurath's cronies, you have that." Thepeiros flicked a glance in the direction of the mage, who was being reluctantly led away by some guild mates. "Still, if you don't mind me asking, what was this all about? Now don't get me wrong, we don't hesitate to take on the lesser guilds when needed, but most unaligned folk would hesitate before making an enemy of any powerful guild."

Gareth eyed Thepeiros, not fooled by the sudden burst of camaraderie. Nor did he miss the steel beneath the velvety soft warning about making enemies. Still, he had Thepeiros to thank for even being here. Gareth wondered how much easier it would make his life if he just gave in and joined the guild. He'd never cared for the power guilds when playing Dragon Epoch because they'd always seemed to attract a certain brand of arrogant asshole. His wife's guild had been a shining example. Or maybe Gareth just wasn't a team player.

Gareth started his bluster with a deep breath. This was going to take some quality ass-kissing to accomplish. "I was waiting around over there, hoping to bump into you. This jerk-wad showed up and started abusing some poor little gremlin. I didn't care for it, so I tried to intervene. Things went downhill from there."

Thepeiros frowned, staring at Gareth. "You challenged a member of the second-ranked guild in town on behalf of a *gremlin*? How very…unique. You'll definitely need to curb the tendency to interfere if you want to survive here. Still, you did well." He stopped and turned to Gareth as if to ensure he had Gareth's full attention. "May I ask why you were looking for me?"

Gareth bit his lip, then proceeded. "I've been thinking over your offer from the training grounds. Maybe I was too hasty in turning you down." He looked down and tried to slump his shoulders, as if appearing penitent. "I figured I should at least gather more info and ask to see your guildhall before I make my decision."

Thepeiros paused as if taking all this in. "Most people require no more than a guild invite to join. The honor of being asked is sufficient in and of itself. After all, once an invite is turned down, it may never be offered again." His eyes then flicked again to where the bodies of the three slain mages lay in the street. "Still, since you're new here, a bit of caution on your part is not unwarranted, I suppose. I warn you, though. *If* we make you a second offer, there will *not* be a third." Thepeiros snapped his fingers. "Timsom, Brownear, come! We're heading back to the guildhall."

Gareth stiffened, startled. "*What?* Now? Aren't you headed to the club? Couldn't we just schedule something for…tomorrow, maybe?" Gareth swept his eyes around surreptitiously to see if he could spot his vanished companion. He hadn't seen Kara since the middle of the battle. But his plan to infiltrate the Elite's guildhall and steal back the axe wouldn't work without her. He had to push back at Thepeiros and this sudden urgency to go do this now.

"Our leader, Lord Slaughter, has had me running around all day looking for you. I'd finally given up and gone to get a drink and then here you were. Another thing you'll find about us: we value obedience as well as power. You need one to successfully use the other."

Sounded like a full-blown cult to Gareth. Damn, this conversation was going to leave him with teeth marks all over his tongue from biting it. Instead, he faked a grin. "*Great.* I'm looking forward to meeting your leader and seeing your guildhall. I need to grab my bag, though." Gareth pointed toward the table where he'd been sitting with Kara before the whole fracas had started.

"Fine, fine." Thepeiros waved his hand dismissively. "But *hurry.*"

Gareth's walk was measured as he made his way over to the table, with eyes darting around to find evidence of Kara's whereabouts. She had to be nearby, didn't she? There wasn't much he could do to search for her now, with Thepeiros and his goons watching him closely.

However, once he'd hit the table, he was far enough out of their earshot to hiss out a quick, "*Kara!*" under his breath while he fiddled at the buckles on his backpack.

After the third time he called out to her, he'd almost given up before feeling a distinct nudge against his shin. "Under here, dummy."

Gareth paused. She was under the table somewhere. He glanced back just as Thepeiros and his guildmates headed in his direction. Gareth opened the top flap of his backpack and pretended to drop it on the ground.

As he bent to fetch it, he muttered quietly. "Shit, we're out of time. Drink the potion and hop in the bag."

"*What?*"

"He wants to take me to the guildhall *now*. Apparently, his guild leader sent people to look for me because he wanted to meet me. Thanks to you, Thepeiros thinks I'm some sort of badass for killing the other mages in the fight. I still don't know how you avoided being seen when Meldurath started looking around for you."

"I hid under a body. Okay so, we don't know exactly how long this potion will last. I was supposed to drink it right before you entered the hall, remember?"

"Yeah. That *was* the plan. Circumstances require a new plan."

"What's the problem, Gareth?" Thepeiros called from about ten feet away.

"*Shit*. they're here. Get in the bag. I'll walk fast."

A glug and a slurp, and a few seconds later, Gareth felt the weight of Kara climbing into his pack. Tying the cover flap down, he left it loose enough to provide her an exit when she needed it. The original plan had seemed genius, but now he felt they were just being dumbasses. This could only end badly. The one thing they had going for them was the arrogance of The Elite themselves. These people could never imagine someone actually attempting to *steal* from them. In his UI, Gareth set a timer to count down for sixty minutes. Mabel had said the potion should last at least that long. *Let's hope she was right.*

Then, he straightened and turned to Thepeiros, who waited imperiously, hands on his hips. Gareth slipped the pack onto his back and collected his shield. "Ah—sorry about that. My bag was open. Had to make sure no one took anything."

The Elite recruiter frowned. "Packs are sacrosanct. It takes a highly skilled thief to even open one that doesn't belong to them." He regarded Gareth with no small amount of suspicion on his features. "Why would someone like that be rooting through your bag?"

Shit. "I didn't know that backpacks are protected like that."

A dark eyebrow climbed Thepeiros' forehead. "Another reason you should join us. You are in desperate need of *education.*" But there was hidden meaning in his words—especially the gleam in his eyes when he said the word *education.* Gareth suppressed a shiver down his spine when thinking about what this creep had in mind for 'educating' the new human.

Against his best instincts, Gareth placed a dumb grin on his face—the good-natured-but-dumb hick was a role he'd had to play many times back home. Hopefully it would work in this situation as well. Then he made a wave as if to say, *I'm following you,* to set them on their way as quickly as possible, the timer countdown in the corner of his UI ever-present, urging him on. "Well, my mom always said, when you have to learn something, learn from the best. Speaking of which, what the fuck is a *Loghtning mage?*"

Much to his relief, Thepeiros started walking, leading them away from the Harpies and their odious tower nest. In response to Gareth's question, he only sighed, glancing at his companions who were in tow with a look that said, *Can you believe this guy?*

"I'm assuming you inspected Meldurath, so I guess you're not a complete idiot. Your log records everything you do, so open it to where you did the inspection. Then, select the class and it will give you an explanation. The information is entered by other players, with the exact information you have available, determined by your class, race, and *guild.*"

Gareth puzzled that out. "What...?" Might as well keep up the dumb-hick appearance, especially now that he was actually feeling the part.

Thepeiros continued, disregarding Gareth's follow-up question. "Given your lack of guild and the *stature*"—he said with a sneer—"of your race, I'm guessing you'll get something like *a magic-using class* . Yet another reason you should join us—our data files are extensive."

Gareth's eyes narrowed. "You can't just tell me? As a small courtesy, a one-off?" What a dick. Nevertheless, Gareth searched his UI, as Thepeiros had instructed.

A popup quickly appeared:

Loghtning mage:

•A form of mage who specializes in the use of fields of force.

•**Their attacks superficially resemble lightning, hence the name.**

•**Be aware that while the spells resemble lightning, lightning-based protections will have no effect.**

•**They are also known for use of force shields to protect both their person and larger areas. Proceed with caution.**

•**Recommended use of magical artillery with piercing modifiers. If that is not available, closing to melee range rapidly combined with enchanted weapons can work, though it is not recommended.**

Octavius Benedictus, scribe.

Hmm, well that was quite a bit more informative than *magic-using class.* at any rate. There appeared to be no end to the arrogance of this Thepeiros character.

Thepeiros gave him yet another haughty look, clearly unaware of the wealth of info that Gareth had just gleaned from his own UI. "Information must be earned." Thepeiros gestured to wave the subject away and then changed it altogether. "I'm interested in learning about your home world. No one has been there for ages. It must be very different from here."

Interesting that he didn't know—or at least wouldn't admit knowing—about the trips to Vegas that resulted in bringing Gareth here. Thepeiros didn't strike him as the sort to make meaningless small talk, so Gareth spent the walk to the guildhall relating trips to the seedier parts of Vegas—all-night blackjack tables, late-night buffets and strip clubs. What was the harm in those tidbits of info? Besides the general sort of harm to the reputation of humanity as a race, of course.

They'd burned through half the time on Gareth's counter before even reaching the hall. Whenever he tried to quicken their pace, Thepeiros would throw him an inquisitive look that made him feel like he was falling under suspicion and thus, forced to slow down to match the easy stroll of his companions.

Once they reached the place in question, Gareth halted beside Thepeiros to take in the building. The hall itself looked like a cross between the Trump Tower and Caesar's Palace on the strip in Vegas—a veritable catalogue of gaudy crap—lights, garish ornamentation and metallic gilding everywhere. Golden lions reared on either side of the door and bright spotlights shot up into the sky. The stonework of the façade was covered in magical glowing symbols while over the door, stick figures re-enacted what he guessed were famous battles in which the guild had participated. Overhead, the words *The Elite* glowed in giant purple letters that blinked on and off continuously. This place would easily be at home in Atlantic City or The Strip.

"Beautiful, isn't it?" Thepeiros beamed.

Gareth half expected a nod and wink to let him in on the joke. But to his growing horror, he could see that Thepeiros was serious as he stared up at the guildhall with a rapturous look, eyes full of wonder.

Gareth tried to muster as politic a response as he could. "It, ah, certainly stands out. No one is going to miss it, that's for sure."

Thepeiro's side-eye look held a little scorn, as if annoyed that Gareth wasn't as equally taken with the architectural monstrosity. "There's no point in hiding who we are. Why would we? We're the best." Then he stepped forward and put his hand on one of the lion statues that wreathed the doorway. "Come here. You must place your hand on the guardian to receive permission to enter."

Ever conscious of that timer ticking down, Gareth complied without hesitation. He wasn't liking this margin. They now had only thirty minutes to carry out what needed to be done before the potion potentially wore off. That was cutting it more than close.

Who walked into a fully armed fortress to carry out a heist without a realized plan? Had he not watched *Ocean's Eleven* dozens of times, including all the sequels? Biggest rookie mistake ever. And yet, he had no choice.

Gareth approached the guardian statue and did as he was told, half expecting it to animate and bite his hand off. Maybe it had a magical way of reading his intent?

He sure as hell hoped not or this heist would be over before it began.

Chapter
Twenty-Seven
Guild Invite

W HEN GARETH PLACED HIS HAND ON THE GIANT golden lion's paw, he realized that he'd been holding his breath, waiting for some kind of doom to rain down, while simultaneously frantic to get inside due to the timer.

His hand was restrained by a powerful magical grasp that crackled with energy.

A deep voice reverberated from within its maned chest. "What is your name?"

Gareth tossed a glance at Thepeiros, who nodded encouragement back at him. "Just answer the questions and you'll be granted an entry pass. Oh and—don't lie. If you lie, the guardian will eat you."

Eat him? Eat? As in devour and digest, Sarlacc-style? Hopefully not over the course of millennia. Great. Subtly, and almost illogically, he tried to move his hand from the paw, but it was stuck to the statue as if superglued. He gulped, eyeing the thing and decided he needed to be *very* careful with his answers.

"Ah… Gareth Fain." So far, so good, anyway.

"What is your quest?"

"*Quest?* I'm here to meet Lord Slaughter and view the guildhall." Was this for real? Every geek worth his salt knew this reference. He just prayed he wasn't going to be asked about the airspeed velocity of an unladen swallow for that third question or he was hosed.

"Do you intend any harm to this guildhall or to the guild that resides within?"

Gareth hesitated. Did returning stolen property to its rightful owner constitute *harm?* Could doing so actually be considered *helping* the guild by acting to restore its reputation? He straightened and squared his shoulders, mustering the internal conviction to answer, "No."

When he tried to lift it away, his hand remained stuck to the lion's paw. Crap. That couldn't be good. Maybe he needed to elaborate on his answer? "I just want to help." After the longest minute of his life, where he considered becoming a human-sized lion-statue snack, the statue finally released him. But he could have sworn that it was throwing him some side-eye while he stepped back and away from it.

Gareth turned back to Thepeiros, who was now eying him from where he stood beside the guildhall door. Thepeiros's brow shot up. "That took unusually long. Hmm... still, it cleared you. Maybe it's a human thing." He shrugged and opened the front door while Gareth followed him into the building. He was mildly relieved to note that they had, thankfully, kept the gaudiness to the exterior.

The interior reminded him of what was always referred to as *The Gentlemen's Club* in those stuffy English period dramas he'd watched with his ex-wife. Lots of dark colors, wood paneling, leather smoking chairs, and thick carpet.

"Nice. So, where are we meeting Lord Slaughter?" he asked while checking the timer countdown. Only a little over twenty minutes remained to get to the dining hall and get the job done.

"At this time of night, he's usually in the bar."

Gareth raised his brows in inquiring. "Is that anywhere near the dining hall?"

"Why?" Thepeiros's brows dropped, eyes narrowing in suspicion.

"Well, I hate to admit this, but my meal was interrupted due to that altercation with Meldurath. I was waiting for my food, but it never arrived due to the fight. I was kind of hoping I could score a snack."

He hesitated and Gareth rattled on.

"Besides, the sound of harpy crap hitting the cafe canopy killed my appetite."

Thepeiros's mouth twisted as he bobbed his head slightly. "I suppose it could have that effect on someone. Luckily for you, the bar and the dining hall share opposite ends of the Great Hall. I'm sure we'll be able to scare up a snack for you."

"*Great.* Let's go."

They crossed the entryway and entered a long hall toward the back of the building. As near as he could tell, this guildhall was ginormous. Other hallways, doors, and stairways branched off regularly. Gareth tried to memorize the path, in case they'd have to make a run for it later.

After long minutes of walking, they entered a huge room— presumably the Great Hall—at approximately the center of the building. The near end was clearly the dining hall, furnished with large wooden trestle tables that stretched the length of the room. Food was served buffet style from heated trays lining one wall. Across the giant room, at the far end, was the bar where Lord Slaughter awaited. From what he could see from here, that end was furnished with deep wooden booths and small tables, providing a more intimate experience.

Gareth hesitated, giving the dining room the once-twice-and-thrice-over. Somewhere in here, Grifor's totem was hung like a trophy, crippling him and preventing him from being able to train new players. With a deep sigh, he reminded himself of the importance of his mission and imagined the look on Grifor's face when he handed him back his battleaxe. *If you got my totem back, I'd owe you a debt that exceeds training you as a warrior...*

Gareth's eyes alighted on a weapon display high on the wall to his right. A huge battle axe forged in the darkest metal hung there, among others. It formed the shape of a giant bat, with one wing holding the haft, the other wing forming the edge of the blade. It was a beautiful weapon, a trophy indeed. But it was Grifor's mojo, and to finish this quest, Gareth was going to have to walk out of here with it—and his life—intact.

Thepeiros, who'd continued walking into the room, turned and gestured for Gareth to follow him. "Your host awaits. You must be anxious to meet him."

Gareth's eyes strayed from the target for a moment to avoid suspicion. "Just taking it all in. It's all quite grand and I haven't seen anything like this yet. You must be *so very* proud of your splendid hall."

Thepeiros looked around the room, his chest visibly puffing up. "You won't find another place like it. It was designed by our guild leader *personally*."

Gareth's brows rose. "Lord Slaughter designed this?"

Thepeiros adopted that instructional stance once more, and Gareth sensed another lecture coming on. "Lord Slaughter is the guild commander in charge of the Muddy River guildhall. However, our guild spans *many* cities, each with its own commander. Our overall guild leader is Lord Crush." His voice hushed almost reverently at the mention of the name. "You should feel fortunate indeed if you ever meet him."

"Well, hopefully I can someday." *So I can kill his ass.* There was a sharp pinch on the back of his neck. A glance at the timer showed that they had barely twenty minutes left. "I'll just, ah, set down my pack over here. I'm looking forward to trying whatever smells so good." He found a spot under the weapon display and dropped his pack, strategically positioning it on its side so that the flap was down. Since the hall was mostly empty, Kara shouldn't have any problem getting out of it undetected.

Gareth rejoined his guide, and they proceeded across the long room toward the bar. A person, presumably Lord Slaughter, held court, sprawled across a large, thronelike chair. He wore a strange type of plate armor, all tinted in reds and black. Branding, no doubt, to match his name. In the low light, it was difficult to make out his features, but he looked vaguely humanoid, like most everyone else in the town. His skin was jade green, but Gareth couldn't make out any unusual protuberances on his skin—nor any extra appendages. As he got closer, however, it was easy to notice that his teeth were sharply pointed, like a shark. When Gareth tried to inspect him, he again received the message that his skill was too low.

All he could find out was:

Lord Slaughter

- **Title: The Flayer**
- **Guild: The Elite**
- **Class:???**
- **Level:???**

Lord Slaughter straightened in his chair as they approached, appearing to have just noticed them. Perhaps he had been casually watching them since they entered, or maybe he was just too deep in his cups to have paid them any mind. Gareth stopped before the throne like chair while Thepeiros moved to stand at Lord Slaughter's side.

"Lord Slaughter, may I present the human Gareth."

The hulking warrior rubbed at his mouth, opening it just barely enough to flash a sinister, jagged-edged smile. "So, *this* is the newbie who thinks himself too good for our guild?" His voice had an odd resonance, probably due to those pointed teeth.

Gareth suppressed a shiver that reverberated down his spine. His flight-or-fight reflex ratcheted up—breath quickening, heart thudding in his throat, perspiration beading on his forehead, and muscles tensing all over his body. If he'd had any doubts before about joining this guild, they were now completely gone. There was no doubt in his mind that he'd end up dead in a week if he did. *Or worse.*

Ignoring this inner terror, Gareth bowed deeply toward the menacing lord. "By no means, your lordship. Rather than 'too good' for your guild, I am *not* good *enough*. Because I'm so new, I felt I needed to find my proper place in the world before joining a guild."

As he was stringing this long list of flattery together, a thump sounded behind him. What was Kara doing? Not being stealthy, that was for sure. But the two in front of him seemed to be too busy basking in Gareth's ass-kissing to notice.

Nevertheless, there was only so far their luck would stretch.

Lord Slaughter leaned forward, frowning directly at Gareth. "That is for *us* to decide, not *you*. It is good that you know your place, though. That will make life simpler."

For who? Gareth wondered darkly.

"Gareth wanted to look over our guildhall before deciding to join," Thepeiros interjected.

Those bushy brows then climbed his forehead as he leaned back on his throne. "Did he now? And what do you think, now that you have seen it?"

Gareth blinked, mind racing to summon up more bootlicking, unctuous words. "Ah, it is *most* impressive. Splendid, in point of fact. I haven't seen its like." At least not since the last time he'd driven past a Nevada brothel.

A gruesome smile crisscrossed the leader's face. "So, then you *are* ready to join."

***Lord Slaughter has invited you to join The Elite. Do you wish to join? (Y/N)**

Crap. "Well, ah, I need some—"
Thump.

Slaughter jerked his head around from where he'd been focused on Gareth to peer behind him into the greater part of the hall. "What was *that?* Thepeiros, go see what's going on."

Because it might look suspicious if he didn't—and also because he wanted to know what the hell was happening— Gareth turned and searched the room. To his horror, he spotted the great haft of Grifor's axe lift off the wall like someone was tugging on it. The blade, however, remained firmly attached, as if magnetically held there. The blade abruptly detached and fell, crashing to the floor with a clatter that echoed and reverberated for the longest seconds of his life.

Everyone stopped what they were doing to look. Thepeiros, who was already headed that way, stopped and pulled a small transparent sphere from a pouch at his belt. With a flick of his arm, he threw it toward the fallen axe. It exploded with a retina-burning flash when it hit the floor.

With a sinking in his gut, Gareth watched the disaster unfold. The sphere must have been some sort of invisibility purge, as the flash exposed a one-foot-tall Kara lying on the ground beside the axe. With a loud pop, she was her normal size, as the shrink potion chose this moment to expire.

Behind him, Lord Slaughter shot out of his chair and pointed. "You repay my hospitality by trying to rob me? You'll beg for death before we're through. *Seize them!*"

***Lord Slaughter has canceled his guild invite.**

Chapter
Twenty-Eight
Chaos Ensues

With Lord Slaughter behind him, pronouncing his doom, Gareth watched the chaos in front of him—Thepeiros and a couple thugs who'd just appeared were trying to catch the all-too-quick Kara as she expertly dodged them. With some forethought, Gareth had palmed his vial of the *grease* potion the moment he'd watched the axe fall. He now took the opportunity to throw the vial at Lord Slaughter's feet. The look on Slaughter's face as his feet went out from under him was almost worth the pain he'd no doubt be inflicting on Gareth later. Without further thought, Gareth took off running and tackled Thepeiros, knocking him over, as well.

"Kara, grab the axe!" Gareth dodged Thepeiros's prone form and moved past him. Most of the others in the room were headed toward Lord Slaughter, presumably to help him. Two of them—big bruiser types—moved in to cut off Gareth and Kara's escape through the doorway.

Gareth pushed himself to run faster. As he maneuvered his way down the great hall, a notification popped up, telling him that he'd gained the sprint skill. Good, but not good enough. He could already tell that he wouldn't make the doorway before the bruisers got there.

Gareth unsheathed his broadsword and held his stance. Bruiser #1's eyes narrowed for a split second before a gruesome grin spread across his face. He put his hands together, flexing his knuckles as he moved to take on Gareth's challenge.

Remembering that he'd spotted a carafe sitting on a table earlier, he used the sword to flick it at his opponent's head. It was meant to be a distraction, but apparently the carafe held some sort of hot liquid. The bruiser started to scream and claw at his eyes in reaction to getting a full dose in the face. Meanwhile, Kara had used some kind of tangle web to trip up the second thug, giving them both a momentary opportunity to flee the room.

Kara bolted through the door with Gareth fast on her heels. The huge axe obviously threw off her balance, but she was still far nimbler than Gareth. He only made it the length of a man's height down the hallway before skidding to a stop. "Crap!"

Kara, likewise, stopped and turned back to him. "What is it?"

"I forgot my pack."

She scoffed. "Leave the damn pack."

"Can't." He turned and ran back. Who knew what sort of mischief could be done if these people got their hands on his pack?

Magic worked here. He had no doubt some sort of weird voodoo spells could be performed if they had his personal effects in their possession. He reentered the great room and spotted his pack leaning against a chair ten feet away. Unfortunately, he also spotted Bruiser #1 and Bruiser #2. They'd extricated themselves from their respective predicaments and they looked beyond pissed off. Behind them, Lord Slaughter loomed, his cape transformed into giant bat wings. He was flying over the greased floor in Gareth's direction. Gareth started to doubt the wisdom of his decision to fetch the pack.

Still, as fortune favored the bold—or so he'd heard—he darted toward it, grabbed the pack by its strap and beat as hasty a retreat as he possibly could. Something whirled overhead with a loud hiss and he ducked, barely in time to spy the giant spiderweb flying past where his head and shoulders would have been. He frowned at that. They were obviously shooting to capture him but not kill him. Given the tortures they probably had planned, a quick death and respawn was probably the lesser of two evils.

Kara was still waiting where he'd left her in the hallway. As soon as he got within eyeshot, she took off running again. "How do we get out of here, dumbass?"

"What?"

"I was inside the pack, remember? Which way is out?"

Gack! Which way *was* out?

Scouring his recent memory, he squeezed his eyes shut for a moment, trying to remember. "Uh…It's right, left, straight, then right." He frowned, feeling in his gut that those directions were wrong. Just as she was about to make the first right, it struck him. "*Shit.* No. That's how we came in. Leaving will be left, straight, right, then left."

She spun and glared at him, no doubt to unleash another tongue-lashing. He was spared it due to the appearance of an Elite guild member jumping out from the hall next to them.

The dude shouted out, "I've got them!" Then he attacked Gareth with a nasty-looking curved short sword.

Hot pain sliced through Gareth's side and a quarter of his health bar disappeared. Gareth threw his pack at the attacker's face as a distraction and then swung his own sword. *Miss.*

They then traded a few ineffectual blows before Gareth realized this guy was only here to delay them until the cavalry arrived. "Kara," Gareth shouted. "I could use some help, here."

"Busy!" He glanced her way to confirm that she was occupied with a second person he hadn't seen. This guy towered over her, but she seemed to be getting the best of him, and the grunt had a lot of trouble landing a hit as she darted around.

And then, their friends from the main hall finally caught up with them. Gareth heard the clatter of their advance. Kara and he were about to be surrounded.

They were out of time.

Gareth returned his attention to the foe in front of him. Judging by the grin on his face, he'd also detected the imminent arrival of reinforcements.

With nothing to lose, Gareth lunged at his opponent, taking a hit in exchange for landing his own. He gasped, registering the loss of half his remaining health. That left a meager 25% health remaining, *damn it.* Well, that hadn't lasted long. He really needed to up his health regen somehow. At least his mana bar was full again.

Gareth landed another blow, this time scoring a critical hit in the throat. His opponent stumbled backward, eyes widened and blood pouring from the wound.

When he heard a loud thump, Gareth turned in time to see Kara's opponent drop to the ground, the main artery in his leg severed. She turned to Gareth. "What are you waiting for? Finish him!"

Gareth's opponent was still shaking off the stun from the crit. To Gareth's shock, he dropped his sword, raising his hands in surrender. "Please, I can't afford another death."

Gareth lowered his weapon. Two of Kara's daggers whizzed by Gareth's ear and sank into his opponent's chest, finishing him off. She sprinted over to the corpse and retrieved her weapons while shaking her head. "Never leave an enemy behind. What if he'd had a healing potion, or a spell to use against you? Don't be an idiot, Gareth. Now grab that heavy-ass axe and let's go."

Gareth slung his pack onto his back, sheathed his sword, then took up the axe. He almost dropped it however, because the moment his hand wrapped around the handle, there was a thunderous voice in his head. *"Who are you?"*

"What?" Gareth sputtered, staring at the weapon.

Kara scoffed. "I said pick up the axe, and let's go, already."

Gareth waved her down the hall. "Not you, the axe."

Her eyes bulged. "The axe *spoke* to you?"

"Yes."

"That's—"

She never got a chance to finish her sentence. Several darts hit the walls around them. Their friends, the bruiser brothers, had caught up with them. Kara threw a silver sphere down the hallway, which erupted into a giant mass of thick spiderwebs filling the hall, stopping their approach.

"This bullshit is costing me a ton in pricey one-use items, Gareth," Kara spat. Then she turned to run down the hall.

"I'll pay you back, somehow," he gasped, trying to keep up with her quick, relentless pace. As he ran, he turned his attention back to the axe and tried speaking to it again. "I'm Gareth."

That same deep, resonant voice came back. *"Why are you here?"*

"I'm trying to take you back to your owner." At least Gareth hoped that Grifor was its owner. Otherwise, this might get awkward.

A strange sensation befell him—as if a sort of gaze from the axe. *"You speak the truth. I will go with you. That one— "* Somehow Gareth felt the reference was to Kara, *"—Only seeks to benefit herself. That's why I would not go with her."*

"You're the reason the plan went to crap? We'd be out of here by now if it wasn't for you."

"I see little evidence of a plan, human."

The next little while required too much concentration for Gareth to continue his conversation with the axe. He ducked through doorways, rounded corners, and dodged inanimate objects he hadn't anticipated until they ended up at the exit point. And there it was…one of the stone lions from the front door stood guard against them.

"SURRENDER, HUMAN, OR BE DESTROYED!"

Gareth shook his head against the ringing in his brain. *Damn, that hurt.*

"Crap on a stick!" said Kara.

Gareth stiffened, glancing over his shoulder to see if the mob had caught up with them yet. "Can we take it?"

"It's a stone golem. You need magic weapons to damage it." Kara was sizing up the lion, as if trying to judge her chance of sprinting past it.

"That's bad, right?" A sense of doom sank into his gut. He didn't know what rules existed regarding in-game torture, but he was sure he was about to find out.

She threw up her hands. "Do you have one you haven't told me about? I don't have anything that would do more than annoy it."

"Maybe…" Gareth stared at the axe in his hand. "Can you kill that thing?"

"*You are not worthy to wield me.*"

Of all the…

Harumph. This was definitely a dwarvish axe. Every dwarf he'd ever met in his gaming experience had been a stubborn, often grumpy, pain in the ass. He gave the axe a quick shake. "Did you enjoy hanging uselessly on that wall for years?"

The axe was silent for a moment, then replied a bit sulkily. "*I suppose I could let you wield me, this once.*"

"Great, we're in business." He turned to Kara. "This axe, here—"

"*Kieros.*"

"Kieros will let me wield him and help us kill the golem."

Kara shot him a skeptical look. "Is talking with weapons a human skill?"

"It didn't talk to you?" Gareth swung the axe around a bit, trying to get a feel for the differences in balance between it and his sword. He'd need to go all out against the lion.

"*Should* it have?" Kara withdrew her black sword and got ready to fight.

"I guess not. It said it didn't like you and didn't want to leave with you." With one last practice swing, he psyched himself up to attack.

"Is that why it stuck to the wall? Why that miserable scrap of tin." She shot the axe a heated glare.

"Focus, Kara." Gareth crept toward the golem. But Kara reached out and grabbed hold of his leg. He turned to her. "What?"

Kara let out a long-suffering sigh. "Maybe heal up first?"

"Oh, yeah." He chain-cast his spam heal until he'd reached max health. Hopefully that process would improve once he leveled up and got a better heal spell. His eyes wandered back to the motionless lion guardian statue. "Why's it just been watching us this whole time?"

She shrugged. "Probably has orders specifically to prevent us from leaving. If we don't try to leave, it's content to keep us here."

"Until the idiots get through the webs and can grab us."

Kara nodded.

"Nothing for it, then." He adjusted his grip on the axe and advanced on the golem.

As he approached, he heard a *snick*. Silvery metallic claws sprouted from its paws. Once Gareth was about five feet away, it sprang at him without warning. He was barely able to dodge the attack and get the axe up in time to parry the paw poised to strike.

Gareth jumped back to put some space between them. He tried waving the axe around menacingly.

There was a distinct sigh inside his head. *"You'd better let me control this, human."*

Gareth nodded, not knowing exactly what he was agreeing to but desperate enough to try anything. The presence of the axe flowed down his arms, into his trunk and throughout the rest of his body. He found himself in the passenger seat for the rest of the fight.

His body, which suddenly knew a lot more about axe fighting then he actually did, took a lethal stance and readied to attack. The golem seemed to sense the difference. Where before it had been playing with him, now, it was much more defensive in its movements.

Gareth darted forward. The axe, which before had seemed sluggish, flew around like some fancy new power tool. Feinting an attack to the right, it flew to the left and buried itself into the golem's shoulder, removing a large chunk of stone.

The golem emitted a loud scream, then the silvery claws on its right paw flew out and struck him, taking out the majority of his newly regained health.

"Heal yourself, human."

Since he currently had no control of his own limbs, he tried to imagine healing energy flowing from his mana pool and infusing his body with health.

His first try did nothing despite the depletion of mana as if he had, indeed, cast the spell. That had to mean something was happening, right? He tried the same thing again. This time, his health bar did tick up slightly. Encouraged, he tried a third time, pushing himself to focus completely on the task at hand. This time, he was able to heal himself, though it cost him most of his remaining mana. Healing this way, instead of laying on hands to heal, was cool but decidedly less mana efficient.

Gareth turned his attention back to the battle. The golem had several more large gashes in its surface. The silvery claws were missing from its other paw. The axe must have been able to dodge them this time.

Then the lion reared up tall on its hind legs and pounced, trying to pin him to the floor. Gareth looked on in shock as his body pulled some serious Kung-Fu moves. He slid forward under the rearing golem and struck the back leg as he passed, nearly removing it. The lion came down, stumbling, as the rear leg refused to carry any weight. This seemed to trigger the front door to open, and the lion retreated, dragging itself through the doorway. Seeing this as a concession, Gareth's hope surged. He and Kara wasted no time in following it through to freedom.

"That was amusing, human. I have not had the chance to see battle in a great while. Thank you. However, I exhausted myself in the fight. From here, you must use your own talents."

"That's it for the magic axe." Gareth told Kara. "Let's bugger off."

•Skill Gained Battle Axe (Apprentice 0)

Oh, a new skill. Apprentice 0 sounded like it sucked, though. It was possible it meant that he could increase the skill now, if he worked at it.

Kara nodded and took off toward the right. Gareth followed her without question.

It had gotten quite dicey there. Thanks to the axe cooperating, they hadn't ended up as prisoners of the Elite... or worse.

But worse—as always, he was learning—was yet to come.

CHAPTER
TWENTY-NINE
A NEW ARRIVAL

ROM THE GUILDHALL OF THE ELITE, KARA BEAT A circuitous path through the city, first ducking down an alley, then weaving through a short stretch of a busy street before sidling into another alley. She never slowed her pace, and it took everything Gareth had to keep up with her.

"Hold up," Gareth rasped, stumbling to a stop and leaning heavily on the alley wall. "I need a minute to catch my breath."

Kara somehow managed to hear Gareth's hoarse plea and complied, looking back at him with disgust. "Put some points into stamina, for gods' sake. We've hardly been running at all."

"I don't have any points to allocate yet, thank you very much." He turned his attention to the stamina bar, watching it refill and noticing how his panting eased as it did so. It was amazing how the game translated stats into what felt like real-world effects.

Gareth took a moment to go through the notifications that had popped up during the fight. Most were just spam. "You have taken damage blah blah blah." He'd need to filter those out, somehow, going forward. Otherwise, he stood to miss the more important notices, like gaining a new skill.

"I gained a skill in battle axe when we were fighting just now. Does that happen often?"

"Sometimes, if the fight is significant enough." She peered at him intently with narrowed eyes. No doubt doing her version of inspecting him. "I thought you were fifth level? You get to add attributes every fourth level."

"Yeah. Well, it must not let you allocate more stats points until you allocate your levels. I'm fifth level, but I've only allocated three."

She frowned. "Why would you do that?"

"I want to multi-class—Warrior/Cleric. I'm saving my next two levels for Warrior."

Kara put her face into her hands and shook her head. "You *never* save levels, human." She pulled her face up and looked at him. "First off, the game measures your level as your *absolute* level, not your allocated levels. So, contested skills and abilities will be harder for you. Second, and more importantly, if you die, you'll lose those unallocated levels."

He shook his head at her. "I was told the death penalty was an increase to the pain modifier. They didn't say anything about losing levels."

"They left some things out, then. When you die, everything is reset to your last level-up. You lose all unallocated levels, skill progress to your next skill-up, any progress toward gaining a new ability *and* any experience you've earned in your current level. In short: dying sucks. Didn't you read your startup guide before making your character?"

Gareth frowned. "There was no startup guide."

Kara's brows knit in puzzlement. "There *had* to have been. Every race has their own startup guide and at least one FAQ on how to play, oftentimes more. It's true no matter which race you play."

"I was told that all the information had been lost when my— or rather the *human* —side lost the great war. The race was set to inactive in the game." Gareth's stomach churned. He hadn't learned much so far, but if he couldn't trust the little that he had, his life had just got even suckier.

Kara shook her head. "Nope. You can lose all your racial perks and unlocks, but your knowledge base stays."

"But how would you know? Clippy was quite clear when I was making my character." Gareth grimaced, desperate for assurance that Clippy hadn't screwed him. What could he do, if even the AIs were against him?

"You have *no idea* how much I know." Kara stalked over to him, visibly angry. "Yours isn't the first race that has ever had to restart. Pixies were wiped out and had to start over. I can assure you we kept our knowledge-bases when we did. Whoever this Clippy is, he lied to you."

Gareth put his hands on his hips. "Then how come I can't access any of this knowledge in game now?"

Kara waggled a finger at him. "Now *that* is a very good question. You might consider that for a while, instead of blindly trusting what you've been told."

"*Human!*" The axe spoke up inside his head.

Why did everyone call him that? "What?"

Kara opened her mouth, not doubt on the verge of saying something sarcastic, but Gareth held up his hand to forestall her.

"There are several people approaching from each end of the alley. I recognize them from the guildhall where I was imprisoned."

Gareth looked up at Kara with a grimace. "The axe says we have members of The Elite coming at us from both ends of the alley."

"Well if the *axe* says it..." Kara shook her head and then stopped and looked like she was listening intently. "Huh, the axe is right. There's four—no, *fiv* e of them. Two to the north and three to the south. Your ignorance of the game is about to cost you your two levels."

Gareth couldn't spot any escape. The buildings to either side of the alley were at least three stories tall and made of stone. The few doors nearby were of thick, banded iron that did not lend to being quickly forced open. Certainly not in the time they had. And there were no access ladders at all. Maybe he should just go ahead and put his two levels into cleric? That would be better than losing them, anyway. But...since he'd put all this work into getting the axe, he was almost there. All he had to do was get the axe back to Grifor and the warrior class was his. And worse case...how hard would it be to gain the two levels back? Besides, a level 5 cleric, level 1 warrior seemed like a bad idea. His instinct was to try and keep the levels as equal as possible.

He held the axe out to Kara. "Here, take this and climb up the wall. I'll buy you some time to get away. Take it to Grifor at the Orc Piss Tavern. Hopefully, he'll still want to train me after I regain my levels."

Kara just shook her head. "I'm not leaving you."

Gareth thrust the axe at her again. "Look, I'm not thrilled about this, but I can't climb, not these walls, anyway. We can't let the axe fall back into their hands. Not after everything we went through to get it."

Kara backed away holding her hand up to him. "Look Gareth. I'm no hero, but I don't desert my friends. There's only five of them. Maybe we can take a couple of them out and make a break for it. It's *your* quest. Store the axe in your bag. That way, you'll still have it when you respawn."

"I hadn't thought of that." He dropped his pack off his shoulder and opened it. But when he tried to put the axe in, it was as if it had hit an invisible barrier, preventing it. No matter how he tried, he couldn't get the axe to go in. Finally, he gave up, shrugging. "No good, it won't go in."

Kara's eyes bulged. "Gareth, an item has to be artifact class or higher to be bag-banned. It's supposed to keep them in circulation, or something."

Gareth frowned, looking down at the axe in his hands. "Well, that would explain why it talks."

"It also means they are not going to give up trying to get it back. Not unless something makes them. This is bad. *Very bad.*" Kara looked towards either end of the alley, as if reassessing the threat level.

Gareth blew out a breath. "I'm not giving it back. Maybe they'll give up after we get it back to Grifor."

"*Maybe.*" Kara looked unconvinced in her reply.

He held the axe out again. "So, we're back to you taking off with the axe while I slow them down. It's a good plan."

Kara cocked her head again. "They're almost here."

Gareth closed in on her, still holding out the axe.

Kara backed up and readied her weapons. "Too late. There's something above us now, anyway. I can't climb and fight."

Gareth looked up but couldn't see anything beyond a thin crescent of sky above the alleyway. His attention was quickly dragged back to the ground by a shout to the left.

"There they are." Bruiser #1 and Bruiser #2 entered the alley from one side. They were now wearing mail shirts and were armed with a wicked-looking flail and a barbed mace, respectively. They returned Gareth's shocked reaction with gruesome smiles. He sighed heavily. "This is going to hurt. A *lot.*"

"Well, well, well. It's Gareth." Thepeiros and two more guild members, casters to judge by their equipment, entered from the other side. "Using me to gain entrance to the guildhall so you could steal from us was clever, I'll give you that. But you made me look foolish in front of Lord Slaughter. *That* I can't forgive."

Gareth and Kara stepped back, heads swiveling from one set of attackers to another. They moved to stand back-to-back, so that, between the two of them, they could keep an eye on all five opponents.

Gareth called out to Thepeiros. "I'm just trying to return the axe to its rightful owner. You know it doesn't belong to your guild."

"It belongs to whoever has the power to keep it. Which, right now, is *us.* I'll tell Lord Slaughter that you stole the axe with righteous motives, though. Maybe he'll let you die quicker." He paused and let out an evil laugh worthy of any Bond villain. "Probably not, though. He does have a reputation to maintain."

Gareth gritted his teeth and held out the axe in front of him. "Axe? *Kieros?* Now would be a good time to help again." For an answer, all he received was silence and a vague sense of encouragement.

"Appealing to your stolen axe for aid? How pathetic." Thepeiros looked at his companions. "Take them both."

The caster to the left of him, wearing voluminous aqua-blue robes, gestured in a circular motion and shouted a command word. Instantly, a force wall appeared so that it was surrounding both attackers and prey. The second caster, wearing bejeweled ivory robes, pointed at the two bruisers. Their skin glowed briefly. Once the spell was complete, they attacked.

Gareth readied the axe in both hands, bracing to take on Bruiser #1. Once within range, the bruiser swung his mace with an overhand attack, leaving himself obviously open to a counter-attack but apparently not caring. Gareth took advantage of the oversight and swung.

Bang! The axe bounced off his opponent's skin like he'd struck a wall.

Shit!

As another attack came in, Gareth tried to dive out of the way. Apparently, he was too slow because Bruiser #1 managed to clip him with his mace. The spikes ripped through Gareth's side, and blood splattered onto the stone at their feet. Thank the gods for the low pain setting. Gareth checked his health bar, noting that a large chunk was now gone. Why was he even wearing chain mail?

Staggering back to his feet, he held up the axe again. Out of the corner of his eye, he saw Kara launch a speedy combo attack with her daggers—*clang! clang! clang!* The daggers bounced off Bruiser #2's skin. "What the hell, Kara? They weren't like this before."

Kara never took her eyes off her opponent as she tried for another attack. "That skinny dipshit over there must have put runes on them. He must be an Enchanter. You need to do enough damage to exceed the hit point protection of their rune shield."

Swoosh! In his distraction, Gareth hadn't noticed his own attacker closing in again. He'd nearly gotten another clip from the mace. Fortunately, the attacker had overextended himself, giving him an opportunity to put some space between them. Gareth took the moment to heal, bringing his health bar back to almost full, and moved back beside Kara. This time, the two of them put their backs to the alley wall. The bruisers, being oversized in the somewhat cramped quarters, would hopefully get in each other's way while they combatted their smaller prey.

Gareth muttered, "New plan: we both beat on your guy until the rune is expended." Kara gave a quick nod, dropping her daggers and pulling out her black sword, sacrificing the possibility of a ranged attack in favor of inflicting more damage. Her height was an advantage now, as she could attack low while Gareth went over her head to attack high. Bruiser #2 had trouble defending against both their attacks. As his opponents were smaller and nimbler, it was no easy task to land a blow against them. For his part, Bruiser #1 was blocked by their constant shifting to keep his ally between them.

The plan seemed to be working okay, but Gareth could tell that Bruiser #1 wasn't trying very hard.

Bang. clang. clang ! Kara and Gareth found their rhythm and were able to take down the rune of protection in short order. The first hint of blood drawn from his companion, however, led Bruiser #1 to dart back in and—*wham!* His mace landed on Gareth, taking a quarter of his life bar with it. He was now at around two-thirds his full health. Gareth tried to force Bruiser #1 to back off by swinging the axe once more. At the same time,

Kara struck out at him and landed several more hits. Each one of them bounced off his rune with no effect.

Bruiser #2 sidled up to the white-robed caster and his skin was covered once more with a brief shimmer. Well, *fuck*. With a seemingly infinite supply of these protection spells, they'd be able to run Kara and Gareth down just from sheer exhaustion.

"They're playing with us," Gareth said, and Kara nodded agreement. Nevertheless, she never stopped her attacks on Bruiser #1. For lack of anything better to do, Gareth joined her.

Shifft! A dart sank into Gareth's left shoulder and his health bar dropped another 10%. A bright, sickly green, icon blinked in the corner of his vision then his health bar began to pulse with smaller losses every few seconds—a damage over time (DOT) affect. Poison, in this case. Thepeiros stood to the side behind Bruiser #2, holding a dart gun. His arms straightened and he closed one eye, taking aim at Kara. A dart flashed out, sinking into Kara's side. Desperately, Gareth healed himself and, momentarily, his health bar shot back to 80%. The poison icon, however, still flashed as strongly as ever.

Thepeiros reloaded his dart gun and pointed it straight at Gareth once more. "As fun as this has been, it's time to end it. You are both to be taken back to the guildhall, where you'll be the night's entertainment at the after-dinner show."

Gareth gritted his teeth, and with a free hand, flashed Thepeiros the bird. "If it's all the same, I'll pass."

Thepeiros quirked his mouth to the side. "Sorry, not sorry." He braced his arm to pull the trigger. Whatever it was on the new dart was bound to hit hard.

Gareth reached down and touched Kara's shoulder, landing a heal on her. It was the least he could do to help them go down fighting. He was making his peace with their inevitable end when the light in the alley was dimmed by a hulking shadow from above. Gareth glanced up just in time to see a massive figure leap into the fray, landing beside the two casters. Gareth's jaw dropped. It was an eight-foot-tall wolf-like monstrosity, all fur and fangs and claws, but in a vaguely humanoid form. The creature wielded the biggest battle axe Gareth had ever seen, making the one he was carrying look like a toy. The Enchanter's head went flying across the alley, very noticeably separated from its shoulders. Blood shot into the air like a gruesome red fountain, spraying everyone.

Gross. This game really, really, needed a gore setting.

"*RAWR!*" The beast raised its muzzle and roared.

Well, *shit.* It had just made very quick work of the Elite Enchanter, but Gareth had no idea whether it was friend or foe. And if it was a foe, he wouldn't last a fraction of a second longer than that Enchanter had.

With a tight swallow, he straightened and took a defensive stance against the new arrival, for whatever good it would do.

Chapter Thirty

The Wolfinator

GARETH COULD ONLY LOOK ON HELPLESSLY AS THE HUGE, armored wolf-beast hovered over the bloodied body of their enemy. A stun icon appeared next to the poison one in his UI—he couldn't move!

The beast reached out to the mage standing nearby. He was shivering in fright but unmoving, clearly also stunned. Using its long sharp claws, the beast thrust them deep into the mage's chest and ripped out his still-beating heart. It turned and hurled the bloody organ into Thepeiros's face.

The stun icon faded in the corner of Gareth's vision, but he was at such a loss for what to do, he may as well have still been stunned. He stood watching with mouth a gape.

Kara, on the other hand, was all too quick to spring into action, launching into Bruiser #1, who was still standing right in front of them. "Don't just stand there, dipshit," she said to Gareth. "Hit something!"

Gareth came to with a shake of his entire body. He stepped forward and swung on the same bruiser that Kara now fought.

307

But he couldn't take his attention away for too long from the wolf creature. It had closed in and started attacking Bruiser #2 while Thepeiros fired dart after dart at it. Sadly for him, the beast's plate armor had no problem resisting the darts.

Gareth and Kara soon rediscovered their rhythm and blew through the new rune shield placed on their opponent. Gareth was impressed with their progress. Impressed, that was, until he glanced over at their new unlikely ally and saw that not only was Bruiser #2 already dead, but the wolf creature had made significant progress on Thepeiros as well.

Kara and Gareth finally polished off their shared opponent, though the steady ticking down of their health bars from the poison DOT made things dicey for a bit. He'd had to drop a couple more heals in the middle of the fight, until they did, finally, prevail. Part of the reason it had been easier to take their opponent out was that he'd clearly lost hope around the time the beast shredded his friends to bits.

Gareth couldn't blame him for that.

With one last flourish of its axe, the wolf monster took Thepeiros' head off with a single, mighty blow. Gareth suppressed a gag as he watched the thing tumble along the alley ground like a bowling ball. The creature seemed to have a fondness for beheading. Though he supposed it was better than ripping hearts out. That was a little too *Temple of Doom* for him.

Silence descended upon the back alley now that their last opponent had fallen. Gareth refused to take his eyes off the wolf creature, certain that he and Kara would be its next victims. But it never struck.

Meanwhile, their stamina bars began to refill. Gareth used the last of his mana to top off their health bars, carefully watching the poison DOT count down. The poison should be gone soon, and he'd be able to heal them back up to full again as soon as he regained some mana. Though, in all honesty, he could hardly see the point of it. Even at full health, they were zero match for this creature.

Still, it didn't move, appearing to slowly regain its own stamina as its breathing grew less labored. Gareth decided to do a quick inspect before he almost certainly became its next victim.

Xena Porteur de Mort

•Level: 5

•Guild: None

•Class: Deathbringer

What the hell? *Xena?* Like his dog?
And this hellacious beast was only *level 5*?
And… what the fuck was a Deathbringer?

In response to that almost rhetorical mental inquiry, new text flashed across his vision:

•Deathbringer – Fuck, Fuck, Fuck, run away. –Sir Robin.

•System note: this entry is quite old and might be in need of update.

Gareth read it twice while his brain tried to process what had just happened.

But before he could even draw a breath to start pleading for his own life, the ferocious beast's mouth opened. It growled, "Come with me, if you want to live."

"Huh. A *Terminator* reference." Puzzling but cool. "Thank you."

The wolf creature didn't seem to know how to deal with his gratitude. It fidgeted in its space, muzzle opening and closing several times before finally speaking again. "*Really.* We must go. More are coming."

"Sure. Just a sec." In the games he played, PVP kills always dropped coin and normally the chance for an item. He wasn't passing up the chance of loot if this game acted the same.

He scurried from corpse to corpse to pick up what he could. "As I was recently taught, the first rule of adventuring is to *never ever* leave the loot." The total tallied in the corner of his UI as he picked it up, totaling no less than 193 gold crowns. He ordered the UI to divide it equally into three piles. Kara made hers disappear quickly, but their new ally merely stared at the pile in its massive paw. Then, it slowly tucked the coins into a belt pouch. Gareth felt a bit of relief as the upkeep counter spun up for once.

"Just one more thing." Gareth bent to grab Thepeiros' head, artfully placing it in his corpse's crotch.

Kara's pixie brow arched high in her forehead. "*Classy.* Gareth."

He shrugged. "People are stupid when they're angry. The angrier, the stupider."

Kara put her hands on her hips. "You didn't do that for any sort of strategic move. Don't bullshit me."

"Okay, I didn't. But just picture his face when he finds his corpse. More than worth the laugh, right?"

A growl and a foot stomp drew their attention back to their new "friend." It was growing more impatient by the minute.

Gareth walked over to the imposing wolf-man creature. "Why?!" he shouted up at the fang toothed face.

Kara tried to step between the two. "Gareth, this isn't the time."

He shouldered his way past Kara. "No, now *is* the time." He looked back to the creature. "Why did you save me? This is the third time someone has jumped in to save me since I entered the game. It's only been a couple of days. This doesn't make sense. I'm not leaving until I know why."

Gareth saw the creature's eyes dart back and forth. "I had to save you." Gareth glared up, demanding more. The creature's voice dropped low, and Gareth was almost sure it mumbled, "You're my human."

"*What?*" He asked, "I'm your human?"

Kara chose that moment to push between them again. "*Because* you're human, dumbass."

Gareth looked down, confused. "Why would that matter? Who cares that I'm human?" Kara just stared at him, and his eyes darted between both of them. "Okay, what am I missing?"

Kara huffed. "Look, humans are almost legendary here. You've been gone for millennia. Tell me, what would you do back on Dirt if you came across an elf being assaulted."

"An *Elf?* Tolkien or Santa?"

Kara just glared at him.

"Okay, well after I got over the shock of seeing a real elf, I'd help him."

Kara nodded. "There you go."

"So, you're saying, I keep getting saved because I'm like an elf?" Gareth wasn't sure he bought this. "Elves would be awesome. I'd kill to meet an elf. Humans are…"

Kara snorted, "Humans are *what?* Boring? Get your head out of your ass." Kara poked him in the side. "Humans back on Dirt are boring. Humans here are *unique.* maybe even legendary. Everyone here knows stories about humans, from the old days—from better days. You need to realize you're not on Dirt anymore. And to be honest…elves are pricks. You'd better hope you don't meet any."

Gareth held out a placating hand. "Okay, okay, I get it. People are saving me because humans are cool."

Kara shook her head. "That might be overstating things."

"I've never been awesome before. I could get used to this." Gareth looked around, and beamed at the world, the wallflower made Prom Queen.

"Don't let it go to your head," Kara stomped her foot, glaring up at him.

Gareth looked down and sighed. "I'm just putting you on. I know my place." Gareth looked up and nodded at the wolf creature. "Let's get out of here."

They headed out of the alleyway and, in silence, winded their way down several streets, using other back paths to distance themselves from the scene of the carnage.

Long moments later, when they'd slowed their pace, Gareth turned to their new companion. "So, I'm Gareth and this is Kara."

A loud snort came from its muzzle. "Xena."

Gareth shook his head in disbelief once more at the coincidence. "My dog's name is also Xena."

Xena kept glancing around, never focusing too long on any one spot. "It's a good warrior name. Xena was a warrior goddess who defended the weak and killed the unworthy. I am a she-warrior, like her."

Huh. Maybe the old TV show, from which Gareth had pulled the name to bestow upon his beloved husky girl, was actually based on some long-established universal mythology? He didn't recall any wolf creatures on that show.

"Well, I'm in debt to you, Xena. We certainly would have died without your help." Gareth nodded towards the large creature.

Another indiscriminate snort. "You still will."

"*Well.* that's cheerful." Gareth rubbed at his jaw. "Anywho, we have an axe to deliver. Kara, lead the way."

Before Kara could do so, however, Xena took off down the alleyway. She called over her shoulder in her gruff voice, "Follow me."

Gareth shouted at her rapidly retreating form. "You don't know where we're going."

She spun and growled back. "Are we not going to the Tavern of the Orc Piss?"

Gareth nodded and the large creature spun and continued her path. As the other two followed, Gareth turned to Kara. "How did she know where we're going?"

Kara stared at the wolf warrior's back. "The operational security on this job is shit." She paused for a minute, then continued, "What's a *Terminator?*"

"It's a movie, back home. One of my favorites."

Kara frowned. "And it doesn't strike you as strange that she quoted that?"

Gareth tilted his head in acquiescence. "It does. Bear in mind, I'm currently running down a back alley, following an eight-foot tall wolf-person in company with a diminutive blue pixie. I buried the needle on *strange* a while ago. The guys who dragged me to the station in the first place brought movies along with the coke. I just assumed Earth movies were a thing here."

Kara shrugged as she ran along. "It's more of a niche thing. There's a Dirt movie club that meets once a month to screen those movies. Mostly comedies. You know, like *Alien, The Thing, Lifeforce...*"

"*Comedies?*"

"Oh, yeah. Your peoples' depictions of aliens are hilarious. And humans dying in hideous ways make it all the more entertaining."

Ahead of them, Xena cut through the open-air corner of a shop, and they struggled to keep up. Gareth glanced around as he raced along, noting he was less winded than he'd been before he'd picked up the sprint skill. Even at his current horrible skill level, it was helping. They appeared to be getting near the midden, the part of the city where the Orc Piss tavern was located.

"Our depictions of aliens are funny because we tend to make them xenophobic and deadly right? Real aliens *have* to be more civilized than that." Gareth took a second to step around some questionable looking refuse before turning to Kara.

Kara spared him a look. "Uh, sure."

They dodged a pile of debris in the alley. Beyond the end, toward the street, Gareth caught a glimpse of the sign denoting the Orc Piss.

"Your wolf friend knows what she's doing." Kara huffed. "We're here. Let's dump the damn axe and go."

Xena held up her paw to stop them before they could step out into the street from the alley. Instead, she crept forward, searching all around to make sure there weren't any members from The Elite lying in wait.

But with the coast apparently clear, she waved them forward to follow her moments later. The three of them entered the pub. Gareth started searching the dark, murky surroundings for Grifor. Heads turned to look them over—or rather, look Xena over. Not one of them attempted to disguise their reactions when the majority of them shifted their chairs away from the newcomers.

Gareth soon became aware of a forceful tugging motion from his back, where the axe was strapped to his pack. After checking to see if someone was pulling on it and finding nothing, he decided that the axe was nudging him toward the rear of the tavern. With a sigh, Gareth followed the direction into the darkness at the back of the room. There sat Grifor, deep in his cups.

Six feet from the table, the axe somehow freed itself from his pack and flew toward the dwarf. Without looking up, Grifor shot his hand up and snatched the weapon out of the air.

A brilliant, silvery shimmer washed over Grifor's body like a rain shower the moment he grasped the axe's handle.

Afterward, Grifor didn't look any different, yet he seemed completely changed, a sudden transformation from a harmless drunk into someone he'd cross a street—nay, even go around the block—to avoid. The sheer menace of him was undeniable.

Had he not witnessed it with his own eyes, Gareth would hardly have believed it possible.

Grifor blinked, staring at the weapon in his hand. "Well, I'll be dipped in pig shit. You did it."

Gareth and Kara pulled out chairs and sat down at his table, but Xena remained standing, putting her back to the wall and surveying the room for threats like a furry, self-appointed bodyguard.

Gareth turned from her back to his would-be mentor. "It wasn't easy by any stretch, but yes, we did it."

"Why should it have been *easy?*" Grifor chortled to himself. "I bet those Elite dicks are shitting themselves right now."

"Ahh, yeah. I'd say they're pretty pissed." Gareth made a motion with his hand as if to hurry things along. It's not like they had all day to reminisce about this, with the guild members still theoretically hot on their heels.

Grifor waved Gareth's obvious apprehension aside. "Oh, don't worry. They won't come here. I doubt they'll come anywhere near me now that I've got Kieros back. Still, a promise is a promise." A slow smile crept across the dwarf's face, half hidden by his dark, unkempt beard.

•Quest complete: "Recover Grifor's mojo"

•Quest reward: Experience

•Quest reward: Faction with Grifor increased to ally

**** Level up ****

- **Welcome to level 6!**

- **You now have 3 unallocated levels.**

Gareth's jaw went slack as he read through the plethora of messages popping up on the UI. *Crap.* How much experience was that quest even worth? His exp bar was almost halfway to level 7. Glancing at Kara, he noted equal surprise that reflected she must also have gained a significant chunk of exp.

"Did you get a quest reward too?" Gareth asked.

Grifor snorted. "Why wouldn't she? She helped on the quest, didn't she?"

Gareth scratched his jaw. "I thought I was the only one with the quest."

"What's that have to do with anything?" The dwarf looked puzzled.

"Gareth has a problem with reading the FAQ for the game. He apparently just likes to learn things as he goes." Turning to Gareth, she said. "The quest notifications are mostly symbolic. They're just a notification of actions you'll be rewarded for. Anyone actually participating in the action will get rewarded for success."

"Does it work the other way as well? It said I'd lose faction with Grifor if I didn't complete the quest. Can others be likewise penalized?"

Kara frowned. "I never told him I'd help, so why would he think less of me if I didn't? You risked losing faction with him because you promised him you'd aid him. If you went back on your word, why wouldn't he think less of you?"

"I guess that makes sense, but it seems unfair. Like I took the risk, but we both gained."

Grifor shook his head. "Now, whoever told you life was fair, sonny? But in this case, you're the one who said you'd help, so you're the one to whom I owe a debt. The lassie helped you, so I paid her off with some experience points. However, the other rewards are yours alone." His smile deepened. "Speaking of which, I believe I owe you some training."

Grifor slid back his chair and stood and placed his hand on Gareth's head.

A prompt appeared in his UI:

***Grifor would like to train you as Warrior. Accept (Y/N)?**

The moment Gareth clicked *yes*. Grifor's hand started to glow. A shimmer of light and a shivering feeling swept over Gareth's body. It felt almost like he'd imagined what beaming somewhere in *Star Trek* would feel like. Once it faded, his UI display updated to show:

•Overall Level 6

•Cleric 3

•Warrior 1

•Unallocated 2

Gareth quickly put his two unallocated levels into the Warrior slot, evening the score. No time like the present, and he didn't want to risk losing them.

- **Stamina pool increase x3 (warrior)**
- **Health pool increase x3 (warrior)**
- **Weapon Use, General Melee gained**
- **Weapon Use, Simple Ranged gained**
- **Armor Use, Medium gained**
- **Weapon Use, Sword upgraded to Weapon Specialization, Sword**

Once the level allocation was done, another message popped up:

- **You have two attribute points to allocate.**
- ***Where would you like to place them?**

Given his character build, the answer to that question was easy. Gareth assigned one point into *Strength* and one point into *Wisdom*.

- **Strength has increased to Above Average.**
- **+1 damage class when wielding melee weapons.**
- **+20kg maximum load**

•Wisdom increased to Above Average.

+10% mana pool maximum

+10% health healed by healing spells

Gareth scanned the notifications quickly, but his eyes stopped on the one that noted his three warrior levels. They'd increased his total health by 30%. He still wasn't sure about this hybrid half class- and half skill-based leveling system in this game. He was feeling a little better about himself, still, he'd kill for some actual numbers rather than this *average. above-average.* and *+percentage* bullshit.

Gareth opened his mouth to thank Grifor but stopped when the gnarled dwarf held up a hand. "Kieros is insisting on giving you a reward as well. Or rather, he's insisting I reward you on his behalf."

Kieros? Oh…the axe. The very grumpy, very dwarvish axe Gareth had been so certain didn't like him. He had pulled his bacon out of the fire, though, so he was still grateful for that.

Grifor was studying Gareth intently, an expression that Gareth had grown to associate with character inspection. He waited patiently while Grifor got the facts he needed.

"Hmm, I see you are apprentice, level one in broadsword, longsword, and apprentice, level 0 in battleaxe. I can reward you with an increase of your skill in either Longsword or Battleaxe to journeyman, level one."

Gareth lifted his brows in question. "Is that good?"

Grifor tilted his head deprecatingly. "Well, each apprentice level adds 1 point to the damage class of the weapon. Journeyman levels add 2 points. Bumping you up to journeyman

1 will add 4 apprentice levels and 1 journeyman level. So, this will give you +6 to your damage class and increase your damage by about 30%."

Gareth blinked, impressed. "Okay, so that's *definitely* good. But you can't level up my Broadsword skill?"

The dwarf shook his head. "I'm afraid I specialize in offensive weapons. Broadsword is more of a generalized weapon for offensive or defensive builds."

Gareth nodded, absorbing the plethora of info. "Okay, so give me Longsword then."

A burly brow climbed Grifor's forehead. "You sure that you wouldn't rather do battleaxe?" He patted Kieros's haft. "Axes are cool."

"Nah. No offense to Kieros, but I'm more of a sword guy." Gareth nodded toward the axe, hoping the axe knew how much he appreciated all its efforts today.

Grifor shrugged. "Your loss."

Once again, a tingle passed through Gareth's body and a new notification popped up, stating that his longsword skill was now journeyman 1.

Gareth nodded in acknowledgment and gratitude. "Well, I guess we're done here. Thank you, Grifor, for all your help."

Grifor stood back from the table and bowed low to Gareth. "You have restored my honor. It is *I* who thanks *you*." When he straightened, his eyes wandered to the other patrons of the main hall of the Orc Piss. "It might be best if we concluded your visit. Your, ah, tall wolfish friend is making people nervous. These customers are the sort who like to express their nervousness with sharp-edged weapons. But don't forget, if you need *anything*, just send word. It might be better if we met somewhere else, though."

Gareth grimaced and looked toward the door. "Understandable. I certainly don't want to start a fight."

When Gareth stood to leave, however, Grifor grabbed his arm and leaned in. "If you should see, ah, that *other* dwarven fellow who helped you out earlier. Please make sure and tell him that I stand ready."

Gareth's brow furrowed briefly, but he nodded. "Got it. No problem."

And just like that, Gareth had walked into a tavern a level three cleric and walked out a level 6 adventurer, both cleric and warrior. Two parts of a bar joke.

And 30% tougher. He had the almost certain feeling that he was going to need that added toughness. And all too soon.

CHAPTER THIRTY-ONE

AN INDECENT PROPOSAL

ONCE AGAIN, XENA LED THE WAY, THIS TIME OUT OF THE Orc Piss Tavern. Just outside the front door, however, Kara turned to Gareth. "So, what now? We finished your quest."

Gareth considered, once again scratching his jaw while the other two patiently waited. "Well, the three of us have worked pretty well together in a short period of time. I was hoping we could form a more permanent group. We could work on levels together, crank out some quests. Besides, those Elite bastards are pissed at all three of us. There's strength in numbers and all that."

Kara looked around the street, checking for threats, then turned to face Gareth. "That sounds good and all, but I was hoping you had a better idea of what to do next besides 'let's go level up.' What about that missing guildstone to unlock your guildhall?"

Gareth's brows bobbed up in surprise. It seemed a challenging feat for their fledgling levels. "Well, yeah, there is that. Let me check my quest list." He pulled up the quest log in his UI and skimmed through it. Not that it took long, He hadn't managed to find that many quests yet. "Shit, I forgot. Chief Bureaucrat Smith gave me a quest to look up Lord Smith here, in the palace."

Kara's brows knit and she chewed at her bottom lip. "The Chief Bureaucrat gave you a quest *in meatspace* …to meet with Lord Smith *here?*"

"Yep. He said his brother has been bugging him because he needs someone to do a job." Gareth ran the conversation through his head again, "Odd thing was I couldn't refuse the quest. Is there something wrong with that? It seems strange now that I think about it." Gareth felt the stirrings of unease. How'd he get involved in so much odd crap so quickly? He just wanted to earn some crowns so he could pay his upkeep. Just be a normal, bland gamer.

"*Very.* You're *never* offered quests outside the game." Kara studied him, as if she was trying to figure out what was so "special" about him that Chief Bureaucrat Smith was singling him out. "And a mandatory quest? That's even odder."

"Well, I need to do it. I don't want to annoy the man—creature—ah, being?—*person* who can kick me off the space station." Gareth gave a mental command to close his quest log. Hopefully, he could cross this one off quickly and move on with his day. Still…he remembered Mabel saying that only significant quests made it into the log. He just hoped this one wasn't too significant.

Kara blew out a breath, her face clouding. "Fine. Let's go see him, then. But I don't like *strange*."

As he turned to head out, a notification popped up. He'd set a timer to remind himself to check on Xena. "Oh, jeez. I'm going to have to log out for a bit."

Another frown. "*What? Why?*"

"I, ah, need to check on my dog. I set an alert to message me when she woke up and another to go off if she didn't wake up after eight hours. It's not like her to sleep this long. I need to make sure that she's okay after her trip to medical. Also, she'll need to go out to pee." Gareth sighed. How could he have spent so long in the game already? He'd nearly forgotten about Xena. How neglectful would he be if things got really intense in the game? He'd hardly gotten into anything yet. Thank goodness for the alarm feature, anyway.

Kara muttered under her breath, before grumbling out a short, "Fine."

They headed back toward good ol' Blacl's inn. Kara and Xena both assured Gareth that he could log out most anywhere safely, but it felt wrong to him to not go back to home base for the transition. Maybe because this game was so real. Having his virtual body phase out in the same place where his real body would be somehow felt reassuring. Though he suspected this was a newbie thing and, as things progressed, he might not even be able to do so once he was traveling much further afield from here.

However, Xena was actively discouraging him from doing it in the first place. "Gareth," she uttered in her growly voice. "The time to strike is now. The Elite guild is in disarray. If you give them time to regroup, they will be able to run you down."

Gareth shot her an annoyed look. "Strike? Strike at *what*? I'm staying far away from those jerkwads. Look, I appreciate what you did. If it weren't for you, they'd have killed Kara and me, for sure." He stopped when Kara snorted very loudly, then cleared his throat and continued. "Well, they would have killed *me* for sure, anyway. I really have no desire to start a war with that guild. This operation was a one-off thing to get Grifor's axe back to him so I could get trained. I've got my fighter levels now. Hopefully if I avoid them long enough, they'll forget about me."

There was a slight snarl to the wolfish words that Xena uttered next. "I fear you are overly optimistic, friend Gareth. You have bloodied their snout, and rumors of it will spread throughout the town by end of day. They *will* be forced to respond or suffer detriment to their fearsome reputation."

Gareth waved a hand as if to blow away a bad odor. "All the more reason to avoid them, then. If I'm not here, they can't come after me. Besides, no one saw the fight in the alley so no one will know what happened."

Xena shook her head. "There is always someone who knows something and will talk. The lure of being in-the-know is too great to ignore."

Gareth bit his lip. "We'll just have to agree to disagree. I'm going to get my poor dog. She'll be waiting for me. Then we'll eat some food, and I'll sleep in a real bed. When I log back in, this will hopefully all have died down."

Xena blew out a breath and Gareth interpreted the whuffle as one of frustration. "I'm sure your companion will be fine. At least leave the city before you log out. Someone will have seen you entering the inn. They'll be lying in wait for you when you come back."

Gareth waved her off again, feeling his irritation grow. "Drop it, already. Blacl's inn is neutral territory. They won't violate that. I don't even know if they *can*, to be honest." He turned the next corner before continuing. "Xena will go nuts when she wakes up all alone. I can't let her suffer like that—wondering where she is and where I am."

"I thought you said your pet wasn't sentient?" Kara chimed in from the other side.

"Well, that depends on what you mean by *sentient*. She can't speak, not using words anyway, but she gets her point across. I always thought she was more intelligent than people normally give dogs credit for. And that was before she was put into that machine and 'repaired.'"

"You think she'll be self-aware now?" Xena asked.

Gareth shrugged. "Nah. She's still a dog. It was weird though, the medical computer there said it needed to install a Network Access Node as part of its repair. Potato guy said that was normally just for sentients."

Xena gave Gareth a look he couldn't interpret. Then she tried a different tack. "I'm sure you will be notified in-game if there is a problem with your pet in your room. You will have plenty of time to go to her." Gareth tossed her a questioning glance, wondering why she refused to give up on talking him out of logging out from the game. "Come on. Your pet will be fine. Let's get out of the city and hide somewhere safe."

Gareth shook his head. "I can't leave the city yet. I still need to see Lord Smith regarding that quest I got in meatspace. Also, I have to find out where that guildstone is for the Vagrants guildhall, so we can finish restoring it. *Then* we can leave the city."

Xena growled. "This will not end well, friend Gareth."

He shrugged, palms up and open, glaring his annoyance. "It will be *fine*. Like I said, I need to get my Xena. Once she's had some exercise and food, I'll log back in and we can take off then. Anyway, we're here."

They exited one more of the countless alleys in this town. Maybe the residents had some sort of aversion to large, open, thoroughfares. Gareth frowned at the thought. Perhaps being out in the open wasn't as safe as he assumed.

Before them stood the welcome sight of Blacl's inn, his current home for who knew how long. From the street, they looked up the three steps to the half-timbered, mullion-windowed building before them. Above the street, the sign depicted an adventurer's sword and a stylized bright red dragon painted on a shield.

The three of them entered the front door and were promptly greeted by Blacl himself, who manned the counter. "Gareth, Kara, Xena, welcome. Just help yourself to a table, we have mutton stew tonight." He waved them toward the dining area with a friendly but toothy smile.

Gareth stepped toward the stairs instead, turning back to his companions. "You two, go eat. I'll treat. I'm going to log out and see to my doggo. I'll grab something to eat with her."

Blacl's brows knit as he looked from the two females to Gareth and back again. "Gareth, you should know that my food is as nourishing as anything you can find—in the game or out."

Gareth smiled back to placate the innkeeper. "Well, yes, that's very true. To be honest, that fact still blows my mind. But I need to take Xena out, and I'm sure she'll be hungry after whatever that machine did to her and sleeping all day."

Blacl looked at Xena the warrior, raising an orcish eyebrow.

"I mean Xena, my dog, not this Xena, the warrior. She's obviously quite capable of feeding herself."

"Right." Blacl looked like he was going to say something else but closed his mouth instead. To Gareth's right, there was a blur of motion from Xena's direction. He turned to see what it was, but the wolfish warrior merely turned to him, staring blankly. She was probably still upset that Gareth had chosen to ignore her advice. He shrugged it off, hoping the warrior Xena wasn't the type to hold a grudge.

"Okay, so I'm heading up to my room. I'll ping you both when I get back in game."

Gareth waved to his companions and headed upstairs. Once at his room, he unlocked the heavy wooden door and peeked inside before opening it all the way. All that talk of the ruthlessness of The Elite had him a little jittery. Laughing quietly at himself, he opened the door all the way and entered the room.

The dog bed was now gone. The game must have figured out that Xena was just a dog and not a player. He puzzled for a moment at the thought that Xena the warrior and his dog shared the name. Perhaps that was the translation of her actual name into his mind—because her name was likely long and unpronounceable. His UI must have picked a familiar name to substitute in its place.

God, this was confusing. He'd have to come up with a different nickname for Xena-the-warrior. In his mind, Xena-the-dog had the prior claim on the name.

Realizing how exhausted he really was, he laid down on the rustic bed and logged out.

Moments later, he awoke in meatspace. With a blink, he thought the log-out hadn't worked. It appeared to be the exact same room. He sat up and went to the door. That would be the easiest way to see where he was—to see who was manning the downstairs desk. Just before his hand connected with the doorknob, he turned to check out the rest of the room. To his shock, Xena, his dog, was sleeping on her bed still. He'd figured she'd have woken up long ago and be bouncing around the room.

He literally wiped his forehead with relief. He'd been feeling guilty that he'd abandoned his only friend to go play in the game. The fact that he needed to do that in order to pay their upkeep didn't help as much as he'd thought. It also didn't help that she had to be shut in a room without even a yard to play in. Whatever that machine had done must have really exhausted her for her to sleep through his arrival. Normally, any slight noise and she was after it like it was a fat squirrel. He'd let her sleep a couple more minutes, then he'd wake her up, if she didn't wake up on her own. She had to be hungry by now.

He looked around the room again. Other than Xena, it was an exact duplicate of his room in game. It had been so cool when he'd discovered it, to make the real world look just like the game. But now, he was coming to understand that he needed a bit of disparity between the two, for transitioning purposes. He wasn't a young buck, after all, and his brain didn't shift gears as quickly as it used to. His brain was already thinking of the game as real. Having meatspace match it exactly was just confusing.

Gareth quickly pulled up the overlay menu and started flipping through the options. He needed to select something radically different from the fantasy settings. He was dithering over the options *cave man chic* and something called *post apocalypto town* when his eye caught upon a setting for a sci-fi show he'd loved as a kid. One of the alien smugglers, like his 'buddies' Ygurthngjix and Steve, must have grabbed a copy of the show at some point and brought it here.

When he selected this new option, the wood and stone chamber quickly transformed into a stylish chrome room, furnished in shiny enamels in shades of blue and gray. The door lost its handle and hinges, transformed into a blank sheet of burnished metal.

Without realizing what he was doing, Gareth reached out to the door. It obediently slid open with a *swoosh.* disappearing into the wall on the left. When he pulled his arm back, it did the reverse, swooshing closed again.

There, that should help him separate the real world and game world. After playing with the door a few more times, he forced himself to stop. He smiled, thinking about how much he'd wanted to be on that ship as a kid, exploring the galaxy. It was no wonder that he took a moment to indulge his inner child for a minute or two.

"*Arooo.*" A cold wet nose poked his leg. All the goofing around had woken Xena up. Thank God. He'd been starting to worry.

"Sorry, girl. Just playing with the overlay settings." He bent over and ruffled her soft fur. "You don't seem worse for wear. How about we hit that little park out front? After, we'll get something to eat."

As they approached the new fancy futuristic door, Gareth wondered how Xena viewed the world. In theory, she had the ability to use an overlay as well. Did she see the basic, stripped-down version of the 'real' world, or did her implant feed her something else? Maybe a dog's version of paradise?

"How about it, girl? What does this all look like to you?"

Dogville.

Gareth did a doubletake, wondering just what kind of effect the game was having on him. He'd been talking with so many strange beings that his brain was now filling in Xena's half of the conversation.

The little park nearby was much as Gareth had remembered it, not huge but plenty big enough for a sniff, a little trotting around and a couple of bushes to pee on. Then there was Xena's favorite game, *Chase.* Gareth got some good cardio in while spending a good half hour pretending to catch the much-faster husky while she easily darted around him, tail wagging the entire time. His dog loved this game, and they'd played it since she was a wee pup, even though they both knew he'd only ever catch her if she allowed it. Or if he cornered her somewhere, as had happened at home a time or two when she'd run out the front door. Huskies were born to run and watching her in motion, it showed.

Finally tired out, Gareth doubled over, hands on his knees to brace himself. He called her over. "Xena, come." The dog knew that meant the game was done, and she trotted over to his side. "Let's get some dinner, girl."

She smiled a doggy smile, tongue lolling as she panted. Then she nudged him with her nose. He took that to mean she was ready for her dinner, too.

They reentered the inn and made their way to the dining area. It was as empty as usual, so they had their pick of tables. Gareth found a seat and Xena curled up under the table. This time, he couldn't see where he should place his order. But, remembering the change in overlay, he looked at the far wall and spotted the familiar row of small doors. Food replicators. He stood and approached, then peered at the control interface before straightening to order. "Burger, medium, with a side of fries." Then he glanced back at his dog who was watching him. Her tail thumped on the ground. "Also, a Ron Swanson—steak with a side of steak."

With a beep, the door opened, presenting a plate with a burger and fries for him. He pulled it out, and it closed to fill out the second order—a plate covered with two steaming, perfectly prepared steaks, rare. Not a veggie in sight.

Gareth took the meals back to the table and set about cutting the steaks into bite-sized chunks, giving them time to cool a little before placing the plate on the floor for Xena. She daintily picked up each piece of steak with her teeth before tossing it up and grabbing it in midair.

"Showoff." Gareth muttered as he watched her eat for a minute before turning to his own burger. "You know, girl, this place is damn strange. But it's not horrible. I wonder if we could get used to it."

"I'm sure you can!"

Gareth nearly levitated out of his chair in shock. He fought to regain his balance before he slid to the floor as he turned to a huge figure beside him. Looming there was Chief Bureaucrat Smith, in the massive flesh. There sure was a lot of him to loom.

"My apologies, I didn't mean to startle you. I was notified you had exited the game, and I decided to come...see how you're doing."

"It's okay," Gareth said after spitting out the piece of burger he'd nearly choked on.

Chief Smith walked around to the other side of the table, pulled out a chair and sat a good few beats before asking, "Mind if I sit down?"

Why was Gareth being reminded of a random scene from *The Godfather*?

He merely nodded in response while using a glass of water to wash down any excess bits of food he'd almost asphyxiated on while warily watching the Walrus-like creature. He remembered Kara's concern—about being given an in-game quest from meatspace. And how unusual it was.

And now this.

"So, have you had time yet to speak with my brother?"

Gareth reached for his napkin and wiped his mouth. "Well, you see, it's like this—"

"You *haven't* then. I'd hoped to discuss this with you after you'd met him, but we'll make do." He exhaled sharply, which blew his large mustache out. Under the table, Xena was watching him intently. Maybe she was hoping some food would come flying out of his mustache.

"*Not.*"

Gareth stared at his dog, practically certain that thought had come from her. But she was now curling up, her meal finished, her eyes closed. She actually looked bored.

Maybe he'd drop by the medical bay to get his interface checked out before logging back in. After all, it had been a long time since they'd injected a human with these things. Who knew exactly what their effect was having on his brain? Hearing thoughts from your dog couldn't be normal.

Mr. Smith harrumphed to regain his attention. "I noticed that you've managed to annoy one of the big power guilds in town already. I commend you on that. Fast work, indeed."

Gareth look askance at the walrus man. How'd he know all that? *Curiouser and curiouser,* as Alice would say.

"Well, ah, they'd stolen something that wasn't theirs." Gareth poked at his food. He just wanted to eat his burger in peace. Was that too much to ask?

The huge walrus-like head nodded. "It's all over the game boards. You're a hero to the underclasses in the city. I must warn you, though. The Elite are favorites of my brother. He's likely to act on their behalf."

Well shit, wasn't *that* just great. "Do you still want me to go see him, then?"

"He contacted me and requested your presence. But that was before your assault on the guildhall. He might want to see you for other reasons now." The walrus let out a throaty laugh. "Sadly, you won't be able to avoid him forever. Best to get it over with." The Chief Bureaucrat looked disturbingly at peace with the prospect of his brother venting his spleen upon Gareth. "It's out of my hands now. Still, it's possible that we can be of service to each other."

This whole thing was definitely sketchy. "How so?" Gareth's half-eaten burger had now cooled on his plate, his appetite vanished. As he stared into the alien eyes of Mr. Smith, he had a lot more sympathy for the squirrels Xena used to hunt.

"My mother was the lord of this place before me—before us. Back then, there was just one lord. The job wasn't split into Lord of the Town and Lord of the Station. The Chief Bureaucrat was merely the functionary who oversaw the station while Mother was in-game."

The room was completely silent and while it had never been busy, Gareth could clearly see that it was completely empty now but for the three of them. It took a minute, but as his eyes roamed back across the table to his newly arrived companion, Gareth realized what was being asked of him.

"You want me to kill your brother."

Chapter
Thirty-Two
A Dog's Breakfast

Xena, lying curled up with her tail over her nose, peered up at the other two through her eyelashes, pretending to sleep. She liked to think of this as her "cute and harmless" pose. Everyone overlooks a sleeping dog.

Bureaucrat Smith, or as she like to think of him: *Someone who can't be dismembered yet,* reared back in horror at Gareth's suggestion that he wanted his own brother killed. Xena's eyes settled on her human, that familiar warm glow of fondness settling in her chest. Gareth still required some training, and he really needed to listen better, but he was coming along nicely. His suggestion showed he wasn't completely out of touch with the game realities, even if he still had a disquieting tendency to want to "help" people.

Bureaucrat Smith's eyes went wide as his hand shot to his mouth. "To suggest such a thing! By no means would I ever, *ever* act in such a way against my brother. Besides, he'd just respawn, only angry." He looked carefully around the empty room before proceeding. "In any case, my mother made quite sure that if either of us managed to settle our differences that way, we would *both* suffer that fate."

Xena sniffed, a little too loudly, as it caused Gareth to glance over toward her. It wouldn't do for him to figure out too quickly that both Xenas, in-game and in meatspace, were one and the same. She knew it had to happen soon, but she'd miss the innocent relationship they had now, along with their games of chase. Gareth was truly horrible at it, being a human with only two legs, but there was something magical about the connection between a dog and her human, something she would miss. Things would undoubtedly change when Gareth found out the truth of just what she was.

Gareth looked at the creature across the table, confused. "What do you want then?" Clearly, he wanted her human to *deal with* his brother, just not in a way that triggered whatever his mom did.

"I'm getting to that, dear boy." Smith reached into a pocket and pulled out a small tablet which he placed upon the table. He flicked the middle of it with his finger and an image formed above it of an ornate brass clock—one with no hands. The face had a complex black-and-white pattern on it, resembling the yin-yang symbol on Earth. No doubt an artifact of some kind. Xena stored an image of it in her UI. She quickly composed and attached a message, to the image, sending it off to the grasseaters:

Give me a full report of the attached object. Also include everything we know of the beings known as Chief Bureaucrat Smith and his brother Lord Smith of Muddy River.

The gods knew Walrus-boy wasn't going to tell them everything they needed to know. Her thoughts drifted once more to just how much she was going to enjoy ripping him apart when the time came. Adrenalin coursed through her veins, and she could feel her body start to shift. She quickly fought down the urge. No, not here, not now. Her human would freak out if she assumed her combat form here in the physical world. That revelation needed to be carefully managed to preserve their relationship. Still, the thought of this odious fool's limbs strewn around the room did bring her a measure of joy.

The idiot continued, "As you can see, half of the face is black, and half is white. My mother was no fool, she knew what kind of people my sib and I are. He and I were to split our time between the station and town, switching off when our time was up. This clock was created to enforce that."

What kind of people you two are? Really? Your whole race, more like. Who did they remind her of? They were on that show her human loved to watch. Yes, *the Ferengi.*

"I take it that it didn't work out that way."

Xena sighed. Her human, pointing out the obvious again. He was adorable, but sometimes a little slow.

Smith gave a snorting bellow, blowing his mustache out again. "It did not. My brother convinced me to allow him to be first as lord of Muddy River. When the time came for the switch over, I remained here, chief of the station. I reached out to him to find out what had happened. I received back a message stating that the in-game world was much too dangerous, and that for my protection he would forsake the real world, leaving it to me."

"Well, that was generous of him," Gareth replied, dripping with sarcasm. "Did you ever find out what happened to the clock?"

Bureaucrat Smith looked at Gareth intently. "I was hoping you would be able to tell me. Up 'til now, I have never been able to get one of my agents into his office to find out."

So, you're sending my human in to try? You probably figure it's no skin off your back if he fails and your brother kills him. You'll quickly find out how wrong you are about that if anything happens to Gareth. Xena let out a little growl, which caught Gareth's attention. She quickly twitched her paws a few times. *Nothing to see here, just chasing rabbits in my sleep...*

Gareth looked back toward the large creature. "It's probably gone by now, anyway. He wouldn't just leave that laying around."

"Oh, it's still in the office, I'm sure. The enchantment our mother placed on the clock would have assured that." Bureaucrat Smith leaned back in his chair, finally taking his gaze from Gareth. "No, it's there. It's just being prevented from working somehow. Which brings us to *you*."

***bing* Message from headquarters received.**

That was quick. Xena opened the message. A swath of smells ran through her olfactory senses. Plastic, metal, body odor, remains of lunch....

Who was manning that place?

Agent, it is not our job to look up things for you. –HQ.

Xena let out another growl. Once again, Gareth's attention was drawn, and he took another quick look under the table. She did her best 'sleeping good dog,' but wasn't sure she'd pulled it off this time. The sheer effrontery of the reply had her raging. Just who did they think they were? They didn't even have the courage to sign the note personally, just using a generic HQ. Trying to find safety in a group no doubt. Just like prey.

Gareth looked at her for a moment longer, his face appearing puzzled. Finally, he turned his attention back to Bureaucrat Smith. "So, you want me to find this clock and fix it."

"Succinctly put, but yes."

Sure...just fix the clock.

"And how am I to do that?"

By feeding his brother's soul to it?

Xena focused on her UI and bit off a quick reply back to *HQ.*

I'm combat branch. You're support. Your job is what I tell you it is.

She added the smell of blood to the message, just to make sure they didn't miss her point.

"That is entirely up to you. You have shown yourself to be resourceful, when you wish."

Now Gareth leaned back in his chair. He stared at the ceiling for a minute, while he mulled over his reply. He appeared fascinated by the perfect replica of a starship ceiling it was now, instead of the smoke filled, exposed timbers and thatch it was before. Xena yawned. Augmented Reality will be Augmented Reality. It still smelled the same to her.

Gareth leaned forward. "I'd like to help you, I really would. But as you said, I've made enemies enough already."

There's my boy, good human.

A loud booming laugh rang out. "And you think if you're a good boy now, all will be forgotten? Your only hope is to help me. The Elite are my brother's enforcers. He'll countenance no slight against them. He *can't*. If people stop fearing them, the city might start to resist his rule. You'll be hunted down and made an example of. Over and over."

Smith leaned in, putting his face close to Gareth's, clearly making him uncomfortable. "Your only hope now is to replace him with me. I will cut off support of The Elite and enforce the neutrality rules once again, restore the city guard. You won't be safe from retaliation, but at least it will be a fair fight."

He might have a point there. There's a limit to how many Elite goons even Xena could kill. It would be good exp, but...she glanced over at Gareth. He's not ready for that level of conflict—not yet, anyway.

Gareth swallowed a couple of times, then replied. "I see your point. But won't he just throw me in jail if I show up at his office?"

The walrus man's eyes glinted in triumph. "Not yet. He needs you for something. You'll be safe until he gets it."

He'll be safe. Xena's lips pulled back exposing her fangs. *You and your brother won't be, but Gareth'll be safe.*

Gareth sighed. "That's reassuring."

"I'm sure." The Chief Bureaucrat replied. He stood up, picking up his tablet and returning it to his pocket. "I'll know if you succeed. No need to seek me out. Come see me in the palace once you do." With that, the creature turned around and left.

***bing* message from headquarters received.**

Be civil, or we will terminate contact.

On this message she caught hints of...yes, that was fear. Xena smiled as she sent her reply.

If you're not helpful, I will come there to find out why.

Once the message was sent, Xena stood and nosed Gareth's leg. Feeling her prod, he looked down at her.

"Well girl, I think I've really stepped in it this time." He reached down and scratched her head. "I'm sorry. I know I've hardly spent any time with you, but I think I need to get back into the game. Hopefully Kara and Xena—not you, a big warrior named Xena—are still around. I'm going to need all the help I can get."

***bing* message from headquarters received.**

There's no need for that. Expect your report soon.

Xena looked up at her human, wagged her tail and grinned. No one—*no one* —messed with her human and lived to tell the tale.

CHAPTER THIRTY-THREE
TOWARD VICTORY OR DOOM

GARETH STOOD UP, SNAKING XENA'S TRAY FROM UNDER the table along with his and made his way to the trash receptacles. Everyone in the Inn had been mostly nice to him so far. No reason to annoy them by being sloppy. Gareth started to wave to the desk clerk, then remembered he still didn't know the clerk's name. Determined to rectify that, even if he was in a rush, Gareth walked over to the desk.

The unnamed desk jockey with the orange skin and large ears looked up from his tablet, where it appeared he'd been managing his fantasy hero team again. "Well, well, well. If it isn't the man of the hour. Your hijinks earlier earned me a healthy return."

Gareth's jaw dropped. "Does *everyone* know what happened? *How?*"

The clerk waved an orange arm in the air. "Don't worry. It's mostly just the fantasy servers. They need to keep up on game events so the leagues can be scored. Hardly anyone in game ever logs out, so your secret's safe. *Mostly.*"

"So, here you can see what goes on all over in the game, but in game you're limited? How does that work?"

"Well, it would hardly be fair if you had knowledge of happenings all over Muddy River, wouldn't it? It's just one of life's little *screw-yous:* we who can't play in the game have more knowledge about it than those who can."

"So, you could tell me what The Elite are planning?"

"Sorry, can't do. That would be cheating. I'd be thrown out of my league for influencing events. I could feed you information and that would feed my score. Others would start feeding information to their picks. It would be chaos. We have to stay purely neutral."

Like the Watchers. Still, he thought there was a way this information could be used to his advantage. It wasn't the time to push, though. "I guess I see your point. Anyway, I came over here because I realized I never got your name last time I was here. I can't just keep yelling 'hey you' when I want something, can I?"

"Well, I'd prefer if you didn't yell at me at all. It's hardly polite. My name is Charon."

Gareth's remembered his last tabletop gaming session, where a particularly sadistic dungeon master sent the party to Hell. "Charon? Like... the Ferryman?"

All expression left Charon's face, and he stared at Gareth with eyes gone dead. His voice developed a deep reverb as he said, "I have no idea what you are talking about. There are no rivers here."

Gareth felt Xena bristle next to him, and she let out a low rumbling growl that made the hairs on the back of his neck stand up. Charon's gaze darted down to her. Gareth looked on in amazement as Charon's face reanimated. His voice returned to normal, and he let out a hearty laugh. "Sorry, I was just screwing with you. There was a time…" He shook his head, as if dispelling some old thoughts. "People used to eat that bit up. I'm glad we could formally meet."

"Yeah, great. Very funny." Xena let out one last growl, sat back on her haunches, and licked her front paw. Apparently, she felt that the situation had been dealt with.

Gareth turned away and headed over to the stairs. He turned to look back over his shoulder. "Hopefully I can earn you a bunch more points today. Have to keep your win streak going."

"Oh, I've dropped you. I have a bunch of Elite players this week. No offense, but the smart money is on them now. You pulled off a longshot, but the odds of that happening again are pretty slim." Charon gave him a jaunty smile and a slight bow.

"Good to know. I hope you won't be offended if I disappoint you." Gareth gave one last wave to Charon and went up the stairs to his room.

He was halfway up the stairs before he noticed he had a new blinking icon in the corner of his vision. Focusing on it enlarged it until he could see that the icon depicted an exaggerated yawning man.

- **You are fatigued.**

- **Until you rest, mana regen is at 50%.**

- **Intelligence and wisdom are reduced.**

•**Penalties will continue to accrue until such time as you rest for a duration of at least eight hours.**

•**This duration can be reduced by resting in an above-average or greater sleeping area.**

Well crap. There went his plan to log in right away. He was bone weary, though worried about what kind of response The Elite were planning for him—all of them. That bit about penalties accruing had him worried, however. This wasn't a good time for him to not be at his best.

Gareth finished his climb up the stairs and reentered his room. He still couldn't get over the swooshing noise the door made when it opened now. Despite being so tired, he was tempted to open and close the door a few more times. Xena gave him a doggie look that could only be interpreted as derision, so he contented himself with doing it just the once. Inside, he quickly lay down on his new SciFi-styled bed. Xena was already curled up on her dog-sized mattress. All the running around at the park must have tired her out.

He pulled up the main menu to see if he could set an alarm. He wanted to get rid of the fatigue debuff but didn't want to waste the day sleeping in. He'd been known to do that from time to time—and all this running around, virtual and otherwise, was really hitting him now that he'd slowed down for a minute. He found an alarm while also wondering what an alarm inside your head would sound like. More interestingly, he found an option to wake up in the game after being fully rested. He selected that option, then rolled onto his side, blanking his mind so he could fall asleep.

Sometime later, he opened his eyes and instantly knew he was back in the game from the change in interface—wood frame and thatched roof instead of sleek SciFi décor. Having the real-world and game-world interface look different was definitely less confusing.

He checked his status logs and noted that he'd slept for a little over 7 hours and got a rest bonus for staying in an above-average sleeping area. Way to go, Blacl! He'd have to remember to mention to the innkeeper how comfortable his beds were.

Before rising, he pulled up his friends list and saw that both Kara and Xena were still—or had already—logged in. He sent off a quick message to each of them suggesting that they meet up downstairs. Both replied they were on their way.

Xena the dog had seemed happy enough to curl up and go to sleep in the real-world. He still felt bad, though. She didn't deserve to be ignored while he was in the game. Maybe there was a way to get her in, so at least she'd be with him here. Or at the very least, maybe the space station had some sort of pet daycare where she could run around and play. They could care for her properly while he was logged in. But did people even have pets here? He had no idea.

After taking care of general hygiene needs, he gathered his equipment and headed downstairs to wait for the others. At the bar, he picked up a glass of something called *mulled chokto* while he waited. He normally started his day off with coffee, so he figured a glass of *something* would help kick-start his brain. With just one sip of the steaming drink in his mug, he concluded that *chokto* was basically hot chocolate.

A few minutes later, the zing in his brain told him that it was heavily caffeinated hot chocolate. He decided then and there to make a morning cup of *mulled chokto* his new breakfast habit.

Xena and Kara showed up, almost at the same time just as he was finishing his mug.

"Is the dog okay?" Kara asked.

"Shockingly enough, she was still asleep when I logged out, which was nice. She can get a bit destructive when she's bored."

Xena the Warrior blew out a breath through her snout. "I am sure she is well-behaved for the environment you keep her in."

Gareth looked up at Xena. "Oh, she is. But she's had a mischievous streak since she was a puppy. I doubt that's going to change now. Just let me set another timer so I can walk her later." Xena opened her mouth, no doubt objecting again. Gareth waved her off. "Yes, I know, we need to worry about The Elite, not pets. But I'm not going to let any game, no matter how involving, cause me to neglect my dog."

Xena appeared to reconsider what she was going to say, then she growled out, "No pet should be neglected. We will simply have to deal with the obstacles that present themselves."

"First things, first." He targeted each of them and sent group invites. "No more screwing around. It'll be much more effective to be grouped up going forward."

Strangely, it took a few moments to group up. Xena was first, though she growled a little and shook her head before doing so. Kara, however, seemed to be engaging in some sort of internal debate before finally hitting the accept button and joining. Now Gareth had three sets of health bars at the top of his vision field. He quickly discovered that he could target them by flicking his eye at their name instead of having to look at their person. This would make healing a lot easier.

"So, what's the deal? Do I smell bad or something?" he asked the other two.

Kara still didn't look happy. "Grouping gives away a lot of information. It's not something to be done lightly."

"Well, it makes it a ton easier to heal you two, and I don't see what the big deal is—all I see is your health and mana bars," Gareth countered.

Kara put her hands on her hips. "You can infer a lot by how fast those go down if you're paying attention. Go ahead right now, highlight one of our names."

He did as she asked and highlighted her name. Her entry blew up and now showed her at level 11 and her class: Knife Warden. It also listed a couple of buffs: *Furious Pixie* and *Stabby stabby*. whatever those were.

"Hey, what's a knife—" Kara jabbed him in the gut. He doubled over, groaning. "Why'd you do *that?*"

She muttered between her teeth. "Private information is private."

Gareth coughed, straightening. "What? I could just inspect you."

"You *could* …if you were a douchebag—*or* if you wanted a fight. Inspecting people uninvited is considered extremely rude. Save it for the monsters—or your enemies."

Gareth frowned. "Wait, can you tell if someone inspects you?"

"You can, unless the person inspecting has a really high-level inspect skill. Then, no one would know."

Ack, so he'd been repeatedly, though unintentionally, rude without even realizing it. "Sorry."

Kara huffed at him. "I don't know what kind of worlds you played in before, Gareth, but this one is very dog-eat-dog." Xena let out a growl and Kara looked up at her. "Sorry. What I meant to say is this game is very competitive. Any little advantage could have big consequences, and people guard knowledge about themselves tightly. Even knowing your exact class can allow people to look up your skill lists. That's why people just use general terms, like warrior or scout. It's hard to hide what your abilities are in general, but it's the specifics that really count."

Gareth nodded slowly. "I begin to see. Sorry if I offended."

She shrugged back at him. "You're just ignorant, not malicious."

"Thanks...I *think*." He grinned.

But he couldn't resist the temptation to target Xena's name to read the info: Level 8 and her class was Marauder. Her buff section was grayed out. Interesting—and maybe a bit worrying.

Xena, who had been waiting more or less patiently while he and Kara talked, had had enough and spat out, "Well? What are we doing?"

Gareth considered carefully how much to tell them about his talk with the Chief Bureaucrat in meatspace. He decided they didn't need to know about the whole magic clock thing yet. But they did need *something*. "Lord Smith has a job for me, apparently. I need to go see him."

Kara smacked him on the leg—hard. "Lord Smith is like the patron saint of The Elite. You can't go see him, dumbass."

Gareth rubbed his thigh where she'd hit him. "You're very violent. I know about his relationship with The Elite. I'm not a *complete* newb."

Her pixie brow arched high in her blue forehead. "That remains to be seen."

"I've been told that I should be safe—at least until I've completed this task, whatever it is. He'll probably make sure The Elite leave us alone until then, too."

Kara was bouncing up and down, probably with the desire to tell him how wrong he was, but Xena talked first.

"*Probably* does not make for a good plan, Gareth."

Gareth sighed heavily. "I know. But at this point I don't have a lot of options, other than run into the woods and hide. And I don't like that plan." He looked from one of them to the other. "Look, I know this plan sucks. But the worst they can do is kill me. You two wait here, and I'll go see him. If he kills me, I'll contact you when I respawn."

Xena shook her head. "I will not leave you to face your enemies alone. If we respawn, we respawn together."

Gareth's gaze floated to Kara, who also shook her head. "I'm no fan of respawning, but I'm coming too. Lord Smith requesting a newb is unheard of. Odd behavior is interesting…and possibly profitable."

Huh. And yesterday she'd told him that she didn't like strange. Gareth took a deep breath and straightened. "Well, then. Off we go."

And whether it would be toward their victory or doom, he still couldn't say, but he was proud to have these two beside him, regardless.

CHAPTER
THIRTY-FOUR
WINNER WINNER,
CHICKEN DINNER

GARETH LED HIS COMPANIONS OUT OF THE INN AND onto the street. He spent a minute looking around, then pulled up his map, trying to figure out which part of town would house the palace. As if frustrated with his hesitation, Kara shook her head and headed down the road toward the hill overlooking the town. Gareth started after her, then veered to the left when he spotted a familiar face out of the corner of his eye.

The figure, a tall, weaselly looking fellow with pale yellow eyes, sauntered away in a different direction, and studiously avoided Gareth's gaze. Undeterred, Gareth stomped up and blocked his path so that he nearly bumped right into Gareth's chest.

"Well, well. If it isn't my friend from the training field. I have something for *you*." Gareth practically snarled.

"*What?*" the creature's eyes widened. "I don't know what you mean. I—I've never seen you before in my life."

"Sure thing." Gareth took his pack off and dug around in it. "Here we are." He pulled out a dead rat. "See this? This is what we call a *Rattus rattus.* or your common black rat." Gareth shoved the rat into the creature's face. "You see this?"

Gareth dangled the dead rat before the idiot's eyes, and he reluctantly nodded.

"*Good.*" Gareth dug into his pack again, this time pulling out a dire rat head, which he promptly dropped on the ground at the creature's feet, the blood spattering on his boots. "Now, don't you look away. What do you think *that* is? And I'll give you one hint, it's *not* a rat."

The creature's eyes shifted before he finally sighed and answered under his breath, "It's a dire rat."

"Winner winner, chicken dinner. Yes, it's a dire rat or *rattus gigantus.* Now, before we move onto the ass-kicking portion of the day, would you mind explaining why you sent me to a dire rat lair instead of a rat nest?"

He blew out a breath. "I didn't have any choice."

Gareth glared at him. "Didn't have any choice? I almost died." Gareth drew his sword. "Now *you're* going to find out exactly what that feels like."

The figure dropped to his knees. "F-fine, then. G-get it over with."

Gareth raised his sword over the creature's bowed head, then hesitated. "Okay, so…wait what's your name, anyway?"

"Eugene."

Gareth lowered his sword, "Eugene? *Really?* Eugene?"

"Eugene the Butcher."

Gareth rolled his eyes, stifling a chortle. "That's not better."

The creature made a gesture somewhat like a shrug. "I thought it sounded fierce."

"Well, Eugene the Butcher, before I send you to respawn, I'd like you to expand on the *I didn't have a choice* part of our conversation. Upon reflection, I find that answer…unsatisfying."

Eugene looked up at him wide eyed before deflating. He muttered as if to himself, "What does it matter?" He looked down, refusing to meet Gareth's gaze. "It was Meldurath. He promised me guild membership if I got you killed. Apparently, his guild leader was not amused when he got banned from the training area, after you got him in trouble with Clud."

Gareth let out a sharp laugh, "After *I* got him in trouble? The little fucker shot me. Figures he was too chickenshit to come after me himself." Gareth waved his hand at Eugene. "You're good, go."

Confusion washed over Eugene's weasel-like features, and he didn't move from his kneeling position.

Gareth waved at him in dismissal. "*Really*. we're good. Go before I change my mind."

Looking visibly relieved, Eugene quickly stood and ran—not walked—away.

Gareth turned back to his dumbstruck companions who stared at him with open-mouthed shock. He walked back to them. "What?"

"He tried to kill you," Xena growled.

"Well, yeah—but really, no. He was just the object used by a coward. Meldurath was the one who wanted me dead. Now, *that* fucker I'll happily kill."

Kara just stared at him before letting out a clipped, "You're an idiot." Then she turned and continued up the road.

Gareth followed her through the town, each turn bringing them into finer neighborhoods and better-maintained roads. Finally, they ended up on a pristine cobbled road, bordered by rows of expensive-looking shops on either side. At the end of the road stood a large palace surrounded by a wrought-iron fence decorated with gilded flowers. A large, gleaming gate stood open, flanked by armed guards.

In front of the gate, a frog-like creature stood, wearing an outfit made of crushed purple velvet with a floppy hat on his head. Visible on his chest was a tabard bearing three white flowers topped with a large golden bee. He held a notebook in one webbed hand and a large, plumed feather in the other. A line of people stood before him. He gestured rudely to the first person in line, shouting out loudly, "*Non!*"

The person's head and shoulders sagged dejectedly and they turned to walk away from the palace.

"Ugh, *toads*. I hate toads," Kara sneered without bothering to lower her voice.

Gareth nodded toward the frog. "I mean, he *is* ugly as sin on Sunday morning, but I hardly think that's a reason to dislike someone."

Kara looked at the toad and rolled her eyes. "Wherever you find the privileged and arrogant, you'll find some toady kissing up to them, working their way into power. They get off on lording it over the 'little people.' Let's just stab him and find our own way inside."

"Wow, just *wow*. I'm expected. Surely that will make a difference." Gareth glanced toward the toad, hoping they weren't being overheard.

Kara's high-arched pixie brow climbed even higher. "I'm sure it will get you in—*after* he extracts his pound of flesh. Toads have a sixth sense about just how far they can push someone and not get in trouble. You've been summoned, but you're a nobody. This is going to be painful." Kara's face set and her shoulders tensed.

Gareth studied the line facing the toad. "Screw this. Xena, why don't you go explain to the toad that we are here at Lord Smith's request."

A large toothy grin split the face of Gareth's new wolf- friend as she headed toward the gate. Gareth and Kara followed close behind as the people waiting in front of her slid quickly aside, casting fearful glances at the towering figure. Some of the guards looked over, but they seemed disinclined to interfere.

One particularly obstinate fellow refused to move, despite the epic glare and lip curl that Xena gave him. Gareth intervened before it could escalate. He was fine with using her to intimidate people, but he drew the line at assault. It was a fine line, but it was his, and he was going to enforce it. Besides, pushing things seemed like a sure way to get the guards involved.

"Look, I've been here all day, you all can just bugger off." The resolute fellow was wearing dark robes with a cowl pulled over his head. His face, whatever it looked like, lay deep in the folds and shadows. Gareth figured him to be some sort of caster. However, given his recent education on how rude it was to inspect people without asking, he didn't investigate.

"You will move, small person." Xena sniffed the air in front of her. "You smell weird."

The fellow drew back, presumably to take her in. "I'm not really sure how to take that." He lifted one arm to take a quick sniff of himself. "I don't smell anything. Anyway, I'm not moving. You can wait your turn."

Xena took a step forward, baring her wolfish fangs, but Gareth slid between the two of them. "Excuse me," Gareth said, coughing into a fist. "I really don't want to take your spot, but the lord here has summoned me. We just need to get by you so my friend can make sure our froggy gatekeeper doesn't drag his feet too much."

The person snorted from behind his cowl. "Good luck with that. I was sent here, too. I was told I had to appear before the town registrar and register before I could take any lodging and I've been waiting all night. Eight people have been let in past me, and if they can ever agree on a price, *that* fine fellow there will be number nine. So, you'll have to excuse me if I don't care that you've been summoned by Lord Smith himself. I'm tired, hungry, and *I'm going next.*" He turned away from them and stared resolutely ahead.

Gareth moved up next to him, trying to get a peek at his face. "Look, um, I didn't get your name…."

"Well you didn't ask, did you? My name's Cynddylw."

"*Cynddylw?*" Gareth tried to repeat.

"*No.* Cynddylw. You need a hard trill on the second y."

Yeah, that wasn't happening. Gareth's tongue had never trilled in his life. It wasn't about to start hard trilling now. He accessed the naming interface and designated him as Arvin. He'd known an Arvin in high school who'd been about as pissy as this guy. Hopefully, the name translation worked as advertised.

With a bit of trepidation, Gareth continued. Dr. Head hadn't cared what he was called, but this guy looked like he might take offense if we got his name wrong. "Well, Arvin…" Garth paused to judge the man's reaction, but he merely shrugged back. Taking that as a good sign, Gareth continued, "I think we might be able to help each other out here."

Cynddylw, now Arvin, stood staring ahead without a response. Gareth continued, "*You* want in the palace, and *I* want in the palace. We have a common enemy in the frog over there. If you let us scoot ahead of you, Xena can convince him to let us both in."

Arvin rotated his head just enough to look at Xena, then he returned his gaze forward. Gareth had to lean in to hear his answer. "If you screw me over and make me wait longer in this accursed light, I will find you and ruin your sleep. For weeks."

Taking this as a *yes*. Gareth proceeded. The person at the gate had finally finished their business, so Gareth waved Xena toward the waiting frog.

The gatekeeper's amphibian eyes widened as Xena approached, but other than that, he paid her no notice. Xena stopped inches from the frog and looked down at him. She growled, "Gareth to see Lord Smith."

The frog glanced behind him, as if to assure himself that the guards were still there before he replied. "He'll have to wait his turn. Now get back in line. I'll see if this…Gareth…is on the list when I have a moment."

Xena, who had at least several feet on the much smaller creature, arched her head over him and bared her fangs. A big loop of drool hung off the side of her mouth before it dropped onto the brim of his hat. Gareth's fearsome wolf-friend reached forward and used a claw to poke at his notebook. *"Gareth,"* she said, poking the name again for emphasis.

Gareth suppressed a chuckle, while Kara took the opportunity to elbow him in the stomach. He glanced at her, and she pointed beyond Mr. Toad, toward the gate. Xena's actions had aroused the guards' attention. Several of them approached. Despite this, they weren't moving with any sense of urgency, which spoke volumes about how they felt about the toad.

Gareth nudged Xena, and when she looked up, he pushed himself between her and the toad. The toad gatekeeper stared up at the figure now looming behind Gareth, having affected a weird sort of twitchy movement. Gareth turned to see that Xena was licking her chops. She seemed to be taking quite easily to this part.

Worried that he might have started more than the three of them could handle, Gareth attempted to calm their target down by speaking in a soft voice. "Now, ah, Mister...what is your name?"

The toad's eyes flicked toward Gareth. "Wha—What?"

"Your name? I'd rather not just address you as 'hey you' or 'toad person.'"

The toad cleared his throat. "My name is Leodithas." His eyes darted back up, up, up to Xena.

"Well, Leodithas, your master, Lord Smith, has specifically summoned me. By name." Gareth noted that the guards were almost upon them. "I would most greatly appreciate your checking the list to grant us access. Then, we'll be gone and someone else's problem. Doesn't that sound good to you?" He gave the toad his biggest, sunniest smile, aware that it bared almost all his teeth as if he were mimicking Xena's mute threat.

"Is there a problem here?" One of the guards, presumably the leader, muttered from beside Leodithas. The other two guards lingered behind the gatekeeper but kept their eyes unwaveringly on Xena and their weapons—some sort of halberd—ready.

"No, no problem, officer." To distract the toady gatekeeper, Gareth snatched his hat. Leodithas's hands immediately shot to his head.

The gatekeeper grabbed at his bare head. "*What!* How dare you!"

Gareth squinted at the creature. What he had taken for hair was actually a wig sewn onto the bottom of the hat and the toad was as bald as, well, a toad. Gareth pulled a handkerchief from his pocket and dabbed the hat where Xena had drooled on it.

"Oh, excuse me. It's just that I noticed that my colleague got drool on your lovely hat. It's the fangs, you know—not really her fault. She didn't mean anything by it."

Leodithas grabbed his hat back from Gareth, settling it back on his head with a firm pull. "I thank you for your assistance. Now, good day!"

Gareth smiled humorlessly again. "Thank you for your advice. Don't forget to check us off your list." He turned and started toward the gate.

The frog stuttered in protest. Xena interrupted with a deep bass growl that chilled every spine within earshot. What was more useful, however, was that it interrupted the toad, who gaped at her, wide-eyed, finally resigning himself to wave the three of them through the gate.

"All is in order?" the sergeant of the guard asked in a flat, bored tone. The gatekeeper gave a jerky nod. Shrugging, the guards moved back to their posts beside the gate.

"*Hey!*"

Gareth looked over his shoulder at his newest buddy, now at the head of the line then turned back to the toad. He nodded back toward Arvin. "You don't mind signing him in as well, do you? Get all your headaches out of the way at one time?"

The UI had helpfully translated Arvin's name on the notebook's list as well. "Look, let me help you." Gareth swiped the pen from the frog's unresisting fingers and scratched a checkmark next to Arvin's name. "There, all done! Have a nice day."

With one last squeeze of the gatekeeper's arm, Gareth released the bewildered frog and waved his newest friend up to join them. The four of them passed through the gates together, giving the guards a jaunty wave as they went by.

There. Mission accomplished.

And they had a mysterious new ally, to boot.

Chapter
Thrity-Five
Questing Conflict

Beyond the gate was a cobbled courtyard leading to a large double staircase topped by an ornate formal entryway into the palace.

"I would like to thank you for keeping your promise," their new dark-robed friend murmured as the four of them crossed the yard.

Gareth kept his eyes straight ahead on his target. "I was taught that a person is only as good as their word."

"A sentiment much lacking in this day and age, I'm afraid." The voice was eloquent with clipped, well-enunciated words in a cultured accent. The figure shook his head as they crossed the cobblestones. "You must be new here."

"You could say that," Gareth replied with a chuckle. "I've been here less than a week."

An expulsion of breath betrayed Arvin's surprise. "And already summoned to the palace? You must have done something truly astonishing to warrant that."

Gareth shrugged. "Not unless killing rats counts as astonishing."

Inside, everything was white marble with gold accents. Lilies in vases and growing on plants were on display everywhere, their sickly-sweet scent permeating the air.

Gareth's destination was, apparently, a small door to the left of the stairs. As a guard had mumbled to him when he'd passed through the gate, that door was for those here on business. He surmised that the more formal, decorative entry was reserved for people of greater status than his motley little group.

Gareth stopped to open the door and paused before entering. "Honestly, I have no idea why I've been summoned—or even how I came to the notice of Lord Smith."

Arvin preceded him through the doorway. "Well, I wish you good fortune today. I, myself, am no great mystery. Presenting myself to the registrar is required before I take up residence here."

Gareth looked at Arvin, puzzled. "Yes, you said that before. If I may ask…why must you register? I don't recall being asked to do so myself."

"That is because you are among the living. All undead are required to register in the city."

Gareth blinked, stumbling a step as he followed the figure through the doorway. "*Undead?*"

The figure turned back at him, still cowled so deeply his features were hidden in shadows. "Vampire."

Well, that explained the dark clothing, the deep cowl, and his previous objections to sunlight. Gareth looked back at Kara who just shrugged, unfazed. Perhaps she'd already deduced it.

They'd entered the wing via a hall that, while much less ornate than the main entry, was still more luxurious than anything else they'd seen so far. Clearly, it was good to be the Lord of Muddy River.

Down the length of the hallway, a reception desk sat, manned by a very attractive woman. Gareth couldn't help but stare, then blushed when he finally realized how long it had taken for him to realize she was actually a centaur. The horse-like lower portion of her body was hidden behind the high desk, lying on an embroidered mat. Her thick dark blonde hair on her humanoid head reached clear past her waist, establishing a thick curtain to hide almost the entirety of her chest. She had lilies tucked into the crown of her head and light brown eyes with no whites and slit pupils, like a horse.

She looked up from some sort of magical screen as they approached. It floated in front of her and seemed to be a list of names with notes next to them. Giving them a bright smile, she addressed Arvin first. "Registrations are to the left." She motioned with a long, elegant arm. "Go through the door, and you'll see the sign about halfway down the hall. And you, Mr. Gareth, audiences are toward the right. Go down that hall and look for the blue door. Your friends can wait here." She pointed at a seating area across from her desk.

Gareth turned to Arvin. "Well, it looks like our paths part here. Look me up sometime. Maybe we can work in a group for a bit. I'm staying at Blacl's inn." Gareth could have offered to send his contact info but decided against it until he knew the guy better—or knew more about how vampires operated, at least.

Arvin faced him and gave a short bow. "I will do so. It is not often that people of my kind gain acceptance here. Even if they practice *obonoughtia*. Good day." He turned and headed toward the registration desk.

"*Obonoughtia?*" Gareth puzzled aloud.

"It's a philosophy that prohibits the drinking of blood. Vampires that follow it survive by drinking a sort of blood surrogate. It's said to be one of the most foul-tasting drinks ever invented, which greatly limits the spread of the practice." Kara looked toward the departing vampire. "If he truly practices it, he is a person of great willpower."

"Good to know." Gareth turned toward the audience hallway.

"Vampires are said to be mages of extraordinary ability," Xena added.

"Also good to know. Wait here, I'll be right back. *I hope.*"

Gareth proceeded down the hall and quickly found the blue door. Passing through, he was now in an extremely ornate room. He could only wonder what the rooms on the floors above looked like. Thinking back on the rather plain office Chief Bureaucrat Smith occupied on the station, Gareth began to see why his brother was loath to switch places. That thought reminded him of his errand. Since the room was empty, he gave it a quick look over but saw nothing that could be the clock he'd been told about. Finally, as if realizing he'd taken long enough and might get caught snooping, he forced himself to take a seat in front of the desk he found and laced his fingers together to begin his wait.

And wait.

And wait some more.

Hopefully Kara and Xena didn't get bored or into trouble while he moldered here. Around the twenty-minute mark, it occurred to him that this was probably some sort of test—to see how he handled himself or maybe see if he'd snoop through the desk. Hopefully, anyone watching had long since gotten bored. *Hope you enjoyed watching me sit and twiddle my fingers.*

By the in-game clock in Gareth's UI, he'd waited a good forty-five minutes before the door behind him opened. Gareth stood and turned. A large walrus-like creature stood there, the spitting image of Chief Bureaucrat Smith. Only this one was dressed for the court of Louis XIV. Without acknowledging Gareth, he walked directly past his guest and sank into the large seat behind the desk.

What a dick.

Someone wearing *that* much brocade and silk with a healthy dose of lace shouldn't be pulling that much attitude. Purple and green seemed to be the colors of the day. Gareth hoped wearing the Joker's colors didn't indicate he had a similar mindset. Having a sadistic psychopath for town leader would suck.

"Sit, sit." The Lord of Muddy River waved Gareth to his chair, finally recognizing his existence. Then Lord Smith settled his bulkiness behind the desk. "You must forgive my tardiness. I was on my way here when I was waylaid by an emergency."

Yeah, right... Gareth complied, retaking his seat. "I hope it wasn't too urgent. I can come back later if needed."

Lord Smith shook his head. "No, it was a small matter, quickly resolved. A minor lord found his son in some difficulty. It's all been handled." The walrus man reached into his desk and pulled out a small stack of paper. He then pulled a monocle out of one of his embroidered pockets and put it into his eye, in perfect imitation of his brother. He pored over the top sheet of the stack before continuing.

"I see you come highly recommended by my brother. He has his faults, but being a poor judge of character isn't one of them." He peered up at Gareth with an intensity that seemed to imply he could see into his soul. For long minutes, he said nothing.

It occurred to Gareth that perhaps that monocle of his allowed him to see things magically, like maybe his character sheet or some other vital information. Though Gareth didn't have any big dark secrets—other than his abilities with alchemy— the possibility still made him vastly uncomfortable.

Finally, Lord Smith nodded. "Very well, I will trust you. I have a mission of some delicacy. It requires a special touch, a *human* touch, to complete."

Gareth's brows shot up. "*A human touch?* You must've been waiting some time then."

Lord Smith bobbed his head up and down. "Indeed, indeed. And the last human I approached ended up being...*unsuitable* for the task."

What the hell? Last human?

How many humans were running around this place, anyway? Or was it all this same guy, the infamous Lord Crush, from The Elite?

Gareth tried to keep his face blank, not wanting to give anything away to Lord Smith. He was already suspicious about this task before getting a single detail about it. In fear of scaring off walrus-boy by seeming too intelligent, Gareth gave him his best *I'm just a newbie* look and merely nodded. People were always willing to accept ignorance, even mistake it for innocence. "I'm glad to be of assistance, your lordship."

Smith harrumphed. "I'm sure you are...I'm sure you are. The pay is *very* generous: 1,000,000 gold crowns."

"A *million?!*" Gareth nearly gaped at the walrus-creature. "What do I have to do?" He mentally braced himself for the answer. *This is going to be bad. No one in any game I'm familiar with pays a newbie that kind of loot for just any job.*

Smith made a big show of digging through his papers, pulled one out of the stack and slid it across the desk. "A number of years ago, an item belonging to me was taken."

Gareth reached out and picked up the paper. It was a drawing of a glowing orb held in an ornate frame. Eagles were prominently featured in the decoration. This, coincidentally enough, matched the exact description of the missing guildstone from the human guildhall that had been meticulously recounted to him by Ceasar, the guildhall's keeper.

Well...*fuck.*

"Very pretty. I can see why you want it back. But...why me? For that kind of reward, you could get just about anyone to go after it." Gareth gave the Lord an exaggerated shrug. "I'm barely out of the newbie zone."

When Gareth met Smith's gaze once more, he noted how the lord's eyes darted around the room before meeting Gareth's gaze. "Well, as I said, this particular item needs a *human's* touch. The item in question is protected by wards of great power. It is keyed so that only humans can touch it."

Gareth blinked at him. "And you think *I* can retrieve this item? I'm only 6th level."

Smith blew out a breath through his slit nostrils. "I've already heard of how resourceful you and your companions are. I'm sure you'll manage." Behind Gareth, the door opened once again. Lord Smith glanced over Gareth's head, and then waved at the desk. "You'll join me for tea, of course."

"I…" Gareth had no idea about the protocol of this situation. To be honest, his knowledge of social niceties in general was pretty weak, as his ex-wife had often loved to point out. Was tea normally expected when conducting business here? Gareth had spent one forced vacation in London. They took their tea very seriously there. Hell, English war tanks were even equipped so they could make tea in the field. Gareth regarded it as nasty, hot brown water. He mentally shrugged. Might as well just go along with it, gross brown water or no. God grant the tea hadn't been poisoned, however. "Thank you, I'm happy to have some."

A servant stepped around him and placed an ornate tea service in the middle of the desk. It was made from some sort of translucent white material that almost glowed. The cups themselves were rimmed with gold, and the handles were carved to look like miniature dragons in flight. Lord Smith hadn't pulled out the cheap service to entertain him.

The servant looked mostly human, except he (or she? Or *it?* Who really knew?) was extremely thin and stood about seven feet tall. The servant poured and placed a cup in front of each of them. Then, they withdrew without ever having spoken a word.

Gareth looked into his own cup, almost afraid to touch it because it looked so delicate. It might fall apart if he breathed on it too hard. Noticing his hesitation, Lord Smith waved him on. "Amazing, isn't it? It took me decades to acquire this set once I'd seen it. Its previous owner was very…*reluctant* to let it go. It's made of dragon-bone china. Don't worry, it's virtually indestructible. It also keeps the tea hot for an astonishingly long time."

Gareth studied the cup once more. "That's, uh, truly amazing." He picked up his cup with two fingers of each hand

and took a sip. He was a bit disappointed to find that the tea tasted like, well, *tea*. Not some exotic drink that was merely labeled *tea* here. Just the same nasty, brown water. It was probably made from plants fertilized with unicorn crap, though. Lord Smith didn't seem like a Lipton kind of guy.

The walrus lord seemed determined to continue his small talk despite Gareth's hesitant consumption of the drink. "So how do you like Muddy River? Does it compare to your home back on Earth?"

After gingerly placing the cup back on the saucer, Gareth leaned forward to answer the question in the most neutral way possible. They spent the next half hour like that, sipping tea and making polite chit-chat.

When they'd finished the pot, Lord Smith politely stood and walked Gareth out of the office. At the doorway, he stopped and handed over a map.

"This will show you the way to the item I need retrieved. Go and discuss it with your associates. There's no hurry. Anytime in the next week or so would be fine."

Then he closed the door, leaving Gareth in the hall, frowning at the wooden door, wondering what he'd just gotten himself into.

•Quest: Retrieve the guildstone for Lord Smith. Travel to the indicated location and retrieve the guildstone. Return it to Lord Smith within one week.

•Assistance provided: none

•Reward: 1,000,000 gold crowns. Possible further quests granted by Lord Smith.

•Penalties for failure: banishment from Muddy River.

This is a mandatory quest.

** Quest update: Locate the missing Vagrant guildstone and return it to the guildhall.

•You now know where the orb is located.

•The next step is to retrieve the orb.

•Sadly, Lord Smith has given you a quest for the same item. Choose well, young one. Your future will be determined by the choice you make.

Gareth heaved a great sigh. *No pressure* or anything.

CHAPTER
THIRTY-SIX
MAPPING OUT A PLAN

GARETH FOUND HIS COLLEAGUES RIGHT WHERE HE'D left them, in the waiting room with the beautiful centaur woman. Xena and Kara had apparently passed the time playing a variation of *Marry, Fuck, Kill.* called *Rob, Torture, Dismember.* and were naming people whom they'd encountered in the game. Gareth didn't really press them for details, since he was anxious to leave the palace as quickly as possible.

Once they'd made it safely out of doors, the trio headed through the city streets toward Blacl's Inn.

"So, what did he want?" Kara started.

Gareth pressed his lips together. "He wants me to retrieve some guildstone that only a human can get."

She stopped in her tracks and peered up at him. "You don't mean...?"

"Yeah, unfortunately, that's exactly what I mean. He wants the same item that *I* need to return to the guildhall. Then, we had tea."

"*Tea?*" Xena asked.

"Yeah, he told me what he wanted me to do, then we sat and drank with some super fancy tea set. And made chit-chat." Gareth shook his head at the absurdity of all that had gone on.

Before he could start to walk again, Kara reached out and grabbed his shirt. "What—what did the tea set look like? Did it have dragons on it?"

"Oh yeah, it did. He said it was dragon-bone china. He made a big deal over it. Why?"

Kara was biting her lip, brows furrowed. "Shit." She let go of him and began to pace. Gareth found it mildly amusing to watch her stomp around on her short legs until slowly realizing that she was deadly serious.

Gareth stepped into her path. "What's the big deal? Having tea was weird, but the dude himself is weird, so—"

"It wasn't just *tea.* you idiot!" Kara shouted.

Gareth held up his hands and backed off. "Okay, Okay. *Not* the tea. Then, what was it?

Kara heaved a sigh. "Let me tell you a story. There was a young lord looking to establish himself in his new position as town leader. Now, this lord had an eye for the finer things, and one day he came across a tea set that struck his fancy. The owner, who very much enjoyed the tea set, swore that he would never sell. And he was right, he never did sell. He *gave* it to the lord two years later, before leaving the town, never to be seen again."

Gareth tilted his head at Kara, confused. "Well, that's kind of disturbing. But still, it's a *tea set —*"

"Did I mention that the owner was a dragon? And that the tea set was made from the bones of his beloved grandmother?"

Gareth's stomach dropped. "Oh."

Kara gestured with her tiny hands in tight, agitated circles. "*Tea.* with that particular tea set, is a *message*. A statement that Lord Smith *always* gets what he wants. If he can force a dragon to give up a beloved family heirloom, what can he force *you* to do?"

"Maybe the dragon was old and sick?" Xena interjected.

"I think even an old and sick dragon would be more powerful than we are," Kara replied.

"Well, I'm not giving him my guildstone, but..." Gareth thought back to his encounter with Chief Bureaucrat Smith. "You know, Lord Smith's brother gave me a quest to fix some magic clock. If I can do that, Lord Smith will end up back on the station and his brother will take his place here. That would cancel the quest from Lord Smith, wouldn't it?" Gareth looked at his group mates, who just stared back at him.

"I *guess*..." Kara finally said. "It's a better plan than just hoping he won't get too mad when you screw him over and keep the guildstone."

"*I* think it's a good plan," Gareth groused. "Anyway, Lord Smith gave me a map to the guildstone. So we know where it is now."

Kara's eyes narrowed, hands curled in fists resting on her hips. "The quest giver of a retrieval quest gave you a map, huh? You really must have twisted his arm."

She actually had laughter in her voice. *Mocking* laughter, anyway.

Gareth blinked. "Well, I—"

"Why did you not import that map into your map?" Xena hovered peering over his shoulder down at the quest map.

"My map? You mean the city map of Muddy River? I didn't see any way to import additional maps into it. And it only seems to show the city, anyway. Everything outside the town limits is gray."

Xena blew a long breath out her snout. "Not the city map. Everyone gets that. It's just for Muddy River township. I meant a *useful* map—one that can show the area outside the city." Xena shook her head. "Everyone should acquire a map. Maps are the second thing you should buy, if you don't already have one, after your backpack. How else do you keep track of where you have been and where you need to go? Even I have a map." Xena pulled out a map that seemed to be drawn on the inside of some kind of animal pelt to show him, which seemed to show the areas immediately outside the city.

Gareth held up a hand in concession. "Okay, I get it. I need to buy a map."

Xena gestured at his quest map with a paw. "First, roll that thing up before someone steals it. Maps are bound to their owners. *Quest* maps are not. That's why people buy personal maps."

"Fine." Gareth quickly rolled up the quest map, tucking it into his backpack. "Happy now? Let's go to the map store. Then, we have to see about going to this North Bringer Abbey place that's on the map."

Kara waved to gesture to their surroundings, the nondescript, narrow alley they'd ducked into. "*Shh.* The walls have ears. Do you know nothing, human?" With that, Kara turned and started down the road toward what he hoped was the map store.

He was shortly told it was a *cartographer's shop* not a map store. In a fit of pique, Gareth edited its description to read *Map Store.* He'd be the only one who'd see it, but it satisfied him, nevertheless. This constant feeling of being the village idiot was getting old.

They entered the store to the ring of a little brass bell at the top of the door, just like in those old movies Gran used to make him watch. The store itself was stuffed with maps. There were shelves and cabinets everywhere, all filled with rolled up maps and everything meticulously labeled. Curious, he picked up one of them and started to unroll it.

The proprietor came bustling up from the back as Gareth did so. "A very wise choice, good sir. Maps of the Outer Banks are very rare. You may have that one for a paltry 1,000 crowns."

Gareth almost dropped the map in his hands. "A *thousand* crowns?" He had to admit his voice squeaked a bit. Quickly, he released one side and let the map roll back up. Then he gingerly replaced it on its shelf.

The shop owner released a snort of amusement. Gareth turned to take him in. The proprietor was a goose. Not goose-*like.* but an actual effing six-foot tall goose. With hands at the ends of its wings or feathered arms or...whatever they were. Given that Earth geese were right bastards who'd break your arm as soon as look at you, he silently vowed not to aggravate this one.

The giant goose creature stepped in front of him, a big-ass goose beak inches from his face. This did absolutely nothing for his peace of mind. "How may I be of service, then, if you're not looking for a map of the Outer Banks?"

"I do need a map."

The creature made an indiscriminate sound. "Yes, of course, sir. Your presence here certainly implies that."

Gareth stared. Not only a goose, but a snarky goose.

Kara stepped up to stand beside Gareth. "What he means, is he needs a *personal* map. He doesn't have one yet." Kara poked Gareth in the side again. She seemed to like doing that whenever she thought he was being especially stupid.

The goose gave no indication one way or the other whether it, too, thought Gareth was being stupid. "Ahh, certainly, certainly. Right this way." The shopkeeper led them to the back of the store, where several blank maps were on prominent display. Gareth noticed one particularly ornate map mounted on the wall.

He pointed it out. "What's that?"

"Oh, that is a very special map, friend. It is a *guild* map." At Gareth's continued blank stare, the goose continued. "A guild map compiles all of the information gathered by guild members onto one giant map. Then, if you need to travel to somewhere a guild member has been before, all you need to do is approach the guild map and copy the relevant information onto your personal map. Guild maps are very useful, but very difficult to make."

Gareth's eyes narrowed at the description. "And therefore very *expensive*. I'm guessing."

The goose bobbed its head. "Quite so, I'm afraid." He dug around in a pile of parchments for a minute and produced three blank maps of varying sizes. "Here you go. Maps for every need."

"What's the difference between them?"

"The price, of course." The goose-man let out a number of loud honks, which Gareth took for laughter. "Sorry, a little merchant humor. I meet so few new people, I hardly ever get to use that joke anymore. The difference in the maps is the amount of information they can hold. The bigger the map, the more you can explore before you fill it up. The maps here are 100, 200, and 500 crowns. Each map holds roughly ten times the territory of the previous map."

Gareth frowned. Well, the 500-crown map was out. He didn't have that much gold left. The 200-crown one was possible but would take almost everything he had. Gareth scratched his jaw. "I guess I'll get the 100-crown map."

The goose-man held out one of his weird, feathered hands. "I would caution against that, good sir. That map is only capable of holding the city here and perhaps ten miles out in every direction. It's fine for farmers, but not for an adventurer such as yourself."

Gareth's mouth twisted in thought. "That may be true, but my bank balance says the small map is preferable."

The goose raised his "hand" to stroke his beak and studied Gareth. "Maybe we can work something out. You look like the kind of people that get up to interesting things. Where are you headed, if I may be so bold as to ask?"

Gareth glanced at Kara before replying. She gave a small shrug. Gareth took that to mean that the amount he revealed was up to him. He turnedback at the goose, determined to remain vague. "We're not exactly sure. Somewhere northeast of town."

The goose sucked in a breath. "You're not headed to the Forest of Ill-Intent, by any chance?"

Gareth glanced at Kara, who gave him a subtle nod this time. "Well, yeah. It appears that we are."

The goose waved his hands excitedly. "Well then, I think we can be of some use to each other."

The shopkeeper walked over to a locked cabinet and pulled out a large ornate key, shaped like a goose in flight. He inserted it into the keyhole and turned it in a strange pattern of lefts and rights that Gareth couldn't follow. There were a series of clicks that told Gareth that it was some sort of bizarre combination lock. After a minute, there was a loud *clunk*. as if all the tumblers had moved into place at once. The shopkeeper removed the key and returned it to the inner pocket of his vest.

Then, he opened the cabinet door, which immediately triggered a raucous, ear-splitting noise…

Honk! Honk! Honk!

It was as if a flock of a hundred angry geese were descending on the store. Gareth immediately ducked and covered his ears, but that did little to dampen the sound. The shop owner, almost in a panic, was using his winged hands to frantically touch at various spots on the cabinet. After too many seconds, the racket thankfully abated.

The goose man heaved a great sigh. "Sorry about that, I always forget to disarm the alarm first."

Gareth shook his head, ears still ringing with the sounds of those obnoxious honks. "Quite all right. Just, uh, try not to do that again, *please*." An uncharitable thought crossed his mind, that even if Gareth *had* been trying to memorize the key turns to unlock the chest, the assault honking would have driven all thoughts of it right out of his head.

When Gareth straightened, he noticed that Xena was glaring hard at the goose-man's back, her lip curled. If her hearing was anything like that of the wolves she resembled, just two seconds of that would have been torture for her. Out of the corner of his eye, he spied Kara pocketing what looked suspiciously like earplugs.

Gareth addressed the goose shopkeeper, eager to spur this along. "I think you said something about us, ah, helping each other out?"

The goose nodded while rummaging around inside the cabinet. After a minute, he extracted a rolled-up map tied with a silver ribbon.

He turned back to the group, which had mostly recovered from the recent sonic assault. "Yes, yes. You need a map, do you not?" At Gareth's nod the goose continued. "And *I* need some areas of my map filled in and updated." He unrolled the new map in front of them. "*This* will help with both our problems."

Gareth looked down at yet another blank map and stared, scratching his jaw. His stomach dropped a little as the thought crossed his mind.

Egads, yet another quest?

He might be a newbie, but as a heaviness sank onto his shoulders, he couldn't help but think that he was getting too old for this shit.

CHAPTER
THIRTY-SEVEN
ONWARD

So, I'm a cartographer now? Gareth scrubbed his hand over his face, still unable to absorb the fact that he was having a discussion with a talking goose about mapping out an unknown area of the world…in order to be able to afford a map for himself.

What?

"How do I even do this?" Gareth turned to the goose-creature, shop proprietor and dealer in all things maps.

To his surprise, Kara piped up with the answer. "It's a squire map."

Gareth blinked. Was he supposed to know what the hell that was? "Oh. Great. A squire map."

She heaved a sigh as if trying to explain calculus to a preschooler. "Squire maps are linked to a master map. As you explore, any updates to the squire map are copied to the master."

"So…it's a map? Isn't this how the guildhall maps work? You just said—"

She shook her head. "Normal maps have to be brought next to each other to update. Squire map updates are reflected in the master map *as they are made.*"

"Oh, I see. So, I wander around and his map gets updated." Gareth scratched his jaw, considering. "Seems kinda stalkery to be honest."

"Most people aren't comfortable with that much knowledge about their location floating around. That's why people avoid this kind of map. Even if the price is right"

The goose proprietor threw a feathered hand over his chest. "I would *never!* It's against the Cartographer Guild laws to release *any* information about the location of those who are mapping for us. To give out your location to anyone would see me expelled from the guild!"

Gareth turned back to Kara, who just gave him a shrug. "That's what they *say.* anyway."

Gareth sighed and asked the cartographer, "So, what's in it for me?"

"*Your* map would be linked to *my* master map." The goose creature beamed as if he'd just bestowed Gareth with a pile of gold.

For himself, Gareth felt like he needed a translator for this entire conversation. Kara seemed to have been a good, if impatient, source of information, so he turned to her with his brows raised. She interpreted the gesture immediately. "He means that your map would have no storage limit. It would keep gathering information and updating wherever you went."

Gareth's brows furrowed, considering. Then he turned back to the shopkeeper. "Just one thing, though. I started with more crowns than most, what do others do to get maps? Or am I getting the special human pricing?"

The goose raised its head to the limits of its long neck, clearly affronted. "I assure you, the price is the price. There are no 'special prices' here."

Gareth stepped back, trying to take himself out of wing-smack range. "Then how—?"

"*Most* people either get a map from their guild or start with one as a racial perk. I"—the goose stepped forward—"make my living selling map updates. The sale of basic maps is limited to independents such as yourself. I do *not* cheat people."

Gareth quickly put his hands up, trying to calm the goose, "Sorry, sorry. It just seemed a bit odd that the maps were so expensive, but you had a ready solution. I didn't mean to offend."

"Humph." The goose did not seem mollified.

Kara's mouth opened, and she stepped forward like she wanted to interject. Gareth headed her off, he'd already learned Kara had a talent for aggravating merchants. "*You* both said I need a map. Clearly, I can't afford a decent map. Doing this task for the, ah, kindly gentleman will get me a useful map. If goose-feathers here screws me, we'll deal with him then. Right, Xena?"

The goose startled, staring up, up, up behind Gareth. The shopkeeper flailed his wings trying to put space between him and the towering wolf. Xena nodded her agreement to Gareth's statement, curling her lips back even further to show more fang.

The gooseman's feathers ruffled and he stepped back, taking some calming breaths before he spoke again. "Like I said, your individual information will never be sold. Just the anonymous data of where you've been. Do we have a deal then?" He held out one wing-arm so Gareth could take his feathered hand.

Gareth was about to reciprocate when he paused. "I'm Gareth, by the way."

"I'm Can-da."

"Well Can-da, we have a deal." Gareth reached out and shook the proffered limb.

Can-da handed the rolled-up map to him. As soon as Gareth touched it, a prompt appeared:

***Install and link map module? (Y/N)**

He quickly chose *Yes,* and the map scroll vanished. A new icon appeared at the top of his vision showing a stylized map. He clicked on it and saw the top-down view of a map of the building they were currently in. There were three dots indicating the location of each group member. The new map had much greater resolution than the starter city map when zoomed in and showed the location of each group member, which was useful. Gareth played around with the settings, zooming out to a map of the entire city and even beyond until further zooming out just showed a blank map with a stylized icon for the city with the surrounding area waiting to be filled in.

Can-da explained, "I took the liberty of loading the city map for you. Everything else is for you to fill in. An *up-to-date* map. You can just delete that trash map you started with."

Gareth pulled himself away from his new toy and shrank the map, allowing him to see the shop again. "Thanks, this should be very helpful."

"It only helps us with part of our problem though," Kara butted in.

He quirked an eyebrow at her, silently questioning.

She rolled her eyes. "Now, import your quest map."

"Right." Gareth dug out the map that he'd been given by Lord Smith. Having had enough of the snarky advice for the day, he didn't ask how to copy the quest map into his own map. He figured he could just put out the thought to import via the UI. Surprisingly, this did exactly nothing.

Kara stomped her foot. "We don't have all day, human."

Both Xena and Can-da stared at him expectedly. Desperate, he held out the map and said aloud, "Import." He could almost feel the sigh of exasperation in her response this time. Kara took pity on him, whispering, "In your UI under *Map*."

He quickly found the entry in question and the quest map vanished from his hand as it copied itself into the main map. "It's not my fault. Normally, I just have to click on things. Actually, being *in* the game is different."

"Adapt quicker, Gareth. This isn't a game," came Xena's growl from over his head.

"But it *is* a game," he protested.

"That's not what I mean," she replied. "Actions here have real consequences. The worst thing that happened to you before was that you lost some time and forgot to feed your dog."

He grimaced and shook his head in denial. "I *never* forgot to feed—" under Xena's glare he wilted. "Okay, *almost* never forgot to feed my dog. And she always reminds me if I do with that slimy cold nose of hers. Anyway, I understand the seriousness of my situation here."

"I doubt that. But you will learn. Or die." Xena turned away. Apparently, the conversation was now over.

More than a bit weirded out by the turn of the conversation, Gareth figured it was time to take his leave of Can-da and the cartographer shop.

"That map you loaded is quite old. I'm not sure what use it will be to you," the goose said before Gareth could turn to go.

"What?"

"I was curious, so I accessed the master map to see your map update. It shows North Bringer Abbey. That place hasn't existed under that name for over a thousand years."

Of course it doesn't. He didn't know why he'd expected Lord Smith or his map to be helpful. Not when most of the people here acted like it was the year of *screw the human*. "Why, what's it called now?"

"No one knows what the inhabitants call it. Most maps just label it the Abbey of Death." The goose shook his head, muttering a quiet "oh dear" under its breath.

Gareth's eyebrows darted up. "Well, that's cheerful."

Kara wedged herself in front of Gareth to address the goose. "So, Feathers. How come no one knows the *actual* name for it?"

Can-da's neck coiled, lowering his head to just above his body. "No one who's gone has ever come back."

Kara blinked, then turned and headed toward the door. "Well, don't that just figure."

Xena shrugged and followed her.

Gareth hesitated at the counter, feeling the need to be polite. "Thank you for all your help."

Can-da's neck un-coiled, raising his head up to its normal height, then he nodded enthusiastically. "I look forward to your map updates with great interest. Try not to die too much. Or if you do, at least die somewhere *interesting*."

Gareth's eyebrows arched once more. "I'll—ah—do my best." He bowed toward the goose and followed the other two out of the shop.

When Gareth caught up with them, they were whispering with their heads together—which given their height difference, made for an odd sight—outside the shop. Whatever they were discussing, they cut off abruptly when Gareth joined them.

"Be careful Gareth, that goose is more than he appears," Kara said.

"I concur," added Xena, lip curling to reveal a gleaming fang. "This map he gave you is one of the least valuable things in his locked cabinet. Any typical vendor would have been robbed of it and any of the other items long ago."

Gareth's tone took on a grave note. "Look, I appreciate the warnings, but I knew he could be trouble when he told me his name." They both frowned at him, clearly confused. "Back home, Canadian geese are the assholes of the bird world. This game's been going out of its way to interface with me and present this world in a way I can relate to. I'm sure as hell not going to ignore such an obvious warning as Can-da the goose."

By the way Kara shrugged, he couldn't tell if she understood him or not.

"Look, according to the map, this North Bringer Abbey—or whatever it's called now—is about a week's march north of here, through the Forest of Ill Repute and into the Bog of Unusual Smells." To which Gareth rolled his eyes. "Damn, who names this crap? I need to make a quick supply run before we leave. Meet at the north gate in an hour?"

The two gave silent nods but didn't appear very enthused about the proposed journey. Nevertheless, he headed off toward the Muddy River bazaar to top off his supplies. He whistled a jaunty tune on the way. It would be nice to get out of the city again.

Maybe even safer, too.

Hopefully.

CHAPTER THIRTY-EIGHT

SNIFFING OUT THE ENEMY

Xena watched as her human and the two-legged *not* -human left to prepare for their trip to the monastery. It was with no small relief, since she'd been hoping to have some time to herself. If she was lucky, their preparations would take a while, giving her the perfect opportunity to get down to the business she needed to attend to.

Raising her muzzle to the air, she took in a deep sniff. Yes...*Yes*. North...no, northwest. She sprang into motion, following the scent, only stopping to get another sniff every block or two.

Getting closer. West...now south and...west again. North...east! The scent was strong now. Her target had to be close.

She halted, taking one last sniff, then caught movement of someone walking in the street. There he was, coming out of Exotic Goods for the Discerning Gentleman. Tall, lanky, yellow eyes. She quickly jumped upward and grabbed onto the roof of the building next to her, pulling herself up before her target caught sight of her.

Along the roofline, she followed him for a number of blocks, the close-set buildings providing Xena an easy path. The footing was tricky, but she managed it with finesse, never losing sight of her prey. Finally, her target, Eugene the Butcher, entered a small alley that would provide the measure of privacy she'd require for their "talk."

Moving with dangerous speed, she dropped down behind him, and as she hadn't bothered to be quiet about it, he jumped, banging into boxes piled along the walls. In the process, he lost his balance but recovered quickly, spinning around. His hand reached for the dagger at his waist.

"Look, I don't want any trouble," he started, before catching sight of the large figure waiting behind him. His eyes widened with realization. "Wait... you're that friend of Gareth's. Z-something."

"Xena," she growled.

"Yeah, right, Xena. You should watch out. You could get hurt surprising people like that."

Xena merely returned the stare without reply.

Eugene stammered a bit, clearly uncomfortable under her gaze. "So, ah, was there something I can do for you?" A worried look crept across his features. "Did Gareth change his mind about just letting me go?"

Xena opened her mouth and smiled, disquieting Eugene even more as his eyes flashed with something like fear. "No. Gareth is an understanding and forgiving human. He considers the incident in the past."

Eugene's body language sagged with relief. "Oh, that's great. He's a great guy, that Gareth. I'll, uh, just be on my way then."

Xena's toothy smile widened, fangs on full display now. "*I,* however, am a vicious and vindictive being. Allow me to demonstrate why it's a bad idea to try to get my human killed."

Eugene needed nothing more to cause him to turn tail and run. Xena's axe made a satisfying swish sound as she unsheathed it from the harness along her back. That sound was almost as satisfying as the scream that followed it while she carefully sliced the tendons along the back of both his heels when she executed a snare strike.

With a screech, he went down, then began to drag himself in the same direction while gazing back over his shoulder at her.

"Bad creature," Xena scolded. "I wasn't done talking with you yet."

"Please—please! I had no choice. He didn't even end up getting injured."

Xena tsked. "Only out of sheer luck. We both know that he should have died after you set him up." Eugene's eyes widened in horror as a rope of drool dripped off Xena's fang and hit the ground next to him.

"You said you had no choice, that they would have killed you. Your education is seriously lacking if you think a quick death at the Elite's hands is the worst thing that can happen to you." Xena's eyes narrowed and Eugene struggled in vain to drag himself a few inches away from her, squirming along in the muck like common vermin. "Allow me to demonstrate."

Xena returned her axe to its harness, then reached down to her belt to pull out a knife. She loved her axe, but she needed a bit more finesse for this. After all, she didn't want to cleave something vital and end the lesson prematurely.

The dim light glinted off the shiny, sharp blade, and with a growl, she leaned in to begin the "lesson."

Sometime later Xena exited the alley. She was rubbing the muck off her blade with an old cloth when she noticed a large-eared biped lounging near the alley's entrance. The creature made several darting looks around in every direction before approaching Xena.

"Was that *really* necessary?" the creature asked, presumably in irritation. "I don't like spending this much time in the open. Death is everywhere."

Xena curled her lip as she looked down at a representative of the other race native to her home planet. "Yes. Muddy River is a hotbed of assassinations," she said her voice dripping with sarcasm. "Perhaps you should hop back to your hole if you're so concerned." *Grass-eaters* …Xena gave a mental sneer.

The creature, which still had not introduced itself, just stared at the alley behind Xena.

Xena shrugged, slightly abashed. "There are exceptions." She finished cleaning and stored her weapon. "Why are you here?"

"Because I have the report you requested." He reached into his belt pouch and pulled out a small crystal cube. Tossing the cube to Xena, he turned to leave.

"*Wait.* I may have questions." Xena's hand flicked out and caught the cube, which gave a small flash and vanished as her paw cupped it. This uploaded the report into her UI, where a plethora of text crawled across her visual field.

"Hmm. This report is quite thorough." Xena caught a glimpse of movement out of the corner of her eye and let out a short growl. The creature immediately froze in its tracks.

"It says here that Muddy River used to be a human outpost. I suppose that makes sense, given its location. It continued under human leadership for quite some time after the fall—until the leadership disappeared, supposedly due to some sort of falling out amongst them. After that, the 'Smith' family took over and led various unexceptional lives, taking us to the current 'Lord Smith.' This pattern held until about 187 years ago." Xena looked up at the messenger. "Why? What happened 187 years ago?"

The creature gestured toward Xena's head. "It's in the report." He bounced from foot to foot, taking in their surroundings from every angle. Clearly, it was uncomfortable and wanted to leave.

"Yes, but this report is very extensive. Sum it up for me," Xena growled back.

"One hundred eighty-seven years ago, a human came through a portal. He and the current Lord Smith started a partnership. Then, the city guards started disappearing. Once they were gone, Lord Smith seemed to no longer be satisfied with taking his cut of everything but wanted to actually rule. Players resisted this initially, but eventually they either accepted it or moved on. That's when The Elite became the premier guild in the city and the enforcers of Lord Smith's rule."

Xena stroked a patch of fur on her neck, deep in thought. "What happened to this human?"

The creature gestured with its paws, long ears twitching behind it. "He left eventually, putting his second in command in charge of the local guild. We have no information on what happened to him after he left Muddy River. There are suggestions that both Lord Smith and the current guild commander of The Elite can contact him if necessary."

Xena let out a low growl as she pondered these facts. This really seemed to upset the courier, who was rapidly bouncing from foot to foot, long ears still twitching, nose wiggling. "Very well. You may leave. I can't even think while you're doing that." The courier shifted his weight in preparation for scurrying off, when Xena held up her paw, halting his escape. "Wait, what is your designation? I may need your assistance in the future."

The courier's mouth twisted, clearly not happy at the suggestion of further interactions. Regardless, he grunted out, "Jack," before scrambling down the street, quickly finding a crowd and losing himself in it.

Xena watched his progress. "Jack. How appropriate."

She turned back to the report in her UI once again, before closing it. She'd have to finish her review later. Time was running short.

One thing had stuck out to her, though. A footnote in the city background section noting that while under human rule, the city had a different name. Typically human, the name made no sense as it wasn't descriptive of the city at all. Muddy River, she could understand, since the river was, in fact, muddy.

But *Avalon?*

What could that possibly refer to? Maybe she'd ask Gareth if it meant anything to him. Maybe not, though. Her human knew a lot of things, but it was mostly fiction or Earth-game related. What could he possibly know about a human in-game settlement from thousands of years ago?

Chapter Thirty-Nine

Can't See the Forest for the Trees

GARETH'S BACKPACK HAD BEEN STOCKED FULL OF rations and anything he could remember about the standard dungeoneer's pack from all those years of playing Dungeons & Dragons, including an expandable 10-foot pole that he'd been so proud to find. Every good adventurer needed a pole. Losing the 42-ish crowns had hurt, but better than dying due to a lack of equipment. He glanced at his upkeep counter which currently stood at 118 days. He had 178 crowns in the bank now, but his upkeep had increased to 1.5 crowns a day due to his increase in level.

Currently, he stood at the city gate, where Xena and Kara were to join him, as they'd agreed. In addition to supplies, Gareth had decided he needed a ranged weapon option, so a new short bow and quiver of arrows were now strapped next to his pack.

He'd grown up playing second edition D&D, and bows were a no-no for paladins in that system, so he'd avoided one at first. But the lethality of this game dictated that he couldn't give up an advantage for role-playing reasons. Hopefully if he ever figured out how to unlock the paladin class for humans, having a bow wouldn't be a deal breaker.

He only had to wait a few minutes for Kara and Xena to appear. Kara had changed into a full set of leather armor he could only describe as mottled green, like forest camouflage. Xena had gone the other way, wearing what looked like plate mail and carrying a shield taller than Gareth. All in all, he imagined that they made quite the fearsome-looking group. Well, Xena and Kara did anyway.

"Ready to go? I've got about four hours left to play before I need to logout and see to Xena-the-dog again."

Xena-the-warrior looked like she was about to comment, but changed her mind, looking off toward the gate instead.

"Nothing to add, big-stuff?" Kara asked, arching a brow up at their tallest party member.

Xena shook her head and headed toward the gate.

Gareth stared after her, frowning. What was that all about? They must have had some sort of talk while he was on his supply run. Whatever. If it was important, it would be made clear soon, and if not, then it wasn't worth digging into.

The trek toward the forest went quickly at first. They proceeded down a wide road paved with large, flat stones fitted together expertly. Who built the roads here? This game was ancient. Had this same set of roads existed since the beginning?

Could a group of players get together and decide to build a random road somewhere?

As he walked, Gareth studied the surface of the road directly in front of him, but it stonily provided no clues. He didn't want to ask Kara because he'd had his fill of "you're such a newb" attitude for the day.

Still, being able to permanently change the game world would open up some interesting possibilities. Also, if you could build roads, there almost certainly had to be a dick-shaped one out there somewhere. He'd have to keep an eye out.

The city grew smaller and smaller behind them as they transitioned into farmland soon after leaving the city gates. They passed a few groups headed back toward the city, looking a bit worse for the wear, but other than a few grunts and nods, they didn't interact. There'd also been a few trash mobs, but they'd all taken to their heels at the sight of Xena.

Missing the chance for easy experience sucked. Gareth glanced over at Xena—how could he blame them for beating a hasty retreat? Fleeing mobs were a new experience though. In most games, they were happy to lie down and die in hordes for the players. Evaluating your opponent was normally an intelligence-only thing—reserved for PCs. How would things work with more intelligent enemies? Would the giant spiders use bats to scout for them?

An hour out, their journey brought the party to the edge of the forest. A dirt path branched off from the road and meandered into the heart of the wood.

The forest itself was almost absurdly cheerful looking. All bright, flowery trees drenched in sunshine, with soft-looking grass and scattered wildflowers growing all around, just begging to be lain upon. Gareth's eyes narrowed.

"Anything this innocent-looking is hiding something," he said, scratching his chin thoughtfully.

Kara stepped up beside him. "Well, it *is* called the forest of ill-intent. There has to be a reason for that name."

Xena gave both of them a look, then brandished her axe. "Speculation is useless." With no further words, she headed down the path.

Gareth readied his weapons and trotted after her. "Hey, slow down. We're not all giants, you know. Look at poor Kara, she's going to collapse trying to keep up." In response, Kara shot him a glare.

"Very well. I will moderate my pace. You like to talk too much. We know what we must do, so let us do it." Xena slowed her pace only slightly.

Gareth gestured to the surrounding forest. "We don't even know what's in here."

Xena continued trudging forward, speaking without looking at either one of them. "Talking will not permit us to discover anything."

Gareth squinted up at Xena. "No, but some caution is in order, I think."

"Perhaps," she grunted.

Gareth studied Xena, but it was difficult to read any expression on her wolf-like face. For her part, she made it obvious that she was ignoring him. He cocked his head at her. "What's with you, anyway? You've been fairly mellow up 'til now."

Just when her silence stretched so long that he didn't think she'd reply, she finally spoke. "I haven't been able to hunt properly since we met. I've fallen behind on my leveling schedule." Xena continued to scan the area in front of and to the sides of them, like she was hoping something would jump out and attack.

"*Leveling schedule?*" He cocked a brow at her.

Xena's head never stopped its scan of the area, always vigilant. Probably a good thing, since Gareth had been concentrating on her and had forgotten to do so himself. Darting a look behind them, he realized that Kara had disappeared, though his map showed her paralleling them off to the right of the path. He obviously needed to work on this group leadership thing.

"My people, the lupinii, come with a set of custom titles only visible to other lupinii. These titles are, among other things, tied to leveling speed. Our sojourn in the city was necessary, but now I am in danger of having my current title replaced with an inferior one."

Gareth's brows knit. "That's, um, intense. You're level 8—wait what the—*level 9?* When the hell did *that* happen?" An unwelcome sense of inferiority started to settle over him.

"It happened while you were sleeping. I do not require as much rest as you do." With a snarl, Xena lunged to the left, her axe swiping through the air. A perfectly bisected bird dropped to the ground with a bloody splat.

Xena spat on the ground, grumbling "Five exp! This is intolerable."

Gareth stepped carefully over the bird's pulverized corpse. "When did you create your character?"

"I first spawned about a day before we met."

Gareth blinked. Holy Shit! His jaw tensed, teeth grinding against each other in frustration. It wasn't a race. Anything that made the group stronger benefited them all. *I'm a strong and powerful Fighter/Cleric.*

Then he cleared his throat. "So, you've gone from level 1 to level 9 in, what? About 3 days? I only just hit level 6 and I was power-leveled for part of the time. What is this title you have? Combat fiend? Level master?"

"*Adequate.*" Xena wrinkled her snout as she spat that out.

Gareth blinked again. "And…if you *don't* level up again soon?"

Xena's ears flickered and then lay flat on her head before she replied, "Sub-par."

Gareth could only shake his head. "Your race puts power gamers to shame. What do lupinii overachievers look like?"

Her ears flickered again, and her lip curled. "*Me.* They look like me. We will need to gather power quickly to survive." Xena's ears had returned to what Gareth thought of as her travel mode, each ear turned toward the sides, likely giving her the greatest chance of hearing anything trying to sneak up on them.

They continued in silence for another long stretch. Gareth pondered the realities of the game he'd tied himself to. It was becoming increasingly clear that there was a layer of brutality at the base of this game, and it was much more serious than just a way to make a buck. The forest was pleasant, though, despite its ill-omened name.

Which sparked another thought…

"Why do these look like trees?" Gareth asked.

He'd caught Xena staring at what looked like a fat squirrel before it scurried off into the forest. No doubt, she was weighing the exp potential of running after it. Hopefully she wasn't going to start murder-hoboing all the wildlife. He'd always found killing non-aggro animals distasteful in any game.

"*What?*" she growled as the squirrel bounded off.

"Well, this is a game that was created an ungodly number of years ago. By aliens." Gareth waved his arm toward the woods. "Why does this all look like home?"

Xena shook her head. "It doesn't. Or rather, it just looks that way to *you*. While we both see *trees*. the *trees* I see and the ones you see are different. We both see what's appropriate to our personal frame-of-reference."

Gareth nodded, pondering. "That makes no sense. There's like…what? A thousand different races playing the game? They have a thousand different models for every object in the game, and we all just see something different?" Gareth peered at a tree, trying to catch a glimpse or hint of what a "Xena tree" would look like. And how was she so knowledgeable when she was as new as he was? Perhaps her race—these lupinii—had a very thorough knowledge base.

Xena tilted her axe head to the left and then the right. Gareth took to be her way of indicating "sort-of."

She further explained, "A box is a box, no matter where you come from, so there are fewer models than you'd think at first. It only applies to the low-level areas, anyway. Once you get above level twenty, the game stops catering to your expectations so much. It's to help you focus on learning the game. And to *survive*—at the start anyway. Like I said, it gets harder."

Gareth's eyebrows climbed his forehead. "*This* is easy mode?" He could almost feel the dire-rat teeth ripping into his thigh again and flinched at the memory.

"The MCP, which is entrusted with running the game, decided that having familiar visual cues would allow players to focus on learning the game mechanics. That way, you would have an instinctive idea of how dangerous something is and be able to level up enough to have what it considers a fair start." Xena flipped her axe through the air, end over end, and caught it. Gareth figured it helped her think, but she could do it a bit further away.

He bit his lip, pondering. "Is that why there's a level cap in the town?"

"Yes. Every player has to have a real, if minuscule, chance to rise to the top of the game." This time, she let the axe spin in the air several times before reaching out to catch it. "If high level players were free to butcher newbies in a starting town like Muddy River, the newbies would have no chance of ever leveling enough to succeed in the game."

Gareth promptly scooted a few paces to the left before continuing the conversation. "How can any newbie succeed in a game as old as this one? Starting a brand-new character on an established server back home always put you at a disadvantage no matter what game it was. And they all had maximum level caps. It allowed you a chance to catch up. How can I compete with some elf that's been playing since the days of the Roman Empire?"

Xena sighed as if summoning the patience to explain physics to a child. "Players have a linear power curve. The experience requirements for leveling follows a geometric one. As long as you keep playing, eventually you'll catch up, mostly. In theory, anyway. I expect the existing powers will stack the deck as much as possible against the newer players."

Much to Gareth's relief, Xena stopped tossing her axe.

He scratched his jaw. "I'm sure. This is all very interesting. Who told you all of this?"

Xena shot him obvious side-eye. "The help files."

"Oh. Reading those is still on my to-do list."

She snorted. "I'm sure."

They quickly developed a routine. Travel through the woods during the day, taking a break at noon, when Gareth would log out to check on Xena-the-dog and take her out for a walk and a pee. He'd then log in and they'd continue traveling, making camp shortly before the sun set. Then Gareth would log again to feed and walk Xena, returning to the game in the morning.

It kind of felt like cheating to Gareth. The game world was so real, that logging out and spending the night in the comfort of his bed and his room felt wrong, like he should be sleeping on a bed roll next to the camp fire. He was probably overthinking it, though.

The forest had been growing steadily darker the longer they'd walked. In addition, the trees had grown larger and more densely packed together. It was getting harder and harder to keep an eye out and make sure nothing was sneaking up on them.

Gareth craned his neck to peer around a suspicious-looking bush when Kara raced toward them from out of the thicket.

She came to a stumbling halt in front of them, obviously winded. "Suh-uh-Several creatures approaching. Fro-from the southeast."

Gareth straightened with a swallow…she wouldn't have run up here like this if it were just more trash.

He steadied his shield and his grip on the pommel of his sword.

CHAPTER

FORTY

INCOMING!

GARETH TURNED TO XENA AS HE SCANNED THE AREA from where the breathless pixie had emerged. "Well, here's your chance to get some of that XP you want so much." He asked Kara, "What do you mean, *creatures?*"

Kara shrugged exaggeratedly. "I don't know...*creatures.* What more do you want?" Kara edged around, quite obviously putting Gareth and Xena between her and the approaching hostile mobs.

Gareth's eyes widened in exasperation. "Maybe a little description?"

She sighed heavily as if equally exasperated with him. "I didn't see them. I have a skill that lets me detect things. I sensed them creeping up on me and ran back here. Whatever they were, they tailed me closely as I ran back." Kara bent to peer around them, looking for any sign of the creatures in pursuit.

Gareth's gaze traced the path she'd taken toward them, but there was nothing there. "Is it, maybe, a city skill or something? Could the trees be confusing the skill? 'Cause I'm not seeing a damn thing."

Kara turned to him, reddening. "I'm telling you, *something* is coming. I keep getting pings so they're definitely getting closer."

"Perhaps they are invisible." Xena chimed in. She had her axe and shield at the ready and was actively sniffing the air.

"I don't think so." Gareth pointed to the area in front of them where short scrub grass grew between the trees. "The grass would be disturbed if something was moving through it. How far away are they now?"

Kara's wild eyes locked onto Gareth's face. "About 30 feet."

Gareth waved his hand around the area. "But...there's nothing there. Your skill is on the fritz. Sorry Xena, no experience for you."

"Maybe they're flying invisible creatures?" There was no mistaking the hopefulness in Xena's tone. Kara whisked out sword and waved it through the air.

Gareth just shrugged. "We'd hear something flying around. Come on. Let's go. There's nothing here but trees."

Xena's sniffing became more intense, her eyes narrowing. Then, she began to snarl. "I smell *something*."

Trees ...Gareth looked up just in time to catch a glimpse of something crawling from one tree to the next. And it—whatever it was—was currently one tree away from where they stood. "They're in the trees." His gaze sank to the ground once more, searching desperately for a nearby clearing. And while there was plenty of space at ground level, the canopy above was dense and full, with no breaks in sight. A chill sluiced down his back as he realized that the creatures could be above them—*anywhere*.

Gareth readied his own sword and shield just as he heard a branch crack above. He instinctively whipped his shield over his head as a mass dropped onto it. From underneath his improvised shelter, a veritable horde of legs tried to reach around the lip of the shield toward him. One swiped at his face when he tilted it to dump the creature onto the ground. Four of the legs curled around the lip of his shield and refused to let go, while the rest reached around and tried to attack him.

A meaty thump sounded behind him—followed quickly by a squishing sound as something landed next to him. A quick look down confirmed his fear—*spider*. Or in this case, *half* a spider since Xena had made quick work of it.

Gareth's head swam. *Spiders...why'd it have to be spiders?*

Ugh. Of all the Earth creatures this game could have replicated for this encounter, it had to pick the one that Gareth hated—and feared—the most.

He turned back to the one that had attached itself to his shield. Its fanged head appeared just over the bottom edge of the shield. He let out a high-pitched, less-than-manly shriek as venom dripped off its fang and hit the ground with a sizzle. There was no shame in this—any other man in his place would have done the same with a giant spider eying his junk from only inches away.

He frantically waved the shield around, trying to get the giant arachnid to let go, but to no avail. The spider's legs tensed, as if leveraging itself to scuttle around the shield and sink its fangs right into his not-armored-enough goods. In desperation, he spotted a tree trunk about ten feet away and shot off in that direction. Just as the spider sprang toward its mark, Gareth leapt at the tree, readying the full force of his body against the spider to squish it between shield and tree trunk.

He slammed into the tree with a resounding *thwok*. The spider released its multi-legged grip on the shield and was now trying to flip over from its back, legs thrashing the air above it. Gareth gathered himself and jumped backward, noticing as he did so that he'd lost a little health from hitting the tree.

From this angle, Gareth was able to get a closer look at his eight-legged foe. Its leg span was approximately 4 or 5 feet, and the body was about the size of a large dog. In addition, clear malevolence gleamed in its myriad of eyes as it glared back at him.

Wanting to avoid a lunge from the spider, Gareth took the offensive, stepping forward to stab it repeatedly as it struggled to right itself on the ground. It was very obviously damaged from being sandwiched between the tree and Gareth's shield.

Even after it had stopped moving, Gareth stabbed it a few extra times to ensure it was dead. After all, it was a giant-ass freaking spider. Relief washed over him and his shoulders sagged with it as he turned back to his friends.

Xena was a tower of spider killing fury, whirling her great axe around with abandon, slicing spiders in half whenever they got within her range. Kara huddled between Xena's feet, sinking her sword into anything that survived Xena's axe. They had clearly found a spider-killing rhythm and were quickly taking out the remaining spiders.

He stared down at the pitiful thing that he had killed, hoping the game awarded group-based exp, or he was quickly going to be out-leveled by those two. He decided he should inspect the last spider currently charging at the pair.

Young Aracne Swarm

•**Level: 5**

•**Health: 22**

•**These monsters love to travel in packs.**

•**Warning: don't incite their mom.**

Their mom? What the hell? He turned back to his companions just in time to catch the last spider retreat, heading straight toward a tree.

"*Stop it from running!*" Gareth yelled, as he pulled out his bow. A retreating mob was never good news in any game he'd ever played. He doubted this game was any different.

Gareth took careful aim. He'd taken archery as a Boy Scout and had taught both his sons as well. How hard could this be?

Thwok! The head stuck firmly into a tree trunk, quivering with the impact. Tree...damn. *Thwok.* bush. *Thwok.* ground. *Thwok.* air.

All those legs must have given the spider an uncanny ability to dodge arrows. Gareth glanced over to check on Xena and Kara. Instead of attacking the spider, however, they were bandaging their wounds. Gareth's attention turned back to the fleeing mob. With one final flourish of eight-legged acrobatics, the spider disappeared up a tree and scuttled away. *Damn.*

•**Skill Gained Short Bow (Apprentice 0)**

Gareth dropped his aim and slung his bow, returning the arrow to his quiver. He closed the skill gain notification. *Apprentice 0.* He'd been hoping his real-world skill would count for something, but apparently not. Or maybe the game decided he wasn't as skilled as he thought he was.

He approached the other two, stumbling slightly when he noticed Xena's health bar was flashing and shrinking fast. There was an icon under her name, bright, sickly green in color with a stylized skull-like symbol on it. He recognized that icon from when Thepeiros had shot him with a dart. *Poison!*

Her health bar started ticking down even faster. Xena was looking decidedly green about the gills. By the time he reached her, her health bar was just a tiny red sliver. Slapping a quick heal on her, he was dismayed at how little the spell moved the bar. Either she'd gained a lot of hit points recently or the poison was reducing the power of his healing along with its other effects.

"Don't just stand there. Do something," Kara snapped, waving her arms frantically.

"I healed her. It just didn't do much." He shrugged helplessly even as he examined the debuff, attempting to glean more information. But nothing came up. Either that information was hidden in this game, or more likely, a character needed a particular skill to access it.

Xena let out a sound that could only be described as half groan, half whimper. Then she slumped against the tall tree trunk beside her. Whatever this poison was, it was nasty and fast-acting. He'd seen her take gruesome hits before without making a sound.

"Well, you better figure something out quick, or it's going to be just the two of us out here." Kara revealed her agitation, quickly shifting her weight from one leg to the other.

Gareth tossed another heal on Xena to buy some time, but like before, it barely did anything to move her health bar. "I'm open to suggestions. Unless this poison runs its course soon, I'm not going to have any mana left to cast anything."

Kara stared at Xena, then grimaced. "The poison has a duration of an hour or so. It's also got a 50% reduction on healing."

Gareth's jaw dropped and Kara shrugged. "It's the identify poison skill."

"Well, we're screwed then. I've got four, maybe five more heals left in me before I'm tapped out. Nowhere near enough. I'm sorry, Xena."

Xena lifted her head weakly and nodded. "You two should start running back now. If you leave soon, you might be able to get back to the main road before anything else shows up." Then she stored her axe in her pack and drew a short sword from her belt.

The sword was a wicked-looking thing, with an edge down both sides of the blade. Gareth nodded to it. "And what are you planning on doing with *that*?"

She let out a small gasp before speaking, now heavily slumped against the tree. "This poison is excruciating. I'll meet you back at Muddy River. Please bring my short sword with you."

Kara blanched and reached out to slap Xena's leg. "Now just hold on. The only reason I came along on this is because *you* were going to be here. There's no way Gareth and I can make it out on our own."

Gareth sent her side-eye. "Thanks."

Kara sent him a look of clear, unabashed exasperation. Then she pointed at Xena. "Heal the poison."

"I tried. The heal doesn't do enough. Speaking of which..." He dropped another heal spell on Xena. His mana bar shrank accordingly. At this rate, the conversation was about to become pointless.

Kara shook her head. "No, you've tried to *heal* Xena. Heal the *poison*. Go straight to the root of the problem."

He threw his hands up helplessly. "I don't have a heal poison spell, or I would have used that. I just have: *Heal. Smite. Bless.* and some spell called *Leafy Twig* . I have no idea where I got that one from. Sounds Druidic."

Kara frowned, thick brows knitting. "Take your heal spell and focus it on the *poison* instead of the health bar."

Gareth looked at her in shock. "That *works?*"

"Who in the hells knows? But do you have a better idea?"

He shook his head. "You got me there. I guess I'll give it a try." He squared his shoulders, looked at Xena and tried to focus on the poison buff as he triggered another heal spell. Her health bar jumped a little bit, but nothing else happened.

"No good." Gareth shook his head, completely out of ideas.

"Do you have mana left?" Kara asked.

"About 40 percent."

"Then keep trying, dipshit."

He sighed and then mentally gathered up his heal spell, consciously *pushing* it toward the poison. For a moment, it felt like it was going to work, but then it seemed to slide off. This time, the spell dissipated with no effect.

Gareth groaned when he checked his mana bar once again. It was now down to about 25 percent. That was enough for two more heals *if* he timed the regen right. But to what end? All he could do was buy Xena a few more minutes of life.

Would he have to watch helplessly as his new friend wasted away from poison? Was that what he felt—friendship? His *friend* just might die before his eyes to face the respawn cycle—and whatever that entailed.

This sucked. Hard.

CHAPTER FORTY-ONE

ONE STEP FORWARD, TWO STEPS BACK

GARETH WATCHED XENA SHARPEN HER SHORT SWORD one last time, prepared to speed her end as painlessly as possible. That poison must hurt like a mofo if this was her preferred alternative.

She met his gaze after pocketing her whetstone. "It's okay, Gareth. I've had a good long deathless run, but we're all going to die sometime in this game. We'll just have to reform afterward and try again."

Gareth's brows knit in frustration. He raised his hand. "Here, let me give it one more try. If it fails, we'll all need to bugger off. We're certainly not going to be able to fight our way through the spider infested territory without you."

Gareth took a knee beside his seated friend and forced himself to mentally focus, using a trick he'd learned during a brief flirtation with yoga over a decade ago. Having chosen a mental image to focus on, he took a few deep square breaths, counting to five, holding it, releasing for five and holding it. Rinse, repeat. After feeling the natural calm settle over him, he reached out and touched Xena's leg where the spider had bitten her and injected its venom. He willed himself to inject his remaining mana into her as pure healing energy.

This time, Gareth could feel the spell grab onto the poison, but there was some kind of thick "skin" protecting it. He imagined his healing energy as a needle piercing the poison like a blister and draining it away. With one last mental push, he felt that resistance give way even as his mana bar emptied itself.

"You're doing it! I can see the duration spinning down," Kara shouted breathlessly.

Now it was a race. Would the poison run out first or would his mana?

In the end, it was almost a tie, with his mana giving out first. Somehow, he managed to keep the spell going just long enough to finish removing the poison debuff. His health bar took a similar battering.

•Skill gained Martyrdom (Apprentice 1)

•In extremis you can use your own life force to power your spells to save another.

•High ranks of this skill will increase the mana gained per hit point lost.

•Spell Specialization — Heal poison.

•Heal spells can heal more than just blunt trauma, who knew?

•**I wonder what else you can heal?**

Gareth took a second to marvel at the new notifications scrolling across his UI before he dropped to the ground, exhausted. Apparently, he'd drained a fair amount of endurance while trying to force the magic down a new pathway.

Curious. He was used to games where the different bars didn't interact in any meaningful way. However, this game was turning out to be more complicated, which would make it more difficult, if not impossible, to min-max your character build.

It took a few moments to recover from the initial weakness, but the exhaustion passed after a minute as his stamina bar slowly refilled. At the same time, he watched his mana bar replenish at about the same rate. He supposed that made sense, as he had split his levels evenly between fighter and cleric. His health bar, however, was still down a quarter. He'd just have to take care of that when he had mana again.

He sat up and noticed Xena was downing a number of potions, each one bringing her own health bar up by 10%.

He goggled at her. "You had heal potions? What the hell?"

She shrugged. "There was no point using them if you couldn't cure the poison. We have limited resources and must conserve them."

"Well, don't waste the potions then. Just wait a couple of minutes and I'll heal you up. I just need to regain some mana."

Xena stared off into the forest toward the west, ears constantly swiveling. "We don't have that long."

"What do you mean?" He spotted one of his arrows sticking out of a tree and remembered the spider that got away. "Oh crap, the runner. Maybe it won't come back."

Xena didn't reply as she sucked down another potion, bringing her health bar up to about 70%.

Kara, who'd been walking a patrol around them while they recovered, whistled to get their attention. "Something's coming. Something *big*."

A shiver slithered down his spine and his guts ran cold. Well, fuck. His head turned this way and that, trying to spot whatever big thing might be coming at them.

"More spiders?" he gasped. Please God, no more spiders.

"My skill's not that specific remember. Before it was reading lots of little things. Now it's one big thing." She ran over and took position behind Xena. "You two had best get ready. It'll be here soon."

Gareth regained his feet, then bent to pick up his sword and shield from where he'd dropped them. He took position next to Xena, who had used more potions to regain a full health bar. Just how many potions did she have, anyway? Gareth took a deep breath and tried to fight the panic as he noticed his own mana bar was still not full. They were going to have to be smarter about this fight or they'd all end up in Respawnville.

A minute later, a faint vibration reverberated up through the ground. Huh. They weren't in T-Rex territory—or so he hoped, anyway. There couldn't be T-Rexes in this game, right? *Right?* But the mere fact that he could feel the ground shake at all was worrying. He tilted his head to peer through the trees and thought he could see some sort of vague mass moving toward them at a pretty good clip. He sucked in a shocked breath that felt cold and prickly going down. So much for plan B—run like hell.

Gareth sighed and readied himself for combat. He mentally willed his mana bar to fill quicker, but it didn't seem to want to cooperate.

Their new opponent finally made itself known.

He wished they'd gone with plan B. Even though that would have failed spectacularly. It was indeed another spider—*if* spiders came in elephant size. But with eight legs, a gazillion eyes and clicking mandibles, it sure as hell looked like a monster-truck-sized spider. When it spotted them, it stopped, as if taking a moment to size them up. Gareth shuddered, all but sensing the malevolence coming from those beach ball-sized composite eyes.

A quick flicker of motion caught his attention. "There's the little fucker."

Gareth pointed to the spider that had gotten away, which was currently clinging to the back of its much larger friend. His notice seemed to piss off the giant spider as it let out a hiss and then, to Gareth's horror, a very large stinger dropped out of its belly.

"Oh, *that's* just bullshit," he called out. Kara looked over and he pointed at the stinger, "Spiders don't have stingers, just fangs. They *bite* people. They don't sting them."

Kara just shrugged, seemingly unimpressed. "It's probably too hard to bite little things like us. A stinger must make it easier."

"*Still* …what's next? Flying snakes? That's—" The rant was interrupted as the giant arachnid crouched down and threw itself into the air, aiming right for Gareth.

"Holy shit!" He dove out of the way, barely clearing the area before the spider landed with a crash. Gareth kept rolling to put more distance between them as the stinger spiked into the ground—exactly where he'd been laying a moment before.

He rolled up against a tree and quickly scurried around behind it, using the large trunk as cover so he could regain his feet. With a deep breath, he summoned the will to peer around the gnarled bark to see what was going on. Xena had planted herself in front of the giant spider and was ineffectually batting at it with her axe while devoting most of her attention to fending off the giant fangs with her shield.

Kara used her small size to good effect, running under the arachnid's carapace to keep the stinger occupied. Unfortunately, she wasn't able to deal it any real damage.

He should jump in, because the current stalemate couldn't possibly last. One of them would make a mistake sooner or later and that would spell the end for all of them. But what to do? Run up and chop at a leg? Use his bow and go for an eye? Even he couldn't miss a giant spider.

He pulled his bow out and was snagging an arrow from his quiver when he noticed the spider tilt its head to one side and then the other. Its size and anatomy must be making it difficult to keep track of both Kara and Xena at the same time, given their positions. In fact, it looked like the small spider on its back was directing where the bites should go while the giant spider spent most of its attention on trying to spear Kara.

Gareth nocked the arrow into his bow and prepared to take a shot. That little fucker *had* to die. His dreams of epic Robin-Hoodness faded as the projectile flew off into a random tree. *Shit.* Maybe he should have shot at the big one.

He snatched up another arrow and readied another shot. He had to do something, or this battle was heading south real quick.

In his UI, he eyed his mana bar which had crept up a sliver, and sighed.

"What the hell, might as well." He'd burn most of his remaining mana by casting *Bless* on himself, but in the grand scheme of things, a heal or two wasn't going to matter in this fight. Something had to be done to shift the odds in their favor.

As he added the buff to himself, he could feel the energy of the spell flow through him, permeating his limbs and sharpening his sight. A trembling he hadn't even noticed in his bow arm dissipated, and his aim steadied. This time, when he released the arrow, it sped true, striking the smaller spider right behind its eye.

The vile thing let out a horrid shriek, and a sizeable chunk of its health bar vanished. Meanwhile, the giant spider, either through lack of guidance from the small one, or surprise at the shriek, totally biffed its next attack on Xena, leaving itself wide open to a riposte from her. Her axe sang out, cleaving straight through its right fang.

Gareth quickly readied another arrow and loosed it once again at the smaller spider, hoping to repeat his success. Just as he did, the larger spider tossed its head away from Xena causing the arrow to miss its target, though the arrow did sink into the moldering black and gray flesh around the bigger spider's multifaceted eye.

The greater spider gave a shriek and spun to face him. Its body swelled as it sucked in a deep breath of air. On instinct, Gareth dropped his bow and grabbed his shield from the ground, steadying it in front of him and ducking his head behind it. The spider opened its fanged maw and expelled a huge white mass that went flying out toward him, slamming into the shield. The force of the blow threw him back against the tree. The mass that collided with his shield then exploded into a huge spray of webs, sticking the shield and Gareth's lower body fast against the tree.

He could only stare in horror as the spider returned its attention to the other two. Firmly stuck to the tree, he had only a limited ability to move his arms behind the shield. If only he had a *Flamestrike* spell or some other way to burn off the webs. His sword lay on the ground in front of him, just out of reach. He had no way to grab it, even if it would cut the webs.

Out of sheer desperation he remembered that *Leafy Twig* spell. He had no idea what it would even do, but he had very little to lose in this situation. *Here goes nothing...*

At first, the only effect he could see was the total depletion of his mana bar. Then, the end of the branch over his head started to twitch. Gareth's gaze shot upward, caught by the movement. The branch grew at an alarming rate, the end quickly drooping down toward him and then lengthening until it sent a tendril down between him and the shield which was pinning him to the tree.

Once there, leaves started to sprout. *So many leaves.* At first, it only provided a somewhat comfortable cushion keeping the shield from crushing into his chest. But more leaves sprouted in profusion—and still more. The pressure built and built, pushing against him so that he could hardly breathe, bruising his flesh beneath his armor.

His health bar started to drop from the now crushing force. Maybe the only thing he'd really accomplished was to hasten his end. Just when he figured his only choice was to close his eyes and experience the respawn cycle, the web-clogged shield was flung away from him, taking most of the webbing with it. Well! Not for nothing after all… *Thanks, Leafy Twig.*

Quickly he reached down, took hold of his sword, and used it to free himself from the remaining webs that held him against the tree.

Once free, he took in the circumstances of the current battle between his compatriots and the monstrous spider. The smaller spider had abandoned its perch and was now on the ground engaging Kara. This allowed the monster spider to focus its whole attention on Xena. Judging by the trees in the area, the spider had tried its flying balls of web several times, but Xena's dodge skill must be much higher than his, because all it had achieved was to decorate the area in a lot of webbing.

However, the monster was slowly forcing Xena back into the surrounding sticky mess, making the web attack effective in the end.

What to do? Help Kara or Xena? Whatever action he took, it had to be quick because in less than a minute, this battle would be lost, and they'd all be respawning, *Leafy Twig* or not.

CHAPTER FORTY-TWO
NOT EASY BEIN' GREEN

Xena's luck ran out when she stepped back to evade an attack and her boot landed on a lump of sticky webs. She was held fast to her spot and unable to perform any more of her heroic dodges. Gareth clenched his teeth in frustration, his mind made up. Kara could hold her own for the moment, but Xena needed his help now.

His shield was a giant sticky mess, and therefore useless to him, so Gareth dropped the broadsword and unsheathed the great sword from his back.

The giant spider was focused on pinning Xena down so it could sink its remaining fang into her. As luck would have it, that put its back to Gareth. That disgusting and incongruous stinger hung down right in front of him. There'd never be a better time to go for it.

Luckily for him, the spider's attention was so absorbed by Xena, it didn't notice his loud-as-hell approach. He planted his feet, pivoted, and smacked that stinger as hard as he possibly could. Best nut shot he'd never feel bad about.

Gareth had envisioned being able to lop off the stinger and was all ready to celebrate his marvelous hit, neutering the fucker. However, as his sword bit into it, he only managed to rend it, falling far short of slicing it off.

But it was more than enough to draw the monster's notice. The spider let out a deafening, bloodcurdling shriek, then froze in place. Any male who'd ever taken a baseball to the crotch knew that pain. In other circumstances, Gareth might have even crossed his legs in sympathy.

And apparently, the stinger was a dual-purpose appendage. Or was it? Maybe the spider meant to inject them with something other than poison?

Oh. My. God. Brain bleach, brain bleach! That image was straight out of a B horror movie set in outer space.

The thought prompted Gareth to start hammering on the stinger in quick succession before it could implant its spider babies in him. Each blow caused the spider to slump further. Xena had taken full advantage of this opportunity and was hacking her way through the front end of the creature.

The smaller spider rushed toward Gareth, desperate to save its bigger…sibling? Parent? Who the hell knew?

The tinier spider's push toward him proved to be a fatal mistake, as that opened it up to an attack from Kara. Not one to let such an open opportunity pass, she sprang through the air and landed on the smaller spider's back. She'd dropped her sword for the attack, pulling out a pair of daggers. With a dagger in each hand, she drove them into two different eyes, drilling straight down into its brain, killing it instantly.

Meanwhile, Gareth and Xena continued their systematic teamwork on the larger spider, finally dispatching the monstrous arachnid.

The moment it died, Gareth dropped to the ground. They were all covered in blood, gross spider fluids, mud, and sticky bits of webbing.

As the adrenaline drained from his system, pain and horror from the fight bloomed, only tempered by the nice fat chunk of exp they all received. Gareth blinked, startled. He was actually most of the way toward ninth level.

Gareth quickly allocated one level each to cleric and warrior, keeping Kara's admonition about never saving levels in mind.

•Overall Level 8

•Cleric 4

•Warrior 4

•Mana pool increase x1 (cleric)

•Stamina pool increase x1 (warrior)

•Health pool increase x2 (cleric, warrior)

•You have two attribute points to allocate.

•Where would you like to place them?

Gareth mulled it over. He achieved two ability points for every fourth level. As his role in the party seemed to be developing towards tank, he decided to put both points into Constitution.

•Constitution has increased to Above Average.

+2 hit point bonus per level.

+1 bonus to Constitution based saving throws.

His health bar filled a bit, as the constitution increase added 16 hit points to his build. As soon as he closed that popup, he was greeted by another:

•You have 1 spell slot to allocate

Gareth scanned the list of spells available to him. Aid looked interesting, but that would give him two buffs, and he wasn't sure that was the path he wanted to take. Given that he was the group's only healer, he should just use this opportunity to upgrade his healing spell.

•Spell Healing upgraded to Greater Healing.

With that business done, he was at level eight already. Xena was probably around level fourteen or something, given her relentless drive upward.

"Gained two levels from that fight! Nice," he said, still astonished at the exp they'd received.

"Don't get too excited. You level pretty quick up 'til you hit twenty." Kara quirked her mouth in regret. "Slows down a lot then."

"Well, Xena got her wish for some experience, anyway," he said, turning his gaze to her. She was currently slumped down on the ground, using a large branch as a backrest. "Though maybe this was a little more exp all at once then we'd want."

Xena lifted her head. "One hopes that these spiders require a large hunting area. Another encounter like this one, and I fear for our ability to reach the abbey."

Gareth's mouth tightened. "Well, that's a cheerful thought. Lunch break, anyone? We definitely need a rest and recover period. A short one anyway."

Xena sniffed the surrounding air, face screwing up tightly. "There's a stream over to the right of us. Maybe we could clean up first? It's going to be hard to sneak up on stuff smelling like *this*."

"Sure." He eyed the giant corpse, remembering Kruger's advice. "But first, there's something I need to do. You might want to scoot back if you don't want to get any messier."

He grabbed his broadsword and started hacking his way into the spider's lifeless form. It took a quarter of an hour, but he finally made it to the stomach, which was full of all manner of disgusting things. He did spy a glint of metal among the bones and fur and other partially digested remains.

All told, he was able to pull out some 300 gold crowns, a few platinum oriels, several gems, and one very interesting-looking hat. It was large, made of leather and had a wide brim, sporting several feathers of different sizes tucked into the hat band. It was also almost pristine, despite having been marinating inside the spider's gut.

He held it up and looked toward the other two with a huge grin on his face, "Loot!"

Xena was looking decidedly greenish as she waved off any desire for the hat. "All yours. You, ah, earned it."

Kara just made some gagging noises.

Gareth looked down at himself, realizing for the first time that he was covered from head to toe in spider offal. He'd also waded into the middle of a chopped-up spider corpse. It didn't present the most appealing appearance, but the loot was worth it.

"Okay, well if you guys are sure?" They both nodded vigorously.

"Can we go wash off now? Maybe *you* could go first?" Kara covered her eyes and pointed toward the stream with her other hand.

"Sure, I guess." He shrugged. Weird that they weren't as excited about the loot, but hopefully they'd come around. This hat had *cool* written all over it. He'd die on the hill that it'd been worth it to hack his way into the monster's innards to get it. It was a bit disappointing he couldn't determine any stats for it. Maybe "evaluate treasure" was yet another skill he needed to unlock.

Gareth gathered his equipment. Fortunately, the webs had disintegrated on their own after ten minutes. He hadn't been looking forward to scraping them off the shield. Then he headed to the stream to wash off.

Once there, he peered into the rushing surface hoping there wasn't something deadly beneath it—like death piranha, murder eels, or something worse. But it appeared safe, so he finally stripped off his equipment and jumped into the water, washing off most of the gore, which headed downstream. Then he took a minute to scrub his armor, releasing another clump of gore into the water. Huh, he'd been filthier than he thought.

Shortly afterward, Xena and Kara joined in. Gareth's eyes narrowed when peering at Xena. Spider guts were stuck to her thick fur everywhere, which she scrubbed frantically. And she was very obviously *not* a fan of being wet. She spent less than two minutes in the drink before scrabbling back up to the bank and shaking herself off vigorously, spraying Kara and Gareth with a sheet of water.

Not unlike his dog, Xena. *Huh.*

"Hey, watch it, giant," Kara called to Xena, her eyes squeezed close against the spray. "I have enough of my own water, I don't need yours."

"Sorry," was the only reply.

Their moist misadventure was quickly interrupted when out of the blue, a voice called out, "Yo, giants! Why don't you go crap in your own yard?"

Startled, Gareth scanned his surroundings frantically trying to spot whoever had just shouted at them but seeing no one. Xena and Kara seemed just as confused.

Regardless, he shrugged and called out. "Um...hello?"

"Down here, dip smack."

Something sharp jabbed him in the ankle. He bent low to stare down into the burbling surface again. Something that looked like a frog stared back at him, standing on its hind legs. And comically, he wore a kilt and what looked to be a bird nest hat. *He* —well Gareth assumed it was a *he* —wielded a long needle in one hand like a spear. No doubt this was the source of the jab in his ankle.

"I'm sorry?"

"Well, you should be, making a mess in someone's yard like that." His tongue darted out of his mouth agitatedly and the spear waved through the air in an angry gesture. "How would *you* like it if I relieved myself in your mouth while you were sleeping? I'm sure you wouldn't be pleased."

Gareth blinked, taken aback by the image the frog presented. "Well, no, I can't say as I would." He crouched to get a better look at the frog creature. "I'm not sure what we've done, though. I certainly didn't see a yard. Or a house for that matter."

Raging Kermit crossed his arms and turned to glare at the mess floating down the stream, gesturing with a long, slender arm. "What do you call *that?*"

Gareth drew back. "Your house is in the stream?"

"I'm a frog, not a fish. My house is on the bank. The stream is my yard. Where I nap sometimes. Which I was doing when this filth suddenly appeared."

Gareth took in the kilt once more. If he hung out long enough, would Miss Piggy and Fozzy Bear be joining them?

"But…you're wearing clothes."

The arms flailed, once again putting Gareth in mind of the iconic Muppet. "Of course, I am. I'm not an *animal.*"

"But…" Gareth scratched his jaw.

"Gareth, we have stuff to do," Kara yelled at him from the bank. "Who knows if there's more spiders out there?"

Gareth turned back to Kermit. "Well, I'm sorry for making a mess in your yard. It certainly wasn't on purpose. We were just so filthy after the battle and needed to wash off all the guts."

The frog reached out and grabbed his leg to stop him from joining his compatriots on the bank. "Wait—what did she mean by *spiders?*"

"Oh, that. We ran into some spiders over in that direction." He waved toward their battle site. "A bunch of little ones and one big ol' mother."

"You *killed* them?" Kermit looked taken aback.

"Yep, they're all dead."

Kermit let out something that sounded like a gasp. "*All* of them?"

"I think so. That pack, anyway." Was pack even the right word? What did you call a horde of spiders?

The frog let go of his leg and stared at the ground. "So Bismiq is dead."

"Friend of yours, was she—he—*it?*"

The frog's head shot up. "*What?* No? Bismiq was a plague. It used to come by and use its web to stick frogs to the trees so they'd die in the sun. Just for amusement. We'd have to sit in the water and listen to their calls for help. Half the time it would wait, hidden, ready to pick off anyone who tried to rescue the victim." He let out a large sigh. "I can't even imagine what the world will be like, going back to normal. For a little while, anyway."

Gareth frowned, truly moved by the frog's story. "What do you mean, *back* to normal?" He gestured around them. "*This* isn't normal?"

The frog snorted. "What—you think wandering swarms of giant spiders are *normal?* What kind of place do you think this is, anyway?"

A game? A tier 2 leveling area? Gareth shrugged. "Well, I just assumed..."

Kermit scoffed, a weird sound, coming from a frog. "You *assumed.* Typical. No one cares about the little people in the world. If you can't run around wielding some giant piece of metal, no one gives you a second thought." Kermit began pacing in the stream, legs sloshing through the slow-moving water, clearly agitated. "No, giant, this was once a nice place. Sure, we had problems arise from time to time, but your lot—"

"You mean *adventurers?*" Gareth interjected.

"Yes, *adventurers.* You came around every week or so and *handled* the problems. The monsters that make our lives hell, they come from the mountain over there." He pointed deeper into the woods, which from here, even in the bright light of day, looked dark and foreboding.

It was also, unsurprisingly, in the exact direction the abbey was supposed to be. *Figured.*

"The adventurers were to go *there* and battle them in their home territory. It worked out for everyone. We had a nice home. The adventurers were able to earn treasure and renown, and the monsters…well, they really didn't get much out of it. But they're monsters, so screw them."

Huh, not only raging Kermit, but skeptical and downtrodden Kermit as well.

Gareth scratched his jaw, mulling this over. He knew from previous games that gamers loved nothing more than finding a good farming area. They'd never leave as long as the exp or loot kept flowing. "So, what happened? Did the loot over there suck?"

The frog halted, stood stock still, tensing. "The loot was fine. *Better* than fine, in fact. Some of the best loot in the area."

"Really? Like this cool hat I found?" He pulled it out of his pack to show Kermit.

Kermit hopped toward Gareth to get a closer look. "*Ahh.* You got the Hat of Inattention. It's an uncommon drop. Too bad, really. Those named spiders drop some really good loot."

"Hat of Inattention?" Gareth's brow shot up as he regarded his prize once more. "What does it do?"

Kermit blinked up at him, tongue darting in and out of his mouth with disturbing quickness. "When you wear it, the hat becomes so fascinating that anyone who sees it will fixate on it and remember nothing about the wearer besides the hat. Back when we saw a steady stream of adventurers, they caused a lot of confusion. Certain hat wearers were blamed for the actions of other hat wearers. One criminal made his career from robbing banks while wearing his so he could cast blame on others who owned the hat. A number of innocent adventurers were imprisoned before it all worked out. The hat is now banned in Muddy River because of it."

Gareth bit his lip and looked once again at the stylish and near-pristine fedora. That newfound knowledge certainly put a damper on his excitement.

Nevertheless, he shrugged and tucked it back into his pack. "I'm sure I can find a use for it."

He sighed and pulled out his canteen, unscrewing the cap while he turned back to the subject at hand. "So, if the loot was good, how come the adventurers stopped coming?"

Gareth tilted his canteen to his lips.

"It's all because of Lord Smith."

Water shot out of his nose as he choked on that last gulp.

Fuck. This shit ran deep, didn't it? And when it was said that he had his fingers—*flippers?*—in everything. They weren't lying.

Which made him really start to worry about this latest quest.

CHAPTER FORTY-THREE

ZOMBIES & GHASTS & GHOULS, OH MY!

"WHAT DO YOU MEAN, LORD SMITH IS responsible? What does *he* have to do with this? He's back in Muddy River."

The frog's arms flailed in the air around him. "Bah, you know nothing. Yes, he's in Muddy River. But where do you think the adventurers come from? Smith sent a bunch of his henchmen one day to talk with the forest council. They told us that since the Lord of Muddy River was doing so much for us, providing us with adventurers and all, that *we* needed to do something for *him*."

Gareth glanced at Kara, hoping she knew something. "That doesn't sound—"

"It would have beggared us!" The volume of Kermit's voice increased alarmingly. "He wanted 90% of our income. He also demanded we send some of the comelier dryads to the city to become his 'assistants.'"

Gareth turned back to the frog, considering his words. "What did he want them for? Aren't dryads kind of…*woodsy?*"

To the side, Kara huffed, rolling her eyes as she looked away.

The frog continued. "We didn't bother asking why he wanted them. We just told him to fuck off. A week later, Lord Smith enacted at 120% tax on all earnings made in the woods."

"*A hundred twenty percent?* That makes no sense. You'd pay more in tax than you brought in."

Kermit gestured again emphatically. "Exactly. And the adventurers promptly went elsewhere, leaving us where we are now—play toys for the spiders, among other things." Now the frog just looked dejected. Gareth would be too, if he was 6 inches tall and had giant 20-foot spiders wandering around where he lived.

"Lord Smith is not honorable," Xena chimed in on the conversation for the first time.

Gareth shrugged. "Well, we knew that. That's why his brother gave me the quest."

The frog's eyes widened with sudden interest. "You've met his brother? He actually *exists?*"

"Yeah, sure. I've met him a couple of times."

Kermit sighed heavily. "The elders cast a spell once, at the beginning of all this, asking how we could deal with Lord Smith. The response was to enlist the aid of his brother. We could never find him. But *you* have…" The frog peered at him for a long moment. "Where is he? You must take me to him."

Gareth grimaced. "That will be, um, difficult." How did you explain out-of-game to an in-game NPC? If he was an NPC. Given the advanced AI in the game, how would you even know?

"*Why?* Are you in league with Lord Smith?" The frog's flipper gravitated to his needle.

Gareth held out his hands, startled. "No, no. Lord Smith is a massive douche. His brother..." His mind raced to think of a way to explain it in a way Kermit would understand. "His brother is trapped in a—a magical dimension. No native of this land can get there. Only adventurers."

The frog looked at him dubiously. "I suppose."

"If it makes you feel better, Chief Bureaucrat Smith has given me a quest to free him. So hopefully everything will get put back to normal and Lord Smith will be banished."

The frog just shrugged noncommittally. "I wish you well, but I don't hold out much hope that you can topple Lord Smith. Many have tried over the years."

Gareth inspected the stream, taking in the bucolic area before letting out a loud sigh and replying. "We can only try. However, we need to get to the abbey first. Taking out Lord Smith will have to wait 'til after we've done what we came here to do." Gareth sloshed toward the bank and began to gather up his equipment. After donning his chain mail and slinging his backpack onto a shoulder, he turned back to his new amphibian acquaintance. As interesting as this conversation had been, they'd rested long enough.

"The abbey?" Kermit said, eyes narrowing. "Why are you going *there?*"

Kara coughed loudly, but Gareth ignored her. He doubted the frog was itching to betray them. "We need to retrieve an item that was hidden there."

The frog fidgeted where he stood. "Will that help you defeat Lord Smith?"

"Sure," Gareth hedged. *Kind of, anyway.* From a certain point of view, anything could help them defeat Lord Smith in the long run.

"Well, I suppose I owe you for killing the spiders, anyway." The frog motioned for him to approach again, which he did, though Gareth held himself ready to spring back in case the frog tried to take advantage of his proximity to pull some surprise attack.

Kermit spoke quietly. "If you head up the stream, you'll come to a waterfall—"

"And there's a secret path behind the waterfall?" Huh, go figure. Classic quest update.

The frog scoffed once again. "No, don't be stupid. Who'd hide a path behind a waterfall? That's the first place everyone looks." He made a sweeping, dismissive gesture with a long, green limb. "No, you turn left at the waterfall and follow the ridge. You'll come to a cave with a dead-looking tree out front. The hidden path is there. Just remember once you're on it to go left, right, left, left, right, straight—"

Gareth drew back, momentarily overwhelmed. "Ugh, wait a second. I need to write this down." He dug through the side pocket on his pack and pulled out a small notebook and pen. Then he asked the frog to repeat the directions. There were thirty-seven in all, ending with an exit through a door that led into the abbey's basement.

A secret entrance!

"Well, thank you." Gareth straightened, closing his notebook. "This will help a lot." He nodded at the small creature.

"Don't thank me." Kermit said in a deadly serious voice. "I'm just helping you toward your death. The abbey is full to the brim with the non-living. You'll likely be joining them before dark."

"Wait, what do you mean by *the non-living?*" But Kermit had already turned and with a splash had disappeared below the surface of the stream.

Gareth scratched his jaw and studied the spot where the frog had been moments before.

On the bank, Kara threw up her hands. "Well, that's just great."

"What?" He moved back to the bank toward her, searching the ground to ensure they'd picked up everything before heading out.

Kara busied herself with covering up traces of their existence, sweeping tracks and moving broken branches and leaves. "Fighting undead sucks. *Big time.*"

"Why?"

Xena shifted the massive pack on her back, brimming with all her gear. "They can be splattery."

"*Splattery?*"

Once Kara finished her tidying, they set off along the bank of the stream. "Yeah. Zombies continue to *ripen* even after they're animated. After long enough, they tend to pop when you hit them. It's quite disgusting. *You'll* be handling that part if we run into them."

"So, the abbey is full of zombies?"

She shrugged, palms up. "Could be skeletons."

"Skeletons are better," Xena added from his other side. He threw her a questioning glance. "Less splattery. Quite dusty, though."

Kara's face screwed up tight. "Yeah, and it gets all up your nose. You'll be sneezing skeleton dust for weeks. And *everything* smells like mold. Still better than rancid, juicy zombie."

"So…we have zombies and skeletons to look forward to. Doesn't sound too bad." He shrugged. He was continually scanning the surrounding area, the surface of the rivers, the banks and what he could make of the woods beyond the trees. His biggest fear was more spiders. God, how he hated spiders.

"Well, and maybe a ghoul." Kara amended. "Anything else would be well out of our level range. Ghasts would be bad."

"As would Ghosts," Xena added.

"Specters." Kara shuddered.

"Vampires?" Gareth interjected so as not to be left out of the conversation.

Kara whacked his leg. "Don't say the V-word. Those creatures are the *worst.* They like to keep you around for a while to use you as a refillable blood bank. The other things we've talked about are bad, but…vampires are cut-your-own-throat and hope you die before they get to you level of bad."

Gareth looked down, having almost tripped over a stone. It'd certainly suck to twist an ankle because he wasn't paying enough attention. "The one we met outside the town hall didn't seem too bad."

"He swore off blood, remember." Kara arched a brow. "The blood drinkers are uncontrolled balls of rage."

"Right." Gareth cringed at the thought. "*No vampires.* Got it. They're too high-level for this area anyway, right? *Right?*"

Xena shuddered. "Vampires would be *bad.*"

They followed the stream for a few hours, till finally they could see a bog ahead. Up until now, Gareth's map and the frog's directions coincided. But here, they diverged, and Gareth wasn't sure how much he trusted a random disgruntled frog person, anyway.

"Gods, what's that smell?" Kara pulled out a cloth and held it to her nose.

"Must be the Bog of Unusual Smells." Gareth pulled off his pack and started digging through it to find something to cover his nose. He glanced over at Xena, knowing her sense of smell was probably much more sensitive than his. Though she didn't complain, tears leaked from her eyes.

"What's unusual about a bog smelling like crap?" Kara groused.

"Maybe it gets worse?" Xena let out a slight whimper. He sighed heavily, slamming his pack closed. "I give up. I've got nothing that will help with the smell. Need to add that to the list of things to buy later."

"Smell protection?" Kara laughed.

"Given all that adventurers have to deal with, there must be something for that purpose." Gareth looked over the bog. "The map says we have to go through there. But Kermit said to keep following the stream."

"We should do what the frog person said," Xena managed to grunt out, while trying to stuff her paws into her nostrils.

Gareth inspected the map again. "Well, Kermit did say that his way led to a hidden entrance."

"Yes, the frog is wise. Hidden entrance," Xena retorted.

"Sure, let's keep follow the stream, then." Gareth had to admit, that choice didn't make him sad at all. He stowed his map and turned away from the bog.

Xena nodded and took off at a trot. A few hours of trekking later, they finally reached the waterfall. It was a massive spray of water tumbling down at least one full story from above them, white water gurgling and bubbling just below their feet on the bank.

"Are you sure we shouldn't check behind the falls?" Gareth asked.

"Go ahead, if you want to be wet." Kara shrugged. "I'm too small, and I bet Xena doesn't want to smell like wet dog again." They stared at him expectantly.

Gareth approached the falls from the sides, leaning in sharply to peer behind the massive sheet of water. As far as he could tell there was no cave—nor even a niche—on the other side.

"Well?" Kara asked when he returned to them, dripping with the spray.

He shook his head. "I can't see anything, and I'm not getting soaked just to take a look."

"Great." Kara pointed left. "We still have to find that dead tree."

They continued along the bottom of the ridge until they came upon what had to be the landmark described by Kermit. It was an old, massive trunk of a tree with only a few branches remaining. The few brown leaves clinging to them rustled in the breeze. Most of the tree was covered in a sickly green moss.

A red alert flashed in the corner of his eye. "Shit!"

Kara turned to look at him, "What, did you see something?"

Gareth shook his head, "No. It's time to walk my dog."

Kara's mouth just hung open, like she couldn't think of what to say. Xena stopped and turned to face him, a scowl on her face.

Gareth looked around and then held up a placating hand. "No, don't bother. I can see this isn't a good time. She'll have to wait, I guess. I just hope she doesn't get up to too much trouble."

Gareth turned his attention back to the tree and began to scan the surrounding area. "This has to be the dead tree. Start looking for a cave."

They spread out and searched along the ridge wall. Every one of them gave the tree a wide berth. It might be dead, but it definitely filled them all with a sense of dread.

Though they spent a considerable time combing the area, none of them could find the cave.

"It has to be in the ridge behind the tree." Gareth turned to stare at it from a safe distance.

"Well, go look then. I'll stay back here and supervise." Kara folded her tiny arms over her chest and shifted her stance.

"It's just a dead tree." Gareth gestured at it dismissively, yet he still didn't move any closer to it. None of them actually thought it was just a dead tree.

"Did the small creature say 'dead tree' or 'dead-*looking* tree?'" Xena asked.

"I think…" Gareth replayed the conversation in his head. "I think he said dead-looking tree."

"You know, there's two ways to take that," Kara said.

Their gazes all gravitated back to the ominous tree. "Is it a really a dead tree, or some kind of living tree monster that only *looks* dead?" Gareth asked.

"Time to go find out." Kara pointed at the tree.

"What am I supposed to do?" Gareth shook his head.

"I don't know. Go talk to it. You like to talk a lot—to anything and anyone. I'd think you'd jump at the chance to talk to a tree." Kara attempted to nudge him toward the tree.

"Okay, okay. I'm going." Gareth sidled toward the tree.

"I do not think talking with the tree is a good idea," Xena chimed in.

"It can't hurt, I suppose." He shrugged, then approached slowly, stopping well out of range of the large branches. Gareth had seen the *Harry Potter* movies, after all. "Hey, tree? Mr. Tree? Can you hear me?"

There was no response, no movement—not even a twig wiggle. Gareth looked over his shoulder at the other two and shrugged. Unwilling to give up so soon, however, he reached down, picked up a rock and lobbed it at the tree, to see if that got a response. Other than a dull *thunk*. nothing happened.

"That throw was *pathetic*." Kara heckled from her safe distance behind him.

"Well, I don't want to hurt it. That could make it mad." Gareth peered at the tree, unsure if he saw movement or not.

"I really think it's just a tree. Go up to it and touch it." Kara made a shooing motion with her arms.

He threw a dirty look at her over his shoulder. "*You* go touch it."

Predictably, she didn't move.

"I'll see if the tree responds to *this*." Xena whipped out her ax.

Gareth's hand shot up to stop her. "*No*. If it is alive somehow, that'll only piss it off."

"Well then, what do you suggest? We can't wait around all day." Xena waved her axe back and forth for a moment, then reached for her belt. "Maybe a dagger? It might just annoy it."

"No. Calm down with the weapons, already." Gareth let out a loud sigh. "I guess I'll walk up to it and see what that does."

He slowly crept up, keeping a close eye on the tree, should it decide to animate at any time. He'd read too many stories about plants that kill things so the blood can water their roots.

Nevertheless, once he reached the tree, there were no signs of mobility or awareness. "Well, I feel like an ass," he said. Looking back, he gestured for the other two to approach. From this angle, he could spot the entrance to a tunnel just beyond, the very one they'd been looking for.

The moment the other two arrived at his side, the tree started a cacophony to wake the dead and non-living alike. "*Aroooooo Aroooooo.*"

A blue shimmering dome appeared, encapsulating all three of them.

Kara turned and tried to leave, bouncing off the shimmering barrier as if she'd hit a wall. "Force wall. This sucks."

They were now magically trapped in a tiny area with a possibly angry tree.

Great. Just great.

Chapter
Forty-Four
The Wannabe Whomping Willow

THE TREE CONTINUED ITS WILD AND EAR-SPLITTING moaning while the three of them scanned the surrounding area.

Xena had taken it upon herself to poke at the glowing dome surrounding them with her axe. She took a few tentative swings but gave up after her axe bounced off for fear of hitting someone.

Kara stationed herself across the tree from Xena as she continued to push back at the barrier.

Gareth tried moving around and poking at different parts of the transparent dome, in case there was a hidden door or something. Xena had abandoned the axe and was now slamming her large body against the barrier.

Meanwhile, the moaning and howling continued, to the point where they had to shout at each other in order to be heard.

"What the hell is the point? To annoy us to death? Who would set up a trap like this?" Gareth ranted.

"It's to keep us contained while that thing," Kara waved at the tree, "summons someone or something to deal with us. I'm sure it will get more interesting whenever they get here."

Gareth studied the dome, feeling stupid that hadn't occurred to him. "We need to get out of here before that happens."

"Captain Obvious." Kara looked back and waved her hands around. Xena had given up her assault on the dome and pulled a shovel out of her pack. In short order, she'd dug at the base of the dome, to try and get under it. Unfortunately, the dome soon proved to be a sphere that continued under the ground, curving under their feet.

Gareth glared at the cave entrance just beyond the barrier. "You know, it would have been nice if Raging Kermit had mentioned *this*. We might've been able to drop in from above the cave mouth to avoid triggering the trap."

Kara gave a little shrug. "People can be assholes."

"Yeah, but he seemed happy with us for killing the spiders. Why screw with us now? We must be missing something."

"You *hope*." Kara fired back.

Gareth ignored her and examined the dead-looking tree more closely. They'd already covered the energy barrier, and other than it being basically a force field, there wasn't much to do about it.

Gareth's eyes narrowed. While the tree did, indeed, look dead—or at least very unhealthy—the look wasn't uniform. Closer to the ground, the trunk of the tree looked worse. Further up the trunk, it gradually looked healthier, with newer, fresh bark instead of the rotted, warped wood along the bottom. Near the top, some of the twigs at the ends of the branches looked normal and alive, with a few small leaves, even.

"Xena, let me see your shovel for a minute." He held out his hand and she quickly passed it over.

"What did you find?" Xena asked.

"Not sure yet, but the tree gets sicker the closer to the ground it is. Maybe there's something buried underneath it."

"And you want to *dig it up?*" Kara asked, wide-eyed.

Gareth shrugged and set about digging around the tree, taking care not to hit the roots. It was hard going until Xena pulled a pry bar out of her pack and broke up the dirt for him. Combined, they were able to quickly expose the roots around the base of the tree.

He leaned heavily on the shovel for a moment to catch his breath. "Man, I need to get a better kit for my pack. I don't have any of these handy tools."

"I have found that the right tool and application of strength resolve most problems." Xena finished cleaning off her pry bar and put it back into her pack. It was bizarre to witness a four-foot-long bar disappear into a three-foot long pack.

Game logic.

"Let's see what we've found...if anything." He dropped to his knees to examine the now-exposed roots. One of them was more shriveled and gnarled than the others.

"Here, look at this." Gareth pointed out the root.

"Gah, its *oozing*." Kara's face twisted in disgust as she drew back.

"Perhaps we should cut it off from the tree." Xena snatched up her axe.

"Why is your response always immediately using your axe?" Gareth held out a hand to stop her.

"Because it normally works."

Gareth kept his arm out, palm facing outward. "Just hold off a minute. I want to dig around the root to see what's there before we start cutting things off."

"Don't get any ooze on my shovel." Xena shook her head, clearly thinking this was a waste of time.

Gareth sighed. "I'll do my best."

It took another fifteen minutes—all while the tree emitted more ear-splitting moans and howls—but he finally found something. A part of the oozing root had, of all things, a large, yellowed claw stuck into it. Gareth reached out to remove the claw when Kara grabbed his hand.

"*Careful.* that's a basilisk claw. It's poisonous."

"Really? It's been buried for a while. Wouldn't the poison have dissipated by now?" Kara said nothing, merely pointing at the very visible effects on the tree. Gareth gave a short nod. "Good point. We do need to remove it, though. Any suggestions?"

"Yes. Get out of the way and let a professional do it."

He didn't have to be told twice, shuffling aside to let Kara approach the exposed root. As she examined the claw, Gareth took the opportunity to close out some notifications that had popped up recently.

He'd been keeping them minimized to reduce screen clutter—or more realistically, *eye* clutter. He usually minimized everything to keep his vision as clear as possible. The notifications liked to flash repeatedly until he opened them. It was annoying, so any quiet moment he got, he systematically cleared them out.

"That's weird," he remarked aloud.

Xena turned to him. "What?"

"I got a couple of points in Diplomacy from trying to talk with the tree. My skill level has moved up from non-existent to horrible."

Xena frowned, if he was reading her expression correctly. "Diplomacy is a skill that only applies to sentient creatures." She angled her great wolf-shaped head to peer closely at the tree. "Most trees are not sentient."

Gareth grunted and turned back to watch Kara. Hopefully this new mystery would resolve itself without killing them.

Kara had taken off her pack and set it on the ground. Then she pulled out a long, black box, which she laid on the ground beside the diseased root. When she touched the top of the box, it split down the middle. Then she flipped it open like it was a fishing tackle box.

Each leaf of the lid flipped up two more times, leaving a box with three levels of trays on each side. Kara dug through the contents, extracting tools and then shaking her head and putting them back. She finally ended up with a telescoping monocle, what looked like a pair of long scalpels, and a device she set on the ground that had a stand with a clip on the end of a long, articulated arm. She set it up, bent the arm over and attached the clip to the end of the claw.

With the monocle and tiny blades, she looked like a jeweler about to cut a priceless diamond.

"You might want to stand back. I don't know what's going to happen when I cut into the root." She hunched over the root, inspecting it closely. "I can see what appear to be veins running through the root, starting from the claw. They look like they're...*pulsing*."

She scrambled around the root, looking at the claw from several different angles before settling on one and setting herself up next to it. "Okay, I'm going to make the cut now."

She reached down and made a small cut into the thick root beside the claw. Immediately, a black, tar-like substance oozed from it. She gagged and coughed, waving a hand in front of her face. "Damn, that smells like ass. I hope the fumes aren't poisonous."

Kara continued making small, precise cuts into the root, all around where the claw dug into it. As she did, the branches over their heads started to tremble. Gareth pointed out the branches to Xena. She nodded back at him, and they both put their shields above their heads, like umbrellas. They moved to cover Kara in case of an attack from above.

The twitching and trembling grew worse the more Kara cut into the root, with some of the branches actively swaying as if caught up in a gale force wind. The continuous howling now increased to a deafening volume. Gareth looked around nervously. All this noise had to draw attention to them sooner or later.

"Um, you might want to hurry," Gareth urged.

"Shush," Kara said without looking up from what she was doing. She had a small hammer out and was tapping the claw on different sides.

"*Whomp!*" What felt like an anvil landed on his shield. *What the...?* A heavy branch had seemingly gone limp and was now laying across his shield.

"*Whomp! Whomp!*" Two more branches slammed down on Xena's shield. She merely grunted in response. Gareth's jaw dropped. She was supporting what had to be over a hundred pounds of wood. Luckily, the tree seemed to be relying upon gravity to do its damage, with the tree limbs just going limp and falling.

The limb on his shield started to twitch and squirm a bit, which alarmed him. Trees shouldn't be able to move like that.

Gareth braced himself, fearing more vigorous attacks to come. Maybe this was the tree 'waking up' in response to what Kara was doing to its root.

As feared, the repeated assaults on them grew more substantial. As the branches beat down on their shields, both Xena and Gareth started losing health. He had to resort to using both arms to support his shield and Xena mirrored him.

"I hate to be a pest, but faster would be better," Gareth barked at Kara.

"Do *you* want to do this? This claw has barbs that stick into the tree root. If I just yank out the claw, they'll stay behind, and who knows what that will do."

"Just—" He stopped as the branches beat down still harder and his health bar dropped again. "We're on a clock, here."

"I know! Now shut up and let me concentrate."

She'd pulled out a small drill and seemed to be excavating the root from around the claw.

The limbs had set up a steady beat-down rhythm now. *Wham, wham, wham.* Brief pause. *Wham, wham, wham.*

Their health dropped at a steady rate with each blow. Kara yelled out, "Got it!"

An even stronger torrent of blows rained down on his shield, rattling him thoroughly.

And in seconds, everything went black.

Chapter Forty-Five
Things Are Not Oak-Kay

When Gareth opened his eyes, Kara was leaning over him as she capped her healing potion bottle. Gareth blinked, checking the blinking health bar in his UI which showed him at 1%. His head was throbbing, and looking around, he determined that he was now lying just out of reach of the tree. The tree itself, thankfully, was now standing immobile, and—even better—silent. Xena towered over both of them, looking much worse for wear.

"Thanks for the heal, but *really*? You left me at 1%? Couldn't you heal me up a little more?"

Kara straightened and shook her head. "Healing potions are expensive, and I don't have many. You can handle it from there."

Gareth slowly pushed himself to his feet and scanned the surroundings for his shield. It was lying just under the death-tree. "What? You left my shield."

"Well, we were more worried about getting *you* out from under the tree un-splatted, but if you'd rather we waited and grabbed your shield, we'll be sure to do that next time," Kara snarked back at him.

Gareth laid hands on his own chest to heal himself—*go spam heal, go.* He quickly blew through his mana with each pulse of increase to his health bar. But with each tiny pulse, he found himself feeling much better. He took a deep breath. "I'll be with you in a minute, Xena."

She replied with a distracted grunt, looking back at the tree and sniffing.

"What's going on?" he asked.

"There is a large amount of fluid coming out of the root— from the hole where the claw was. And the tree looks much better."

He followed her gaze. The tree had, indeed, transitioned from *dead looking* to just *dying.* "Could the poison be leaking out?"

"That's not normally how it works." With hands on her hips, Kara had joined them in studying the tree. "But then trees don't normally attack you, either. We're in unknown territory."

She'd noticeably managed to grab her tools when they'd retreated from the tree. Now, she bent to scoop up her box and fold it up for storage in her backpack. After having stuffed it there, she rummaged and removed a retractable spyglass, which she put up to her eye and pointed at the tree.

"There's *definitely* a steady stream of black fluid coming out of the root. And look, as it spreads out, the grass it touches is withering. I'd suggest avoiding that stuff."

"No crap." Gareth stared at the tree, squinting. It was continuing to green up as the ichor left it. "So, you think it's safe to pass the tree now? We still need to head to the Abbey, but there was all that noise."

"You just want your shield back." Kara gave him side-eye.

"Well, I *did* use that shield to protect your little butt. I'd think *you'd* want me to have it back too," he groused.

"We'll retrieve the shield," Xena interceded. "I suggest we wait and see what happens when that flow of goo stops."

"*Ichor.*" Gareth corrected.

"What?" Xena's ear pivoted for a moment, then pointed forward again.

"It's coming from a living thing, so it's *ichor*. Goo would be from a non-living thing."

Xena just stared at him, then repeated, "Goo."

Their attention returned to the tree, which looked healthier with each passing moment. There was no doubt now that the tree was on the mend.

After nearly half an hour of them watching this process, Xena spoke up, "I think the flow of goo is slowing down. Yes, see? It has stopped." They all stared expectantly at the tree.

After a couple minutes with nothing happening, Gareth decided to move things along. "This is stupid. It's a tree. The whole moving limbs around was probably due to the ichor. I'm getting my shield."

"It's *not* a tree. It's a dryad," came a soft voice from behind him.

The three of them spun around. Gareth's sword slithered from its sheath as they faced the creature, or rather, person who'd approached them so silently that not one of them—even Xena—had noticed.

This person was very beautiful—with long black hair and striking green eyes. If he didn't know better, he'd think it was someone cosplaying a cute anime elf girl at a Comic-Con convention or something.

"Oh, wow," Gareth muttered, jaw gaping.

"*Smooth*." Kara said snidely.

There was a thump at the back of his head. He glanced behind him only to see Xena glowering at him.

"Enemies can look nice, too," she reminded him.

The girl in front of them cocked her head. "Why do you suppose that I'm an enemy?"

Xena gave a loud sniff. "You hide your scent, and you snuck up on us."

The girl shrugged. "I could have attacked you while you were retrieving your friend. Instead, I waited until the situation had calmed down to approach you. These are not the action of an enemy."

"She's got you there, Xena."

Xena glared down at Gareth, then sniffed at the air again. "I can smell your attraction to her. Your analysis is not reliable in this situation. We cannot trust her." At Gareth's lack of reaction, Xena shook her head and moved away, muttering. "Don't come complaining to me when you're missing a kidney."

Gareth held out a hand to their surprise visitor. "Her hostility is unwarranted. I assure you I'm no threat." The girl—well, woman, now that he was getting a close enough look at her—walked up to stand beside them and take in the tree.

His eyes traveled down her form, taking her in. She was slender, not tall but not too short. He'd guess her age—though he was typically pretty bad at that—at somewhere in her mid-thirties. Her long glossy black hair was loose about her face but primarily tied into a loose braid that hung between her shoulder blades. She wore no armor on her slight form, just a bohemian-style dress in shades of green with a small tan-colored suede pack slung over one shoulder and matching leather bracers around her wrists and boots under the long hem of her dress.

What caught his eye, and had him blinking, were the very long—and pointy—ears gracefully arching up along her head—like an anime elf. Her skin was smooth and glowing, but she wasn't pale. She was rosy-cheeked and healthy looking.

And just flat-out stunning. Gareth blinked again.

Kara stepped up, addressing her while gesturing to Xena. "She's just mad because Gareth is *her* human."

"What? I'm not her human. She's my *friend*." The thought crossed his mind again, might in-game Xena and out-of-game Xena be related somehow? Nah, it couldn't be. Given the things his dog had seen…well the thought of her walking around and talking made him more than a little uncomfortable.

Though being able to talk with his dog like you would a person would be beyond cool. He shook his head. There was no way that the same universe that spent the last couple of years crapping on him would do anything as awesome as upgrading his dog to this Xena.

"Anyway, I'm an independent human." He continued and bit his lip self-consciously. Then he lowered his eyes to the ground for fear that the newcomer would dazzle him again, and he'd either come across as a creeper or a lovesick puppy. Neither option was good.

Frustrated and flustered, he turned back to the tree.

"So, it's a *dryad*. you said?"

She followed his gaze and nodded, turning back to look at him. "Yes, a young one if I'm not mistaken." Her elegant, dark brows drew together in concern. "And it's in great pain." Her large, crystal-clear eyes clogged with unshed tears as she shook her head and turned back to it.

"Well, we just removed a basilisk claw that had been driven into its root, poisoning it. I'm guessing that's the source of the pain," Gareth said.

"A basilisk claw?" Her large eyes widened impossibly bigger. "Those are very dangerous. You must be very brave."

Gareth's chest puffed up with pride even as his cheeks heated under his stubble. "I have my moments."

"*Actually. I'm* the one who removed—" Gareth roughly bumped Kara as he turned to extend a hand to the newcomer.

"My name's Gareth."

She smiled up at him fetchingly, dark lashes fluttering. "Saoirse."

"Not that anyone's asking, but *I'm* Kara. The tall and furry one is Xena." Kara turned to Gareth. "I hate to interrupt, but we were kinda in the middle of something."

"Yeah…" Gareth tore his gaze away from Saoirse back toward the dryad. His shield still lay at the base of it. "I should grab my shield, and then maybe we should try to talk with the tree again."

"Okay. *You* do that." Kara jutted out her hip and folded her arms across her chest, arching an expectant brow.

Gareth took a deep breath, considering. Should he do this? Would it attack him again? And what would attacks coming from a healthier dryad be like, if he got multi-thumped into unconsciousness from a dying one? He glanced at his two colleagues. "Either of you want to go with me?"

"*No.* But we'll come grab you if it knocks you down again." Kara pressed the spyglass to her eye, inspecting the dryad once more.

"I no longer feel any hostility from the dryad," Saoirse added.

"Thanks, I guess." Nevertheless, Gareth stepped slowly toward his shield. Once he got within range of its branches, he crouched down and shuffled forward in a weird sort of crab walk. It probably didn't look very impressive but left him ready to spring back at any hint of the branches reanimating. To his surprise, he arrived at the shield with no sign the dryad was even aware of him. Which might have been insulting, given the beat-down it had just landed on his head only an hour before. Gareth scowled. *Honestly.*

With no small amount of relief, he grabbed his shield and stood.

"It's okay, you guys. I don't think—"

"*Whoosh!*" Before he could even think, Gareth threw himself flat on the ground, whipping the shield over his head to protect it. He lay there for several minutes, waiting to feel the tree limbs thumping heavily on him again. Or for Xena and Kara to run up and drag him to safety. After a slight delay, he realized neither of these things was going to happen, so he lifted the shield and peeked out.

His eyes landed on a tiny pair of booted feet. His gaze moved up only a few inches to tiny legs clothed in brown pants.

"Are you okay, Mister?" a high-pitched voice asked.

It sounded like...a kid?

Gareth pushed to his feet and turned back to the tiny, slight figure who made even Kara look like a body builder. It *was* a kid.

And the dying tree was now gone. He goggled. "What—what happened to the tree?"

The kid, who stood about three feet tall, and looked remarkably like a Keebler cookie elf, looked down at the ground. His clothing favored several different shades of brown. Dark coffee-brown pants, chocolate-brown shirt, light brown hair, mahogany brown skin, amber-brown eyes. The kid took *brown* to a whole new level.

With the tree gone, it was easy to see the entrance to the cave. That had to be the one they were looking for!

The boy's shoulders hunched. "I'm really sorry about that, Mister. I honestly didn't want to hurt you."

"Wait, what? *You're* the tree?" Gareth choked out.

"*Dryad.*" Saoirse corrected as she approached.

The kid looked at him sheepishly. "Yeah, I'm a dryad."

Kara and Xena now approached as well. The young dryad lifted his head to take them in, eyes widening in fear and tensing as if he might bolt. Gareth held out a reassuring hand. "You're safe with us. We're just a little...confused."

Saoirse said something in a musically lilting voice in a language that Gareth's UI didn't translate. Whatever she said caused the tension to dissipate from the child's form. He blinked and took a deep breath before letting it go.

But his eyes sank to the ground once more, head bowed. "My mama told me not to wander too far, but the bunny was so cute, I had to chase it. I just wanted to pet it, maybe feed it something. Then..." The bottom lip curled into his mouth, and he bit it, looking troubled.

"Then...?" Gareth prompted. "It's okay. You're safe now."

The young dryad looked around, taking in the woods, the hill looming above, the sky, anywhere but at them. Finally, he scuffed his boot in the dirt, and continued, in a whisper. The group leaned in so they could hear. "That's when *he* caught me."

"He?" Gareth looked at Xena, then Kara to see if they might know who the kid was talking about. His colleagues merely shrugged.

"The vampire." His whisper was almost inaudible now.

"*Vampire?*" Gareth repeated, his voice rising so fast it ended on a squeak. "What do you mean *vampire?* I thought we were talking about skeletons and zombies in the abbey. Fuck vampires."

"Hush, Gareth. You're frightening the child." Saoirse's thin, dark brows drew together in disapproval.

"Sorry." Gareth shuddered, "The whole blood sucker thing gives me the willies. Besides, what level even is this place? You can't tell me there are level 8 vampires running around."

"No, there aren't." Kara waved him off and turned back to the dryad. "What happened then, little one?"

"*He* brought me here and forced me to take my tree form. Then, he stuck that *thing* in my root. It—" The boy shuddered and stopped talking.

"It's okay." Gareth patted the child's shoulder, then realized he didn't know what his name was. "What's your name, son?"

"Birch."

"Well, hello, Birch, I'm Gareth. These are Xena and Kara. Our new friend, here, is Saoirse." Gareth studied the boy, struck with sympathy at his obvious fear. Poor thing. He was reminded of his own sons when they were little. "We're headed up to the abbey through that cave you were guarding. But I'm sure we can take a small diversion to walk you home. Would you like us to?"

Birch shook his head. "That's okay. I was able to call out to my parents as soon as I wasn't trapped in tree form anymore. They'll be here soon."

Gareth put his dad skills to good use, squatting beside the boy to put himself on the same level. "Well then, we'll just wait here with you until they get here, so you won't be alone."

Birch nodded quietly, his eyes flitting away, and Gareth sure as hell hoped that Mom and Dad dryad were not aggressive or this could go bad really, really fast, given what a child dryad had been able to do to them.

A few minutes later, they all looked up, startled as the ground shook. Then everything grew chilly as they found themselves in the shade. Gareth looked up and blinked as he found himself under a massive oak tree. A *very angry* massive oak tree.

Xena and Kara jumped back from the furious foliage, but Gareth was too overtaken to move. The outraged oak was able to reach out and snatch him up in one of its massive branches. With no questions asked, it then proceeded to squeeze him... *painfully.*

Saoirse bravely moved to the base of the tree and rattled off another stream of words in whatever language she'd spoken earlier.

She was quickly joined by Birch, who ran up and started yelling at the tree "Uncle, *no!* Put him down. They're the ones who rescued me."

The tree's branch tightened rather than loosened, and Gareth saw spots swirling around the edges of his vision. It wasn't going to listen to reason, clearly.

But Saoirse pressed her open palm to the great oak's bark. She uttered what was clearly a powerful command in the musical tongue. With one last shake, the tree loosened its grip and dropped Gareth to the ground.

Birch appeared at Gareth's side, reaching out a hand to help him sit up. Xena and Kara remained well out of reach of the tree.

"I'm so sorry." Birch uttered frantically. "You're not hurt, are you?"

"I'm okay. I'm okay. Just a little bruised." Gareth glared at the tree looming over him.

Birch brushed the dirt and leaves off Gareth, then turned to face his uncle. "You change right now and apologize to him."

The massive tree shook its leaves a few times before finally acquiescing to Birch's demand. Gareth blinked at what he was witnessing. The tree's form flowed into itself before finally morphing into a middle-aged looking man with dark brown skin and impossibly bulging muscles.

When it spoke, it was in a very deep voice. A voice of something ancient. "Come, young one. We must leave. Your parents have been distraught since you disappeared. Every day, they wander the woods searching for you." He reached down and tried to take hold of the boy, who easily dodged him.

"Uncle Greenbark, first, you must apologize to Gareth. Then I can go."

Gareth wasn't particularly upset by the uncle's man-, uh, tree-handling of him. Heaven only knew, he would've reacted similarly if someone had tried to snatch either of his kids. But he found the child's persistence charming. It was always good to be appreciated.

The tree-man looked them over indifferently, then spoke to his nephew. "I'm sure the human knows I meant him no harm. We assumed the worst when you went missing."

"Well, he *was* kidnapped. Just not by us," Gareth said before realizing he might re-anger the older dryad.

Greenbark stared at Gareth, eyes alight with fury. "Who would dare to take one of our kind?"

Gareth pointed up the hill. "Apparently, the vampire in the abbey did."

Greenbark looked back at his nephew. "Is this true?"

"Yes, uncle. He grabbed me and made me stand guard in tree form over the tunnel." He pointed to the cave mouth before turning pleading eyes back at his uncle.

"Vampires have no power over us, child. How could he force you?" Greenbark's bushy brows creased.

The boy hung his head and kicked at the ground, clearly flustered by his uncle's unspoken accusation.

"They used *this*." Gareth pointed at the basilisk claw on the ground. "Its poison prevented him from changing form or calling out to you. Or moving." Greenbark's tree had appeared over them. Now that he had a moment to think about it, Gareth realized they must be able to move while in their tree form, like Ents from Middle Earth.

Greenbark studied the claw with rage crisscrossing his strong features. A thin tendril of a green vine sprouted from Greenbark's forearm and extended toward the claw, snatching it up. The vine promptly shriveled and sickened where it held the cursed thing.

"Be careful! We're not sure what exactly it is," Gareth cautioned.

"*I* know what it is, human." The dwindling vine deposited the claw into his large, callused hand. "And I will *not* allow you to have it."

He grasped the claw in his hands. Both arms started to bulge as he put great pressure on the thing. With a loud grunt, he snapped the claw in half. A dark energy emerged from within, spreading out toward them.

A sickness washed over Gareth, and his skin felt like it had been dipped in a foul, oily substance. He struggled to breathe. It felt like his soul was recoiling from whatever had come out of the snapped claw.

Was he about to pass out again—for the second time in fifteen minutes?

CHAPTER FORTY-SIX

CURTAINS IN THE BASEMENT

GARETH WHEEZED AS THE SICKLY, FOUL-SMELLING cloud engulfed them all. It was like a combination of skunk spray and the rotten-egg smell of sulfur—and it had a thick, unctuous quality about it. A familiar feeling roiled in his innards and his mouth watered. He turned his head to dry heave for a moment before suppressing the gag reflex enough to talk.

"Why would you think I wanted *that* thing?"

Greenbark answered without hesitation, punctuating his words with a cold stare. "All your kind want control."

Gareth shook his head, "Not me. My wife was the one with the control issues. I'm always happier just getting along." Greenbark, however, appeared unmoved by Gareth's pronouncement. So, he gestured with a little desperation. "Look, all we want to do is find a tunnel into the abbey. We were searching for it when we came across your nephew and helped him out."

"To further your own goals," Greenbark sneered.

Gareth threw up his hands with a dramatic shrug. "Helping someone and helping myself aren't mutually exclusive." Heat rose to Gareth's cheeks in uncharacteristic frustration—and annoyance. What bug had crawled up this guy's butt?

Greenbark began, "Still—"

"Uncle, stop it. They didn't have to help me." Birch turned and handed Gareth an acorn. "If you ever need help in the woods, just crush this and throw the dust in the air. We'll come find you. Now, Uncle, let's go home. I am longing to see my parents."

"Elder," Saoirse interjected. "May I have a word?"

Greenbark turned to study Saoirse, then let forth a long string in that same language they had spoken before. Dryadish, he supposed.

Saoirse's reply came in that same language. The discussion went back and forth for a while and Gareth was almost tempted to ask Birch to translate for him.

Finally, Greenbark nodded. "Very well."

Saoirse glided toward Gareth with that same elegance she did everything. He had to admit, if even to himself, that his heart sped up a bit even as he locked gazes with her.

She smiled, lighting up everything around her, it seemed. "I'm sorry to leave you so soon after our meeting, but I must travel with them back to their village."

Gareth's heart dropped. He blinked. "But—but you just got here."

"I know, and I am sorry. I have been looking for the dryads for a very long time. Now that the chance has come, I cannot let it pass. Our paths will surely cross again, perhaps after you've completed your adventure here."

Gareth blew out a breath. "I guess. If you're ever in Muddy River, look me up. I'm staying at Blacl's inn. You can leave me a message there." Gareth tried—and failed—to manage a smile.

Saoirse's smile widened. "I will. And good luck restoring the guildhall."

The three then turned and sauntered into the woods. Greenbark gave Gareth one last stink-eye glare over his shoulder before they disappeared into the dark foliage. Gareth frowned, staring after them for minutes after they'd vanished.

"That tree-person has much anger." Xena stood at his shoulder, staring off in the same direction.

"Yeah. Thanks for all the help with that, by the way." Gareth scowled, disappointed in his friend. He hadn't known her long, but she'd had his back up until now.

Xena's shoulder slumped and she looked abashed. "Trees shouldn't move. It's unnatural."

He goggled at her. "You're scared of trees?"

She growled, clearly affronted. "I am *not!* I just prefer to keep an eye on them from a distance. That way, I have more options on how to respond."

"Uh huh." Gareth was oddly comforted by the fact that the eight-foot-tall wolf of death had her own quirks and fears, just like everyone else.

Kara stuck her head out of the cave mouth from where she'd disappeared minutes before. "The entrance to the tunnel is here, just like the frog said."

"Well, let's get on with it, then. Still not happy about the whole vampire thing. At least it's just one." Gareth slung his pack onto his shoulder and started into the cave. Xena trailed right behind.

"*That we know of.*" Xena added helpfully.

When he caught up with her, Kara said, "I have something else to upset your day… a red flag kind of thing. I don't recall any of us ever mentioning the guildhall quest to our new flirty, tree-loving friend. Do *you?*"

Gareth froze, blinking. He scanned through his memory of the conversation they'd had when she'd first shown up, the interaction with Birch and his grumpy-ass uncle, everything. Kara was right. They'd never mentioned the guildhall and yet… she'd wished them luck with that very quest when she'd left. He scratched his jaw, befuddled. "No, I don't."

Kara shrugged, looking out of the cave towards where the trio had entered the woods. "I'd accuse her of being a stalker, but stalkers don't usually take off with another group of people within minutes of making contact, so who knows? Maybe she can read minds or something."

Gareth shuddered at the thought. Hopefully she hadn't read too much of his, because his thoughts hadn't stayed exactly G-rated.

With a long-suffering sigh, Kara turned back to the cave, motioning for the two of them to move past her so she could take up the rear position.

Like this, the three entered the cave, Gareth in front, and Kara bringing up the rear. Within just a few steps, it grew so dark they couldn't see their hands in front of their faces. They had to resort to lighting up their torches, the acrid black smoke rising and curling in the stale air above their heads.

From years of playing D&D, he would have expected more from torchlight. But in reality, it sucked, just giving off a dim dome of flickering reddish-orange light to a small area around them. Bits of burning hot tar dripped off the end, forcing him to hold the torch at an angle to avoid getting it on his gauntlets. The flickering caused the shadows to jump around, which had him startling at first. This was definitely going to make it hard to spot any creatures in the area.

"There's got to be something better than this for light," Gareth grumbled.

"Oh, there definitely is," Kara replied. "The other options are costlier. There's a store off Delving Street in Muddy River that specializes in dungeoneering gear. If we're going to keep doing this, we should drop in."

"I hadn't really thought about it, but in most games I've played, the best loot is always in some kind of dungeon," Gareth mused.

"It's the same here," Kara added from behind him.

"Great," he huffed, ducking around some roots hanging down from overhead. "Gah, I hope we hit a real tunnel soon. This is too damp, drippy and mucky for me. All roots and worms and shit. Next thing I know, Darth Vader's going to be coming at me from around the corner with his light saber ignited."

"I don't know who that Dark Vader person is, but at least there're no spiders." He could all but hear the smirk in Kara's voice.

"Or worm-spiders. Those would be really bad," Xena added from behind.

Gareth spun, halting her in her tracks. "*What* are you doing?!"

Xena stared down at him, dark eyes widening. "Just teasing."

Gareth stiffened with frustration. "Well...*don't*. Things *listen*. I once made an off-handed comment in a D&D game. I was joking about how it was great that the trolls we were fighting weren't armored. An innocent-enough remark, right? Do you know what happened?"

"No."

"The GM snickered and wrote something down. The very next game, we got our butts thoroughly kicked by *armored trolls*. Don't give the universe any ideas."

"Yes, but this isn't a D&D game. This is..." Xena waved her hand. "A world."

"*Right*. And yet, there's nothing *running* this world? No computer game master who can hear something and go, 'Wow, that's a good idea, let's do that?'" Gareth fumed.

"I don't think the game's controller pays any attention to us." Xena held her torch up, trying to peer past Gareth.

"Still, let's not tempt things, shall we?" Gareth raised his brows and Xena nodded.

He turned around to continue forward once more.

After following the quite-lengthy instructions given to them by Raging Kermit, they came to an obviously constructed tunnel that ended in a stone door.

Just in front of the door, a large yellow gem set into the ceiling glowed brightly. Gareth quickly threw his hand up to halt the group.

"Trap!" he hissed.

"Oh, get out of my way." Kara pushed her way toward the front of the group. "I'm on traps. You're here for hitting things."

When she reached the front, she looked around. "Okay, where's the trap?"

"What, are you blind? It's right there." He pointed up at the brightly glowing gem. "The glowing thing. It has to be a trap."

Kara shook her head and let out her 'you're such a newb' sigh. "*No*. That's just a save point."

"A *save point*? Really." He walked forward and touched it, expecting a flash or something. He was disappointed. "So, if we die, we'll respawn here?"

"No, if we die, our last memory will be from here," Kara replied.

Gareth searched her face, trying to see if she was putting him on again. "*What*—how does that work?"

"Long ago there was an adventuring group that was famous for taking down the biggest bosses in the game. They had come across an artifact that allowed you to change your spawn point to any location. Then, they'd just attack the encounter over and over again until they figured out how to beat it."

"Huh. They Zerged it."

Kara looked at him quizzically but didn't bother asking the question, so Gareth took his own opportunity to be informative. "It's a common tactic in online games back home. You get a big group and just rush in over and over until you can kill the boss mob. Those who think of themselves as *real gamers* look down on it. But it got results." He shrugged.

"Yes, well the MCP that maintains this world agrees with your *real gamers*. Save points appeared. They're explicitly there to prevent you from just assaulting an encounter over and over to gain knowledge. All memories from after the save point will be deleted if you die. Each attempt has to be encountered fresh."

Gareth peered at the glowing save point with narrowed eyes, his jaw setting. "That's hardcore. I dub this the 'shit's about to get real' point."

Kara nodded while making sure her sword wouldn't stick in its sheath. "The presence of a save point almost always means you're about to get your ass kicked."

"True excellence in battle is shown by your ability to adapt and overcome your opponents. This *Zerging* is clearly a technique for the weak," Xena opined.

"Games are about defeating the content, not proving how studly you are," he replied.

"I think *you've* missed the point, Gareth. This entire world was created when two ancient powers decided individual achievement mattered more to them than group goals. Its entire existence is a paean to the supremacy of the individual," said Kara.

Gareth shook his head. "Sounds to me like they were just a bunch of twelve-year-olds that got off on tea-bagging their defeated opponents. And to think—they had a galaxy-wide civilization. I would have thought the ability to travel between solar systems would require a certain amount of maturity."

"Others have made that observation." Kara shook her head and sighed. "Well, this discussion of game philosophy is great and all, but we have a door to open and a power core to steal." Kara approached the door and began inspecting it. "I don't see any traps. And..." She tried the handle. "It doesn't seem to be locked."

She looked back, waiting for something. Then, she picked up her trap detecting tools and moved to her position behind Xena and Gareth. "I just unlock them—I *don't* open them. That's *your* job." Kara nodded meaningfully at the door.

"Oh, okay." Gareth readied his shield and made sure his sword was loose in its sheath. He turned the knob and pushed against it. It didn't budge. He pressed a shoulder against it to give it more muscle. "It's jammed or something."

Xena squeezed past him and put her shoulder against it. "Let me," she snapped. After nearly a full minute of straining, she managed to move the door inward about an inch. "There is definitely something behind this door" she growled.

All three of them rearranged themselves to give it a team effort, shoving with all their might and weight against the door. They eventually managed to widen the gap enough so that they could each squeeze through, though for a moment, things looked sketchy for Xena. But with some relief, she was able to somehow twist her body around and snake through the opening that should have been way too small for her.

The three of them found themselves in what looked like a basement, just as Kermit had explained. After everything, the frog's directions had ended up being remarkably accurate. Gareth huffed. Nice that there was one creature in the world that wasn't out to screw them.

He coughed, and Kara spat on the ground beside her. Furniture covered in ratty dust cloths and cobwebs filled the room. A massive, pockmarked oak desk had been shoved up against the entry door to bar the way.

"Why's it always a dusty basement room filled with old furniture?" Gareth bitched, peeking under a dust cloth.

Xena and Kara both looked at him quizzically. He sighed. "In *every* game I've played, a secret tunnel always enters into a room filled with dusty furniture. I dunno, it just seems a bit...*unoriginal"*

Kara blinked, then shrugged and looked away. "Just be happy there's no ambush waiting for us." She poked around a bit, looking under the tarps. "After all, someone here knows about the tunnel, or they wouldn't have bothered to put the kid at the entrance."

An icy shiver crawled down his spine. "I hadn't thought about that."

Xena pushed farther into the room. "Indeed? I just assumed you had planned a counterattack. An ambush seemed inevitable after we found the guardian at the entrance."

Gareth's brows knit. "I guess I was just too worried about saving the kid to think about the implications of him being trapped there." He felt his face burn with frustration—and not a little embarrassment.

"It's okay, humie. That's what you have *us* for," Kara replied as she finished her survey of the room. "Once again, no traps. How am I ever going to skill up if I can't find anything to disarm?"

"I'm sure there'll be plenty of deadly traps ahead for you." Gareth poked under some more of the sheets. All he found was old furniture.

"You think so? I only need two more points to make Master. That will allow me to unlock grade-five magical locks." Kara rubbed her hands together in glee at the thought.

A set of doors sat closed in the opposite walls of the room—one a large wooden double door, which was undoubtedly how the furniture had been brought in. The other was a normal sized door to their right.

Kara headed toward the larger door while Xena and Gareth continued to poke around under the sheets and tarps. The pixie fiddled with the door for a minute before letting out an exasperated sigh.

"What?" Gareth looked up.

"Unlocked and untrapped. *Worthless.*" She moved to the other door.

But Gareth was too distracted by his latest discovery. Pulling the tarp the rest of the way off, he leaned in to get a better look. Under the tarp sat an intricately carved desk made to look as if it were a dragon skull. The detail and craftsmanship was stunning, down to chips and scars in the skull as if it had taken battle damage. He could almost feel ghost eyes in the sockets glaring at him.

Gareth caught his breath. He been in love with dragons since his character had died to one when he was twelve years old. He had to have it.

"Say, do you think I could fit this in my pack?" Gareth asked.

Xena looked up briefly and shook her head. Kara ignored him. Well, screw them, then. He whipped off his pack and tried to fit it under one end of the desk.

"*What* are you doing?" Kara snapped.

Gareth cringed, then looked up at her, abashed. "Well, since the guildhall is looking so bare. And you know, I need a desk…"

"Gods, Gareth, will you just read the manual already? You can just store housing objects in your pack. Pull up your storage menu and select *Store in pack.* You don't have to actually *stuff* it in." She blew out a breath but at least managed to hide rolling her eyes as she turned back to her work on the smaller door.

She'd pulled out a lot more equipment this time. "Locked *and* trapped," she informed them over her shoulder.

Xena finished her inspection of the room and walked over to Kara, watching over her shoulder.

Gareth silently complied with Kara's directions, quickly finding the storage menu in the UI and storing the desk with no problem. It did take up over half of the pack's slots, which left him very few slots free. Hopefully the power core wasn't too large for the remaining space in his pack.

Kara worked for a while, while muttering to herself. Apparently, this door was being an "inconsiderate bitch" and a "son of a syphilitic whore." Finally, she asked Xena to pick her up so she could reach out with a slender metal probe and adjust something at the top of the door.

"*Finally!*" She let out an explosion of breath.

"You disarmed the trap?" Gareth scanned the door, looking for evidence of her success. It looked exactly the same.

"*No.* I finished the dusting. Of course I disarmed the trap. Now I need to unlock it." She bent and placed two probes in the keyhole. There was an audible click seconds later. "*There.* That part was easy."

Kara stood back from the door and waved Xena to it. Once Kara was out of the way, Xena turn the knob and swung it open. Just past it was the heavily worked and mortared stones of a very solid wall.

"What the hell?" Gareth scowled, joining them after storing the desk. "Who puts a trapped door in front of a blank stone wall?" He reached out to touch it just in case it was an illusion. Nope, just a regular old stone wall.

"Some sadistic fuck, *that's* who." Kara shook her fist at the wall and made a few other gestures that he assumed were rude in her culture. "The other door was just so obviously a trap, the locked door *had* to the be way to—"

"Ohh, crap." Gareth sighed. "I've got a real bad feeling about this. We spent a lot of time dicking with that door. What if it set off some kind of alarm?" Gareth searched the dark room around them as if somehow that would yield answers to his questions.

Kara shook her head with conviction. "Nope. I would have detected any sort of alarm on the door. It's what I do." As if to double check, she turned back to the door to give it another inspection.

Xena pointed. "There could have been a light-sensitive rune on the wall. You wouldn't be able to detect that. Opening the door would set it off." She growled, sniffing the air. Her pointed ears swiveled to either side as if listening intently to hear anything approach.

"*Well.* thanks for the cheerful thought, Xena." Gareth moved to the double door to open it. The door wouldn't budge, no matter how much he rattled the knob or pushed his shoulder against it. "Shit, we *definitely* set something off."

Both Xena and Kara turned to look at him, so he pointed at the double doors. "Locked now. We're stuck down here."

Kara spun around, rapidly looking at every side. "My threat detection skill just went off the charts. Things are coming...*lots* of things."

"Back into the tunnel," Xena barked out. "We can ambush the ambushers."

Or run like hell. the option Gareth preferred. He turned to sprint across the basement toward the hidden tunnel when something loud thumped above them.

The ceiling, which had looked like a solid vaulted stone cellar, now had several gaps in it. "Oh, *shit.*"

He had only a second to feel something icy cold slice into his body. Then, everything went black.

***** You have died *****

CHAPTER FORTY-SEVEN
LIVE TO FIGHT ANOTHER DAY

KARA'S STOMACH CONVULSED, AND HER LUNCH splattered on the ground in front of her. "Gods, I hate that skill." She wiped her mouth with the back of her hand. "Still better than dying, I guess."

"I should say so, Agent 99!"

Kara's head snapped up to take in her erstwhile superior, a fellow pixie. But where Kara was lithe, he was stocky, possessing an expanding gut he failed to control with a girdle, the top of which peeked out of his waistcoat. "*Great.* I was hoping you'd be gone, Harkness."

His eyes narrowed. "Agent 5, if you please. You know the rules. No names here. Still, I suppose some forbearance is warranted. I know the toll that evacuating takes on you." He gave her a smirk. "I'll overlook the fine *this time*." He waved towards the mess on the ground, "After you finish cleaning that up, come to my office. I want to hear about everything you've been up to."

Kara watched him head towards the door to his office as she ground her teeth and curled her lip. "Dick," she muttered, grabbing a rag and bucket from the stack helpfully placed next to the portal area.

The Lair, or the *Righteous Center of Enlightened Thought*. as Harkness liked to style it, was located in a subterranean complex somewhere underneath Muddy River. Where exactly, she didn't know. Her head had always been covered with a black sack while entering or leaving on foot. It was only the exception when, like today, she used her get-out-of-deep-shit skill to bring her here.

Her personal theory was that the sickness from sudden evacuation into the Lair was caused by the protection wards that had been cast to keep the location secret. She'd used the skill a few times when she'd first acquired it and hadn't suffered any adverse effects. It was only after she'd been required to rebind the target of the skill to this location that her stomach started rebelling each time. Changing the locus had supposedly been for her safety. She figured it was really that they didn't want her to be able to use it to get away from these assholes themselves.

She swiped the ground one last time with the rag, then tossed it and the bucket into the corner. With a deep sigh, Kara headed toward Harkness's office, forced to weave through the maze of supply boxes dropped at random. She suspected that, like so much in the *Glorious Service Against the Over-heighted*. the actual purpose was to hinder anyone attacking through the portal entry.

The office door was an ostentatious thing, all polished wood and shiny brass, with a gold nameplate that read *Beloved Leader*. The office, in sharp contrast to the rest of the place, reeked of wealth. They were all equal in the organization, but some were definitely more equal than others.

Kara paused for a second before knocking, hoping she might overhear something interesting from inside, but the only sounds were from the other agents working out of sight across the room. Finally, she pulled out a dagger and used the hilt to knock on the door, knowing it would irritate Harkness immensely.

"Come!" was the immediate reply.

Kara opened the door, slipping the dagger back into its sheath as she entered. The room inside matched the entry. Mahogany bookshelves loomed behind an imposing desk, its surface pristine except for a gold pen set in a stand in the center. Harkness sat high in an overstuffed leather chair, which must have been specially made, as it allowed him to loom over his guests from behind the desk. A low stool sat in the room in front of her, awaiting its petitioner.

Huh. *Subtle*.

Kara strutted in and flopped onto the stool, refusing to be intimidated by such classless showmanship. "Okay, so I'm here."

Harkness opened a desk drawer and pulled out a folder. He spent a few moments flipping through it, carefully ignoring the other pixie. Finally, he closed the folder with a sigh and looked down at her from his perch. "I see you have missed your last four check-ins. We were starting to wonder if your heart was in this mission."

Kara blinked, folding her arms across her chest. "I was busy. *You* try spying on someone you adventure with all day, then sneaking away to report. I don't know why I needed to come in person, anyway. I left detailed notes at the drop-off."

Harkness pulled a sheet out of the folder and read, "The subject is named Gareth Fain, a human. Entered the station by mischance. Mostly harmless." He looked up, sighing. "As detailed as your notes were, I would have still appreciated a chance to ask some follow-up questions. Like, for example, *Why the fuck is he still entering the game?*" The pixie leader pushed himself to his maximum height in the chair as he screamed down at her.

Kara glared back at him. "I did my job. I arranged a partnership with him, which wasn't easy, by the way. Only then could I find out why he was here and what his plans are going forward. It's all in my reports. He's *harmless*."

"*Harmless?* Listen here, humans have *never* been harmless. Were you hit on the head and forgot what they did to us? How they betrayed and abandoned our kind?" Harkness sat back in his chair and glared at her. "Investigating was just the *first part* of the assignment. Once you'd learned all you could, you were supposed to make his life such living hell that he'd never want to log in again. You seem to have completely failed *that* portion of the assignment."

Kara pulled a dagger out and started cleaning her close-clipped nails with the tip. "I remember my history just fine. Wasn't it like six thousand years ago that they abandoned us? And wasn't their planet basically destroyed? And I seem to remember that the humans who survived here worked with us, until they vanished. I think it's time we moved on, don't you?"

Harkness peered back, shaking his head and sighing. "*Vanished?* More like they ran away, taking the city treasury with them. And what about the legion? A group of humans finally came back, pretending to be our friends. And what happened? Once they got what they wanted from us, they abandoned us *again* . No doubt they're out there, living the good life, a ready supply of life-prolonging potions at hand. It doesn't take an oracle or a mage to see the pattern here, does it? Weren't your family in their employ? Did they take them along? Or were they left to deal with the fallout?"

Kara's grip tightened on her hilt. "You know they were left here." Kara looked away and answered Harkness with pretended nonchalance. "Still, that was two thousand years ago. Ancient history."

Harkness looked down, fake sympathy on his face, "And in all that time, have your family fortunes recovered? Your home restored, your position in society reestablished? Or are you still suffering from their betrayal?" He scolded, shaking his head before sinking into his chair. "But if you insist on a current example, what about Crush? He was all charm and friendliness…until he *wasn't* ."

A tiny drop of blood beaded on the tip of her finger, a result of her distraction when the name of The Elite's guild leader was mentioned. "Crush is on *you* . And Gareth is *nothing* like him."

Harkness's features sharpened, his eyes narrowing as he looked down at Kara. "Oh, I see. You *like* the human."

Kara set her dagger in her lap, pondering carefully how to answer this. "I don't know what those other humans were like, but Gareth is honest and cares about people. He didn't hesitate to risk himself and jump in to save Spartacus in front of The Harpy's Nest."

Harkness's features clouded and he growled out, "*You mean* Agent 102."

Kara rolled her eyes and echoed her superior, "Yeah, him. Agent 102."

Harkness shuffled through the papers in the folder until he found the one he was looking for. After a brief read, he said, "From your own report, it seems *you* are the one who saved Agent 102, not the human."

Kara shook her head. "The skill I used has to be used from behind the target. Without Gareth drawing their attention, I would never have been able to use it. Besides, Gareth doesn't know what my abilities are. He had no idea I'd be able to help him when he tried to protect Spar—ah, Agent 102."

"And thereby endangered his mission. Agent 102 was supposed to gain employment at the Harpy's Nest, and keep a low profile, thereby allowing him to pass amongst the patrons and report on what he overhears. The human's actions risked *all* of that."

"Agent 102 was stuck working on the street cleaning up harpy shit. The only thing he overheard was 'splat!'" Kara sneered, glaring at her superior.

Harkness blinked, momentarily taken aback. "It was a work in progress. He would have made his way inside, eventually. Now, his employment is under review. The management is wondering why the human risked his neck for a gremlin. Better if 102 had received his beating and not had the extra attention drawn to him. He understands what is required of him." Harkness gathered up the papers, carefully straightened them and set them all neatly back into the folder.

"Easy to say when *you're* not the one getting the beating," Kara muttered.

"What was that, Agent 99?" Harkness shot her a look.

"There's no guarantee he would have survived the beating. And AI's don't respawn, remember."

"Agent 102's death would have been unfortunate. However, drawing attention to our efforts is *unforgivable* ." He shook his head at Kara. "I'm getting the feeling, Agent 99, that you wish to terminate your assignment with the human. You have that right, as a free being. Unfortunately, given our limited resources, I would have to reassign the assets currently working on retrieving your parents *if* you choose to sever our relationship. Is that what you wish?" Harkness turned to fiddle with something inside a drawer on the right side of his desk, weirdly focused on the task as he awaited her response.

Sure, pretend you don't care asshole . Kara shot a heated glare at the pixie leader, still sorting his collection of girly magazines, or whatever was in that drawer. After a long, thick silence, she finally grunted out, "*No* ."

He finally looked up at her. "Then *do your job* . This venture to the monastery was a good start, if your presence here indicated it failed?" Kara waited a minute before giving a sharp nod. "*Good* . See to it that he *keeps* failing until he gives up. Once he ceases logging in, we will consider your contract complete." He stared at her until she gave another quick, grudging, nod of assent.

"And my parents?"

"Unfortunately, the circumstances aren't quite right to retrieve them yet. I'm told that *should* change soon." His smile dripped with insincerity. "After all, we mustn't do *anything* to endanger them. It would be a shame, after all this time, if something terrible were to happen." He raised an imperious hand and waved toward the door. "You can see yourself out."

Kara stood, spinning stiffly so that he wouldn't see her fuming and left the room.

When the door slammed behind her, she satisfied herself with sending it the rudest gesture she could possibly muster.

She was really, *really* sick of this asshole.

CHAPTER FORTY-EIGHT
YOU HAVE (NOT) DIED OF DYSENTERY

GARETH CAME TO IN A DUSTY, GRAY SPACE. HE WAS wearing his jeans and t-shirt from the camping expedition in the desert. Blinking as the world came into focus, he wondered for not a few moments if it had all been a dream—armor and swords and fighting, a pixie thief and a giant wolf warrior that might or might not be his dog.

If it was a dream, it had been one hell of one. He patted himself down, wanting to make sure everything was where it should be, with no bits missing or leaking blood. It was strange, but he felt almost naked without his armor and weapons. How much had he changed in the last week?

He remembered making his way down the tunnel, reaching that glowing spawn point thing. Then — he was here.

This place reminded him of the DMV. A place which he'd had dwell inside for all too many hours. Drab, dull, and with empty desks as far as his eye could see. Glowing crystals in the ceiling gave off a wan yellowish light, which flickered like fluorescent lights in movies when they want to establish that some place is rundown.

The serial killer horror movie vibe was strong here.

It didn't help that he couldn't see any type of exit—to say nothing of the fact that there was not a single other soul here, even to man a desk.

First, he had to deal with the annoying red flashing notification that was giving him a serious headache. Apparently, it hadn't been a dream, or maybe the dream was just continuing? When he selected it, a giant wall of text sprang into his field of vision.

•You have died.

•Experience has been reset to last level up, you are level 8.

•Skill progress has been reset to last skill increase.

•Combat skill progress has been reset to last skill increase.

Gareth scanned all the details of the skill progress he lost. Losing that progress hurt more than losing his exp, and he'd earned most of the way to level 9. But it was taking forever to increase his skills. Each and every skill point was hard earned. Well, this sucked. He pulled up his character sheet, just to make sure he'd hadn't lost anything else:

Name	**Gareth Fain**
Level	**8**
Class	**Cleric 4**
	Warrior 4
Deity	**Unaligned**

AC 14

HP 96

Strength	**Above Average**
Intellect	**Average**
Physicality	**Average**
Constitution	**Above Average**
Wisdom	**Above Average**

Spells

Bless 1
Greater Healing 1
Leafy twig 1
Mending 1
Smite 1

Talents

Natural Alchemist (Apprentice 1)

Skills

Diplomacy (Horrible)

Inspect (Horrible)

Knowledge of potions (Horrible)

Martyrdom (Horrible)

Search (Horrible)

Skinning (Horrible)

Sprint (Horrible)

Combat Skills

Battle Axe (Apprentice 0)

Broadsword (Apprentice 5)

Kite Shield (Apprentice 5)

Longsword (Journeyman 1)

Short Bow (Apprentice 0)

Abilities

Armor Use, Light

Armor Use, Medium

Armor Use, Heavy

Shield Use, General

Weapon Use, Simple Melee

Weapon Use, General Melee

Weapon Use, Simple Ranged

Specializations

Spell Specialization - Heal Poison

Weapon Specialization, Sword

Everything else still seemed to be there. But he was pretty sure his combat skills had been about to increase again—especially Broadsword and Kite Shield. He let out a long sigh.

Ugh, he needed to stop brooding about this and get on with things.

"Hello?" he called out, answered only by the faintest echo smothered in the industrial gray carpeting.

This was the worst afterlife ever.

Gareth blinked, rubbed his eyes, and had to stop himself after spinning around trying to spot someone, anyone, amongst the sea of desks. He looked down to regain his bearings and fight off a wave of disorientation.

That's when he noticed that he was standing on a blue line marked on the floor. With a shrug, he sighed. Keeping with the DMV theme, he found himself walking along it, winding through the arrangement of desks until the stripe ended. The desk before him was familiar-looking, all too similar to those he'd used during his time in IT—a chest high, gray plastic counter, suspended between equally grey fabric walls. Modular office hell. *A gray fabric cage for a gray fabric life.* he'd always thought. Still, it was better than the open office super hell that became all the rage later on. He looked up and saw a number two in black, gothic lettering hanging on a dull silver panel suspended from the drop down tile ceiling. A smaller sign, hanging below it, simply read *Readmissions*.

Was this the part where some friendly, loveable but painfully slow anthropomorphized sloth came out to help him? God forbid.

The counter in front of him was bare, save for a large brass bell with a small hammer next to it. He did the obvious and rang it.

"May I help you?" came a dry whisper before the bell had even stopped ringing.

Gareth let out a shriek and jumped back. There was now someone at the desk—or rather, some*thing.*

Behind the desk sat a robed and skeletal Grim Reaper.

Nope. *Hell to the nope* .

Gareth chose to back away until he was outside of arms' reach—if the arms' reach belonged to a mega-giant or Godzilla. Everything in him tensed, preparing to flee, if necessary.

The empty eye sockets stared calmly back at him.

God, this was so weird.

Gareth frantically searched the surroundings once more, hoping for any other option to present itself. Nothing did. So, he girded his loins, gritted his teeth, and stepped forward again.

Having watched plenty of slasher movies in his youth, he made sure to keep ample fleeing room available. You never knew when you'd have to bugger off in a hurry.

The...*thing* merely turned its head to look up at him. It smelled of ancient dust on the cobwebs of old tombs and his great-aunt's dank old basement—all rolled up into one.

The eyeless, silent stare was really starting to freak him out. He almost—*almost* —wished it would just leap at his throat and get it over with. Every scary movie he'd seen left him with no doubt about where this was going.

However, it didn't move. Didn't even speak. It just stared him down.

With an exasperated sigh, he braced himself to try a new tack. As he scrambled for what to say, his eyes landed, once again, on the sign. "I guess I need a readmit?"

"Of course, sir." The voice was flat and deep, gravelly and indifferently ominous. From somewhere, the creature pulled out a sheet of paper and a giant plumed feather pen. "I see here you recently died of multiple stab wounds, followed by dismemberment. Very gruesome, if I do say so myself. Still, as they say, any death you can walk away from is a good one."

The skull tilted up to regard him as if waiting for a response.

Gareth blinked, fumbling for a reply and failing to come to one quickly. To be honest, he was still just trying to absorb that horrific description of his death.

After a few minutes, he still found himself unable to process it. One second, he's about to enter a basement, the next he's in the afterlife with the word *dismemberment* running through his brain over and over. Finally, he swallowed. The skeleton was still standing there, patiently waiting. No use trying to win a staring contest against a being with no eyes.

He scratched his jaw. "I, ah, have no idea what to do here. This is my first death."

The skeleton nodded. "Right. First, you'll need to—Wait, *what?*" The skeleton's arms flew up into the air. The hands detached from the wrists before coming back down and resuming their proper place. "This is your first time? Where did I...?" It lowered its arms and started rummaging through various cubbies under the counter and around the cubical before extracting what it was presumably searching for. "Here we go, sir. In honor of your first visit with us." It proffered a large metal button and pushed it across the desk toward him.

Gareth gingerly leaned forward to pick up the item. It was about three-inches wide, perfectly round, and all done up in purple and gold. Across the top, it read, in the same gothic lettering as the sign above: *First visit!* At the very bottom, it read, *I'm celebrating* !

The worst part? The eerily smiling skull in the center with a burst of flowers—lilies, of course—behind it.

"It's, uh, *nice*? Thanks," Gareth offered nervously.

"Well then, pin it on, sir! We are very proud of our first timers here." The skeleton grinned at him. Gareth stifled a visible cringe. Not at *all* disquieting. *Yikes* .

He glanced around at this mention of *we*. As far as he could tell, it was just Mr. Reaper and himself. Under the skeleton's repeated urging, Gareth unhooked the pin on the back of the button and attached it to his t-shirt.

"There, isn't that nice? Now, as I was saying, first you need to fill out your readmission paperwork. Then, we can see to your rebirth. Easy peasy."

Gareth shook his head at the bizarreness of it. The skeleton did *not* just say *easy peasy*. "Why do I need to fill out paperwork to respawn? I've never heard of that before." Maybe it was to prevent spawn-rushing, a tactic he particularly despised from his old *EverQuest* days.

"To be honest with you, sir, this is all a bit new to me as well. Our previous human guests—"

"*Human?* This is all just for human players?"

"Each race has its own processing center. This—" The skeleton waved its fleshless hand around. "Is the human one." Then it leaned forward and whispered, "I'm not sure I care for the new look. The previous center was much more atmospheric.

Imagine a plain where everything has been laid to waste, bordered by a sooty river flowing through it—all in dark grays and black. There was even a ferry all made of bone. You rode on it by making a ritual payment to the ferryman for ceremonial transport across the river. *Very* moody."

Gareth blinked, jaw agape. "The River Styx?"

The skeleton seemed to brighten—if that was even possible to discern. "Oh, so you've heard of it?"

Gareth took a deep breath and fought to choose his words carefully. "I'm, um, somewhat familiar with the lore. The planes of Hell were popular with my D&D group. So, what happened to spur the, ah, redesign?" It was kind of a bummer, really, now that he thought about it. He would have liked to have seen the setup that ol' Skelly was describing. It would've been cool to throw a doubloon at the Ferryman for the ride.

The skeleton pulled back to sit up straight. "You are the first visitor here in quite some time. It was deemed more appropriate to base the theme upon an association more familiar to you."

Gareth looked around. This came from *him?*

"I believe this is to reflect a place called *The Department of Motor Vehicles.* Your subconscious seemed quite positive that it was a place very close to Hell."

"Well, I can't really argue with that."

"We appreciate your feedback. We'll be sure and take it into account upon the event of your next death."

His next death. Those words brought his current situation crashing back to the forefront of his brain. That's right—he'd died in the game. But what had become of Xena and Kara? His heartrate shot up and his breathing quickened with anxiety. He had to get back!

He made grabby hands toward the skeleton. "Give me those forms. I need to respawn ASAP. "

The skeleton pushed across a pile of forms over an inch thick. *What the actual fuck?* "Here you go, sir. Please let me know if you have any questions."

He blinked, eyes sizing up the pile. The top form was just… He blew out a breath, eyes widening. "My mother's aunt's maiden name? My father's social security number? The name of my third pet? What the Hell?"

"Exactly, sir." Skelly nodded.

Gareth rolled his eyes and commenced flipping through the pages. "This is going to take me all damn day."

"Don't worry, sir. It will only *seem* like that. You will still respawn in the game the standard one hour after you died."

"Well, that's *some* comfort, I guess." He plucked up a pen from a nearby cup and began filling it out. Fucking infuriating, if you asked him. But of course, no one was asking…

A subjective eternity later, he pushed the completed stack across the desk, vigorously shaking out his hand cramp. "Here you go."

"Very good, sir. Now that you have finished the introductory section, we can get to the main form."

He could feel the blood drain from his face. *Introductory section?*

Hell, indeed. Bureaucratic hell.

A stint on the ferry with Charon was starting to look like a joyride compared to this.

As he silently grumbled and felt sorry for himself, the skeleton searched through the area behind the counter. Then it looked up at Gareth with a loud cackle. "Just a bit of a joke, sir.

It's been a while since we've had anyone to talk to here. You'll have to excuse us."

Gareth's jaw tightened as his eyes goggled, relief and annoyance warring with each other in his mind. "It must be hard to be here all alone," he bit out. Then reminded himself to release his hands from their fists and just relax, no matter how much he didn't care for Skelly's little joke.

The skeleton nodded. "It is good to have company again, sir. It's very lonely when it's just us. And more than a little boring, if I do say so. New people are always a breath of fresh air."

Gareth worried his lip. He supposed that must really suck. Astonishingly, a wave of compassion for the creature washed over him. Now he felt bad for being so annoyed by the joke. He might have acted similarly in such a situation. He knew from experience that day after endless day of the same boring nothingness was depressing beyond belief.

"How do you deal with it?" he blurted without realizing he wanted to ask the question aloud.

"Well, we do have quite the lively Bridge club." Skelly brightened once more. "But now that you're in the game, we have great hopes of being useful again."

Gareth studied the skeleton, feeling ambivalent. The skeleton so clearly just wanted some company. If only he didn't have to die to get here. "Well, I hope you don't take this the wrong way, but I was planning on dying as infrequently as I can."

The skeleton laughed, its teeth clattering as its jaw opened and closed. "Of course, sir. We wouldn't expect anything less. We like our patrons to have great success in the game. I would be remiss, though, not to mention how much we'd appreciate it if you could recruit some more of your kind into playing. Variety is the spice of life, after all."

Recruit more humans? He'd been so focused on just surviving the day to day—the game, the station—he hadn't given any thought to what would come next.

If he could get back home, back to Earth, what would he do? Would he choose to keep playing the game? He'd have no problem getting recruits. Hell, he'd have to fight people off.

But he couldn't just recruit people and then leave them to their own devices here. He'd have to stay and play with them, mentor them. He'd definitely feel responsible for them and not want them left to their own devices, as he had been.

But...did he want that?

And what about his boys? He hadn't been seeing them much anyway, since the divorce. That was how he'd ended up in the desert. Another custody hearing hadn't gone his way, and he'd been drowning his sorrows around his campfire. And if he failed again, the ex could take it all—and maybe he wouldn't see them again until after they'd turned eighteen. And really, what could he tell the judge? "Your honor, I make my living playing a space game with a bunch of aliens..." That would go over well. He'd be lucky to stay out of a mental institution.

He shook his head, blinking. All of these things weighed heavily on him, but he fought to set them aside. They were problems for future Gareth to resolve. Today's problem was getting back into the game, so he could find a way to go home. Eventually.

He couldn't help but think, though, that bringing back some of his old guild buddies to take on the content would show these people a thing or two. They'd show those Elite fucks how a real guild should function.

His ex, Matilda, and he had their problems, but the thought of unleashing her on some of those shitheads in Muddy River caused a warm, happy glow in his stomach. They'd played many hours together, back during the good times. And while he'd objected to her power-gamer tactics, there was no arguing with their results.

"I'll do what I can about recruiting. Problem is, I don't currently have access to Earth, so that makes it pretty impossible. But if and when I figure that out, I'll see about recruiting some more humans."

The skeleton leaned back, "Oh, I am sorry to hear that, sir. We just assumed that the reactivation of the Londinium gate was due to you passing through it. Please, forget I asked."

Gareth goggled at the skeleton. "*Londinium* gate?" He blinked, mind racing. What the fuck? There was a gate into this game from *somewhere in London?*

"I really can't say any more, sir. We are forbidden from interfering with the game or divulging information about the game to players." Gareth's eyes narrowed. His spidey senses were tingling. The skeleton did not really seem all that sorry to have let that tidbit slip.

His brows furrowed. He must have imagined it winking at him at the end there. Huh. He held out his hand to make a wave of dismissal. "Sure, it's forgotten."

But his mind took that little tidbit to the races and let it go, full speed. An Earth gate was now active? Why did Earth even have a gate into the game? This must have something to do with those ancient humans that had supposedly played the game.

Were there other secret gates that had never been discovered? And why was this Londinium gate "recently reactivated?" Just how long ago had it been created? It couldn't possibly be six thousand years old, could it?

He took a deep breath and let it go, ordering his overclocked imagination to take it down a few notches. "It's been fun, but I need to get back into the game. How do I do that?"

The skeletal arm reached out with a two-fingered gesture off to the left. "Just head through the exit." The skeleton indicated a door with an industrial-looking, standard glowing green EXIT sign over it. Gareth blinked. That hadn't been there a minute ago.

Without another word to Skelly, he turned to head toward it.

"Profitable adventuring and easy deaths," the skeleton called after him.

Gareth turned and waved. No point in being rude, after all. "Ah, thanks. Until next time." *Until next time?* What the fuck had he just said?

When he turned back toward the exit, however, there was a man—this one nonskeletal—sitting in a leather overstuffed chair right in his path.

Gareth halted to take in this new development. The man—for he did appear human—was good looking: short brown hair, stone-gray eyes, dressed in a gray frock coat, with a black waistcoat and matching trousers. A black cravat finished off the look that was markedly Victorian in flavor. Beside him on a small table sat a complete silver tea service. There was a matching chair across the table from him.

"What the—! Where the fuck did *you* come from?!"

The man didn't get up to greet him but reached to brush something nonchalantly off his coat. His flinty eyes flicked back to meet Gareth's gaze. "I hardly think that sort of language is warranted." He gestured to the chair across from him. "Please, join me."

A markedly erudite British accent. Stuffy and poised. As if from centuries gone by.

Gareth glanced back over his shoulder, as if hoping to get some sort of explanation from his skeletal friend. No such luck. The dude had vanished.

"Do not concern yourself with *them*. They're incapable of interfering, in any case." He repeated his gesture toward the empty chair. "Please."

Gareth remained standing, holding his hands up. "Look, I don't know who you are, and I'm pretty sure you're not supposed to be here. So, please don't take this the wrong way, but I'm gonna head out. I've had enough strangeness for one day."

"My apologies, I have been remiss." The stranger stood and promptly buttoned his coat before giving him a little bow from the neck up. "Crush, at your service."

Gareth stiffened, blood freezing in instant recognition of the name.

Crush. As in Lord Crush.

As in leader of The Elite. As in the guy who had painted a target on him and his friends. As in thief—and presumed current holder—of The Vagrants guildstone.

Gareth froze in place, jaw dropping and not caring that he probably looked like an utter fool.

He wondered if it was possible to die again before even respawning.

CHAPTER
FORTY-NINE
CRUSHED

GARETH STARED IN OPEN-MOUTHED DISBELIEF, NOW face-to-face with his heretofore unseen nemesis. Lord Crush himself stood beside his tea table, staring at him with a haughty, expectant expression.

Gareth took a deep breath and somehow managed to speak in a civil voice. "What do you want?"

Crush made an appeasing gesture. "Please, have no fear. I'm merely here to talk. You've made quite an impression in Muddy River. After the report I received from Lord Slaughter, I decided I must make your acquaintance. And so, here we are." Crush unbuttoned his coat to return to his seat. Then he took up the silver teapot. "Tea?"

Gareth's hand twitched as the adrenaline kicked in and his body went into fight-or-flight mode. Though now it was currently in freeze mode. Could he turn and walk away? The exit was just past Crush, but would Crush try to stop him if Gareth tried to get by?

How was *he* even here unless he was dead, too? Gareth scratched his jaw, skin crawling under that flinty stare.

Deciding that his distaste for Crush was outweighed by his curiosity about why he was here, Gareth finally decided to take the empty seat.

Crush poured tea into Gareth's empty cup. He kept a careful eye on it, hoping this wouldn't devolve into a Vizzini versus Dread Pirate Roberts Iocaine powder situation.

Crush started talking. "I find there is no situation in life that isn't improved by a good cup of tea. Milk?"

Gareth shook his head.

"Suit yourself." Crush set down the teapot and added a healthy dollop of milk along with a cube of sugar to his tea. He plucked up a tiny silver spoon and stirred three times before carefully placing it on the table beside his napkin. This all had a ritualistic feel. Gareth sipped at the piping hot liquid before setting the fine china cup down on its saucer.

"Ahh, that hits the spot." Crush sat back after having sipped at his cup. "Some associates of mine bring me a regular shipment of leaves from time to time. I'm afraid the local varieties just don't measure up. It's possible, of course, that I am biased."

Shipment? Gareth's brow furrowed. "Aren't we still inside the game?"

Crush held up one hand and rocked it from side to side. "Technically we are in a *between state*. Neither in the game nor in the real world. Though, increasingly I find the distinction between the two meaningless." Crush paused to take another sip of his tea. "Take this, for example," he held up his teacup. "In theory, this is a virtual cup of tea, its flavor entirely provided by the wondrous machines that oversee this realm. But does it really matter if the *taste* of the tea is provided to our brain by our tongue or by our mechanical friends?"

Gareth pondered this, suddenly recalling that scene in *The Matrix* where Morpheus is trying to teach Neo the nature of how things work in the programmed reality. *Do you believe that my being stronger or faster has anything to do with my muscles in this place?*

Crush was still monologuing. "If the taste is equal, the reality of the tea must be equal. Further, to access *this* tea, I must secure an amount of it to deposit into the game. Much as you did with your gold coins. The only conclusion I can reasonably draw is that real world reality and in game reality are more fluid than has been previously thought."

Gareth hated to admit the point, but he couldn't deny it either. He, himself, had already found it hard to separate the game world from the real world. Everything a person experienced came via electrical impulses provided to the brain. Did it matter where the impulses originated?

Gareth's eyes darted back to his companion. Crush hardly seemed like the figure Gareth had been imagining. He almost seemed...reasonable.

Maybe it was wrong of him not to try to work with the guild. Had this all been a needless conflict? Who could he really trust? He thought he could trust Kara and Xena, but he'd been wrong before in the real world.

Crush took another long sip of tea, then refilled his cup. "I do love a good philosophical conversation. I'm afraid the company I keep back home tends toward more practical matters. Thoughts on exploring the meaning of our existence are sadly foreign to them. However, I must put this conversation aside. As pleasant as the company is, I didn't expend the effort to appear here merely to make your acquaintance."

Gareth set down his cup. This tea was actually quite good. Definitely better than Lord Smith's blend, for sure. It didn't have to be nasty hot brown water after all.

"I'm afraid that I must ask you to put an end to your recent endeavors. As stimulating as this world no doubt is, it is *no* place for you. Your actions are already starting to cause too much disruption and will draw unwanted attention." Crush stirred his tea and stared at Gareth directly. "You must forget this place and return home."

Gareth's brain, initially stunned by the abrupt left turn in the conversation, finally started functioning again. He sat back in his chair and narrowed his eyes at the man across the table from him. "Well, I *do* desire nothing more than to return home. But I *can't*."

A crease formed between Crush's dark eyebrows. "Just return via the gate from which you entered the game. *Voila.* you're home." Crush spread his fingers in the air with a flourish, as if embellishing a magic trick.

Gareth stiffened in annoyance at the flippant response.

He took a deep breath and responded in as calm a voice as he could muster. "I'm afraid I didn't enter the game through a gate that I can use to return home—as in Earth. I was abducted from Earth and brought to a space-station. I entered through one of *their* game portals."

A flicker of annoyance crossed Crush's features before they settled back into a composed mask. "Well, that is rather unfortunate. You'll have to confine yourself to the domain of the

Muddy River Township, then. Its society is somewhat savage, but it is not uncomfortable."

Gareth blinked, then shook his head. "I can't do that, either. Maybe I'd hang out for a little while, but the upkeep, you know. Rather hard to earn a living if I constrained myself to the town. I'd rather not face the alternative and be forced to take a walk outside the station without a space suit."

Crush studied him intently before breaking the silence again. "I'm afraid I really must insist."

The thin veneer of Crush's civilized bullshit was already showing in spots. Gareth chided himself at how quickly he'd been taken in, despite having entered this encounter on his guard. *And* despite having met scant few beings who didn't want to take advantage of him here. It wouldn't be long, maybe just minutes, before those lily-white calfskin gloves of his came off.

Gareth leaned back and squared his shoulders. "And *I'm* afraid I really must say *no*. I have people who depend on me."

"And *I* have an entire planet depending on *me*." Crush snapped back. A faint hint of color appeared at the carefully manicured neckline of his white shirt.

Gareth frowned but didn't reply. Crush took a deep breath and centered himself. "I'm not used to having to explain myself."

Gareth raised his brows. "Sorry, not sorry?"

Crush's eyes leveled on Gareth. "The depths to which the English language has debased itself, particularly in the hands of you colonials, never ceases to amaze me." His eyes flicked away and, almost as if to buy himself time to regain his composure, he made a big production of fixing himself a fresh cup of tea, from the seemingly endless—and endlessly hot—teapot.

As he did so, his voice took on a level, even and almost instructional tone. "About six thousand years ago, our planet, Earth, was attacked. Ancient beings—the very beings who created this game world we find ourselves in—decided that humanity had overstepped and had to be put back into place. They dispatched a fleet of ships that flew through the heavens between distant stars rather than upon the water. These ships destroyed the advanced civilization that resided upon our world, a civilization of such wonder that can hardly be imagined. It was reduced to nothing, its memory wiped or faded into legend."

Gareth took up his cup and tried to take a sip, finding it empty. "Hmm. That's an interesting story but…do you actually *believe* that? Clippy told me we had some kind of base back then, but his story never made sense. Wouldn't we have noticed the remains of some high-tech civilization on Earth? Even after 6,000 years, *something* would remain. Some CDs, maybe a Twinkie or two."

Crush's brows furrowed in puzzlement. "I don't know these *Twinkies.* and I sense you are making light. I assure you that it's the truth. The invaders used an ingenious device called *nanobots*, extremely small machines, capable of disassembling—"

"I know what nanobots are," Gareth huffed.

"You do? How extraordinary. Well, they used these nanobots to disassemble everything on the planet not constructed of natural materials. Everything was broken down back to its basic elements." Crush took another sip of tea.

Dread settled into Gareth's innards. "Even if they managed to destroy everything, they couldn't have killed everyone, or we wouldn't be here. *They* would have remembered the past and written it down again. There'd be stories, scrolls, cave paintings…something."

Crush looked off to the side—a gesture which was now reminding Gareth of someone accessing his or her UI in the game. "They employed the nanobots alongside another weapon, something called a *retrovirus*. It was created to rewrite everyone's memories. They simply forgot all about any higher civilized existence and were placed firmly back into the stone age. Their entire existence was erased. Still, the people on Earth are in for quite the shock if they ever visit the Moon."

"We've already been to the Moon," Gareth said. "Several times. The Apollo missions in the seventies."

Crush, despite his Victorian dress and old-fashioned manner of speech, did not appear surprised by this news. "But never to Fra Mauro."

"Fra Mauro?"

"Yes, I understand there is a large base there, covered in…regolith, I believe it is called. It will undoubtedly be discovered once someone lands there." Crush watched Gareth carefully.

Gareth scratched his jaw, thinking, playing with his beard that he'd been letting grow out. "Fra Mauro…Fra Mauro. Where have I heard that from? Isn't that somewhere we visited on one of the Apollos? One of the landing sites."

He wracked his brain trying to pin down the reference. His mind drifted back to his eldest son practicing for a middle school science presentation about the Moon and the space race. He'd suggested, afterward, that they watch a movie together, *Apollo 13*. Tom Hanks had said something about the Fra Mauro highlands.

"That's where Apollo 13 was supposed to land."

"And they were prevented from doing so, were they not?" Crush raised his teacup, as if he had scored a point.

Gareth rolled his eyes. "Now you're telling me the malfunction of that mission wasn't an accident?"

Crush shrugged. "I have no evidence. But a seeming accident that prevents a well-hidden secret from being revealed to an entire planetary civilization…Well, you must draw your own conclusions."

Gareth carefully replaced his teacup on the table, then he turned his attention back to Crush. "This is insane. I'm supposed to believe these ancient aliens destroyed human civilization over a *game*? And that the human civilization was so advanced they had a moon base? One that's been kept hidden by sabotaging NASA missions?"

Crush tilted his head to the side in acknowledgement. "It does beg credulity, I will admit. But you must understand just how important this game is. It's certainly the single most important aspect of their society. Virtual warfare, if you will, taken to the extreme."

Gareth blinked, reminded of his younger son's penchant for watching Twitch gaming streamers on the internet. What these aliens had done was the cosmic equivalent of calling the SWAT team—swatting—on their opponent.

But Crush was still yammering on. "Given what they've done in the past, you must see that we cannot risk anything that might draw their ire toward Earth once more."

Gareth frowned, still skeptical but willing to entertain these alternative facts for the sake of conversation. "Assuming these beings exist and what you said happened actually did happen, it would be prudent to avoid their notice, yes," he conceded.

Crush's eyebrow rose and he stared pointedly at Gareth. "Wait…you mean *me*? I cannot possibly be that important."

Crush fought a condescending smile and shifted in his chair to cross his leg. "I agree, you're not important. Given the severity of the response, however, I find myself loath to entertain *any* risk, no matter how small. You've certainly stirred things up, even if only in Muddy River, a town of admittedly no consequence."

"So, we're back to my confinement."

Crush tilted his head. "A small enough price to pay, to ensure the security of Earth."

Gareth pondered this tale but found himself heavily distracted by the thought of his friends waiting for him in the game. He couldn't—or wouldn't—leave them behind. Not for anything. Fuck this dude for even asking.

He steeled himself, then shook his head vigorously. "Nope, not buying it. You're just trying to scare me off. Even if these alien overlords are still out there, they have long since moved on to other things. There's no way my killing some rats is going to draw their attention and bring down Armageddon onto Earth again." Gareth's mind ran a mile a minute, trying to make it all make sense. Everything circled back to those two wildly conflicting quests—the one thing he was involved with that had real value in the game. "You…you're just trying to protect the guildstone, after stealing it in the first place!"

Crush hardly moved, but he made that chair of his seem like a royal throne with all the haughty arrogance that radiated from him. "I assure you that everything I've told you *is* true. Your actions have the potential to bring disaster back to our common birthplace. I am disappointed that you are so ready to endanger *everything*. all so you can see to your own comfort."

Crush set his cup down on the table and waved his hand, causing the entire tea service to disappear. "As for your allegation, you're correct that I did appropriate the guildstone, but I did not *steal* it. You can't steal something that already belongs to you. I was offered the quest and offered the guildhall, same as you. I just chose to take what I needed from it and leave the rest. Or did the guardian not mention those details?"

"No," Gareth's voice faded out. Then he used his own UI to pull up his quest log. He scrolled through it quickly in order to refresh his memory, his eye landing on the quest from Caeser. "Wait...in order to take possession of the guildhall, you would have needed to pay off the taxes, which are still owed. Meaning you never did. Which means the guildstone wasn't yours to take." Gareth's eyes narrowed in accusation. "You're a *thief*. nothing else."

Crush's eyes tightened and his right hand moved to his waist—and to the scabbard of a dagger Gareth hadn't noticed before. He stiffened, alert.

When Crush spoke, it was with ominous tones. "I let that accusation pass the first time. Now you dare to repeat it. There won't be a third time."

"Touchy," Gareth said, preparing to push out of his chair.

"In the environment we find ourselves in, the only thing that matters is our honor. All else is ephemeral. Even death. I will brook no slights upon mine." Crush leaned forward in his chair.

"Shouldn't have stolen the guildstone then, I guess." Gareth couldn't resist.

Crush sighed. "I can see our conversation has come to an end. I'd hoped to resolve this peacefully in honor of our shared heritage, but I can see that won't be possible now."

He stood. Gareth pushed to his feet at the exact same time, having prepared himself for this. The chairs and the table vanished. Crush drew not one, but two daggers as he stepped toward Gareth, then halted, hovering menacingly there.

"Don't stop on my account," Gareth said when he really wanted to say, *Bring it on, bitch.*

"A proper workman never rushes. He takes the time to do the job perfectly." Crush took a moment to look over each knife before giving them a flourishing twirl. "Flawless."

"Would the three of you like to get a room? What's the point of this showboating? Even if you kill me now, I'll just respawn. Right here, apparently."

Nevertheless, Gareth backed up several paces, reaching for his own sword. He let out an annoyed grunt as his hand only found air, reminding him that he'd appeared here without equipment, weapons or any armor. *Shit.* The fact that Crush had his must have been due to whatever trick he'd pulled to break into this place.

Crush watched this entire process, unmoved. "You really should learn more about how the game operates. It is normally impossible to die in the respawn zone, so there's no procedure in place if you do." He took a step forward. "If you die here, you will never leave. You'll become *a ghost in the machine.* as it were."

"What?" Gareth stepped back again, searching for something he could use to fight this bastard off. But all he saw were empty desks. Even Skelly had disappeared.

Crush launched himself at Gareth, displaying an incredible burst of speed. He closed the space between them in the blink of an eye, lashing out with his righthand dagger. A blazing strip of pain erupted across Gareth's chest, like a white, hot streak of lightning bursting from inside him. He could feel pain? *Here?*

Gareth struggled for breath, sputtering. "What the fuck?"

Crush sneered, inches away from his own face. "Combat isn't normally allowed here. Along with respawn, they never implemented the pain reduction algorithm here either." He regarded the bloody knife, then shook it to flick the copious amounts of blood off it. Gareth's blood, which now soaked the entire front of his t-shirt. Crush's tone grew nonchalant. "I find pain reduction makes in-game combat less satisfying, regardless. So, this is a pleasant side effect—for *me.* anyway."

Crush readied his knives again.

Gareth staggered back, trying to put some space between them. He quickly glanced around, maybe he could find a stapler to throw. Or a paper cutter. "Fucking lunatic!"

Crush swung on him again, and he was just so damn fast—and presumably a much higher level. In short order, Gareth bore wounds all over his body, each carefully scored to cause pain without completely taking him out. A form of torture.

Something Crush appeared to be greatly enjoying. *Psycho.*

Gareth tried to heal himself, but nothing happened. They probably never implemented spells here either

"Just end it, why don't you?" Gareth panted faintly, attempting another dodge behind a desk.

"An opportunity like this is too rare to be rushed." The eyes gleamed with something like madness. "It must be savored."

Crush was a cat playing with its food. A matador toying with a dying bull. Gareth's eyes searched around him, confirming what he already knew. There was nothing here that could save him. He jumped back once more, desperate to avoid another strike, slamming into the desk behind him. He slid down against the desk, causing his shirt to bunch up, and the first-visit button he'd been given whacked him in the face. This last indignity was too much. In exasperation, he ripped the pin off his shirt.

As he did so, heat exploded from it—accompanied by an intense vibration.

Gareth looked up to see what his opponent was doing. Crush stood still, brows furrowed in puzzlement. Then he advanced again, as if to finally end the fight. In a panic and without even thinking, Gareth threw the pin at Crush's face.

Crush flicked a wrist to swat the thing away with his dagger. As if possessing its own intelligence, the pin nimbly dodged Crush's attempt. Then, with a blur, it smashed right into his shoulder, blowing him into thousands of tiny fragments which almost as quickly, faded away into nothingness.

Gareth blinked, wiping his mouth with the back of his hand and panting heavily. Fuck…was it really over?

"Towel, sir?"

Gareth startled. Skelly was back and standing right beside him.

"*What?*" Gareth snapped. "Where were you? He tried to kill me!"

"We are forbidden from interfering with the game." The skeleton repeated.

"I thought this area was *outside* the game?" Gareth took the proffered towel from Skelly and started blotting the sweat and blood.

"Normally, that is true, but when your opponent entered the zone, it became a *de facto* game area. Hence, our normal rules no longer applied." The skeleton held out a bony hand to retrieve the soiled towel.

Gareth shook his head as he handed it over. "So, he cheated somehow to enter the zone, and you can't interfere because of rules, even though *he* broke the rules." Garth felt his wounds start welling with blood again. "Shit, how many times did he cut me, anyway?"

Gareth reached for his mana, trying to heal himself, and once again felt himself cut off. He stood there, dripping blood on the ground, staring at the skeleton.

"Your wounds should disappear as part of the respawn process."

"*Should?*"

"As for the unfortunate events, I can only reiterate that we are forbidden from interfering with the game." Damn guy was starting to sound like a call center representative responding with an obvious script. All that was missing was the bland name that didn't match the accent.

Gareth sighed, then his gaze narrowed at the skeleton. "Wait a minute, what about that pin? You can't tell me that was a normal pin."

The skeleton hesitated. "I must apologize. I must have given you a self-defense pin by accident. It's been so long, and the pins look quite similar. Still, it was an unforgivable mistake. If you wish to file a complaint, I can access the complaint forms for you."

Gareth shook his head. "Your mistake saved my life. I, ah, don't suppose you have any more of those pins handy?"

"I'm afraid not, sir. We're not allowed to interfere with the game." The skeleton stood there, in no rush to get back to its duties, whatever those were.

"Unless you accidentally interfere ahead of time?" Gareth arched a brow. The skeleton opened its jaw to reply, but Gareth waved it off. "Yes, I know, you are unable to interfere with the game. Crush is a bastard. Must have been disappointing for you to have the only two humans in the entire game fighting each other."

"That other creature is not human. It should never have had access to this area. We serve humans."

Gareth wasn't sure how, but he could feel anger radiating from Skelly. "He sure *seemed* like he was from Earth," he contended.

The skeleton refrained from replying.

Gareth tilted his head, studying it. Maybe Skelly would drop some further details if he stared it down? But after only a few minutes had passed, he gave up. He turned his head and scanned the area to locate the respawn door. Ah, there—just behind him.

"Well, it's been fun, but I think I'll be going." Gareth felt more of his blood dripping down his side under the shirt. *Definitely time to be going.*

"Very good, sir. Until next time." The skeleton gave a quick bow.

"Sure, be seeing you." *Hopefully not too fucking often.* This wasn't any fun at all. Gareth gave a quick wave and turned toward the door.

He opened the door right under the bright green EXIT sign, and beyond the threshold, saw his room at Blacl's inn. Ready to be whole again, and to see his friends, he eagerly strode forward.

The moment his foot crossed the portal, a bolt of intense pain swept through him, stealing his breath. When he was a kid, he'd helped his dad rewire their 1920s-era house. He'd accidentally touched a live wire that had sent a jolt right through him. This sensation felt like that—only ten times worse.

His muscles locked up and he fell over, landing half on the bed, the rest slumped to the floor. No one had said anything about respawn being painful.

Maybe it was a bug. Or something to do with Crush's interference.

"Log out," he gasped, barely able to form the words. "Log out *now!*"

The pain surged through his body, waves of agony washing over him and threatening consciousness. Why the hell wasn't the log out function working?

But...he'd forgotten. This wasn't a voice activated game. *Use the UI, dumbass...*

He pushed his pain-fogged mind to find the right menu in the UI. Finally, much to his relief, he logged out.

He awoke moments later, finding himself back in his room on the station replete in all its sci-fi splendor. He spent a moment luxuriating in the complete lack of pain his transfer to the real world had brought. That respawn was seriously fucked up. What kind of sick fuck tortures you for the sin of dying in a video game?

"Ahem."

Gareth's contemplation of the unfairness baked into his new existence was brought short by a grunt coming from behind his head. He sat up and spun around, only to find someone wearing a familiar red-shirted uniform, declaring him to be from engineering, or security. Hopefully not security.

The face was familiar, last seen resting while Gareth hacked his way through dire rat guts. *"Kruger?* Why are *you* here?"

Kruger looked down at him and shook his head. "You're off to quite a start, kid. We seriously need to talk."

.

Geoffrey Brenna is the pseudonym for Jeff and Bren, a husband and wife writing duo. Bren is a USA TODAY bestselling author and Jeff is a lifelong hardcore Science Fiction and Fantasy reader. They are both avid gamers and have played together for decades in all variations of tabletop and computer games--especially MMORPG games.

They live in California with their children, both human and furry. Their most cherished inspirations for writing are the works of Sir Terry Pratchett, Douglas Adams, Robin McKinley and Ilona Andrews. Thus, they prefer to infuse a heavy dose of humor, a deep dive into character and world building and adventures galore in their brand of LitRPG stories.

For more information, visit their website at
www.GeoffreBrenna.com